This book is dedicated to my wonderful and loving Dad, David Broen:

All my life he's always supported my dreams. His love and strength kept me going through the frustrations and difficulties of not only writing this book but life as well. He sadly had to read it up in heaven. I guess I'll have to wait to ask him what he thought of it. He is greatly missed and always loved.

Contents

The Storyteller's Journey

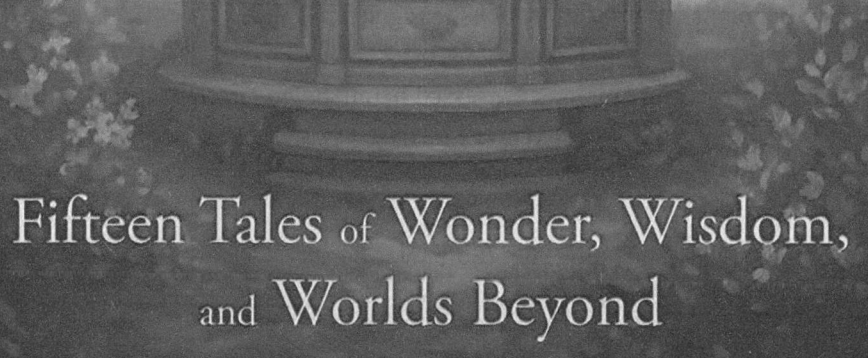

Fifteen Tales of Wonder, Wisdom, and Worlds Beyond

KRISTEN M. BROEN

SILVERSMITH
PRESS

Published by Silversmith Press–Houston, Texas
www.silversmithpress.com

ISBN 978-1-967386-21-5 (Softcover Book)
ISBN 978-1-967386-24-6 (eBook)

Part 4
Fantasy & Legacy

Part 5
Final Reckonings

PART 1

Foundations of Belief & Identity

CHAPTER 1

The Journey

Alicia sat in her friend's living room. Her three oldest and closest friends Jackie, Sadie, and Cindy sat scattered around the room. Cindy had just handed out coffee for everyone. The four of them had known each other since their senior year of high school, which meant they'd known each other longer than any of them really wanted to admit.

"I see you're getting a short breather from your busy schedule, Licia," Sadie commented, while taking a sip of coffee.

"Such is the life of a celebrity," Jackie teased in an overly dramatic tone as she sat back with her cup in her hand.

"First of all, Jack, I'm not a celebrity, and second, I'm not that busy," Alicia replied, tossing one of the throw pillows at her friend.

"Oh really? I happen to remember your picture on the cover of a magazine," Jackie replied teasingly while, dodging the pillow.

"That was Mark's idea," Alicia replied, eyeing the other pillow, debating whether or not to throw it at her annoying friend.

"I've always wanted to know how you decided to become a storyteller," Cindy asked, hoping to forestall the pillow fight and keep Jack from any further teasing.

"It's not that interesting of a story. When I was about sixteen, I was asked to write a story and present it whether in written form or out loud to the class in Career and Trades Class. The story subject was the thing that I hold most dear. It's an allegory which quite impressed my teacher. I ended up presenting it out loud to the class. It was exhilarating, and from that moment on, I knew that it was what I wanted to do," Alicia explained, the joy of that remembered moment in her voice.

"That sounds like an amazing story," Sadie said, getting into a comfortable position.

"You have to tell us that story, Licia," Cindy said excitedly as she shifted to face her friend.

"Yeah we got to hear it," Jackie agreed, just as excited.

"Alright," Alicia replied as she thought back to that long-ago story.

It only took a few minutes for her to remember the story. She really hoped that her friends would like the story because it had always been really special to her.

"Come with me to a land where everyone spends their lives wandering in a forest. This forest is an endless maze filled with never-ending twists and turns," Alicia introduced, as her friends leaned forward with rapt attention.

* * *

One of the wanderers in the Great Forest was a young man named Luke. He, along with everyone else, had spent twenty years of his life hopelessly lost. However, he now knew something that so many people on that journey didn't, that he was, in fact, lost.

As he walked down one of the winding roads he saw someone on the path ahead of him he recognized, his friend, Micheal. Walking a bit quicker, he easily caught up to the other man who was about the same age as him.

"Hello, Luke, how have you been doing?" Micheal greeted, clearly happy to see his old friend again.

"Not very good, I'm afraid. I'm totally and completely lost. Not only that; I've come to the realization that I'll never be able to find my way on my own. I don't know what I'm going to do about it," Luke admitted, hanging his head.

"Do you want to stop being lost?" Micheal asked, his blue eyes locked with Luke's hazel ones.

"Of course I do. Who would want to be hopelessly help-lessly lost?" Luke asked, baffled it was even a question.

"You'd be surprised. Come with me," Micheal said, lightly grabbing his wrist as they walked.

Micheal led Luke around a corner to a crossroad. There were two paths, one that went to the right and the other to the left. The two of them stopped at the crossroad.

"Why are we stopping?" Luke asked as his friend led him down a path he'd never been down before.

"I'd like to give you a copy of the map of the Great Forest," Micheal answered, as he opened his bag and began looking through it.

"You mean you have a map," Luke exclaimed as he watched his friend rummaging through his bag.

"Not just a map, but the map," Micheal replied, pulling a rolled up scroll from his bag, then closed it again.

"What do you mean? There are lots of maps. You can get them almost anywhere," Luke said, looking at the scroll in his friend's hand like it was nothing special.

"That's true, but none of them are like this one. It's very special," Micheal replied, his gaze moving from the map in his hand to his friend.

"Really what's so special about it?" Luke asked, looking at the ordinary-looking scroll slightly skeptically.

"Two things actually. This map was made by the man that created the Great Forest," Micheal answered, watching his friend's reaction.

"Really? That's amazing," Luke replied, with a little awe in his voice.

"Was there anything else that you wanted to know?" Micheal asked, tapping the roll of paper against his other hand.

"Sure is, what was the other thing that makes this map so special?" Luke asked, not sure what to make of the look on his friend's face.

"Oh, the fact is that this map is magic," Micheal replied, as if it was the most simple thing in the world.

"You can't be serious. Surely you don't actually believe that," Luke replied, his gaze darting from the map to his friend's face.

"Actually I do believe it. Here, let me show you," Micheal said, holding up the still-rolled piece of parchment.

Luke noticed the map wasn't very big. The map was about the size of a regular letter. This surprised him, especially considering the sheer size of the Great Forest.

Micheal unrolled the map as Luke walked over to look

over his shoulder. The map was not what he expected. He had been expecting the drawn lines that would be on any other map. As soon as the paper unrolled, the words "Take the right path" appeared in a faint gold light.

"The map will glow like that whenever there are new directions," Micheal explained, turning to face his friend.

"That's amazing," Luke said, astonished.

"There are some things that you should know. If you choose to follow this map, there will be times that the directions don't make much sense. But if you follow them, you'll never be lost again, even when you feel like you are. There will also be times when the path will be difficult, sometimes even painful," Micheal explained, his tone grave and serious.

"I understand," Luke replied in the same tone.

"Do you still want the map?" Micheal asked, his voice just as serious as he met the gaze of his friend.

"I'm tired of being lost. I do want the map no matter what," Luke replied, meeting his friend's gaze unwaveringly, holding out his hand.

With a decisive nod, Micheal touched the cross that was at the top of the map. The instant he did, a glowing ball of light rose from the parchment.

The glowing ball of light floated over to Luke. As soon as it came to rest in the palm of his hand, it solidified into another map.

"Wow," Luke said, staring at the parchment in astonishment as he closed his hand around it.

When he unrolled his map, it to said for him to take the

right path. He turned and headed down that path joined by his friend.

The two of them traveled together for a couple of weeks. During that time, they discussed many of the things Micheal had experienced since getting his map. Right before they parted ways, Micheal told Luke that his journey would likely be very different than his.

After a couple days of traveling on his own, things seemed to be going well. During that time he hadn't felt lost even once. It was wonderful to now have a firm direction and know where he went.

It was now dusk and he'd just followed another direction. A little bit ahead of him off to the side of the path was a bench with a man sitting on it. The man was dressed in black and carried a large bag. Luke could tell this man was a merchant based on the wooden sign sitting next to him listing what he had to sell and the prices.

"Greetings, young traveler," the man said, standing up as Luke approached.

"Hello," Luke said, eyeing the merchant, not really sure what to think about the man.

"As you have probably already guessed, I'm a man of commerce," the merchant said, extending his hand.

"Yeah, I'd figured that out," Luke replied, shaking the man's hand while glancing at the sign sitting on the bench.

"Perhaps you'd like to take a few minutes to peruse my wares," the merchant said, gesturing to the rather large bag.

"I suppose it wouldn't hurt to spend a few minutes

taking a quick look," Luke said, something about the man setting him slightly on edge.

"I knew right off that you were a smart lad. You see, I'm famous far and wide for being an excellent judge of character," the merchant said, nudging the young man closer to the bench. He began taking things out of the bag and placing them on a cloth next to the bench.

"Thank you," Luke said, his gaze darting over the many things laid out on the cloth with curiosity.

While the young man looked over the things for sale, the dark-clad merchant observed him. The instant his beady eyes landed on the map tied to Luke's belt, he got an annoyed scowl on his face. He glared at the parchment as if its very presence offended him.

"You know, young man, I do accept items in trade," the merchant said, his voice silky smooth as he drew Luke's attention back to him.

"Really, that's great cause there's a few things that looked interesting," Luke said, mentally going through the things he had on him that he would be willing to part with.

"I couldn't help noticing that you have one of those Light Maps tied to your belt. I hate to be the one to tell you this, but that thing is quite outdated. There is a bit of good news though; I happen to have a map that was drawn just this year with all the latest information. You'll never get lost if you follow it, unlike that dusty old thing you have now. Since I like you, I'd be more than happy to trade you it for that archaic thing," the merchant offered, holding up one of the parchments that was on his cloth. There was a slight glint of red in the man's eyes.

"On second thought, Sir, you don't have anything that I want," Luke replied, loosening his map from his belt and clutching it to his chest like a lifeline.

Before the now-dumbfounded merchant could say anything, Luke hurried away as quickly as he could. He wanted to put as much space between him and the slimy merchant as he could.

A few days later, his path crossed with another man. This time, it was another wanderer just like him. The two of them were even about the same age. At that exact moment, his map began to glow. Slightly confused, his loosened from his belt and unrolled it. This time, instead of directions, the glowing words read "This man is lost." Thinking back on what it felt like to be lost, he decided that he'd try to help this man if he could.

"Hello, fellow traveler," Luke said as soon as the man reached hearing range.

"Hello to you as well," the man replied, turning his attention from scanning his surroundings to Luke. His eyes were distant, as if deeply considering something.

"It sure is a nice day for traveling," Luke said, glancing around, then turning his attention back to the man.

"Yes, it is. My name is Allen, by the way," Allen said, introducing himself while extending his hand.

"I'm Luke. It's good to meet you," Luke said, shaking the man's hand.

"So, Luke, what direction are you going today? I'm currently seeing where going west takes me," Allen said a bit curiously.

"Well, according to my map, I'll be heading in a similar

direction, at least for now," Luke replied, placing his hand on his map again tied to his belt.

"Map, what would you need a map for? What do you need some dumb piece of parchment telling you where to go?" Allen asked, shaking his head.

"Without a map, how would you know which way to go," Luke said, his expression and tone quite skeptical.

"You should go any way that feels right," Allen said, in a tone that sounded as if it was the most obvious thing in the world.

"How are you supposed to avoid falling off a cliff or into a river or something like that?" Luke asked, sounding concerned.

"Who says that those things can be avoided? If they happen, they happen. Do you really believe your map can help you avoid things like that?" Allen challenged, crossing his arms.

"Yes, I absolutely do believe that," Luke replied instantly with a lot of confidence.

"Well I still say if you just use your brain, you can find your own way," Allen replied as he put his hands in his pockets.

"That still sounds like a very good way to get lost to me," Luke said, shaking his head.

"How can you get lost if there is no ultimate destination," Allen countered with a triumphant look, as if he had won the whole argument.

"Of course there is a destination; all journeys have one," Luke replied, crossing his arms.

"Really, what would that be?" Allen responded, also crossing his arms and scowling as he stared down the other man.

"That's obvious; we're all headed to the Twin Ultimate Gates. The one that you go through determines where you go after you leave the Great Forest. Weather you go to the Eternal Haven or the Eternal Fire," Luke answered, returning the other man's stare calmly.

"You can't possibly believe that old legend about there being more than one gate or that old fable about there being anything beyond the gate," Allen replied with a scoff in his voice while, shaking his head.

"I do believe both of those things," Luke said with complete confidence, the certainty in his eyes boring into the other man's eyes.

"What possible proof of any of that could you have?" Allen asked, not backing down in the least.

"The man that created the Great Forest said so," Luke answered, again touching the map on his belt without wavering.

"That's what you're calling proof? Come on; that's the weakest evidence that I've ever heard of," Allen scoffed a mocking look in his eyes.

"Oh really? What kind of proof do you have that it's not true? Or are you disbelieving because you don't want it to be true?" Luke asked, returning the gaze evenly while being careful to keep any edge out of his voice.

The questions hit Allen like a ton of bricks, making him realize the other man was right about the reason for his disbelief.

"I guess you're right. I am lost," Allen said thoughtfully, then turned and walked away.

Sadness gripped Luke's heart as he watched Allen walk

away. He couldn't help feeling like he'd failed. He wondered if there was anything else he could have said. Or a better way to phrase what he did say.

As he turned the next corner, the sky began to cloud over. How fitting, he thought, considering his current mood. Within a few minutes, it was as dark as twilight and there was a biting chill in the air sending a chill through him. A couple of minutes later, an equally biting wind began blowing, causing him to shiver.

An instant later, he felt the first raindrops hit his head and saw dots appear on the concrete at his feet. Before he could take more than a few steps, it seemed like the sky opened up. The rain came down in sheets. He tried desperately to see through the seemingly endless streams of water coming from the sky. There was what felt like gallons of water dripping into his eyes.

While his frantic search continued, there was a flash of lightning. A split second later, the resounding crash of thunder sounded. It felt as if the explosive sound was right over his head and all around him.

"There has to be shelter somewhere," Luke said, thinking out loud as he shivered, looking around frantically.

Before anything else could happen, he noticed a flash of gold in his peripheral vision. There was a light came from his map. He reached down and removed it from his belt. As soon as he did, he found that the scroll itself glowed. That glow seemed to repel the raindrops, protecting the parchment from the water.

When he opened the map, a new set of directions had appeared. The glowing, gold letters on the parchment caused the raindrops to glitter and sparkle like falling diamonds.

As he set out to follow the directions, the wind picked up as he continued to be pelted by the freezing rain. It felt as if the wind tried to snatch the map out of his hand. As a result, he clutched the parchment tighter as he turned a corner.

Coming to a fork in the road with three paths, he shivered as he looked down at his map. The driving rain in his eyes made reading the words a bit more difficult. Reaching up with his other hand, he quickly wiped the water from his eyes, allowing him to see the words clearly.

Now confident about where he went, he walked down the middle path. As he began walking, lightning flashed, and a few seconds later, thunder boomed. The flash of light and loud noise caused him to flinch.

After ten minutes of walking, the storm still raged. It may have even gotten a little worse. However, there was a slight upside. A huge mountain rose in front of him. As he neared the mountain, he followed a couple more directions. When he reached the mountain, something so breathtaking and amazing appeared before him that for a second he thought he was dreaming.

There, nestled behind some trees protecting it from the driving rain, was the opening of a cave. He walked over to the edge of the cave in an effort to determine if it was real. Much to his great relief, he found out that it was real as he stepped into the cave.

Walking into the center of the cave, he placed some rocks in a circle in which he would start a fire. Once done, he set about collecting tree branches for the fire. It only took a few minutes for him to gather enough wood. After that, it only took a few minutes for him to get the fire going.

About thirty minutes later, the fire burned bright. Sitting next to it, Luke finally stopped shivering as he looked through his pack for a dry set of clothes. A couple seconds later, he found one and quickly changed into it. After he did, he made himself some dinner. After he was done, he laid out his bedroll and went to sleep.

A couple of hours later, the storm had only lessened slightly. Suddenly he shot upright as if struck by the lightening that was crashing outside. He had been awakened by a sound. In the stillness he listened carefully, straining to hear through the sounds of the storm. His heart leaped into his throat as he heard it.

Turning his attention to the mouth of the cave, he froze in his spot. There, just on the edge of the cave mouth, he saw five sets of glowing eyes. In the space of the next heartbeat, a howl shattered the stillness of the moment. That was followed immediately by intermingled growling coming from the five shadowy figures.

In the dying light of the fire, the figures began advancing into the cave. As soon as they entered the cave, he could see that the figures were wolves. Moving further in, they began encircling him while growling and snarling. The predators circled just outside the ring of light from the rapidly dying fire cutting him off from the stack of branches.

Just as the fire flickered for the last time and died, something remarkable happened. The glow of his map became brighter till it extended a couple inches past the limits of what the glow of the fire had been previously.

Suddenly one of the wolves tried to advance into the ring of soft golden light. The instant that the light touched its paw, it yipped and jumped back. After that, none of the other wolves seemed particularly eager to try that again.

Even as the wolves continued to circle, Luke felt an overwhelming sense of safety flooding him. After a couple of minutes, he laid back down. It was only a few minutes later that he was once again sound asleep.

The next morning when he woke up the wolves were gone. He quickly packed up his campsite, making sure he didn't leave anything behind. When he stepped out of the cave, it was all he could do to not sigh in annoyance. While it wasn't the raging storm of the night before, it was, unfortunately, still raining.

Within thirty minutes of him starting out again, he was again soaked to the bone. Thankfully, there was no biting wind this time.

That's why it was such a relief when ten minutes later an inn came into view. Without really meaning to, he picked up his pace a little bit, wanting to get to the building as fast as possible. He looked forward to a roof over his head and maybe a good meal.

When he entered the inn, the atmosphere was warm with a low hum of noise. Spotting an empty table near the back, he made his way over to it. He took a quick look around the room as he sat down in one of three chairs at the table. Just as he sat down, a waitress walked up asking what he'd like, and he told her he wanted a bowl of stew with something warm to drink. She returned with his order within a few minutes.

Just as he was finishing his meal, a man a few years younger than him walked up to his table. As the other man sat down, the waitress came and took the plate away.

"Hello, my name it Matthew, but most people call me Matt," Matt greeted, extending his hand.

"My name is Luke; it's good to meet you," Luke said, shaking the other man's hand, not really sure what was going on.

In the few second of silence, Matt shifted in some discomfort.

"Is there something I can help you with?" Luke asked, noticing the other man seemed to be very excited about something.

"Yes, actually, there is. I couldn't help but notice when you came in that you had something that looked like a Light Map tied to your belt," Matt said, taking a drink of water from the cup in his hand.

"You're right; that it is a Light Map," Luke replied, encouraged by the hopeful expression on Matt's face.

"I was hoping that I could get a copy," Matt requested, looking straight into Luke's eye as he set his cup on the table.

"Certainly," Luke said, taking out his map and touch-ing the cross at the top of the map, causing another map to appear on the table in a flash of gold light.

"Thank you," Matt said, standing up as he shook Luke's hand again.

Matt immediately turned and walked back to his group

of six friends. As soon as he reached them, he showed them the map. After he talked to the others about it for a few minutes, many of the group got copies as well. The group continued to talk as they left the inn.

A disconcerting something drew Luke's attention away from the door after it had closed behind the group. Out the corner of his eye, he noticed someone standing up. That person was a man sitting at a table at the other side of the room, who walked over to the bar and leaned against it.

"It's all just so unnecessary," the man said, shaking his head.

"What is?" Luke asked, as he stared in utter confusion at the other man.

"Relying on a piece of parchment when there is a better way," the man answered, his gaze flicking to the map still open on the table.

"And just what is that better way," Luke countered as he crossed his arms, looking more than a little skeptical at the other man.

"All you really need to do is think for yourself instead of relying on some outside source," the man replied, also crossing his arms.

"Just what do you mean by that?" Luke asked, continuing to look skeptically at the man, with his arms still crossed.

"You see, I got this system to figure out which way to go," the man said, sounding quite pleased with himself.

"How is that working out for you so far?" Luke asked, sounding like he really did care what the answer would be.

"I'll have you know it's been going really well. It's

so much fun being able to go anywhere and do anything I want," the man replied with a confident smirk.

"Have you thought about where you'll end up?" Luke asked, dreading the answer.

"Nope, and I'm not going to," the man replied with the same smirk.

Luke nodded while tossing a few coins on the table. With the sadness and disappointment hitting him just as hard as it did last time, he turned and left the inn. His mood didn't improve as he began walking down the path again.

He'd been traveling for a few hours when he saw a man approach from ahead of him. As the man got closer, he bumped into Luke. When the other man bumped into him, their gaze met and he saw a faint red glow in them. Both of them staggered back slightly at the impact. It only took a few seconds for them both to step back and recover. As soon as the other man had done so, he quickly scampered off like a rat. While that happened, Luke reached down to place his hand on his map. When he did, there was nothing there. The instant he realized, he whipped around in the direction that the man had gone.

"Hey, wait," Luke shouted, before the man had the chance to make it very far.

"Now why would I do that," the man replied without turning around.

"You took my map, and I want it back. You can't take that from me," Luke shouted, holding out his hand toward the thief.

"Oh really, watch me. What just happened!" the man exclaimed as the map disappeared from his hand in a golden light. The second the light began, he shielded his eyes from it as if the light was painful to him.

Just as suddenly, Luke's map appeared in his outstretched hand. For an instant he stared at the parchment in astonishment. By the time he looked up, the man had run off and was nowhere to be seen. He carefully secured the map back where it belonged, then continued on his way.

A little while later, the attempted thief stood in front of his boss. He'd just reported what had happened and now stood stiffly. The boss paced in front of his fearful subordinate.

"How could you be so stupid," the angry boss seethed, storming forward to grab hold of the thief's clothes.

"What do you mean, Sir," the thief asked, not able to keep all of the quiver out of his voice.

"How many times have I told you that those infernal maps can only be removed for the possession of someone who surrenders it willingly," the angry boss rebuked, shaking the thief while his eyes glowed bright red.

"Many times, Sir," the thief replied, sounding terrified.

"That's what I thought. Now get out of my sight," the angry boss said, throwing the thief toward the door.

The instant his boss released him, the thief took the opportunity to escape and scrambled to his feet and fled the room. His boss turned his back on his subordinate and stared out the window.

During a straight stretch of the path with branch-off paths, Luke's map unexpectedly started to glow. Confused he took out it out and opened it. The message inside was even more baffling, which was "Wait there for five minutes." Exactly five minutes later, just as he'd taken out and unrolled his map, two men walked up. The second one of the men saw the unrolled map. He got an angry scowl on his face.

"I don't want anything to do with that thing," the man said, glaring at the parchment with the same angry scowl.

"What is that?" the other man asked, curious, not understanding his friend's angry response to such an ordinary-looking object.

"It's a Light Map. Would you like a copy," Luke offered, his attention turning to the other man.

"I think I've heard of those. Alright, I'll take a copy," the second man said, an open and curious expression on his face. He watched as Luke touched the cross on the top, making another copy, which was handed to him.

"You do whatever. I'm out of here," the man sneered, then stormed away.

The second man watched as his friend walked away. It saddened him to lose his friendship, and he couldn't understand why his friend got so angry. On that note, he and Luke continued on as well.

Many years later, when Luke's journey came to an end a few things had changed, one of those things was that he was traveling with three other people. Over the years, there had been times he'd traveled by himself, while at other times he'd travel with other groups for a time before they parted ways. During that time, he'd also give maps to many people he met along the way.

As the gates came into view in the distance, the path started to go uphill. With each step, it got steeper and steeper. Just before they reached the gate, Luke looked down and saw the other path leading down to the other gate. When he did, his heart ached when he saw the three men that had rejected the map walking through the gate to the Eternal Fire. Knowing he'd done all he could, but wishing it could have turned out differently, he turned his gaze forward. He walked through the gate to the Eternal Haven.

* * *

"And that is the story that started it all," Alicia said when she finished the story, while looking at each of her friends.

"That was amazing," Sadie said, astonished.

"It might take me quite a while to figure out the symbolism," Cindy said, running her hand through her hair.

"Yeah, me too," Jackie agreed, glad she wasn't the only one.

With that, the group made and ate some dinner. Afterward, they returned to the living room and watched a movie.

THE END

CHAPTER 2

Love Across Time

This time Alicia was at her parents' twentieth wedding anniversary. The party took place in a small reception hall in a local hotel. About twenty-five people attended the party.

Her parents had each just made a speech about their marriage. Once the speech was over, her dad, Jack, sat down. Her mother, Stephanie, remained standing with the mic in her hand.

"You all know my wonderful daughter, Alicia," Stephanie said with parental pride in her voice.

Her words were answered by a round of applause from the whole room.

"It seems that she needs a little encouragement to grace us with her considerable talents. What do you say we give her some," Stephanie suggested, sounding excited.

"Yeah," several people in the audience said, accompanied by a new rounds of excited clapping filling the room.

The clapping only died down when the aforementioned woman stood up. Alicia glanced at her mother, then turned her attention to the crowd.

"Alright, as a special gift to my amazing and persistent mother, I'll do it," Alicia said, her statement followed by clapping.

"How about you tell us a love story. That would certainly be appropriate considering the occasion," Stephanie suggested, glancing at her husband.

"You're right; it would be appropriate, and I know just the story. This is a love that overcame every obstacle, including time itself. It all starts with a perfectly ordinary young woman named Jessica and how her life became anything but ordinary," Alicia said. She then launched into the story.

* * *

The winter morning dawned crisp and cool. A young woman named Jessica Brent stepped out of her house and pulled her coat tighter as a gust of cold wind blew. It had to get cold today of all days, Jessica thought as she walked down the street.

The young woman headed to her favorite coffee shop and afterward would head to work. When she entered the small café, a warm feeling engulfed her, caused by not only the temperature but the scent of freshly baked cinnamon rolls and other baked goods. The design and colour scheme was also warm and inviting. She entered just as the last of the three-person lineup was served.

"Good morning, Amy," Jessica greeted as she walked up to the counter.

"Morning, you want the usual," Amy guessed lightly.

"Yes, please," Jessica replied, reaching into her purse for her wallet.

"The cinnamon buns are really good today. Would you

like one of those with your coffee this morning?" Amy asked as she began making the ordered coffee.

"Sure, I might as well have some breakfast for once," Jessica replied, consulting the price list for the price of the cinnamon roll, then placed the right amount of money for both it and coffee onto the counter.

By the time she finished, her coffee was made and the cinnamon roll was right next to it. She picked up both and thanked the cashier. As she left, she checked her watch. She didn't really like what she saw.

She looked up and started walking considerably faster. If she was going to make it to work on time, then she'd have to hurry. It took her about fifteen minutes of fast walking for her to reach the place where she worked.

The building the young woman worked in was called the Dragon's Talon Inn, though it was more of a medieval experience than just a hotel. What made this place different from a regular hotel was neither the staff nor the guests were allowed to have anything modern on the premises. Things like watches, cell phones, or any other technology were to be checked at the front desk. The staff was required to wear period clothes, and the guests were strongly encouraged to also wear period clothes.

Jessica slipped in the staff side door hoping and praying that she wasn't late. The instant she was through the door, she looked up and realized she hadn't made it on time. What led her to this conclusion was when she saw her manager and saw the look on the stern older woman's face.

"You're late, Miss Brent," the woman said with stern

disapproval in her tone as she stood there with her arms crossed.

"I'm sorry, Mrs. Jacobs," Jessica replied, hoping she wasn't going to get into to much trouble for being late for the second time this week.

"Just get changed and get to work," Mrs. Jacobs instructed, sounding resigned.

Jessica nodded and headed to the staff changing room. She got changed as quickly as she could and took her post at the front desk.

In a very different time and place, a young man named Sir Luke Borden of Erith walked down one of the many halls of his father's castle. Each footstep echoed off the stone walls and came to a stop when he heard footsteps. A few seconds later, his squire Elric rounded the corner and walked up to him. The young man was about fifteen years old and had sandy coloured hair that was a mix of brown and blond.

"There you are. I've been looking for you," Luke greeted, eyeing his young apprentice.

"I apologize, Sir; your father is looking for you," Elric informed, hoping that he wasn't going to get into trouble.

"He often is," Luke replied dryly, lightly crossing his arms. He met the young man's gaze with an unimpressed look.

"He wishes to speak with you about a matter that is, apparently, of the utmost importance," Elric added, his tone losing the worry from before, now that he knew that he wasn't in trouble.

"It's not terribly difficult to figure out the topic of

discussion," Luke replied, the frustration in his tone increasing.

"It never is," Elric replied in a tone of voice clearly showing the two of them had had this conversation before.

"I'll go to him and have the same conversation yet again," Luke said, not sounding like he looked forward to it.

The young knight squared his shoulders and continued down the hallway. He grew more annoyed with every step.

It didn't take Luke very long to find his father. His father, Sir Henry Borden Earl of Erith, was in the library reading. When he opened the door, his father looked up from the book.

"Ah, my son, I have been looking for you," Henry greeted, closing the book he was reading and putting it on the small table next to his chair.

"Yes, I heard," Luke said, meeting his father's gaze while crossing his arms lightly as the door swung closed behind him.

"We need to have an important conversation, my son," Henry said, his tone serious as he stood up from the chair.

"So I was told," Luke replied evenly.

"I'm deeply concerned for you, son. You have refused to marry no matter how many perfectly suitable maidens that I find. I'm at my wits end with what to do with you," Henry said, shaking his head as he began to pace.

"It's not that I'm uninterested in marrying, and I know that I must marry a lady of noble birth. It's just that the woman I marry will be one I've chosen, that I love," Luke replied as his eyes followed his father.

"And how long must I wait for you to find this woman,"

27

Henry demanded, holding his hands behind his back to keep from waving them around in the air.

"As long as it takes," Luke replied, his tone firm and unyielding. It was clear that he wasn't going to back down.

"It's only that I want to see the last of my children safely married before I die," Henry said, his tone softening.

"You are as healthy as a horse. There is still plenty of time," Luke replied with a slight smile.

"At the rate you are going, I'm beginning to wonder," Henry replied, scowling at his amused son.

"You worry much to much, father," Luke said, then turned and left.

Henry stared at his son's back in disappointment as the servants opened the door. There was nothing amusing about this situation. His gaze didn't waver till the door closed behind his son.

Back in modern times, Jessica sat at the front desk. She looked through the drawer of the desk for a blank piece of paper. That's when she saw two modern white envelopes, which were an almost-jarring contrast to the off white of the parchment the inn used. When she turned them over to see the side with the address, they were both addressed to her. She scowled at the offending envelope. Both envelopes had been delivered to her at the airport just as she was about to board the plane after a weeklong trip to London. She had just gotten back the day before and must have left them behind by accident.

The top letter was written by pretty much the last person on the face of the earth she wanted to hear from.

That is why neither letter had been opened. Taking a deep breath, she decided to take the plunge and open them.

Just as Jessica picked up the two envelopes, Mrs. Jacobs walked up. The older woman looked at the young woman as she looked at the envelopes. Mrs. Jacobs felt a spark of concern when she saw the dazed and distressed look on her employee's face.

"Mrs. Jacobs, can I have my break now?" Jessica asked, her voice shaking ever so slightly and her hand was also shaking just slightly.

"Certainly, Miss Brent," Mrs. Jacobs replied, her voice tinged with the appropriate amount of concern.

To upset to actually speak, Jessica nodded as she stood up from her chair. She rushed into the back toward the kitchen, getting more upset with every step. As she hurried through the kitchen, she was still looking at the top of the two envelopes. The instant she emerged from the back door, she crumbled onto the back steps. With shaking hands, she opened the envelope and took out the letter. When she was about a quarter of the way through, anger filled her eyes that were glistening with tears. After another few sentences, the threatening tears fell, dotting the paper. When she was halfway through the letter, she couldn't take any more. With anger still bright in her eyes, she crumpled the letter.

Just as she finished, she heard a crash near the end of the ally. Standing up, she angrily jammed the crumpled letter into her pouch attached to her belt. At the sound of another crash, she more carefully put the other still unopened letter into her pouch.

Unable to resist the siren call of her ever-curious mind, Jessica carefully crept deeper into the alley. Her more sensible side kept telling her she should run the other direction. Unfortunately, that side of her was summarily ignored as she took another step deeper into the alley. Just as she reached the spot where the crash had come from, she heard a sound coming from behind her.

Before she could spin around to see where the sound had come from, she was grabbed from behind. A heartbeat later, just as she was about to try to scream, someone placed a cloth over her nose and mouth. The surprise of the sudden onset of her situation caused her to gasp. In that instant, she smelled a sweet smell and knew that she was in trouble. Armed with this knowledge, she tried to struggle. Unfortunately, it was to late. Her limbs felt like they were made of lead as she pushed weakly against the arm restraining her. Sadly, it was no use. It felt like the arm was made of steel to her sluggish brain. Blinking frantically, trying to stay awake, she felt her arms flop uselessly to her sides. Panic surged through her as she succumbed to the heaviness that was relentlessly dragging her toward unconsciousness.

Her attacker smiled maliciously as she slumped unconscious in his arms. In the next instant, a panel van backed into the end of the alley. A man jumped out of the front passenger side and hurried to the back of the van. He quickly opened the back doors and turned to his conspirator.

"Hurry and get her into the van," the passenger said quietly but with a whole lot of urgency in his hushed tone.

"I know, I know," the attacker said in the same hushed tone, but sounding annoyed.

"We gotta get out of here before someone sees us," the passenger said, gesturing for the other to move faster.

Heeding the prompting of his conspirator, the attacker picked up his pace. As soon as the two men got her in the back of the van, it sped off. In doing so, the driver hit several trash cans and barely avoided hitting two other vehicles in their haste to get away.

It didn't take very long for the van to reach its destination. Which was, a rather ominous, old warehouse with discarded, half-broken pallets and trash all around the front of the building. The cracked or broken windows and rusted or dented corrugated metal made the building seem even more imposing.

When the van approached, the massive doors opened, and it drove in. Once inside, the driver turned off the engine and got out. By the time he had run around to the back, the other two had gotten Jessica out and put her on a gurney.

Just then a man in a lab coat entered the cavernous space of the warehouse. He walked over to the gurney and looked down at the woman laying on it.

"Bring her to my laboratory," the lab-coated man instructed, then turned and headed toward the door he had just emerged from.

"Right away, Doc," the driver replied immediately.

The three men quickly brought the gurney down the stairs to the basement room that the mad scientist used as a laboratory. The room was filled to the brim with a wide verity of machinery. Near the centre of the room was a

31

devise that looked like a huge, empty frame with machines on each side. The mad scientist was busy bustling around the room with most of his efforts centred around the frame-like machine.

About two hours later, the mad scientist looked over at the gurney and found it empty. He frowned in annoyed disappointment while shaking his head.

"You lose something, Doc?" a lackey asked, dragging a struggling Jessica over to the mad scientist.

"Yes, thank you, Stewart. Tie her securely, both wrists and ankles," the mad scientist instructed as he adjusted something on his machine.

Stewart did as he was told and tied her up. Just because he felt a bit vindictive, he tied a bandanna around her mouth. Once he was done, he placed her on the gurney.

"You really should be honoured, Young Lady. You're about to be on the forefront of a major scientific breakthrough in time travel. Unfortunately for you, the trip will be one way," the mad scientist said as he powered up the machine.

Suddenly, a whirring sound came from the machine. A few seconds later, a curtain of white light appeared inside the frame-like structure.

The mad scientist monitored the readings on the readouts. After a second, he seemed happy about what he saw and turned toward the gurney and his lackey.

"Throw her through," the mad scientist instructed in a cold voice.

Stewart approached Jessica and reached out to pick her up. She tried desperately but unsuccessfully to squirm away from the man's reaching arms. The lackey didn't seem to even notice her efforts as he lifted her like a sack of flour. He unsympathetically tossed her through the curtain of energy. A brief flare lit the energy curtain before it shut down.

When Jessica came into contact with the energy curtain, a bright light engulfed her. She also was engulfed by a feeling that she was floating. The sensation and light only lasted a few seconds before both faded.

Within a few minutes, Jessica could once again see. She looked around. When she did, she felt utter confusion as she tried futilely to understand her change in surroundings. The cause of the feeling was that she was now in some kind of forest, when just minutes before she had been in the middle of a city.

The young woman's contemplation of her surroundings was cut short when she heard a sound. She held her breath and listened, trying to figure out what the sound was. After a second, she, to her great surprise and confusion, recognized the sound as hoof beats that were really close.

A few minutes earlier, Luke and Elric were out on their afternoon ride. They rode through the north woods of the grounds of Withall Castle. They had just entered a small clearing when something unexpected happened, there was a bright flash of light.

When the light died down, they were yet again surprised to find a young woman. The second Luke saw that she was tied up, he immediately jumped off his horse. As soon as his feet hit the ground, he took a step toward her.

The instant he did, she scrambled back away from him till her back came in contact with a tree.

"Madam, you need not be afraid. We mean you no harm," Luke assured, trying to calm the clearly frightened woman.

As the young knight had hoped, the woman seemed to calm at his words. He again cautiously approached her. This time she didn't shy away.

"Please remain calm while I cut your bonds," Luke requested, pulling his dagger from the sheath on his belt.

At the woman's nod, the knight made quick work of the ropes around her wrists and ankles. With a slightly shaking hand, she pulled off the cloth around her mouth. Just as she did so, Elric got off his horse and rushed over.

"Are you alright?" Luke asked, still in his crouched position.

"I think I'm mostly alright," Jessica replied, trying to determine if she had any injuries more serious than a few scratches and scrapes.

"Are you hurt anywhere?" Luke asked, sounding concerned as he helped the woman to her feet.

"No, just some scratches, scrapes, and bruises. I'm also pretty sure that I hit my head as well," Jessica replied. She wrapped her arms around herself to stop herself from shivering. Though she wasn't sure why she was shivering.

"Here, you can use my cloak," Luke said as he took off his cloak and wrapped it around Jessica's shoulders.

"Thank you, my name is Jessica Brent," Jessica introduced, as she pulled the warm wool cloak tighter around herself.

"My name is Sir Luke Borden, the youngest son of the Earl of Erith, and this is my squire, Elric," Luke introduced, gesturing at himself, then the young man standing next to him.

When Luke said this, it immediately caused Jessica to go even paler, which confused both of them. They were even more confused when she looked like she tried to comprehend what she'd just been told.

Jessica tried desperately to figure out if this was a dream or if she'd hit her head a lot harder than she'd thought. After all, this man had just introduced himself as a knight. Now that she thought about it, they were both wearing period appropriate clothes as well. Suddenly it hit her that one of the last things the lunatic in the lab coat had said was something about time travel. At the time, she'd thought it was nothing more than the deranged ramblings of a mad man. Now much to her astonished confusion it seemed to be true.

"Sir, we should get her back to the castle. It looks as if she is about to faint," Elric suggested strongly, watching concernedly as Jessica swayed slightly.

"You are correct; she does seem to be quite shaken from her ordeal," Luke agreed, also sounding concerned.

"Thank you both for all your help," Jessica said, looking between the two of them with gratitude in her expression.

"I'm glad that we were able to assist you," Luke replied, sincerely.

Luke helped Jessica up onto his horse. At this moment, she was very glad that she had learned how to ride sidesaddle. She had learned when she had taken a summer job at a medieval fair two summers ago.

It took the three of them about thirty minutes to reach the castle. The beautiful, bright, gleaming, white structure towered majestically over the land. When she'd visited a castle in her time, she had thought that they were impressive. That didn't even hold a candle to what they looked like in this time. The crenellated towers and walls gleamed in the bright sunlight.

As they approached, the soldiers on guard opened the gates. Henry looked out the window of his chambers as the gates opened. When he did, he saw his son leading his horse while a young woman with long, braided, blond hair wearing a bright gold dress rode it. A few seconds later, Elric rode through the gate before it was closed again.

The elder knight turned and headed out, intending to greet his son. As he navigated the many maze-like hallways and chambers of the castle, he wondered who the young woman was. It didn't take long before he crossed the Great Hall to the door. Just as he stepped through the doorway into the courtyard his son, his son's squire, and the mystery woman came to a stop a few feet away. The two of them both got off their horses. Luke walked over and handed the reins of his horse over to Elric, who then led both horses away.

"How was your ride, my son?" Henry asked as he watched the woman walk over to stand next to Luke.

"Greetings, Father, it went quite well mostly," Luke greeted, inclining his head slightly out of respect.

"And who is this charming young lady?" Henry asked, turning his attention from his son to the young woman.

"This, Father, is Miss Jessica Brent," Luke introduced, gesturing toward Jessica who was standing to his left.

"Greetings, Lord Borden," Jessica said, stepping forward and curtsying to the Earl.

Henry noticed the red marks on Jessica's wrists. This as well the way she swayed just slightly caused concern to bloom inside him.

"Come, let us discuss this in the drawing room," Henry said, then immediately turned and reentered the keep.

The three of them followed the Earl into the closest drawing room. As soon as they entered, Henry and Luke each took a seat.

Luke asked that Jessica be shown to a guest room and received a nod from his father. A second later, a maid entered and led Jessica out of the room. As soon as the door closed, Luke sat down in the chair next to his father's chair.

The knight told his father how they found Jessica. Henry asked if she had been set upon by bandits. They told him they didn't know because Jessica had been to shaken from her ordeal to tell them. The discussion ended with the two of them deciding to help her.

About an hour later, Luke and Elric were in one of the private solars with Jessica. She had agreed to tell them what happened, but she wanted to do so somewhere private.

"What I'm about to tell you will seem unbelievable. I'm having a hard time believing it myself. All I ask is that you give me the chance to prove it. Because I promise you that it's absolutely true," Jessica said, touching the tips of her hair nervously.

"I will give you that chance," Luke assured, not sure what she could say that would be so shocking.

"I will as well, Madam," Elric agreed as soon as the knight finished talking.

"Near as I can tell, I'm from around a thousand years in the future. I was abducted and sent here by an evil man. He did it just to see if he could. Whatever he did to send me here is what caused that bright light that you saw," Jessica explained, holding her breath, terrified at what their reactions would be.

"You are quite correct, Madam; your story does seem quite unbelievable," Luke said, skeptical but trying to sound not to be entirely closed to the idea, an effort that was mostly successful.

"Even in my time such a thing would be viewed as totally impossible. So I can't really blame you for not believing me," Jessica said, sounding resigned.

There was a brief silence as the two men absorbed the information. Neither were really sure whether they believed her. The most obvious conclusion would be that she had gone mad. If that was the case, they weren't really sure what they were going to do. However, they had given their word that they'd give her the chance to prove what she said was true.

"Like I said, I do have proof here," Jessica said, reaching into her pouch and pulling out the envelope from one of the letters.

"I do hope that this proof you have will be quite

significant to prove such an astounding claim as this, Miss Brent," Elric said, sounding skeptical.

I hope that she really isn't mad, Luke thought. There was something about this unusual woman that drew him to her.

Jessica handed the envelope to them. They each took a good look at the envelope. There in the corner was the date that the letter was sent. The paper was also unlike any they'd seen before. Those two things combined proved to be quite compelling proof.

"I can never go back," Jessica explained, her tone a combination of sadness, loss, and a significant amount of fear.

"You needn't fear, Madam; I'll help you in any way that I can," Luke said, gently touching the back of her hand for a second.

"Thank you, Sir Luke," Jessica said, feeling warmth growing inside her at his words that she couldn't quite identify.

"It must be terrible to have been separated from your family in such a way," Elric said, sympathy clear in his voice.

That I'm afraid already happened, Jessica thought. Just thinking about that particular situation caused a stab of pain, sadness, and loss.

"This could be a chance for a fresh start," Luke said encouragingly to get rid of some of the sadness in her bright-blue eyes.

"I know you two have already done so much for me, but I have one more favour to ask of you. Please keep where

I come from a secret," Jessica requested, looking between them.

There was a brief pause as the two men thought about her request. After that few-second pause, Elric glanced at the knight, who nodded, then they both turned their attention back to Jessica.

"I swear on my honour that I will never divulge this information," Luke said, realizing the danger of such information in the wrong hands.

"I too swear on my honour that I will never tell a single soul," Elric said seriously as he locked eyes with the young woman.

At their words, Jessica's eyes brightened significantly. Just as she was about to respond there was a knock on the door. At the sound, she quickly returned the envelope to her pouch.

"Come," Luke said, once they were sure everything futuristic was out of sight.

A servant girl entered and curtsied to the three people in the room. Her eyes flicked around the room briefly.

"Apologies for the interruption, but dinner will be served soon," the servant girl said, hoping she wasn't about to get in trouble.

"Thank you for informing us. We will be down shortly," Luke said kindly.

"Yes, Sir Luke," the servant girl said, then curtsied again and turned to leave.

"Wait. Could you find something for my guest to wear to dinner," Luke said, just as the servant was about to head to the door.

"Certainly," the servant said after turning around to face the knight.

The young girl turned her attention to Jessica, who also stood up and turned her attention to the young woman.

"Do you think there's time?" Jessica asked, thinking about how long it took her to get into her work clothes.

"Oh certainly, Madam," the servant girl assured with confidence.

"That is one thing that always confounds me is how long it takes a woman to get ready," Elric said quietly, intending for only Luke to hear.

"Really. And just how long does it take for you to get into your armour," Jessica replied, having heard what he said.

"I, um, see your point, Madam," Elric replied, his tone indicating he'd learned his lesson.

Luke tried to hide a chuckle behind his hand at Jessica's mischievous reply. When Jessica heard him, she turned a bright smile on him that seemed to light up the room.

"Right this way, Miss," the servant girl said, indicating for Jessica to precede her out of the room.

On that note, the two ladies left. As the door closed behind them, they were already talking about dresses.

Later, Henry, Luke, and Elric sat at the table. When the door opened, Jessica entered and began making her way to her seat at the table. Both of the men looked up. Jessica now wore a beautiful blue dress. From the moment that the door opened to when she sat down, Luke couldn't take his eyes off her. Henry took special notice of his son's attention to this mysterious woman.

"Miss Brent, I would like to formally welcome you to Withall Castle," Henry greeted, raising his glass.

"I thank you for your kindness and hospitality, Lord Borden," Jessica replied, respectfully inclining her head.

"It is our pleasure to have such a lovely and charming guest," Henry replied, even more curious about the young lady.

The rest of the dinner went really well. There was unsurprisingly quite a lot of curiosity about Jessica, all of which she handled well. After the meal ended, Jessica retired to the guest room where she was staying.

Elric had also noticed the attention his teacher had paid Jessica. He figured he would have to wait and see if anything came of it.

A week later, the Earl was having a party at Withall Castle. The evening had seemed to drag on forever with a seemingly unlimited stream of people that Luke was obliged to talk to. Elric was equally bored with the supposed festivities. That is why the two of them decided to take a little break in the form of a walk through the grounds. Only a few minutes into their walk, they noticed Jessica, who clearly had the same idea.

"Greetings, Jessica," Luke said as they approached while she examined a particularly beautiful flower.

"Good evening," Jessica said, standing up straight from examining the flower and turning to face them

"Have you been enjoying the party or just enduring it?" Luke asked, a bit of mischievousness in his tone.

"Somewhere in that range," Jessica replied, picking up on and returning the mischievousness in his tone.

"Jessica, have you seen the roses over there?" Luke asked, pointing to the rose bushes a couple feet down the path.

"Not yet, but I'd love to," Jessica replied, looking at the indicated bushes, then looking back at the knight.

"Shall we," Luke said, offering her his arm.

"We wouldn't want to neglect your squire," Jessica replied uncertainly, torn between being worried about if it was proper and wanting a little alone time with Luke.

"You needn't worry about me. I'll be right here," Elric assured, silently reassuring them both that he would chaperone them.

"In that case, I'd love to," Jessica said with a pleased smile on her face.

With that the two of them continued down the path. As Jessica admired the flowers they passed, she kept sneaking glances at Luke. A couple of times when she did this, she caught him doing so as well.

"You know, these gardens are the handiwork of my mother," Luke explained, as he glanced at some of the flower beds.

"Really. Well she did a good job. These flower beds are absolutely beautiful," Jessica said as she admired a particularly beautiful blue flower.

"Perhaps when she returns from her trip in two days, you can tell her. I'm sure she'd be glad to hear it," Luke replied, his gaze on the flowers that he pretended to be interested in, when he was far more interested in the beautiful and intelligent woman next to him.

"I'd be happy to," Jessica replied brightly.

"How are you adjusting, considering your unusual circumstances?" Luke asked, sounding concerned as he changed the subject to something more important.

"Fairly well, I think. What do you think? How am I doing at blending in?" Jessica asked, slightly nervously.

"You're doing really well. There hasn't been anything that one would notice unless they were looking for it," Luke assured, with a reassuring confidence.

"That's good because it's so different here, almost like a wonderful dream," Jessica commented, slightly lost in thought.

"What is it like so far into the future?" Luke said quietly, being careful even though they were alone.

"I come from a world where everyone is totally focused on the future. They're in such a hurry trying to grasp the next minute that they never take the time to truly live in and appreciate the one that they are in," Jessica replied as they came to a bench that was next to the rose bush Luke had pointed to earlier.

"I can't even imagine such a thing," Luke said, shaking his head.

"You should count yourself forever blessed that you don't. It's a disappointing and empty way to live. In fact, that's why I started to study this time. Hoping maybe to get back some of what was lost in the name of progress," Jessica explained, lost in thought.

"I guess that explains why you're blending in so well," Luke commented, finally understanding something he'd been wondering for quite a while.

"You know, I don't think that I'd go back even if I

could," Jessica said. It made her sadder that she felt that way than she was about losing everything that she'd ever known.

After that, the two of them started talking about a wide variety of things. Luke loved how she opened up like a blooming flower, so precious, delicate, and beautiful. He found himself wanting to protect her. The rest of the world seemed to fade as he listened to her describe the world he'd lived in all his life in ways he'd never imagined.

As they sat on that bench together, Jessica felt warm and safe. The reason was that she could tell that he was really listening to everything she was saying. She listened to everything he said with equal attentiveness. Jessica found herself hoping one day she could be there to support and encourage him the way he'd done for her.

It was as if there was a bubble around them keeping the rest of the world out. As the two of them talked, nothing else seemed to exist. Suddenly the illusion was broken by the sound of approaching footsteps. Simultaneously, in perfect sync, the two looked up at the source of the sound.

"Sir, Madam, the party is ending; perhaps it's time we went inside," Elric suggested, taking his chaperon duties very seriously.

"You're quite right," Luke said as the two of them stood up.

The three of them turned and headed back to the castle. Once inside, they each retired to their respective rooms for the night.

The next morning Henry was angrily pacing one of the lesser halls. His youngest son was once again causing him great frustration and quite a bit of anger with his antics. He'd gone missing halfway through the party last night and never reappeared. Henry decided to see what he could find out before talking to his son about it.

"Lad, go find my son's squire and tell him that I need to speak with him immediately," Henry said to the servant who had just started the fire in the fireplace

"Right away, M'Lord," The servant replied, bowing slightly, then hurrying off to do as he was instructed.

It wasn't very long later that the servant returned with Elric. Henry dismissed the servant back to his duties with a wave of his hand. His gaze never left the young squire.

"You were with my son when he left the party," Henry began. It was definitely a statement, not a question.

"We'd only intended to step out briefly for a breath of air," Elric explained, sounding slightly nervous.

"Then what happened? Neither of you were seen for the rest of the night," Henry responded. His tone was tense as his sharp gaze locked onto the young man.

"We came across Madam Jessica in the gardens. She and Sir Luke began talking while he showed her the flowers. They ended up sitting on a bench talking," Elric explained as best he could.

"The two of them spent slightly over three hours sitting on a bench talking," Henry said thoughtfully as he eyed the young man.

"You needn't worry, M'Lord, they were within my sight the whole time," Elric assured quickly.

"You may go and resume whatever my son had you

doing. It seems I need to have a talk with my son," Henry said, his tone once again thoughtful.

They both turned and left the room, each going in different directions. Just minutes after the Earl left the room, a servant approached him with an urgent message. It seems my talk with my son will have to wait, Henry thought after he read the paper.

A while later, in another part of the castle, Jessica was sitting in the top room of one of the towers. She had wanted to find somewhere to be alone. Something she hadn't thought would be that difficult, considering the size of the castle. However, much to her surprise, it turned out to be. She'd finally decided to finish reading the letter to finally close that chapter in her life permanently. When she was done, she angrily crumpled the paper into a ball. With a mist of tears in her eyes, she blindly tossed the paper ball. It hit the wall next to the door just as it opened. Luke and Elric entered the room. The knight's concerned gaze was fixed on Jessica.

"What's wrong, Jess?" Luke asked as he picked up the paper ball.

"I just finished reading the letter that came in the envelope that I showed the two of you before," Jessica said, the tears in her eyes finally dropping as she glared at the paper ball in his hand.

"Is it something you'd like to talk about?" Luke asked, his concerned gaze still fixed on her.

Jessica nodded and told him the story. How her father, the son of a minor but wealthy nobleman, met and fell in love with a regular girl. His father gave him a choice, the girl or his inheritance. They were married the next day.

The young woman told them how both her parents had died two years later. With their last breath, they asked her to tell her grandfather they forgave him and he should forgive himself too. She went to London and delivered her parents' message. It turned out that he'd been notified of her parents' deaths. Just as they had predicted, he blamed himself. While he'd still wished he hadn't missed his son's last years, knowing that his son didn't die hating him brought him a lot of peace. Over the next two years, the two of them became really close.

"May I read this," Luke asked, holding up the crumpled paper ball, hoping it would help him understand what was upsetting her so much.

"Alright," Jessica answered, trying to pull herself together.

Luke uncrumpled the letter so that he could read it. As he began reading, feelings of sadness, then anger began welling up inside him. By the time he finished, he found himself fighting a rather strong urge to punch something.

There was a good reason for the even tempered and disciplined knight's reaction. The first few sentences of the letter informed Jessica that her grandfather had died. The anger was caused by Jessica' grandfather's family called her and her mother gold-diggers that were only interested in the family money. To make matters worse, they went on to say that they were going to make sure she never saw any money.

Knowing Jessica was of noble birth didn't really help their situation because her relative wouldn't even be born for hundreds of years. It was frustrating to feel as if the answer was just out of reach.

Pushing that matter aside for now, Luke noticed Jessica still seemed really upset about the letter. Looking around the rather uninteresting room for something to distract her, he spotted another letter from her time that must have fallen out of her pouch when she pulled out the other one.

"Perhaps you'd feel better if you thought on something else," Luke suggested, hoping to get her mind off the hurtful words in the letter.

"You know, that sounds like a good idea," Jessica said, looking up at him, her eyes brightening with the barest hints of happiness.

"How about you open this letter," Luke suggested, picking up the letter, then handing it to Jessica.

"I'd almost forgotten about this. A few months back I decided to find out about my mother's ancestry. I hired someone to do some research; this is what they found out," Jessica explained as she opened the envelope and took out two sheets of paper.

There was a brief pause as Jessica read the paper. Sure enough, whatever the paper said did cheer her up. Her eyes lit up with excitement as she finished.

"According to this, my mother was related to a man named Thomas of Belmont. A fifth-century Count that renounced his title and became a lay brother at a monastery," Jessica explained as she put the papers in her lap and looked up at him.

"I remember reading about him in my history studies.

If I remember correctly, he married and had at least five children," Luke said thoughtfully.

"That is a lot of children," Jessica commented, more than a little surprised, especially considering the time period.

"This is very important. How certain are they that this information is accurate?" Luke asked, a hopeful tone in his voice.

"The birth records were very accurate. I do not see how this is all that important," Jessica replied, not understanding the serious look on Luke's face nor his hopeful tone.

"There are things that must be attended to first, but I promise that I will tell you," Luke assured, lightly touching the back of her hand.

"Alright, you can tell me whenever you feel the time is right. I trust you," Jessica said, her smile, though not quite as bright as usual, was sincere and filled with love.

"I'm sorry to interrupt, Sir, but we really should be training," Elric said, after clearing his throat.

"Unfortunately you're right," Luke said, standing up and turning to him.

While Jessica quickly put both letters back in her pouch, Luke and Elric headed to the door. Both men said a brief goodbye as they left the room. A few minutes later, Jessica left the room too.

As Luke walked out onto the practice field after getting his armour on, the words in that first letter returned to his mind. When they did, the anger they had inspired the first time returned. He proceeded to channel all his anger and frustration into sparring, a fact that the knight's sparring partners were soon not going to appreciate.

"Do you yield?" Luke asked, holding the tip of his sword to the neck of his opponent who was lying on his back and panting.

"I yield," the other man said, sounding a little frightened and very very tired as he stared up at his victorious opponent.

"Couldn't you go easy on them once, little brother?" Renard asked, noting that something seemed to be bothering his younger brother.

"Why would I do that?" Luke asked as he sheathed his sword and turned to face his brother.

"You seem bothered by something," Renard commented, tinges of concern entering his voice as he eyed his brother.

"I am, but I cannot speak of it," Luke relied, sounding slightly apologetic.

"Alright, Father would like to speak to you. He is waiting in the Lesser Hall," Renard said, a little surprised since Luke had never kept many important things from him.

Luke nodded and left, heading for the armory to take off his armour. As he and Elric took off his armor he realized he was feeling better for having the opportunity to burn off his anger. Once they were done, they headed off to meet with the Earl.

It didn't take long for the two of them to reach their destination. As soon as they reached the hall, Luke opened the door to find his father pacing back and forth.

"There is something I need to tell you," Luke said as

he strode confidently into the room, drawing his father's attention.

"Really, what would that be," Henry asked curiously, a bit surprised by the determination that he saw in his youngest son.

"I am in love with Madam Brent," Luke stated with confidence and conviction.

"And what do you intend to do about these feelings?" Henry asked, not sure what to think about the situation.

"I intend to ask for her hand in marriage this very afternoon," Luke said, just as confidently as he stared down his father.

"Is she of noble birth?" Henry asked, a little surprised that things had gone this far.

"She is descended from Thomas of Belmont from her mother's line," Luke explained, dreading the question that he knew was coming.

"What of her father's line?" Henry asked, noting the look of dread on his son's face.

"On my honour she is of noble birth through that line as well. Beyond that, I can't tell you. I keep this secret only to protect her," Luke explained, placing his fist over his heart.

"You have seen proof of this?" Henry asked, not pushing for more information, not wanting to put the young lady in danger.

"I have," Luke replied immediately and with certainty.

"As have I, M'Lord," Elric added with equal certainty.

"And she feels the same about you?" Henry asked, pretty sure she did, but he needed confirmation.

"She does, Father," Luke answered with equal certainty.

"In that case, I give you my blessing, my son," Henry said, his heart filled with happiness that he might actually see his youngest son married.

"Oh thank you, Father," Luke said, his eyes, along with the rest of his face, lighting up with more joy than he'd ever felt.

Henry watched as Luke and Elric rushed out of the room, likely going to find the young lady. I truly hope the two of them find happiness, Henry thought as the door closed.

It didn't take very much looking for them to find the lady. Jessica sat on the bench where they talked the night of the party. As they walked up to her, she looked up at them. Luke sat down next to her.

"I have something important that I need to ask you," Luke said, gazing lovingly into her eyes as he thought about what he was going to say.

"Alright," Jessica replied, looking into his eyes with every bit as much love.

"Jessica, you have lit up my life since the moment that you entered it, and I love you with everything in me. Will you accept my hand in marriage?" Luke asked, taking her hand in his, his voice filled with the love he felt.

"Of course I'll accept because I love you with my whole heart," Jessica said, her tone filled with just as much love.

As the sun set, they stood up still holding hands. The setting sun silhouetted them as they gazed lovingly into each other's eyes.

* * *

Alicia looked around the room as all the couples began holding hands. The best part was that her parents gazed lovingly at each other.

"And that is how the love story that crossed a thousand years began," Alicia said, excitedly glad about how people enjoyed the story.

The whole room applauded as Alicia handed the mic back to the MC. The evening ended with a toast to Alicia's parents and their enduring love.

THE END

PART 2

Secrets, Shadows & Truth

CHAPTER 3

Murder at Moonlight Castle

The dusk had long since given way to the black of night. The bright moonlight and the soft glow of a campfire broke up the darkness. Six people sat staring at the flickering flames. Of the three men, two were young, in their twenties. One of the women was in her early thirties, one was in her early fifties, and the third was in her twenties. Five of the people turned their attention to the thirty-year-old woman.

"Come on, Alicia, tell us a story," one of the men requested eagerly, as those around him nodded in eager agreement.

Alicia's eyes were fixed on the moonlit sky above them. "Alright. They say long ago there was a place called Moonlight Castle. It was called this because the stone that the walls were made of seemed to sparkle in the moonlight. A day that started out perfectly normal quickly became anything but."

* * *

Inside the majestic stone walls of Moonlight Castle there was the usual hum of activity. What, with the many servants bustling around getting a jump on the day. All the while, Sir Philip and Lady Nichol, who owned the castle, were still sound asleep. Suddenly, a piercing scream reverberating down the countless halls and throughout the castle shattered the peaceful, mundane scene. The scream sent the guards rushing to its source.

The scream came from one of the guest rooms. When the guards arrived, they found one of the male servants lying dead. A maid sitting on one of the couches with her arms wrapped around herself, trembling and staring at the wall.

Jemma, a traveling merchant of exotic fabrics, who had been staying at Moonlight Castle for about a week. She had long, bright-red hair that kept getting in her green eyes if she didn't tie back the strands closest to her face. On this particular day she was wearing a red dress, which she herself had made out of one of the fabrics she sold. The reason for this particular visit was Lady Nichol wanted a new dress. She was looking for just the right fabric but as of yet hadn't found it. The nobel woman had blond hair that reached all the way down her back when it was loose, which was not very often since it was always worn in a braid. Her stone grey eyes were kind as she looked over the fabric. She currently wore a sky-blue dress with a light-blue flowing skirt and silver accents on the bodice. Sir Philip was also wanting a new cape.

The morning had been quiet. She had been looking through her stock that was in the back of her covered wagon. She was looking for something new to show to Lady Nichol. When she found what she was looking for, she headed back inside.

When she had just arrived at the Lady's private sitting

room, the scream rang out. Instantly her attention turned in the direction the sound came from. The cloth merchant's curiosity was piqued, as well as her concern. She wanted so badly to go find out what the cause of the scream was she could barely stand it. It took all her willpower not to rush out of the room. However, she managed to avoid it and got back to showing her ladyship the fabrics. About a second later, when they were again in deep discussion, there was a knock on the door.

"Enter," Lady Nichol said, turning her attention from the cloth to the door just seconds before it was opened.

A young soldier entered and walked up to Lady Nichol and told her about the murder. He also told her that the victim was one of the male servants. Lastly, he told her that a young maid had found the body and may have seen something else. However, they weren't sure whether she did or not because the maid was so traumatized she wasn't talking.

"Jemma, if I recall correctly, your father is a circuit judge," Lady Nichol said, turning her gaze to Jemma.

"You are correct, M'lady," Jemma replied. She had a strong feeling she knew where this conversation was going.

"I would appreciate it if you'd look into this matter," Lady Nichol requested, taking a sip of her tea while she glanced at Jemma.

"I'd be honoured to assist you in this matter," Jemma replied, her mind already buzzing with what she needed to find out.

"Should someone send for the Coroner and the Undersheriff," The young soldier asked, drawing attention back to him.

"That would be wise," Lady Nichol agreed, confident that between the two of them the killer would be found.

The young soldier told both of them where the crime had happened. Once he was done, he was dismissed to return to his duties.

Before another word could be said, Jemma rushed out of the room. As she rushed down the cavernous hallway with archways on either side, each footstep she took echoed almost ominously. With each step, she hoped that she was up to the challenge placed in front of her. Her father had taught her much about investigating crimes such as murder. What she hadn't learned from her father she'd learned from watching the sheriffs in the towns where her father had held court. The fact that there were guards headed in the same direction only further confirmed this. When she rounded the next corner, she noticed there were a bunch of guards outside one of the guest rooms. As she approached the room, a guard stepped in front of her.

"Ma'am, this is a restricted area," the guard said, blocking her path with a fairly stern look on his face.

"Her Ladyship asked me to find out what happened," Jemma said, with as much confidence as she could muster.

"I'm not sure, Madam," the guard replied. The uncertainty of his words were echoed by the look on his face.

"Allow her through," the constable instructed, just as he'd stepped out of the room that was now the crime scene.

Immediately the guard stepped aside, allowing her entry to the room. The room that she entered was ornately decorated, though for the moment she paid little attention to the room in general. Instead most of her attention was focused on the maid sitting on one of the couches. The young woman was very distressed, still staring at the wall. Jemma walked over to her and sat down next to her. She recognized the young maid who's name was, Alice.

"Alice, can you hear me?" Jemma asked, trying to gain the traumatized young woman's attention. To this end, she placed her hand on the maid's hands that were clasped in her lap. When she did, she noticed that they were trembling.

"Richard is dead," Alice said, her voice trembling worse than her hands as she turned her tear-filled eyes on the woman sitting next to her.

"Did you know Richard well?" Jemma asked, gently trying to coax information out her before she shut down again.

"No, not very well. He'd only been working in the castle for a few weeks," Alice answered, still shaking like a leaf.

"What was his job?" Jemma asked, her voice calm and gentle. She hoped she could get more information from her.

"It was his job to light the fires in the rooms in the morning," Alice relayed, tears still in her eyes as she looked at her hands.

Jemma took a moment to consider everything she had just been told. She carefully filed away each piece of information, certain that most, if not all, would be helpful later.

"I can't believe Richard is dead. I just saw him twenty minutes ago. Now that I think on it, he did seem a mite out of sorts," Alice said thoughtfully as she turned her attention back to the wall.

"In what way? Was he upset or angry?" Jemma asked,

intrigued by this new bit of information and hoping to learn more.

"He seemed frightened, kept looking over his shoulder like he was scared that someone would be there," Alice replied, sounding like she was about to cry again.

"Thank you for your help. There may be more questions later, but for now, you can go back to your duties," Jemma said, feeling bad for the distraught maid.

"Oh thank you, Miss," Alice said, then stood up, hastily curtsied, and rushed out of the room, clearly wanting to get as far away from there as she could.

As the door closed behind the maid, Jemma stood and set about examining the room for any clues. The first thing she did was walk over to the fireplace. She carefully examined the area for any sign that there had been a struggle or of who the killer was. Sadly, her efforts were unsuccessful. Not only were there no signs of a struggle or the killer, there weren't even any signs that the victim had reached the fireplace at all.

Just as her fruitless search of that particular area came to an end, the door opened and two men entered accompanied by a soldier. When she heard the sound of the door opening and the men entering, she turned her attention to them. One was about her age with blond hair and blue-green eyes wearing clothes of varying but complementary shades of dark blue. The other was older with dark-brown hair and eyes. He was wearing clothes ranging from sand coloured to dark brown.

"Madam, I'm afraid that you'll have to leave this room," one of the men said, taking a step further into the room.

"Let me guess, you are the undersheriff and you the Coroner," Jemma replied, completely ignoring his statement and pointing from one man to the other.

"That's correct, Madam; I'm Undersheriff Robert Bartly, and this is Jacob Borden the Coroner," Robert introduced. While he observed the young woman that was clearly not a servant, surmising she was likely a guest of Lady Nichol.

"A pleasure, Sirs; my name is Jemma Alden. I'm afraid that I won't be leaving just yet," Jemma said, watching the two men carefully.

"Really, why is that?" Robert asked, not having expected that response, certainly not from a lady. He'd have thought she would be eager to leave the room where a man was killed.

"Her Ladyship has asked me to assist you in looking for the perpetrator of this horrible crime," Jemma replied as her intelligent green eyes met those of the undersheriff's.

"Why would you even wish to assist in such a troubling matter?" Robert asked, not quite sure why this lady had been allowed in the room to begin with.

"Because someone's life has been taken away, and I know I can be of help. Also, as I said, Lady Nichol asked me to," Jemma answered. There was also the reason that she was insatiably curious and never could walk away from a good puzzle, but that reason she'd keep to herself.

"Also in what way could you possibly assist me?" Robert asked, quite certain that he in no way needed assistance to do his duty.

"Tell me, Sir, how good are you at getting information

from maids that are on the verge of tears? Also, I'm quite observant and tend to notice things others miss," Jemma answered sweetly.

"I'm not going to be able to convince you to leave this to me and go about your business, am I," Robert said with a sigh, pinching the bridge of his nose.

"That is a very astute and accurate assessment of the situation," Jemma replied, with a sweet smile on her face.

"At least if you're assisting me I can keep you out of trouble," Robert responded, though his gut told him keeping this firebrand out of trouble would make solving a murder look like child's play.

While they were discussing this, the coroner had gone over to examine the body. The dead man was about thirty-two and in good physical condition. That is with the obvious exception of the stab wound in the side. The wound was to his upper chest just slightly below his armpit and likely punctured his lung. The blade was likely of medium length. Looking closely, the coroner could just see some bruising around the victim's mouth that, indicating the killer had placed his hand over the man's mouth to silence him just seconds before the fatal blow was struck. It also indicated that the attack had likely been from behind.

"Were you able to learn anything?" Robert asked, turning his attention to the coroner who was examining the body.

"It was an attack from behind. He was silenced with a hand over his mouth, then stabbed in the side. The blow punctured his lung. He would likely have been dead within minutes," Borden explained as he stood up and turned his attention to the undersheriff.

Robert began looking at the area of the room right around the body. Especially the area directly behind where the victim lay. That's when he spotted the faint impressions of a man's boots in the rug. The impression was to faint to tell anything about the man that made it.

As the undersheriff turned his attention to the room at large, his assessing gaze stopped on one spot in particular. Specifically a spot less than a step away from where the body lay, there were signs something had been removed. Based on the other contents of the lavishly decorated room, he figured that it was likely something valuable. This caused an idea for a possible motive to form in his mind.

Meanwhile, Jemma had begun her own examination of the room. She was looking over by a small table that had a pitcher of water resting on it. The table sat on the opposite side of the room than the body. As she examined the table, she noticed a piece of torn cloth. It was caught on a loose nail in the front of the table. She carefully disentangled it. Once it was loose, she took a close look at it. The fabric was not what she had been expecting.

"Excuse me, Lord Robert. I believe I found something you should see," Jemma said, turning her attention to the undersheriff with the scrap of cloth still in her hand.

"Really, what is it, Madam?" Robert asked, pausing his examination of the room and walking over to where Jemma was standing.

"I found this piece of cloth on a loose nail on that table

over there," Jemma answered, pointing to the table where she had found the cloth.

"That scrap of cloth could have been there for any length of time," Robert replied, skeptically eyeing the bit of cloth in the woman's hand.

"I happen to know that it was not there yesterday evening when I was in this very room," Jemma replied, sounding certain.

"You believe it to have been left by the killer," Robert stated; he received a nod anyway. He was beginning to agree that Jemma might be able to help him after all.

As the two of them resumed their examination of the room, Jemma slipped the scrap of cloth into a small bag hanging from her belt. After a couple of minutes of looking, the three of them decide to head down to the servant's quarters to search the victim's belongings for clues. On the way there, Robert decided to ask a question that he'd been meaning to for a while.

"The sergeant mentioned you questioned the maid who found the body. I need to know what she said. It could be very important," Robert requested as they walked down one of the many hallways.

"Certainly. She said that she didn't know the victim very well, only that his name was Richard. That his job was to light the fires in the morning, and he had only been at the castle for a short time. Also that, in the days leading up to his death, he was scared and constantly looking over his shoulder, as if he expected someone to be there," Jemma explained as they neared their destination.

"Hmm," Robert replied thoughtfully as he considered

this new piece of information and its implications. As he did this, a frown began to form on his face.

"Does something about what Alice told me trouble you?" Jemma asked, noting the look and wondering what had caused it.

"I had thought that Richard had been killed because he'd surprised a thief. However, this new information about him being frightened casts a bit of shade on that notion," Robert answered, still thinking through the information.

"What led you to believe that it was theft in the first place?" Jemma asked, going over everything she'd seen.

"There was a missing object near the body," Robert answered, watching her reaction to this information curiously.

At just that moment, another servant ran up to the group. "Sir, we found it this morning," the servant said, holding up a vase.

"That was the one that was missing from the scene of the crime," Jemma commented, all three of them stopping to examine the vase.

"What was it doing in the hay loft, Madam?" the servant asked, his gaze moving from Robert to Jemma with a questioning look.

"Perhaps the killer took it to try to make us think that the victim interrupted a thief," Jemma suggested thoughtfully as they began walking again.

A few minutes later, the group entered the servant's quarters. It was a cavernous room lined on either side with very simple wooden beds with small, plain, wooden chests at the foot of each one. Every one of them looked exactly the same as the others. A servant pointed to the bed belonging to the victim. The three of them walked over to the bed, while glancing around the room.

The first thing that Jemma did was open the small chest and begin to look at what was inside. Most of the space inside it was taken up by clothing. There were also a few personal items, which she placed on the bed as she took them out of the chest. Once she was done searching, she decided to take a closer look at the clothing, hoping to learn something that could be helpful in solving this mystery. As she was doing this she noticed that Robert was looking at the few personal items. By the time she was nearing the bottom of the chest, she had as of yet found nothing of interest. The instant she touched the last item of clothing, she knew something was wrong.

"That is most interesting," Jemma commented absently as she examined the cloth more carefully with a surprised look on her face.

"What have you found?" Robert asked, looking up from what he was doing at the unexpected comment.

"This fabric is of far better quality than what a common laborer could afford. Also, based on the fading of the colours I'd have to guess that the garment was purchased about five years ago," Jemma commented, holding up the jacket.

"Are you certain?" Robert asked, looking closely at the item of clothing in the lady's hand with an unsure look on his face.

"Sir, for your information, I'm a cloth merchant by trade, and I know my business," Jemma replied with a vehement look on her face.

"I was not aware," Robert responded, a question popping into his head that he decided he'd ask at another time. The undersheriff looked around the room for anything amiss. As his gaze traveled around the room, there didn't seem to be anything wrong. However, something did catch his attention. On the other side of the room there was a door.

"Where does that lead?" Robert asked a servant who was heading toward the door they'd entered by pointing to the door he had noticed.

"It's a back way that leads outside though the kitchens, Sir," the servant replied respectfully.

"If the motive was personal, it would have been easier to get in here. Why would the killer sneak into the keep when it would be much easier to get in here," Robert asked thoughtfully.

"It could be another misdirect," Jemma suggested, though she sounded kind of skeptical about that idea herself.

"Perhaps it would have been to conspicuous for the killer to be seen in the kitchens and servants' quarters," Robert suggested, his instincts telling him this was important.

"That would have been the case if the killer was a high-end merchant," Jemma suggested thoughtfully.

"Why do you suspect a merchant? It could be any high- or middle-station visitor to the castle. That is if your theory is even correct," Robert replied, not certain of all the conclusions she was drawing.

"Because the jacket we found is something a that

high-end merchant would wear," Jemma answered, fairly confident in her theory, though she'd need more evidence to be certain.

Before they could do any more theorizing or investigating, they were called to the afternoon meal. Afterward, the two walked down a hall, headed to talk to someone who knew the victim. The man they were going to talk to was one of the grooms. In the time the victim had been working at the castle, the two of them had gotten to be close friends. The man's name was Joshua, and they were told he was in the stables. A fact the two of them found to be accurate when they stepped into the stables. When they entered the stables, the rugged-looking man with brown hair looked up at them. Who was, forking straw into a freshly cleaned stall.

"Are you Joshua?" Robert asked, watching the man straighten from his leaned forward position and begin walking toward him.

"Aye, that would be me, Sir," Joshua replied as he stabbed the pitchfork into a nearby haystack, then crossed his arms.

"I'm Undersheriff Robert Bartly. I have some questions regarding the murder of Richard," Robert explained simply.

"I heard about that. It's a right shame; 'e was m' mate," Joshua said, sounding sad while bowing his head in very real grief.

"What kind of a man was Richard?" Robert asked, needing to know more about the man who's death he was investigating. He was also hoping that the information would lead him to a suspect.

"Hum, 'e was a decent enough chap. We got on real

well. He was real quiet, didn't talk much to anyone else. Always said that was one a the best parts a his job was that there wasn't anyone about where he was working most of the time," Joshua replied with fondness in his eyes.

"Is there anything that you can tell me about him that would aid my investigation?" Robert asked, watching the man's reaction.

"Not sure, 'e never did talk about himself very much," Joshua replied, leaning against the fork stuck in the hay bale.

"Did you notice anything about Richard's behaviour in the last few days?" Robert asked, trying a more specific question.

"I'd say so 'e been in a right state for the last week," Joshua replied after thinking on it for a few seconds.

"Can you think of anything that happened that could account for the change in his behaviour?" Robert asked, crossing his arms.

"There was that dustup with Roger. Though getting in a dust up with anyone is a might unusual for him," Joshua replied, trying to think of anything else that happened that could be classified as unusual.

"What is this Roger's job?" Robert asked, wondering if this man could be a potential new suspect.

"He's a handyman. Often he is either helping lift things in the kitchen or chopping wood for the fires," Joshua replied.

"Were you there when this dustup happened?" Robert asked, wanting to know more about this new information.

"No, I was here in the stable, and it happened in the courtyard," Joshua replied, recalling what he had heard.

"Did you hear what caused the fight?" Robert asked, wondering if this new suspect also had a motive.

"Yeah, Roger is a right disagreeable fellow, always picking on someone. He's one of the gardeners. When he'd get a mind to, he'd target some poor sod and make their lives miserable for a few weeks. Before he'd get bored and move on to someone else," Joshua explained.

"I see," Robert replied, taking careful note of the obvious dislike that the other man held for this Roger.

"Honestly, I'm surprised that Roger isn't the one that got himself murdered," Joshua continued with obvious venom in his tone.

"Do you think that this man would be capable of killing someone?" Robert asked, wondering what the man would say.

"So far, Roger hasn't actually hurt anyone. I'm not really sure how far he'd take it, but I wouldn't put anything past him," Joshua replied, crossing his arms.

"Do you remember seeing him talk to any of the merchants that have been to the castle?" Jemma asked, drawing the man's attention to her.

"I seem to recall him talking to a merchant that came here about a week ago," Joshua replied, after thinking for a few seconds.

"Did you get the impression that Richard knew this man?" Jemma asked, paying close attention to what the man was saying.

"I think so, but it was from a long ways back," Joshua answered, thinking back to the interaction that he'd witnessed.

"How did they seem to be getting along?" Jemma

asked, needing to learn more about the days leading up to the crime.

"The other guy seemed right angry with Richard. I thought for a second the other guy was going to hit him," Joshua replied, shaking his head.

"Did you hear what this argument was about?" Jemma asked hopefully.

"Sadly no, I was to far away," Joshua replied, sounding like he wished he could be more helpful.

"Can you describe this man?" Jemma asked thoughtfully.

"He was about as tall as the undersheriff. Had brown hair that was starting to turn grey and green eyes. Was dressed like one of the better-off merchants," Joshua answered, thinking back on the encounter.

"Thank you for your help. I may have more question later," Robert said, pondering all the new information he had just gotten.

"I hope you catch whoever killed Richard," Joshua said, his voice sounding both sad and vehement.

With that Robert and Jemma turned and left the stable. Once outside, the two of them headed toward the keep, considering what they had just learned.

As they were walking back to the keep, Robert decided to ask Jemma a question. It was something he'd been wondering about for quite a while. In fact, he'd been wondering it since they first met.

"Jemma, why did her ladyship ask you to assist me in this investigation?" Robert asked as they walked.

"My father is a judge, and he taught me a lot about

criminal investigation. What he didn't teach me some of the sheriffs he dealt with did," Jemma answered happily.

"Let me guess, your father wanted a son," Robert remarked dryly, not sounding very impressed with the entire situation.

"Nope, I have an older brother who was just appointed as an undersheriff," Jemma answered with a smirk on her face.

"Then why did he indulge your interest in such unladylike pursuits?" Robert asked, sounding totally baffled.

"He always said that if the Almighty had wanted me to be a delicate flower, He'd have made me one. After all, who was he to question His plans," Jemma answered, her love for her father very clear in her expression.

Robert just shook his head, completely speechless. He was totally unable to come up with any reply to that. Of all the answers he could have received, he hadn't been expecting that.

"So we've got two suspects, a bully and what might be an old enemy," Jemma summed up thoughtfully.

"We should probably talk to the one suspect that we have identified," Robert said, also thinking through the situation.

"In that case, Roger is likely in the kitchen or near there chopping wood," Jemma explained, indicating to that part of the castle with a wave of her hand.

"Lead the way, Madam," Robert said, indicating in front of him.

Together the two of them headed to the kitchen in the back of the keep. When they rounded the corner, they saw a tall, strongly built man chopping wood. He wore a tan shirt, light-brown vest, and stone-gray pants.

"Is your name, Roger?" Robert asked when they got close enough.

"Yeah, what of it," Roger replied, stopping what he was doing.

"I'm Undersheriff Robert Bartly, and I have some questions for you concerning the murder of a man named Richard," Robert said, watching the man's reaction.

"We were told that you didn't get along with the victim," Jemma added, crossing her arms.

"What of it? I didn't like the arrogant little twit," Roger replied, sticking the axe in the chopping block.

"So you're not denying that you had a motive," Robert said, his suspicion of the man growing.

"I ain't denying anything, but I didn't kill him," Roger replied indignantly.

"Why should we believe that?" Jemma asked, sounding skeptical.

"Missy, you should stay out of man's business," Roger said with a sneer.

"Have more care how you address a lady," Robert said, glaring at the man as he placed his hand on the hilt of his sword.

"Fine, as I said, I didn't kill the twit," Roger replied, scowling.

"Where were you this morning?" Robert asked, still glaring at the offensive man taking his hand away from his sword.

"Out in the forest gathering wood," Roger replied, crossing his arms.

"Was anyone with you?" Robert questioned skeptically.

"Nope, was by myself ,didn't see another soul the whole morning," Roger replied, pulling the axe out of the chopping block.

"That's not much of an alibi," Jemma commented, looking about as impressed as she sounded.

"Didn't know I'd need one. How was I supposed to know that the annoying little twit would go and get himself killed or that I'd be blamed for it," Roger replied, scowling as he rested the axe against his shoulder.

"As of yet, you haven't been blamed for anything," Robert responded, just managing to keep his tone calm and professional.

"But I am a suspect though," Roger replied, glancing at the undersheriff.

"Yes," Robert confirmed evenly.

"That's what I figured," Roger said, not sounding terribly happy about it.

"Attempting to flee the area will be taken as an admission of guilt. If you do so, you will be hunted down and arrested," Robert informed, glaring at the man.

"Yeah, yeah, I ain't going nowhere," Roger replied testily.

"Good," Jemma said, just to annoy the dislikeable man.

"If that's all, I've got work to get back to," Roger said, scowling at the two before placing a block of wood on the chopping block.

"That will be all for now," Robert said with barely restrained distaste.

With that the two investigators turned and walked

away, both more than a little happy to be away from the thoroughly unpleasant man. Both of them were simultaneously thinking that he was now the prime suspect.

"What a horrible man," Jemma commented, all her frustration and distaste clear in her voice.

"I agree, but we have no proof that he's the killer," Robert replied. He clearly did not like the man any more than she did.

By this time it was coming upon evening. The sun was beginning to set behind the massive stone walls of the castle.

"What is our next step?" Jemma asked, changing the subject.

"Well I'm going to check in with Jacob, then return to my room to write out a report of what we've learned so far," Robert answered, already beginning to gather his thoughts.

"While you're doing that, I'll ask around among the servants and other guest. See if we can find out who was the man Joshua saw arguing with the victim," Jemma said, already figuring out who she would talk to first.

"In the morning we'll meet up tomorrow after the morning meal in the Great Hall and discuss what we have learned," Robert explained as they walked through the doors of the keep.

"Hopefully, by then, I'll know who the merchant was," Jemma said with a bit of determination.

With that the two went their separate ways, each going in opposite directions down two hallways. They returned to their rooms to get ready for the evening meal.

Jemma spent the rest of the evening talking to both

the other guests and servants. She asked them whether they had ever seen the merchant that had been seen arguing with the victim. Most of the people that she talked to had never seen him. Some of them had seen him but didn't know anything about him. Finally things started to look up when she was talking to a young maid. She listened as the maid told her that his name was Steven and he was from a town two counties away. The maid also told her that he seemed to be a pleasant man.

The next morning, right after the morning meal, Jemma found Robert had just finished talking to the coroner. As soon as she walked up, the undersheriff turned his attention to her.

"Good morning, Lord Bartley," Jemma greeted, so excited to tell him what she found that she almost forgot the pleasantries that were necessary, especially in a setting as public as the Great Hall.

"A good morning to you as well, Lady Jemma," Robert returned, easily picking up on her excitement.

"How about the three of us take a walk around the bailey," Robert suggested, not wishing their conversation to be overheard.

"That sounds like a splendid idea," Jemma replied cheerily.

The three of them made their way out of the Great Hall, down a couple hallways, and through the door of the keep. Once the three of them began walking, Jemma turned her attention to the two men.

"I take it your inquiries were successful," Robert commented knowingly.

"Yes, they were. I was able to find out the name of the man that the victim was arguing with. His name is Steven, and he's a merchant from two counties away from here," Jemma explained happily.

"Did anyone you talked to know what the argument between this Steven and the victim was about?" Jacob asked thoughtfully.

"Unfortunately, no," Jemma replied, shaking her head.

"So we still have no idea what the argument was about," Robert said, sounding a little frustrated.

"Is this Steven still staying in the castle or has he left?" Jacob asked as they continued walking around.

"Yes. He's planning to leave tomorrow. Which is odd because he'd originally planned to stay for another week," Jemma answered, a little suspicious of the man's intended sudden departure.

"In that case, we should have a talk with this Steven," Robert said, not liking the fact that one of the suspects was about to leave so soon after the murder.

"I'm afraid I won't be able to join you," Jacob added, having some of his own responsibilities to take care of.

"That's alright; we'll keep you informed, my friend," Robert replied easily.

Jacob nodded just as easily, pleased that he wouldn't lose touch with the investigation. With that the three of them turned and headed back to the keep. Once inside, they split into two groups, Jemma and Robert going in one direction and Jacob going in another.

The two investigators caught up with Steven just leaving one of the guest rooms on the south side of the castle.

The man was about average in height and build and had dark-brown hair that was smoothed back. His eyes were a curious hazel that seemed to be assessing the two people standing in front of him.

"Would I be correct that you are the undersheriff that is investigating the unfortunate death of the servant yesterday?" Steven asked, his tone pleasant and slightly sympathetic.

"You are correct," Robert replied neutrally.

"Which means this must be the lady merchant that is assisting you," Steven said, his eyes flicking to Jemma.

"That is correct. My name is, Jemma Alden," Jemma replied evenly.

"It's a pleasure to meet you, M'lady," Steven replied, inclining his head.

"We have a few questions concerning the murder," Robert stated calmly, not giving anything away.

"Of course I'll help in any way I can," Steven replied immediately.

"A few days before his death you were seen arguing with the victim. What was the argument about?" Robert asked, watching the other man's reaction very carefully.

"It was nothing of any great importance. The man dropped something on my foot, and I got upset about it," Steven replied dismissively.

"The witness to the interaction said that you were considerably more than upset. In fact, this person said you were angry nearly to the point of striking the victim," Robert countered. He was trying to determine whether the man was attempting to downplay the incident for appearance's sake or if this man was intentionally trying to deceive them in an attempt to conceal involvement in the crime.

"Regrettably, I got a little more worked up about the incident than I really should have. It was quite improper of me to have nearly struck the man as I did," Steven replied, sounding embarrassed.

"Did you know the victim?" Robert asked, changing the subject, at least for now.

"No, Sir, I'd never laid eyes on the man," Steven replied with great conviction and certainty.

"In that case, why did you get so angry with the man," Robert asked, not entirely convinced.

"I must confess to that having been a rather awful day. First, I lost several rather prominent clients. About an hour later, I receive word that one of my establishments burned down. To my shame, I took my anger and frustration about my misfortunes out on the fellow," Steven replied, sounding genuinely regretful.

Before either could say anything in response, a servant came to fetch the merchant's bags. He told the young servant in what order the different bags were to be taken from the room. Immediately the servant turned toward the guest room the merchant had been staying in and reached for the door knob.

"I'm afraid that I must insist that you remain at the castle till this matter has been resolved," Robert informed, stopping the servant just as he was about to turn the knob.

"Whatever for?" Steven inquired, looking each of the investigators in the eye.

"I apologize for any inconvenience this may cause," Robert replied, completely ignoring the question.

The only response Robert got from the frustrated merchant was a curt nod. His apology was also completely ignored due to its purely perfunctory nature. Without another word, the merchant reentered the guest room to unpack, much to his rather obvious annoyance.

The two of them turned and began walking down the hall away from the room. About halfway down the hall a servant walked up to them. It looked like the young man had been running based on the fact that he was breathing slightly faster than normal.

"Sir, Madam, the coroner would like you to meet him in the servants quarters right away," the servant replied, urgently.

"Did he mention what was so urgent?" Robert asked, curious.

"No, Sir, he didn't," the servant replied instantly.

"Thank you for delivering the message so promptly," Robert said, dismissing the young man back to his other duties.

"You're most welcome, Sir," the servant replied, then walked away to get back to his other duties.

The investigators again turned and walked down the hallway. This time they were headed to the servants' quarts. When they got there, Jacob was just standing by the victim's bed. He was staring at something in his hand and looked up when they entered.

"What have you found, old friend?" Robert asked as they approached.

"I found these in a secret pocket in one of the victim's cloaks," Jacob said, handing the documents in his hand to Robert.

Robert accepted the documents, then began looking through them. He wasn't to happy with what he saw at all. The documents were contracts forming a business partnership centred around a store. The thing that the undersheriff was not happy about was the fact he couldn't make out the name of the second of the two people forming the partnership. He could only make out the first letter of the name, and even that was not very clear. It could be either an S or an R. It galled him to be so close to the answer yet not be able to grasp it.

"What is it?" Jemma asked, noticing the angry look on the undersheriff's face.

"Here, look," Robert said, handing her the document while glaring at the bed for lack of a better target.

Jemma took the document from Robert and began to read it. She didn't like being that close to the answer but have it elude her either. We just need a plan, Jemma thought. This caused her to get a thoughtful look on her face. An idea began to form in her mind. She just hoped that Robert would agree to her idea. However, she knew convincing him to do so would not be easy.

"I believe it is time to have another talk with both of our prime suspects," Robert said, tightly controlled anger in his voice.

"I think that may not be the best idea. It is unlikely that they will be any more honest with us than they were before. Also, it will give away what we know," Jemma explained, crossing her arms.

"Then what do you suggest?" Robert replied, sounding annoyed.

"That we get someone to tell both suspects that the document was found by a servant that can't read, who gave it to me and that in the morning I'm going to give it to you," Jemma suggested, pretty sure what reaction she was going to get.

"You do realize that will instantly make you a target," Robert replied, disapproval in his tone.

"I'm aware of that," Jemma responded, not sounding at all phased.

"Of course you are. It's far to dangerous," Robert replied, not liking the idea of a lady being in such danger at all.

"We don't know which of them is the killer. It's the only way to force the guilty one's hand," Jemma replied, meeting his disapproving gaze without hesitation.

"It is far to dangerous for a lady," Robert said, crossing his arms, not in favour of this idea one little bit.

"The very fact that I'm a woman would make the killer more likely to make a move. He won't see me as much of a threat," Jemma replied, hoping that would convince him.

"And who would we get to pass on this information?" Robert asked, his tone clipped due to his intense dislike of this whole idea.

"Marla, she's a maid and the castle gossip," Jemma answered with determination shining in her eyes.

"Fine," Robert said, correctly interpreting the look in her eyes as saying that if he refused, she'd just do it by herself, and that would be a thousand times more dangerous.

Jemma folded the document up and put it in her pocket. While she was doing that, a young maid entered the room. Robert walked over to her and asked her to go get Marla. A few minutes later, Marla entered and walked up to them.

"I was told you wanted to speak with me, M'Lord," Marla said, looking between the two people in front of her.

"That's correct," Robert replied evenly.

"We need your assistance," Jemma added just as calmly.

"Of course, anything I can do to assist you would be an honour," Marla replied, her gaze darting between the two of them.

"We need you to pass some information to two men, Roger the handyman and a merchant named Steven, who is staying in the castle," Robert explained, watching the young woman.

"It is very important, Marla," Jemma added, her eyes fixed on the maid.

"Under no circumstances are you to tell these men that we told you to give them this information," Robert said, pinning Marla with an intense stare.

"Certainly, M'Lord," Marla replied without hesitation.

"You are to inform them that was I given this document by one of the servants that doesn't know how to read, and I'm going to do some research in the library late this evening before turning the document and anything I've found over to the undersheriff," Jemma explained, her eyes fixed on the young maid.

"It is vital that they both believe you," Robert added, pinning the maid with a piercing look.

"I will do my best, M'Lord," Marla replied with certainty.

"As soon as you have completed your task, you are to bring a tea tray to my rooms and report how it went," Robert instructed, stern but not unkindly.

"Yes, M'Lord, I'll do so most promptly," Marla replied instantly.

"We really appreciate your help, Marla," Jemma added with a kind smile.

"It's an honour to be of assistance, Madam," Marla said eagerly.

"That will be all," Robert said, dismissing her.

Marla curtsied and hastily left the room. She was so excited that she had opportunity to assist the under-sheriff with a murder investigation. So she resumes her chores, keeping a look out for an opportunity to pass on the information as she was instructed. She found the perfect opportunity when she and another maid were in the merchant's room laying a fire. Just as they got started, Marla heard the door open and close. About a minute later, she heard the man's footsteps approach from the side where there was a bookshelf. Hoping that the merchant was listening she began telling the story that she'd come up with containing the information. To her relief, as soon as she mentioned Lady Alden, she heard and felt the man shift closer to listen. By the time they were done building the fire, she'd relayed the information that the undersheriff wanted him to have. With their task completed, the two maids hurried out of the room.

Next she headed to the kitchen. To her great relief, when she entered she saw Roger stacking firewood. Her task was made even easier by the fact that Roger had a reputation for listening in on gossiping maids and cooks. She walked over to one of the prep cooks that were stirring a pot of soup on the stove. The two young women started giggling and chatting about the latest gossip. Again, as soon as Marla was sure that Roger's attention was on their conversation, she slipped in the information from the undersheriff. As instructed, Marla immediately brought a tea tray to the undersheriff and told him that she was successful.

That evening Jemma entered the library carrying a candle. She lit the candle on the table, then started walking around as if she was looking for a book. As she did so, she went over her plan in her mind again. While the name of the second partner was unreadable, the rest of document was quite legible. She hoped to use the information contained in it to trick the killer into confessing. The library was dark, and with each step the floorboards creaked ominously. She picked up a book from the shelf and began walking back to the table. Just as she was about to enter the circle of light cast by the candle on the table, she heard someone come up behind her. The next thing she knew, she felt the sharp blade of a knife being pressed against her neck and a hand on her shoulder.

"Give me the document, or I'll kill you," Steven hissed into her ear.

"Here," Jemma said, taking the document out of her pocket and holding it out toward the hand on her shoulder. Steven removed the hand from her shoulder and snatched the document out of her hand. Instantly he began moving the document toward the flame of the candle in her hand intending to light the parchment on fire. His plan was thwarted when she blew out the candle. The murderous merchant made an angry sound in the back of his throat.

"I should kill you for that stunt," Steven threatened angrily.

"You mean like you killed the servant Richard?" Jemma asked in reply.

"Yes. He cost me a lot of money because of his stupidity. He had to pay for that," Steven replied, no small amount of venom in his voice.

"The fire that destroyed the store the two of you owned wasn't his fault, and there was nothing he could have done to stop it," Jemma replied, trying to remain calm and mostly succeeding.

"It would appear that you know quite a lot about the situation. I was going to let you live; unfortunately, it would seem that is not possible," Steven said, shaking his head in mock regret.

At that second, there was the slightest of sounds of shifting a little further outside the glow of the candle. Less than a heartbeat later, Steven felt the tip of a sword pressed against the back of his neck.

"Let her go or lose your head," Robert threatened coldly.

The murderous merchant instantly dropped the dagger

like it was white hot and would burn his hand. He was in no hurry to die; though, he realized that it was only delaying the inevitable.

As soon as she was free, Jemma took a step away from her former captor. She then spun around and snatched the document out of the man's hand.

With a single gesture from Robert, the soldiers stepped out of the shadows. The soldiers took Steven into custody, tying his hands behind his back. Next, they less than gently led the murderer out of the room.

The next morning, Robert was about to leave with the murderer. The undersheriff led a group of soldiers that were restraining the murderer. They just stepped out of the keep and were headed to the waiting prison wagon. A groom stood nearby with Robert's horse.

Jemma was standing on the front steps of the keep to see him off. While the soldiers loaded the prisoner into the wagon, Robert walked up to her.

"Your assistance in this matter has been invaluable, Lady Alden," Robert said, inclining his head slightly.

"Thank you, Lord Bartly," Jemma replied, curtsying just slightly.

"Perhaps we will have the chance to work together again," Robert added sincerely.

With that the undersheriff turned and walked over to his waiting horse. He got on his horse, waved at Jemma still standing on steps, and rode away. The prison wagon followed after him as they headed toward the gate.

* * *

As the story came to an end, Alicia turned her gaze from the sky to the people around the fire. "That is how the murder at Moonlight Castle was solved. Proving that you can't judge a book by its cover," Alicia said in conclusion. She was met with applause by her attentive audience.

THE END

* * *

CHAPTER 4

Hide and Seek

Alicia had been hired to tell a story at a celebrity party. Though what said party was about she wasn't exactly sure. When the woman who hired her had explained it to the storyteller she'd been talking in so many circles that she had stopped listening after the first few minutes.

The only thing that Alicia knew about the party was that it was spy themed. It was this very fact that gave her an idea on what story to tell. She decided to tell a spy story; she figured it would be quite appropriate due to said theme.

"What do you guys think of hearing a spy story," Alicia asked the fifty or so people that were around the room.

"Sounds like a good idea," one of the women in the crowd agreed, liking the idea and also considering it quite fitting.

Similar agreement came from the rest of the people in the room. It sounded like a good idea to them too.

"Today's story of espionage, intrigue, action, and hopefully more than a little excitement all started in a perfectly ordinary downtown condo. The person who lived in this condo was one Violet Beck. By all appearances, she was a completely ordinary young woman. If one were to ask her neighbours about her, they would tell you that she was a nice, though slightly shy, young woman. If you asked them what she did for a living, they'd tell you that she was a cosmetics sales person. However, the truth was far, far more interesting. You see, Miss Violet Beck was in fact a spy," Alicia began, drawing the people in the room into the story.

* * *

Violet Beck tied her blond hair into a ponytail as she stepped out the front door of her building to go on her morning jog. Her expert blue eyes quickly and thoroughly scanned her surroundings. As she stepped down onto the sidewalk, she took note of how many cars were parked on the side of the road. All this happened in a little over a minute.

She crossed the street heading to the park directly across the street. Next to the gate of the park was a man selling flowers.

"Good morning, Miss Beck," the man greeted, her with a warm smile.

"Morning, Steve," Violet greeted, returning the warm smile while she stretched in preparation for her run.

After that she took off down the running path. She was making good time, a little faster than she usually did. That's why she reached the halfway point a little ahead of schedule.

There was a bench at roughly the half way point of the trail. The bench was made of black wrought iron that was, as dark as night, and crafted in spirals with darkly stained woodAs she was running near the bench close enough to brush against it, she dropped her sunglasses.

She immediately bent over and picked up her dropped sunglasses. While standing up, she brushed her hand against the coarse wood of the bench that felt like sandpaper against her hand. Once she straightened up, she continued on her run. As she started off again, she briefly put her hand in her pocket for about a second.

When Violet arrived back at her apartment, she took another glance around the area, paying attention to the people walking down the sidewalk. As soon as she did she quickly unlocked her front door and went inside.

Once inside, she quickly showered and changed. When she was done, she reentered her bedroom. Picking up the running shorts, she pulled out the message that she'd retrieved from the drop under the park bench. She unfolded the paper, a light violet colour on. It was two simple words, Grimstone Aerospace.

Before she could think about what the brief enigmatic message meant, the ringing of the phone broke the contemplative silence of the room. She stood up and walked over to the phone with the note still in her hand. Her eyes were still fixed to the paper in her hands as she brought the receiver to her ear.

"Morning, Vi," a man's voice on the other end greeted, sounding an interesting combination of distracted and amused.

"Any specific reason that you're calling me at 7:30 in the morning, Jake?" Violet asked, putting her hands on her hips.

"Is that any way to talk to one of your trusted and treasured colleges," Jake said, putting his hand over his heart.

"If you didn't go out of your way to be as annoying as

possible, as well as calling about an hour and a half before you should, you might get a different response," Violet replied. The tone of her voice softening just a little bit.

"I'll take it under advisement," Jake replied, the amusement still in his voice.

"You still haven't told me what was so important that you had to call me at home," Violet pointed out.

"I guess you're right. The chief wants to talk to you," Jake replied; the creek of him leaning back in his chair could be heard over the phone.

"Did he say what he needed?" Violet asked, her attention was now fully on the phone call instead of the message.

"He didn't say, but I'd suggest that you get here as soon as possible," Jake answered, sitting up in his chair.

"Will do," Violet said, then hung up the phone.

A few minutes later she was driving into the office. As she drove, she gripped the steering wheel with a white-knuckled grip.

Even though it took only about fifteen minutes for her to get to her destination, it somehow felt like hours. She quickly gathered up her stuff, then got out of her car.

As soon as the young woman walked into the office, a door on the opposite side of the office opened. An instant later, a man with grey hair, stone-grey eyes, and an air of authority about him stepped through it. This man was their section chief, Philip Davidson.

"Agent Blue Rose, I need to see you in my office," Chief Davidson said, his gaze locking onto Violet who was still standing by the door.

"Right away, Chief," Violet replied immediately as she quickly began walking toward the office.

As Violet moved across the busy bullpen, Davidson stepped back into his office and closed the door behind him. When she reached the door, she opened it and entered the office, pushing the door closed behind her. As soon as it was closed, she sat down in the chair in front of her boss's desk.

"What did you get at the drop this morning?" Davidson asked, placing his hands on his desk.

"It was just as we thought; it's Grimstone Aerospace," Violet answered, her eyes meeting those of her boss.

"I can't say that I'm really surprised," Davidson commented, steepling his fingers and placing his chin on them.

"At least we can be certain that the tip that we got was credible now," Violet replied, trying not to get to annoyed that she had no new information.

"Alright I've got your next assignment. You're going undercover in Grimstone Aerospace," Davidson informed, picking up a file on his desk and holding it out to the agent.

"What's the cover?" Violet asked, accepting the file and opening it.

"Your name will be Jessica Jennings. You'll be going under as the assistant to the head of the department where the leak is coming from. That department is currently working on a defense contract project," Davidson explained, gesturing to the file in her hand.

"His name is Richard Harris, and he's headed that department for the last five years," Violet read out of the file.

"We're not really sure whether he's in on it, but some-one in his department in definitely leaking information," Davidson added, his tone grave and serious.

"Don't worry, Chief; I'll find out," Violet replied confidently.

"Be careful; keep your eyes open and your head on a swivel," Davidson cautioned sternly.

"Don't worry, Chief; I can take care of myself," Violet said, reinforcing her statement by standing up.

Davidson dismissed her with a wave of his hand, at which point the spy turned and headed to the office. Just as she reached the door and was about to open it, she heard him mutter, "That's what they all say." Walking through the door, she promised herself that she'd take the warning seriously.

On the way back to her desk, she read the file in her hands. According to this, she'd be starting at Grimstone day after tomorrow, which gave her some time to get ready but not much. By that fact alone she could tell two things about the mission: it was very urgent and very important.

The agent spent the rest of the day getting things ready. By the time that she was done she was extremely tired. That is why she went straight to bed when she finally got home.

Early the next morning, she left her apartment with her sample case. She was doing this so that her neighbours would think that she was going on a business trip. Just as she closed the door behind her, one of the neighbour's doors opened and an older woman stepped out.

"Good morning, Miss Beck," the woman greeted with a warm smile.

"Good morning, Mrs. Roberts," Violet greeted her, returning the smile.

"I see you're going on another business trip. How is the cosmetics business anyway?" Mrs. Roberts asked in the way only a slightly nosy neighbour can.

"Really well, sales were up last month and the one before," Violet replied, not really liking lying to those in her life but not having any choice.

"Oh that's good. Well I'll let you go. I wouldn't want to delay you to much," Mrs. Roberts said, glancing at her watch.

"I think you're right. I guess I'll see you when I get back," Violet replied, also looking at her watch and realizing that if she didn't hurry, she would be late.

"I'll see you then, dear," Mrs. Roberts said warmly.

With that Violet turned and walked down the hall. As she was doing that she saw Mrs. Roberts pick up her newspaper and retreat back into her apartment. While she headed down the halls and stairs, she ran through her cover again in her head. By the time she reached the parking lot and got into her car she was confident that she had it down.

Once she arrived at Grimstone Aerospace headquarters, she immediately headed inside. When she reached Richard Harris's office door, she knocked and was asked to come in. She walked in and got her first good look at the man that was hunched over his desk going through the files on it. The man's brown hair shifted as he turned his head. She couldn't tell what colour his eyes were due to the way he was hunched over, but she knew them to also be brown.

"Hello, my name's Jessica Jennings. I'm your new

administrative assistant," Violet greeted, standing in front of the desk.

Mr. Harris looked up at her greeting. "Welcome, Miss Jennings," Richard greeted, extending his hand.

"Thank you, Mr. Harris," Violet replied, shaking his hand.

The department head went through all the things that she was supposed to do, as well as the pertinent details of her job. Once he was done, he dismissed her back to her desk just outside the door to his office.

With that the spy left the office and walked over to her desk. The instant that she sat down she began to go through the documents sitting on it. Unfortunately, there wasn't anything that would be of any help to her investigation among the papers.

The phone rang just as she looked through the last of the papers. She put down the papers in her hand and picked up the phone.

"Grimstone Aerospace, Richard Harris's office," Violet said in a polite, professional voice.

"It's Paul Danvers; he's expecting my call," Paul said, sounding impatient and annoyed.

"I'll check with Mr. Harris; please hold, Mr. Danvers," Violet said, then pushed the button to switch to line two.

"What is it, Miss Jennings?" Richard asked distractedly as he read the papers in front of him on his desk.

"There's a Mr. Danvers on line two; do you want to talk to him?" Violet asked, her gaze fixed on the flashing light on the phone.

"Put him through," Richard answered, sitting up straighter.

"Right away, Mr. Harris," Violet replied, pushing the necessary buttons.

Even after the call was put through, the spy continued to listen. She was hoping that she'd learn something helpful. Though the chances of it being that easy were very small.

"I want that information, and I want it now," Danvers said, with sharp icicles dripping from each and every word.

"And I've told you about a hundred times that you aren't getting it," Richard replied, surging to his feet.

"That is a decision that you really should reconsider," Danvers countered, his voice so cold that it was surprising the phone line hadn't frozen solid.

The only reply that Danvers got was Harris slamming the phone down. He did it so hard that Violet could hear it through the thick wooden door. Idly she wondered if Mr. Harris would need a new phone.

As far as the content of the call, at least now the agent had somewhere to start. This Danvers character seemed like a prime candidate. Which was better than she'd done with all of the looking that she'd done this morning.

The other thing she now knew was that Harris was aware of the leak. Though whether he was involved she still wasn't sure, which was a piece of information that she was determined to find out.

"Miss Jennings, could you run down to the break room and grab me a cup of coffee," Richard said over the intercom.

"Right away, Mr. Harris," Violet said, firmly biting back an annoyed sigh at the request.

She stood from her desk and headed down to the break room. When she got there, three other people were in the room. She hoped that she'd at least be able to learn something on the little errand. Walking over to the counter, she began looking through the cabinets for the coffee cups. As she opened the fourth cabinet, she heard someone walk up behind her. She turned around, carefully suppressing her instinctual response to someone unexpectedly walking up behind her.

"Hello, I'm Hannah Stevens; you must be new here," Hannah said, her hazel eyes bright as she held out her hand.

"Yeah, I am; it's actually my first day. I'm Jessica Jennings, Richard Harris's new administrative assistant," Violet said, shaking the other woman's hand.

"Welcome to Grimestone," Hannah said with an equally welcoming smile.

"Miss Sunshine here happens to be one of our top engineers," a man with black hair interrupted, while leaning against the wall at the other end of the room.

"Well, Mitchel, I'd rather be a Miss Sunshine than a gloomy dark cloud like someone I could mention," Hannah shot back, the ponytail her dark-brown hair was tied into swinging as she turned her head to face the man.

"That cheery one over there is Mitchel Grey, and I'm Jack Simmons. We're all engineers in the same division working on the same project," Jack said, gesturing to the dark-haired man, then to himself.

"I'm happy to meet all of you," Violet said, opening the

next cabinet, pulling out two cups, then pouring two cups of coffee. She was about to turn to leave the room.

"It was nice to meet you as well, Miss Jennings," Hannah said happily as she opened the cabinet and pulled out a coffee cup.

With that Violet headed back to Harris's office and her desk. After delivering his cup of coffee, she sat down at her desk, all the time thinking about the three people she had just met. She decided to at least find out what division they worked in. That way, if they were in a different one than the leak was coming from, she'd at least be able to cross them off the proverbial list. However, if they were from the same division, she'd just have to dig a little deeper like she was going to be doing with that entire division.

Unfortunately the rest of the day was so busy that she didn't even have two minutes to rub together. Let alone find any time to look into any of the three people she'd met. By the time she got to the apartment that had been rented under her cover name, she had a pounding headache and went straight to bed.

Things kept getting worse for the undercover spy. The next two days were just as busy. While also being only slightly productive for her investigation. Much to her frustration, the only thing she'd been able to find out was what division her three suspects worked for, and that division was the one where the leak was coming from. Which meant that all three of them were on her rather large pile of suspects. All of whom would need to have an intensive background check. The only ray of hope she had was that she was going to get some help with that from the office.

That evening, on the way back from work, she stopped at a convenience store. She got out of her car and walked toward the building. As she neared it, she scowled at the bright and cheerful sign that so diametrically opposed her current mood.

The chimes that sounded when she walked through the door sent a spike of pain through her head. With as much speed and efficiency as she could muster, she collected the things that she came in for. Walking up to the counter, she managed a convincing polite smile as she put the things from her basket onto the counter.

"Good evening, Ma'am," the cashier greeted as he began scanning the three things that she had placed on the counter.

"Evening," Violet replied, carefully keeping her tone politely friendly.

"Will this be everything, Ma'am?" the cashier asked as he scanned the last thing.

Violet made a show of looking at everything that was on the counter. "Yes, that's everything."

The cashier told the agent the total, and she handed him the appropriate amount of money. He asked her if she needed a bag, and she said no.

"Would you like a receipt, Ma'am?" the cashier asked, moving the items on the counter slightly closer to her.

"Yes, they make good bookmarks," Violet replied, picking up her items.

The cashier printed out the receipt and held it out to the spy. With her free hand, she took the folded receipt as he wished her a good evening, and she replied with "You too." With that she left the store and headed over to her car.

It didn't take very long for her to get back to the apartment. Once inside, she quickly put the food items away. She also put one of the TV dinners in the toaster oven, not having enough energy to make anything else. After that was done, she picked up the receipt and unfolded it, relieving the reason for the whole trip to the convenience store.

There tucked inside was a note with information from headquarters. Knowing that the message would be in code, she put the note on the coffee table as she picked up her purse. She opened up the secret pocket and pulled out her code book. She quickly decoded the message, then flopped back against the back of the couch.

The intelligence agent found herself in a good news, bad news situation. The good news was that they'd managed to narrow down the leak possibilities to five people. Reading through the list, she noticed that the three people she'd met on her first day were on the list.

The bad news was that they hadn't been able to find anything on this Paul Danvers character at all. That fact alone sent up quite a few warning bells. It seemed that the job of finding out about him would have to fall on her.

The next morning she got up a little earlier than usual. Because of this, she was able to get coffee from a coffee shop instead of at work. She made it to work so early that Harris hadn't even arrived yet. Which gave her a chance to see if she could find out anything about Danvers.

After making sure that no one was near, the agent carefully let herself into Harris's office. She needed to see what she could find before the department head arrived. As soon as she carefully and quietly closed the door behind her, she took a quick look around the office.

She began her search with the desk. The first thing that she checked was papers on top of the desk. While going through them, she sat down in the chair. Unfortunately, there wasn't anything which didn't really surprise her since anything on the desk surface could be seen by anyone in the office. That made it not exactly an ideal place for secret information. However, drawers were a much more likely candidate. The first three cabinets were a total bust. None of them had anything interesting in them. As she opened the fourth one something felt off. At first glance the contents of the drawer looked just as unhelpful as the rest of them. However, when she started moving things around, she found a secret compartment. When she opened it, she found a small paper that had the name Paul Danvers on it, as well as the phone number that he'd called from. Under that was another number that seemed familiar. She knew that she'd seen numbers like it and recently. As she tried to remember where she'd seen it, she looked around the room. When her eyes landed on the file cabinet, it clicked. The number was a file number. Photographing the paper, she quickly but carefully put the paper back into the secret compartment.

Walking over to the filing cabinet, she quickly looked through the labels and found the drawer that according to the number was the one with the file she was looking for. Opening the drawer, she quickly began to flip through the files. Glancing at her watch, she realized that her time was rapidly running out. This caused her to flip through the files even faster. After rapidly flipping through about fifty more files, she finally found the one that she was looking for. Moving quickly, she pulled out the file and set it on the top of the cabinet. Flipping it open, she realized that it was a file about Danvers, including a picture. She quickly took a picture of each page of the file. Just as she closed it, she heard something that made her gaze snap to the door to the office. It was not a sound that she really wanted to hear right at this exact second. As quickly as she could, she put the file back into the cabinet and closing the drawer. Moving quickly she slid through the door and, every bit as quickly, scrambled behind her desk as fast as she could. She made it behind her desk just as Richard Harris walked through the door.

The reason she was in such a hurry was that the sound she heard was her early warning system that she set up to warn her when Harris was coming.

"Good morning, Mr. Harris," Violet greeted, carefully hiding her reaction to the fright-induced adrenaline rush. Based on his lack of reaction, she was successful.

"Good morning, Miss Jennings, you're here early," Richard greeted, only glancing at her, then returning his gaze to the papers in his hand.

"I figured it would be a good idea to get an early start," Violet replied in a calm and professional tone.

"That's what I like to hear. There's some dictation that needs to be done, so if you'll get your notebook and follow me," Richard said, then turned and walked over to his office door, confident she would follow him.

"Certainly, Sir," Violet replied, picking up her notebook. She followed her boss into his office. As she listened to the reports that her boss was dictating she listened for anything that would be useful. Unfortunately there wasn't anything. It took a couple hours for the dictation to be finished.

"As soon as you get those typed up, I'll need you to run a few errands. Here's the list," Richard said, handing her a slip of paper.

"Certainly, Mr. Harris, this shouldn't take very long," Violet replied, accepting the list.

"Good. That will be all, Miss Jennings," Richard said, dismissing her.

Violet nodded, then turned and headed to the door to leave. She left the office and sat down behind her desk. It didn't take her very long to get all of it typed up.

After she was done, she grabbed her bag and left to run the errands. Once she was done with those errands, she needed a cup of coffee. So on the way back to the office, she stopped somewhere and got a coffee.

When she got back, Harris gave her some filing to do. Which gave her an opportunity to get a look at the employee files of her suspects. In doing so, she was able to learn some very interesting information.

That evening when she got home, she was feeling better than she had for the last few days. As she stepped into the apartment, she picked up her mail, which included a seed catalogue. She took this opportunity to go through the files on her suspect from HQ that was hidden in said seed catalogue.

The first one that she was looking through was Hannah

Stevens. What she found was quite interesting. The thing that got the spy's attention was the engineer's financials. According to her history, she was barely making ends meet. About a week after the most recent leak, there was a suspicious transfer into her account.

As she was looking through the records of the other three, she found something quite interesting, though not very helpful. It seemed that all three of them had the same transfer on the same day.

While she was trying to figure out what the implications of this could be, something interrupted her contemplation. That thing was the sound of her secure phone ringing. She walked over to the bookshelf and pulled out the third one on the waist-level shelf.

"Good evening, Blue Rose," Davidson greeted as she answered the phone.

"Evening, Chief," Violet greeted, sounding cheerful.

"Have you found out anything?" Davidson asked, sounding tense and a little impatient.

"Sure did, I found a file on the mysterious Paul Danvers. It was in Harris's file cabinet under a file number but without a name on it," Violet answered contemplatively.

"Who do you think that this Danvers is?" Davidson asked, his tone serious.

"At this point, if I had to guess, I'd say that he's the handler," Violet answered thoughtfully.

"Did the records that research division dug up give you anything?" Davidson asked, while making a note to have someone get eyes on Danvers.

"Yeah they gave me some things to look into," Violet

replied, looking at the other books on the shelf, the beginnings of a plan already forming in her mind.

"Such as?" Davidson asked, wanting more information.

"About a week after the most recent leak all the engineers in that division got the same payment from the same shell company," Violet answered, still considering the implications.

"Do you think that the whole division is in on it?" Davidson asked, sounding alarmed because if they were, it would be a much bigger problem than they had first thought.

"No, I think it's just a misdirect. Whoever is behind this probably figured that because of how important that last leaked bit of information was, someone was bound to start looking. They figured if they sent money to everyone in the division, no one could tell who their real inside man was." Violet explained her theory, which seemed like the only other explanation.

"That seems like an awfully expensive smoke screen," Davidson replied, sounding a bit skeptical.

"I guess they thought it was worth it to keep their inside man in play," Violet replied with a shrug of her shoulders, even though her boss couldn't see it.

"Look into it as soon as you get anything definite, report in," Davidson ordered, hoping that what she found would lead to something.

"Will do, Chief," Violet agreed, then they both hung up, and she put the phone back in the book and put the book back in its place.

Over the next two weeks, she worked to get close to her

suspects. By the end of that time, she had managed to get to the level of acquaintance with all four of them.

Monday morning of the third week she didn't get to work early. In fact she barely made it on time. That is why she had to make do with the breakroom coffee for her morning cup before she began her exhilarating day of filing and typing.

It wasn't till nearly lunchtime that she managed to emerge from the abyss of paper. She rubbed her temples as she made her way to the breakroom for the sandwich that she'd put in the fridge and another cup of coffee. The instant she entered the room, she noticed that someone else was there. Despite the pounding in her head, she easily identified the other person as Hannah Stevens. She decided to use the incessant pounding in her head to her advantage. After pouring her coffee, she glanced at the engineer who was sitting at one of the tables.

"Good afternoon, Jess," Hannah greeted cheerfully.

"Afternoon, Hannah," Violet replied, while rubbing her temples.

"Are you alright? Why don't you come and sit," Hannah invited, pulling out the chair right next her with a concerned look on her face.

"I'll be fine. It's just a bit of a headache. I think I will sit down for bit though," Violet replied, sitting in the chair.

"Maybe you should go home and rest," Hannah suggested, the concern in her tone perfectly mirroring that in her expression.

"I wish I could, but I can't afford to miss the day of work," Violet replied, wincing as she shook her head out of habit.

"Believe me, I understand that situation, but you should take care of your health. I hope it gets better, and I'll be praying for you," Hannah said, correctly guessing that the other woman wasn't going to go home and get some rest.

"I heard this rumour that some of the engineering staff takes outside consulting jobs to make extra money," Violet said, blatantly changing the subject. In an attempt to steer the conversation away from her health to something more pertinent to the investigation.

"It's true; a man named Paul Danvers approached me about doing that. I prayed about it for a week and decided to say no. He tried sending me money to change my mind. When I tried to send it back, they said I couldn't. I didn't feel right about keeping it, so I put it in the missionary fund at church. Figuring it would be better to give it to the LORD," Hannah explained, sounding annoyed at the fact that Danvers thought giving her money would change her mind.

"Do you know if anyone else actually took the job?" Violet asked, sounding like she thought that Danvers was a real jerk.

"Um, I think that someone in my department took the job. I think it might have been either Mitch or Jack, maybe even both of them," Hannah answered after a moment's thought.

"Why do you think it might be one of them?" Violet asked, leaning forward slightly as if the two of them were sharing a secret.

"They've both been acting really weird since Danvers started making offers," Hannah answered, also leaning forward slightly.

"I sure hope they haven't gotten themselves in trouble," Violet said, planning to follow up on this new information. "Yeah, me too," Hannah agreed. Just then her watch beeped, causing her to excuse herself and rush out of the room.

Violet grabbed another cup of coffee and headed back to her desk. In between the ever-exciting administrative tasks, she looked closer at the two men. She checked both of their office phones for any trace of contact between them and Danvers. There unfortunately wasn't any going back as far as three months before the leak.

Hours later Harris sent her to deliver some files to that department. Realizing that this was an opportunity to get more information, she took the files from Harris. As soon as the door closed behind the department head, the under-cover spy stood and quickly made her way to the elevator. Once inside she pressed the down button.

It only took a few minutes for the elevator to come to a stop on the correct floor. Quickly finding the right office, she could see through the window that there was only one man inside. Even though she could only see the back of his head, she could tell that it was Mitchel Grey based on the black hair. As she got closer, she could hear that Grey was on the phone talking to someone. Though it was a bit muffled she could hear what was being said. Being careful not to make any noise, she pulled a small recorder out of her purse and switched it on.

"No, you'll get the information when I get my money," Mitchel said, pacing back and forth as far as the phone cord would allow.

As Grey listened to whatever the other person was saying he turned and paced in the other direction.

"Don't even try to blackmail me. I have as much on you as you have on me," Mitchel replied, his hand tightening around the phone receiver.

As he listened for a second, his expression grew even angrier. After about a second, he slammed the phone receiver down as hard as he could.

She quickly backtracked a little before again approaching the office. Knocking on the door, she saw Mitchel Grey sitting behind his desk, seemingly calm, as he looked through the papers. A second later she went in to deliver the file and left without giving even the slightest indication that she'd heard his conversation.

At last Violet was making progress, and it only took two weeks to do it. Now that she knew that Grey was a leak and had proof, she just had to figure out what was going on with Jack Simmons. There was no way that she was going to walk away from this mission till she was absolutely certain every single leak was securely plugged.

As she was walking down the hall, she contemplated what the next step was in this situation. Having just decided that the best bet was to talk to Simmons and see what she could get out of him. While trying to figure out how to bring that about, she wasn't paying enough attention as evidenced by the fact that she nearly ran into none other the Jack Simmons.

"Oh hey, Jessica," Jack said, stopping short of actually running into her.

"Afternoon, Jack," Violet greeted, a little surprised by his sudden appearance.

"So what brings you to the depths of the engineering department?" Jack asked, appearing casual as he shifted the papers in his hands.

"Mr. Harris sent me down with some papers for Grey. You know, the usual exciting stuff," Violet answered, lightly noting the tension under his casual appearance.

"That doesn't sound terribly exciting," Jack agreed, sounding gently sarcastic, again shifting his papers in what might be a nervous tick.

"I bet your job is a lot more interesting than shuffling papers all day," Violet commented, hoping to learn something.

"From the sound of it, you're probably right," Jack replied, sounding sympathetic. His expression clearly showing that he didn't like paperwork.

"Building things seems a lot more interesting," Violet commented, hoping to steer the conversation toward his job.

"Yeah that's definitely my favourite part of the job," Jack said, the passion he has for that aspect of his job was evident in his expression.

"Since that's the best part of your job, can't help but wonder what the worst is," Violet said, carefully making sure that her voice sounded only mildly curious.

"That, Jessica, is an easy one; it's the stupid, never-ending bureaucracy," Jack answered, looking like he'd just eaten a whole tin of sardines when he said bureaucracy.

"Wouldn't it be nice if dumb bureaucrats would just stay out of it and leave the building things to you guys and stick to whatever it is that bureaucrats do well," Violet commented, watching his reaction closely.

"But if they did that, then they wouldn't do anything at all," Jack replied with a scowl on his face as he stared at a spot on the wall.

"Since you hate bureaucrats so much, why don't you find an engineering job that doesn't involve them," Violet suggested, hoping he'd give something away in his reaction.

"I have my reasons," Jack replied mysteriously.

Violet saw something in his expression that seemed very off and put her on guard. She watched as Jack checked his watch in an exaggerated fashion.

"Look, I've got to be going. They don't pay me to stand in the hall chatting," Jack said, glancing at the door to his office.

"Yeah, me too. If I'm not back soon, Mr. Harris will send a search team out," Violet replied, her light tone giving the impression that everything was fine.

With that the two separated, and she continued walking down the hall. She had definitely not missed the way that the engineer had shut down. Nor had she missed the way that he ended the conversation and left as quickly as he could.

When she got back to her desk there was, a postcard waiting for her. Written on the postcard was a coded message that was a single sentence. She quickly deciphered the message, which was the time and place where she was supposed to meet her boss. Immediately she went and got permission from Harris to take an early lunch.

It didn't take very long for her to reach the park where the meeting was happening. While watching her surroundings and staying inconspicuous, she spotted the two benches that were back-to-back. She also noticed that there was a man sitting on one of them. After another quick discreet glance, she made her way over to the bench. She sat down on the bench opposite the one the man was sitting on.

"Have you found out anything?" Davidson asked without turning around.

"Yeah, I've identified one of the leaks," Violet answered, keeping her eyes forward while reaching into her bag.

"What proof did you find?" Davidson asked, focusing in on the first part of her statement.

"A recording that is about as incriminating as you can get," Violet replied, sounding quite pleased.

"What do you mean by one of the leaks? I thought that there was only one?" Davidson asked, sounding surprised.

"I suspect that there is more than one engineer selling information," Violet answered, sounding more confident than she felt.

"Do you have any proof of this second leak?" Davidson asked, more than a little bit skeptical about the idea.

"Not yet," Violet admitted, dreading what she knew was coming.

"So you don't really know if there is a second leak. I'm tempted to just pull you out of there right now," Davidson said, not sounding very happy.

"I may not have anything definite, but there are some indications, and my gut is telling me that he's dirty. If I leave now, when the leak continues, it'll take months to embed another operative," Violet replied, her voice fervent even though her posture was relaxed.

"Do you have any reason to believe that your cover has been blown?" Davidson asked, needing all the facts before he made a decision.

"Not that I can think of," Violet replied, hoping that the question was a good sign. She really didn't want to leave before the job was done.

"Alright, I'll give you two days. That's it forty-eight hours; after that, we're pulling you out and picking up Grey. That's it, understand," Davidson said, his tone firm.

"I understand. Thanks, Chief," Violet replied, then stood up and walked away.

For the rest of the afternoon, our spy friend was one busy little bee. Harris had quite a few tasks for her that kept her busy. Between them, she tried to do more digging on Jack Simmons. Unfortunately she wasn't able to find anything. Either she was wrong about him or he was very good at covering his tracks. The only thing that kept her going was the awful breakroom coffee. So it was no surprise that by the time that she got home she had a headache.

The next morning, as usual, she went on her run. This time, however, as she started out, something felt wrong, though she didn't know what. Because of this, she watched her surroundings even more closely. A run which was largely uneventful. Arriving back at her apartment, a few people waved to her, and she waved back as if nothing was wrong before slipping inside to change and get ready for work.

About ten minutes later, she left the apartment building and walked down the steps to the sidewalk. She walked up to her car and got out her keys. Just as she was about to put the key in the lock of the door someone walked up beside her. Before she had a chance to react, she felt the barrel of a gun being pressed into her ribs.

"You're coming with us, Jessica," Jack said, being

careful that no one passing could see the gun that was in his hand.

"And where are we going, Mr. Simmons?" Violet asked, her voice as stiff as her posture, knowing if she resisted it could put bystanders in danger.

"We're going to my car. It's the red one two cars down," Jack replied, indicating down the street by tilting his head in that direction.

"Fine," Violet replied, putting her keys in her pocket to curb the temptation to try to stab her kidnapper with them. While she was reasonably sure that she could get away from him if she did that, she wouldn't learn anything.

They began walking down the street. When the two of them reached Simmons's car, Mitchel Grey was sitting in the driver's seat. She was practically pushed into the back-seat of the car. Jack slid in next to her, still pointing his gun at her. As soon as the door closed, the car pulled away from the curb and sped off.

Within about twenty minutes the car pulled up to a hotel. Violet was ushered out of the car and into one of the rooms. As soon as the three of them entered the room, she was shoved into a chair.

"If you know what's good for you, you'll sit there, stay quiet, and do as you're told," Mitchel threatened, glaring at her.

"I'll be as quiet as a mouse," Violet replied with just enough sass to maintain her cover while making it clear that she was going to do as she was told and wasn't going to cause trouble.

With a nod, the two men proceeded to ignore her. As

Mitchel turned to talk to Jack, Violet carefully reached into her pocket and turned on her recorder. When Jack looked suspiciously at her, she pulled out her hand with a hair tie in it. He nodded and turned his attention back to Mitchel.

"Do you want to tell me why we grabbed her?" Mitchel said, crossing his arms as he stared down the other man.

"The Boss wants to find out whether she's just a nosy secretary or if she's an agent," Jack answered, looking really annoyed.

"What does he want us to do till he gets here?" Mitchel asked, sounding really frustrated as he glanced at Violet.

"That's simple; get some answers," Jack replied, walking over to her.

"Well, Jessica, have you just been being nosy?" Mitchel asked as he leaned against the wall next to her chair.

"Or is the answer something a bit more nefarious, like, for instance, you being a spy?" Jack asked, standing in front of her chair.

"I thought you wanted me to be quiet," Violet replied, mimicking his poster by crossing her arms.

"You keep giving smart aleck answers like that and things'll get quite unpleasant," Jack replied, placing his hands on her arms and pushing them down against the armrests of the chair.

"Alright, alright, I was just curious and things didn't make sense so I looked deeper. I've been accused of being nosy before," Violet replied, trying to sound as meek and sincere as she could.

Jack looked scrutinizingly at her for a few minutes to determine if she was telling the truth. After a few seconds he nodded, deciding she was telling the truth, and let her go.

Now that they were both clearly satisfied that they had the answer their boss wanted, they completely ignored her. The two men made sure the door into and out of the room was securely locked. Once they did that they went into the other room and closed the door. She carefully and silently walked up to the door. As she reached the door, she could hear what was being said on the other side, so she placed her recorder against the door.

"Did the boss say when he was meeting the buyer?" Mitchel asked as he took a deck of cards out of his pocket.

"Yeah, he said that the meeting was taking place in about a week," Jack replied as the cards were dealt.

"Are they going to use the Grimstone warehouse on the east side?" Mitchel asked, picked up his cards, and looked at his hand.

"That's what the boss said," Jack replied, rearranging his cards.

Before anything else could be said, there was a knock on the outside door. Violet quickly went back to her chair while turning off her recorder and putting it back in her pocket. Jack put his cards down as he stood up. He walked into the main room just as she sat back down in the chair. The engineer walked over to the outside door and opened it. Danvers entered and walked past Jack just as Mitchel joined them.

Danvers took a quick look around the room before his eyes landed on Violet. After a few seconds, he turned his attention back to his lackeys as he walked around the room.

"Were you able to find out the information that I

wanted?" Danvers asked as he stood in front of Violet with his back turned to her.

As quick as lightning, Violet jumped to her feet, grabbed Danvers around the neck, and pressed the muzzle of her gun against the man's temple.

"Go back to that other room, or you'll lose your paycheck," Violet threatened, pressing the gun harder.

The two men reluctantly filed into the small room while glaring at her. When both of them were inside, she shoved Danvers inside after them. Moving quickly, she shut and locked the door. She wedged a chair under the handle. As soon as she was sure it was secure, she rushed out of the room.

Once outside she pulled out the car keys she'd expropriated from Jack. Slipping into the car, she took off down the road hoping to get as far away as she could before the criminals got loose.

The agent quickly drove to headquarters and headed straight to the chief's office. She immediately reported everything that had happened to the. The chief immediately put an end to the undercover aspect of the investigation.

"Do you know what warehouse this meeting is taking place in?" Davidson asked, tapping the pencil in his hand against the papers on his desk.

"There's only one in that area that is not in active use," Violet said, circling a particular name on the list of warehouses owned by Grimestone.

"Do you know how many people will be at this meeting?" Davidson asked, still fiddling with his pencil.

"No, sorry, Chief," Violet replied, shaking her head.

The two agents spent the next couple days planning the bust. Working out how many teams would be needed, as well as where each team would be positioned.

When the day came, the teams waited out of sight of the warehouse. Suddenly two cars pulled up to the warehouse. Two groups got out of the cars and went inside. The teams waited a few minutes before they moved into position. The tension was thick as the teams waited for the go ahead to storm the building.

The instant the signal finally came, the teams all rushed the building. When they entered, the three men in the centre of the warehouse froze. A heartbeat later, the warehouse erupted into chaos as the three men and their bodyguards began firing at the teams.

Through the noise and general chaos of the fire fight, Violet looked around the room. It quickly became evident that her blue gaze was looking for something. When her gaze landed on the side door, her eyes widened just slightly. She darted from across the room, taking cover behind boxes, shelving units, and even old, abandoned vehicles till she reached the side door. She made it to the door just as it began to swing closed behind the person that she was chasing. She moved quickly through the door before it had a chance to close completely.

As soon as she emerged from the cavernous building, she saw her quarry enter the factory next door. She quickly followed him inside and quietly closed the door behind her. While navigating through the twists and turns of the maze-like building, she listened for any sound that would give any clue where the man went.

"I know that you're in here, Danvers," Violet shouted, trying to get his attention as she continued to look around.

"You're right; the only question is where," Danvers replied, his voice echoing all over, making it quite difficult to tell which direction it was coming from.

"It's only a matter of time before I find you," Violet responded, the sound of each step on the grate echoing off the pipes and other machines.

"Someone's confident, Miss Agent," Danvers said mockingly as he jumped down a flight of stairs, making the grating ring like a bell when he landed.

Violet began moving in the direction of the loud banging sound. All the time hoping that he would keep talking and making noise.

"Tell me, Agent, what agency are you with? The NSA or the CIA?" Danvers asked as he continued to move around, trying to obscure his location.

"Neither, actually," Violet replied as Danvers came into view and took a shot at her.

She immediately ducked behind a machine; the bullet pinged against the metal. The two of them exchanged fire for a few minutes. None of the bullets were hitting their mark. Instead, they were instead pinging off machines, pipes, and metal railings.

"You think you're so smart rooting out both Grey and Simmons, Miss Agent," Danvers said, sounding both mocking and disgruntled as he moved around.

"Just being observant and doing my job," Violet replied, tracking his movements as best as she could and only getting a few glimpses of him.

"You can't be all that observant considering that you missed something quite important," Danvers said, sounding a touch smug as he fired at her.

"Like what?" Violet asked, confused while taking careful steps forward.

"Such as the headaches that you've been having. You mean that you never noticed that you only got them when you had coffee in the breakroom? And you said that you're observant," Danvers said, shaking his head in mocking disappointment while his voice seemed to be moving around.

"You mean," Violet replied, completely astonished.

"Exactly, we have been slowly poisoning you," Danvers said, standing up and shooting Violet in the shoulder.

The agent staggered back a few steps, putting her hand on the wound. Before he had a chance to approach her, she turned and ran in the opposite direction. Within a few seconds, she was out of sight, disappearing behind the pipes and machinery.

Danvers listened as he began moving in the direction that she had gone. He'd only been walking for less than a minute when he heard a loud clanging sound coming from ahead of him. Quickening his pace, he rounded the corner and a malicious smile spread across his face.

"What do we have here?" Danvers asked, with the same malicious glee in his voice.

There, lying on the metal grating under a dented pipe, was the unconscious form of Violet. She was bleeding from her shoulder and completely unresponsive. Her gun was laying uselessly next to her lax hand.

Danvers walked up to her and picked up her gun. With a chilling smile on his face, he crouched next to her still form. Savouring the irony, he placed the spy's own gun against her temple and was about to pull the trigger.

As quick as lightening she grabbed his wrist and pushed it up just as he pulled the trigger. The bullet lodging in a machine off to the side. As the sound of the gunshot echoed, she twisted his arm behind his back while at the same time she knocked his legs out from under him. He landed on his face with his arm twisted behind his back and her knee pressed into his lower back. She quickly cuffed him, the clicking sound was massively satisfying.

"I have to know how soon did you get on to me?" Violet asked as she pulled him to his feet in a less then gentle way.

"I didn't; there was another candidate for the secretary job. She worked for us and was supposed to get the file. Also, she was going to feed us information. So we were trying to get you to quit so she could take over the job," Danvers answered as they walked back toward the door where he entered the building in the first place.

"Mind if I ask you a question?" Danvers asked as they walked down a flight of stairs.

"Fine," Violet answered, not seeing any harm in it.

"Since you clearly didn't hit your head on that pipe, what made that dent?" Danvers asked as they turned a corner.

"I hit it with the butt of my gun," Violet answered, quite pleased about her trick.

Within a few minutes, the two of them emerged from the building. There was a team of agents waiting for them when they did. She handed her prisoner over to the head of the team, who led him to a waiting car. The crook was pushed inside, and the car drove away. As the car drove away, she could see the other two crooks through the back window.

There was a kind of finality to watching the car drive away with the criminals. However, something was different about the close of this case than any other in her career. Normally she could walk away from a case and all the people involved without any regret. That was not true this time. As she walked over to her car, she found herself mourning the friendship that had been developing between her and Hannah. No matter how many times she reminded herself that the engineer was friends with Jessica Jennings not Violet Beck, it didn't make her feel any better this time. There was just something that made her think that they would have been great friends. It had been so long since she had a close friend. On that sombre note, the intelligence agent slipped into her car and drove away.

* * *

Alicia took a step back from the mic and took a deep breath. As she did, another man, the MC, walked up to the mic.

"Did everyone like that exciting story of intrigue and espionage?" The MC asked into the mic excitedly.

"Yeah," the crowd cheered, excitedly.

"Let's give our special guest a round of applause," the MC said, taking the mic off the stand as he gestured to Alicia.

The crowd instantly began clapping. The sound filled the room. As applause followed Alicia as she stepped off the stage, she breathed a sigh of relief.

THE END

CHAPTER 5

Secrets, Lies, and Spies

People filtered into the room of a medium-sized auditorium. An announcer was standing on the small stage of the cavernous open space adjusting the papers on the stand. He adjusted the microphone as the last few people took their seats. Doing so caused an ear-piercing screech to reverberate through the room, making every one wince.

"Ladies and Gentlemen, welcome to this meeting of The Cold Case Club," the announcer greeted the crowd.

The crowd clapped and whispered among themselves.

"As many of you know by now, there's going to be a special guest at our meeting tonight. Join me in welcoming the woman with the golden voice, Alicia the storyteller," the announcer said, gesturing to a door off to the side.

Everyone in the crowd turned their attention to the door. At exactly that moment, the door opened and the crowd started clapping as Alicia stepped into the room. She walked onto the stage and accepted the mic from the announcer.

"Show of hands, how many of you amazing people have seen at least one of those cop shows?" Alicia asked, pretty sure she knew the answer already.

Sure enough, everyone in the crowd raised their hands.

"Then you all know that the quickest way to get on

a detective's bad side is to lie to him," Alicia commented with a slight knowing smile.

"That would sure do it," someone in the front row agreed, shaking his head at the very idea of doing such a thing.

"Well this fine afternoon, I'm going to tell you the story of a man who did that very thing. It all started in the depths of a big city. Far from the glitz and glamour of the prestigious parts of the city the ever-shifting shadows, both real and metaphorical, hid many secrets. In today's tale two of those secrets are on a crash course. When they meet, things are bound to get interesting," Alicia began, the introduction adding a bit more anticipation.

* * *

A chilling late-fall wind blew down a largely empty street. It did little other than flutter discarded newspapers and caused the few people walking along it to pull their coats a bit tighter around themselves.

That included a man with sandy-brown hair wearing a light-brown, moderate-quality suit with a matching top-coat. This man's name was Robert Jenkins. His attention was fixed on a mostly empty lot across the street. As he crossed the street and walked onto the lot, he took a quick glance around. When he did, he noticed something that was both unexpected and not supposed to be there. That something was actually, a someone.

While Jenkins walked into the small shack that was off to the side and halfway down. He was only there for a few minutes. When he stepped out of the shack, he saw some movement out of the corner of his eye. He glanced around the corner of the shack and saw the man from before skulking around. He froze when he saw the man toss an object into a hole and lightly cover it with trash. What made him stop in his tracks was that he could see what that object was, it was a gun. He shifted his stance slightly. In doing so he bumped a piece of metal trash on the ground, making a noise. At the sound, the man looked up and directly at him. After a second, the man turned and ran away, disappearing around a corner.

Robert looked down at the envelope in his hand, then slipped it into his briefcase. As he did, a bad feeling began to form in the pit of his stomach. Turning around, he headed in the opposite direction from the one that he'd come from, and the man left. When he reached the sidewalk, he too disappeared around the corner, not that anyone was looking for him. It only took a couple of minutes for him to walk to his car, during which time the feeling had only gotten worse.

Pulling into his driveway, Jenkins sighed and rested his forehead against the steering wheel of his car. He really hoped the man that he had seen wasn't going to bring trouble. Just that morning, he'd been talking to a friend at the office about how easy this assignment was going to be.

Guess that's the moment that I was well and truly doomed, Robert thought to himself with a slightly self-deprecating smirk on his face.

The next morning, the sound of a firm knocking

interrupted Robert's morning routine. He was not expecting to see two uniformed officers on his doorstep.

"Are you, Mr. Robert Jenkins?" the older officer asked, looking at the notebook in his hand for a second.

"Yes, Officer," Robert said, glancing from one of the officers to the other.

"Were you in the warehouse district yesterday afternoon?" the second officer asked, watching his reaction very carefully.

"Yes, I was. What is this all about?" Robert replied, his questioning gaze still flicking from one officer to the other.

"Some detectives want to ask you a few questions. So if you could come down to the precinct, I'm sure it shouldn't take to long," the first officer said, handing Jenkins the card of the lead detective on the case.

"I was just about to head out to run an errand anyway. I'll stop by afterwards, if that would be alright," Robert said. He had a pretty good idea what the detectives wanted to talk about.

"That would be just fine. Thank you for your time, Sir," the older officer replied as both of them extended their hands.

Jenkins shook their hands and watched them leave. He turned and walked back inside. In a few long strides, he reached his office and walked over to the far side of the room where his safe was located. He began pacing between his desk and the wall. This continued for about fifteen minutes till the ringing of the phone shattered the tension. He talked to the person on the other end of the line for a few minutes before hanging up. With a near-tangible sense of urgency, he walked over to his safe. Quickly entering the combination, he opened the safe. After pulling his briefcase out, he turned on his heel and walked out of the office.

On his way out, he grabbed his keys off the small table by the door and his coat from the rack. He sighed in frustration as he stepped out of the door. After a quick glance around, he walked over to his car with an urgency that made it clear he was in a hurry. Sliding into the driver's seat, he started the engine and pulled out of the driveway.

The errand that Robert needed to run was that he had arranged to meet with the agency chaplain. He desperately needed to talk to someone about this whole mess. Hopefully he'd be able to get some advice on how best to get out of this tangled mess. These thoughts were still swirling through his head as he pulled up to the building, slid out of his car, and entered. It didn't take very long for him to reach the right office. On the door was the name Micheal Stevens. He knocked and entered the medium-sized room. In the centre of the room was a wooden desk that looked to be fairly old. The rest of the room looked about like you'd expect a preacher's office to look like.

"Good morning, Mr. Jenkins, please take a seat," Micheal greeted, gesturing to the chairs in front of the desk.

"Sure," Robert said, sitting heavily in his chair.

"I've heard that you're in quite the predicament. Why don't you tell me about it," Micheal suggested, sounding concerned.

Robert explained in detail the whole mess that he now found himself in.

"That is quite a predicament that you've found yourself

in," Micheal said, sitting back in his chair with a thoughtful look on his face.

"What am I supposed to do?" Robert asked, running his hand through his hair.

"I'd suggest that you tell the truth," Micheal answered after nearly five minutes of thought.

"I can't, and I already told you why," Robert replied, not sounding like he liked the alternative one bit.

"In that case, the only advice I can give you is that you pray and do the right thing," Micheal said, wishing he could be of more help.

"I'll do that," Robert said, sounding slightly hopeful but still stressed while standing up and shaking the chaplain's hand.

With that, the intelligence courier left the office and the building. When he stepped out of the building, the first thing that he did was make a call at the nearest phone booth. The call only lasted a few seconds, consisting of only a few words being spoken by either side before he hung up, walked back to his car, and drove away.

Just as he had told the officer, Robert headed over to the precinct right away. Walking into the controlled chaos of the station, he quickly made his way over to the desk. The desk sergeant directed him to the interview room, where the detectives were going to be talking to him.

Entering the room and taking a seat, he was pretty sure what this was about. However that didn't stop him from really hoping that he was wrong. The door opening and two detectives entering drew him out of his contemplation.

"Thank you for coming by this afternoon, Mr. Jenkins," the first detective greeted, shaking Jenkins's hand.

"I'm Scott Langston, and this is my partner Jake Layton," Scott greeted, also shaking the witness's hand.

"It's really no problem. I only hope I can help," Robert replied sincerely as he took the seat that the detectives motioned to.

"We're glad to hear that, and we hope you can too," Jake replied as the two detectives sat down on the opposite side of the table.

"At this rate, you'll be out of here in no time," Scott said, putting a file down on the table.

"I sure hope so," Robert replied, low enough that he hoped the detectives couldn't hear.

The two detectives shared a look, having heard what he said. They were wondering why Jenkins was so eager to leave before they'd even started the questioning. This was supposed to be a simple witness interview. However, his reaction was really interesting.

"First of all, you're not in any trouble, so you don't need to worry about that," Scott said, trying to calm Jenkins's quite well-hidden nervousness.

"What we need to know is where in the warehouse district were you yesterday?" Jake asked, spreading a map of the warehouse district on the table.

"I'm afraid that there's been some kind of mistake; it was the day before that I was in that area," Robert said, the amount of concern in his tone and on his face seemed genuine.

"That isn't what you told the officers this morning,"

Jake countered, leaning back in his chair, fixing his assessing gaze that held just a hint of skepticism was fixed on the witness.

"I must have gotten the days mixed up when he asked," Robert replied, shifting in his chair just slightly.

"Why do you think that could have happened?" Scott asked, calmly being very careful to keep any skepticism out of his voice.

"I've never had police officers come to my house before. I guess it threw me off balance enough that I got a little confused," Robert replied, a hint of defensiveness in his voice.

"Have you ever seen this man before?" Jack asked, pulling the file out from under the map, taking out a picture, and placing it on the table in front of Jenkins.

"No. Can't say I have," Robert replied without hesitation after picking up the picture and taking good look at it.

"If someone suggested that changing your story would be a good idea, it isn't. Hiding information in a murder investigation never is," Jake warned, pushing just a little.

"I already told you why my story changed, and it had nothing to do with anyone else," Robert replied, crossing his arms.

"I guess that we're done for now," Scott said as they all stood up, and he shook Jenkins's hand.

"We might need to talk to you again," Jake said, shaking Jenkins' hand before he turned and left the room.

The whole interview had been structured to get Jenkins talking by showing that they were on his side. Unfortunately, that strategy hadn't work at all. Everything that he'd told them was a lie. It was clear that next time they were going to need a different strategy.

The instant Robert stepped out of the station he closed his eyes for a few seconds and took a deep breath. Once he opened his eyes he looked around and spotted a phone booth. Entering the booth he hesitated for only an instant before dialing and picking up the receiver. The ringing only lasted about a minute before someone picked up.

"I did it; I lied to the detectives," Robert said, sounding utterly dejected, his head bowed with his eyes again closed.

"I know that wasn't easy for you, and I'm sorry about that, but we both know that it was necessary," the man on the other end replied, firm but sympathetic.

"The fact that it's necessary doesn't make it any easier to take, Peter," Robert replied, raising his head, opening his eyes, and clenching the receiver in a white-knuckle grip.

"You're one of our best intelligence couriers. You know very well why we can't have that drop location burned right now," Peter replied, his voice a little firmer.

"This is a murder investigation. Someone lost their life, and the person who did it could get away with it. If that happens, it would be my fault," Robert said, clutching the receiver so hard that his hand began to shake.

"If you don't, then someone else will lose their life," Peter said sternly.

"I know," Robert replied through gritted teeth, frustration dripping from each letter.

Before another word could be said, Jenkins slammed the receiver down. He really hated being stuck in the middle of a situation where no matter what he did, something bad was going to happen.

About three days later, the two detectives entered the station talking about the interview with Jenkins. Neither of them could figure out why the man had lied. Especially since he wasn't being accused of any crime. They were planning on another interview with him this afternoon.

"Morning, Double L," Officer Mathews greeted, leaning against Scott's desk with his arms loosely crossed.

"Good morning. How did picking up Jenkins go? Did he give you any problems?" Scott asked, moving his friend off the edge of his desk.

"Not a bit. I half expected him to try and run considering the amount of trouble that he gave you two. Gave him a ride to the station because his car died on him. He's waiting in the interview room," Officer Mathews answered, sounding a bit surprised.

As Scott picked up a file off his desk, the officer was called away. The partners each grabbed a cup of coffee before they headed over to the interview room. When they entered, Jenkins was sitting a little stiffly in the chair.

"Thank you for coming in again," Jake said, taking one of the chairs on the opposite side of the table.

"Hopefully this time we'll be able to get a bit further today," Scott added, taking the seat next to his partner and placing a file on the table.

"I'm not sure how much more I can tell you than I did last time," Robert replied, being completely truthful.

"Our biggest problem with what you told us last time

is that everything you said was a lie," Jake said, putting the pressure on from the beginning.

"What makes you think that?" Robert asked, making sure that his expression was innocently neutral.

"This might have something to do with it," Scott said, pulling a picture out of the file and placing it in front of Robert.

"That clearly shows you entering the warehouse district on the day that you insisted you weren't there," Jake said, tapping the picture.

"I guess I was mistaken I was in the warehouse district that day," Robert said, looking at the picture.

"Now we're getting somewhere," Scott said, nodding.

"I still don't see what me being in the warehouse district has to do with a murder," Robert said, shifting his attention to the detectives.

"I'm sure you remember this man from when we showed you his picture last time," Scott said, placing the suspect's picture next to the other one.

"We know that he murdered his neighbour after an argument over a fence dispute," Jake informed, watching Jenkins's reaction carefully.

"I didn't see anyone murdering anyone," Robert said, relieved to be able to answer that one truthfully.

"We know that; in fact, the murder happened in another part of the city entirely," Jake added, flipping to the next page in the file.

"Then what difference does it make whether I was in the warehouse district or not," Robert asked, hoping that this would be a way out.

"We've almost got enough to arrest and charge him. We're only missing one key piece of evidence. That very piece of evidence is hidden somewhere in the warehouse district," Scott explained, crushing his hopes completely.

"What makes you think that I know anything about this piece of evidence?" Robert asked. He'd just barely managed to stop himself from saying gun.

"We think that you saw where our friend here hid it," Jake said, tapping the suspect's picture.

"Really, why would you think that?" Robert asked, crossing his arms as he looked from one detective to the other.

"A couple of reasons, one of them is the fact that you lied to us," Jake replied, it was a simple statement of fact.

"That may not have been a very good idea, but it doesn't prove that I know anything about any evidence in a murder," Robert replied, internally wincing at the truthfulness of the first part of his statement.

"True, but it does make us quite curious as to why you'd do that," Scott said with the right amount of curiosity in his voice.

"You've taken a fifteen, twenty minutes tops witness interview and turned it into a whole lot of trouble," Jake said, pushing a bit harder.

"You seem like a nice enough guy and you've got a clean record. We don't want to see you get into trouble. So why don't you just help yourself and tell us what you saw," Scott said, easing up on the pressure a bit. He could tell that they were losing him, so he decided to switch tactics.

"Do you mind sitting tight a few minutes while we grab a cup of coffee?" Jake asked, standing up and gathering the papers.

"Would you like something?" Scott asked, standing up.

"Some water would be okay," Robert said, after taking a deep breath while uncrossing his arms and relaxing just a little.

With that the two detectives stood up and left the room. Both were hoping that they'd be able to get more when they came back.

As soon as the door closed, Robert ran his hand through his hair. After his first conversation with the detectives, he had hoped that this would be over. He'd known that the detectives didn't believe him, but he'd figured that they couldn't prove it, so they'd try another strategy to get a conviction. He should have been more careful when he was entering the warehouse district.

Why did I have to miss that stupid camera, Robert thought, scowling to himself.

A couple minutes later the detectives reentered the room. Both of them sat down in their previous places. Scott handed Robert the bottle of water, and he took a sip of his coffee. With that the interview started back up again. It went on for about an hour and a half before they ended the interview. The whole time, they kept expecting Jenkins to ask for a lawyer, but he never did.

The next morning, Robert had just finished breakfast and was drinking a cup of coffee. The tranquil atmosphere of the morning was shattered by the shrill ringing of the phone. With a sigh, he picked it up, already nearly certain what this call was about. Sure enough he was told that he needed to come into the office.

When Jenkins arrived, he nodded to the receptionist on his way past. Stepping off the elevator he ran his hand through his hair He only half paid attention to the writing on the wall that identified this section as the offices of the Information Retrieval and Relocation Division.

It only took a few minutes for him to reach the office of his supervisor, Peter Davis. Taking a deep breath, he reached out and knocked on the door. A couple seconds later, he entered the office and was directed to one of the seats in front of the desk.

"Hello, Peter," Robert greeted, a hint of annoyance in his voice.

"Good morning," Peter replied, sounding entirely to chipper.

"It was until it was interrupted," Robert replied, with a slight scowl on his face.

"That couldn't be avoided, I'm afraid. There's something that we need to discuss," Peter said, leaning forward and steepling his fingers.

"I figured as much," Robert replied, his voice as tense as a bow string and his chin resting on his interlocked fingers.

"Figured you would," Peter said with a sigh, not holding his reaction against him.

"Sorry, guess this situation is starting to get to me," Robert said, resisting the urge to run his hand through his hair.

"How far do you think things have gone?" Peter asked, sounding a bit concerned as he observed his friend.

"They're working up to charging me or at the very least threatening to," Robert answered, leaning back in his chair.

"What do you think the charge will be?" Peter asked, not liking the idea of losing one of his best people, who was also his friend.

"It'll probably be obstruction of justice," Robert answered, his tone clearly showing how much he was looking forward to dealing with that.

"That brings us to what I wanted to talk to you about. You haven't asked for a lawyer yet; care to explain that," Peter said, his tone making it very clear that the last part was most definitely not a question.

"Not particularly," Robert replied, crossing his arms with an obstinate look on his face as he met his friend's stern look.

"All you'd have to do is say that simple phrase, and they won't be able to talk to you anymore. That's all it would take to get this off your shoulders," Peter said, compassion and worry for his friend entering his voice.

"We both know that's not true, PD. I almost wish that it was that easy," Robert replied, standing up and moving away from the chair.

"Bobby, you know how important this is and what's at stake," Peter said calmly, his expression still stern.

"Don't you think I know that? I couldn't forget even if I wanted to," Robert said as he began to pace back and forth in the open space next to the door.

"That's why I want to get you out of this whole situation," Peter said, trying to convince him to change his mind.

"No, you just want me out of the situation to make

certain that I won't say anything," Robert replied, his gaze sharpening.

"That's not fair, and you know it," Peter responded, his tone sharpening as well.

"You know me; I'd never say anything. Life would be so much easier if we could just change the drop point," Robert said, a wistful tone in his voice.

"You know that we already thought of that, but SC is far to paranoid about spies infiltrating his operation for us to get away with that. It took us months to find a safe drop point," Peter replied, also sounding like he wished that was an option too.

"Just telling the cops where the gun is isn't an option either, as we've already established quite thoroughly," Robert commented, shooting his friend a meaningful look.

"Because if we do, SC will think that Mark is a police informant," Peter explained, saying out loud what both of them already knew.

"So basically no matter what I do, someone gets hurt. Either I say nothing and a murderer walks free to possibly kill someone else, or I talk and Mark's a dead man. He's got a wife and three kids with another on the way," Robert said, clutching his hair as he ran his fingers through it.

"It does sound pretty bad when you put it that way," Peter agreed, wincing in sympathy at the predicament.

"How exactly do I put it in a way that isn't terrible?" Robert asked, crossing his arms and scowling.

"I guess there really isn't any way," Peter conceded. There was really nothing else that he could have said.

On that oh-so-cheerful note, Robert turned and left the office, knowing full well that nothing was any better than when he'd gone in. He only hoped that the tiny sliver of a plan which was beginning to form in his mind would work.

A couple of days later, Robert walked out of his favourite coffee shop over to the parking lot. He was on his coffee break, something he usually didn't have time for. The only reason he could this time was because he had been chained to his desk doing paper work. After having been informed that he wouldn't be able to do any pickups or drops till this whole mess is resolved. He'd barely gone a couple of feet when he spotted two people leaning on their car. Those people were Detective Langston and Detective Layton standing a few feet away.

"Are you here for a cup of coffee, Detectives? Because it's really good here," Robert said, not really thinking that they were.

"No, but we'll keep that in mind," Jake replied, glancing briefly at the building before returning his attention to Jenkins.

"We were wondering if you'd come down to the station for another chat. There were a few things that need cleared up," Scott said with deliberate understatement.

"Alright," Robert agreed, knowing that if he said no, they'd arrest him, which was something that he had a feeling they were wanting to avoid. Which was, something he too wanted to avoid, though that was looking increasingly unlikely.

"How about you follow us back to the station," Scott

suggested, gesturing to Jenkins' car that was right next to his.

"I'll see you there," Robert said, then walked over to his car, got in, and the two cars pulled out of the parking lot, then drove away.

Not long later, the intelligence courier and the detectives entered the interrogation room once again. The detectives sat down in the two chairs on one side of the table and gestured for Jenkins to sit in the single chair on the other side. Both detectives placed a folder on the table in front of them.

Before either detective could say anything, there was a knock on the door.Neither detective looked very happy about the interruption as someone entered and closed the door behind them. Both detectives had a whispered conversation with the newcomer before he turned and left, closing the door behind him. As soon as the door closed, both detectives turned their attention back to Robert.

"Do you mind hanging tight here for a few minutes?" Scott asked, standing up and picking up the folder.

"Why, what's going on?" Robert asked, sounding concerned. He hoped that the murderer hadn't decided to skip town or something like that.

"Nothing bad, just something that me and my partner have to settle," Jake answered, noticing the concern in his voice.

"Alright then, I'll wait here," Robert said, sitting back in his chair.

With that the two detectives turned and walked out of the interrogation room. As the two of them crossed the bullpen and headed toward the captain's office, they were each thinking about what they were going to say. When they entered the office, there were two men inside. One was the captain, which they expected. The presence of the other man was not a good sign.

"I'm sure you know Mr. Johnson from the DA's office," the captain said, gesturing toward the man that was leaning against his desk.

"We've met," Jake agreed, glancing at the man.

"Have you gotten anything from that witness yet?" the captain asked, pinching the bridge of his nose.

"Not yet; we were just about to try again," Scott answered, not sounding particularly optimistic about their chances.

"Your captain told me this is the third time you've brought him in here. He hasn't told you anything on either of his previous trips. I want him placed under arrest; my office is going to refer charges," Johnson said firmly.

"If you do that, then we'll never get anything out of him," Jake said, sounding frustrated.

"You haven't been doing such a good job of that so far," Johnson countered, crossing his arms.

"Cap, as long as he is willing to talk to us and hasn't lawyered up, we've got to keep trying," Scott said, directing his determined plea to his captain.

"He's right. They've got to keep trying. If he lawyers up, then you can hit him with the charge then," the captain said with finality.

Johnson nodded, stood up, and picked up his briefcase. He knew that this conversation was over if he tried to push;

the captain would just call the DA. The four men talked for a couple of minutes, then the lawyer turned and left the room.

The two detectives were dismissed, and they headed back to the interrogation room. They grabbed another cup of coffee as they crossed the bullpen. When they entered the room, they sat back down and placed the folders back on the table.

"I'm going to level with you. You're in a whole lot of trouble," Jake said, taking a sip of his coffee as he leaned back.

"Yeah, I noticed," Robert replied, glancing around the interrogation room.

"There's only one way out, and that's to tell us where that gun is," Scott said, leaning forward and placing his elbows on the table.

"I don't know what you're talking about," Robert said, his gaze fixed on a spot on the table right in front of him.

"You wouldn't want someone working for the murderer to find out where it is," Scott said, sitting back in his chair.

"That might have already happened," Jake said, opening the folder in front of him and flipping through the papers in front of him.

"What's that supposed to mean?" Robert asked, a touch of sharpness entering his tone, even as he tried to keep his cool.

"All the times that you lied to us made us curious, so we did some digging, and look what we found," Jake said calmly, pulling a piece of paper out of the stack.

"Seems you got ten thousand dollars the day after the gun was hidden," Scott said, pointing to a particular line on the paper.

"What do you think we'll find if we dig into that payment?" Jake asked, also tapping the paper for emphasis.

"This is your chance to tell us your side of the story," Scott added, sitting up straight in his chair again.

"As I'm sure that you know, I'm a freelance real-estate consultant. That money was from a job that I did a couple months ago, but there was a bank error, so it took a while to get deposited," Robert replied calmly. Everything in his tone and body language screaming that he wasn't even the slightest bit worried about them looking into that payment.

Both detectives noticed this reaction and shared a look. Because of this reaction, they decided to change tactics.

"You know me and Jake are more than willing to talk to you for as long it takes. However, it seems the DA's running out of patience, and he wanted us to arrest you," Scott explained, not very happy about the ADA pulling that.

"I figured that would happen," Robert said with a resigned tone of voice.

"But we went to bat for you with the DA and managed to get him to change his mind. Now we need you to do something for us. We need you to tell us where that gun is hidden," Scott said, tapping the folder in front of him with his pen.

"There's nothing I can tell you about that," Robert said, turning his gaze from the table to the detectives.

"Do you really want to be the reason that a murderer gets away with it?" Jake asked, leaning forward in his chair.

It was all Robert could do not to flinch as the detective voiced his worst nightmare. That was the very thought that kept him up at night.

"The DA okayed us offering you a deal. If you tell us what we want to know, you get immunity. That means no obstruction of justice charge," Scott said, hoping he goes for it.

"That deal goes away the instant that we leave this room," Jake added, a strong note of caution in his tone.

"There's nothing that I can tell you," Robert said as truthfully as he could.

The interrogation went on for another hour and a half, but it felt much longer. Much to the frustration of both detectives, Robert never told them anything. Neither detective could figure out why this man was withholding the information so determinedly.

A week later, Robert was pacing in his living room. He knew that it was only a matter of time before he was brought in for questioning again. Which was something that he was not looking forward to even a little bit.

The shrill ringing of the phone shattered the tense atmosphere like an ice pick. Its sound seemed three times as loud in the quiet of the room. He picked up the phone on the end table near the big chair.

"Hello, Bobby," Peter greeted, a note of excitement in his voice.

"I hope your day's been better than mine," Robert said, tension dripping off every word.

"Well it's about to get better. We got him, and his entire network is gone, every last bit. Spencer Clifton is now sitting in a holding cell while a bunch of countries fight about who gets to prosecute him," Peter said, excitement filling his voice.

"Really," Robert said, his voice slightly breathless.

"The best part is that Mark is safe and home with his family," Peter added, happiness entering his voice.

The relief that he felt at those words was so great that he basically collapsed into the chair behind him. Any other words that came from the receiver in his trembling hand were just a faint buzzing sound. When the sound changed to a dial tone, it took him two tries to hang up the phone.

For the next fifteen minutes, he stared blankly at the phone trying to process what he had just heard. His stunned haze was broken by a firm knock on the door. Before he could stand up there was another one. Which was followed by a voice identifying the knocker as Officer Mathews. When he opened the door, the officer asked him to accompany them down to the station. A request that he was more than happy to agree to.

About twenty minutes later, the detectives again entered the interrogation room where Jenkins was waiting. They both expecting more of the same of what they'd gotten the other three times. However, the instant that they sat down they could tell that something was different, though they had no idea what that difference meant they had no idea.

"How about we start at the beginning, the morning of the eighteenth," Scott suggested with a notepad in front of him and a pen in his hand, which he used to tap the pad.

"Certainly, Detective. I got up at about seven, did my usual morning routine. After which I went to an empty lot on a job. While there, I saw a man hiding a gun," Robert said, being very careful not to specify what kind of job.

"Is this the man that you saw hiding the gun?" Jake asked, showing him a picture of their suspect.

"Yes that's him," Robert replied instantly after studying the picture.

"What is the address of this lot where the gun is hidden?" Scott asked, certain that this question would put an end to this surprising cooperation.

"Of course," Robert answered instantly and gave the address.

Both detectives looked up in surprise after hastily writing down the address. Neither had been expecting that answer. Shaking off their surprise, Jake stepped out to ask someone to go find out if the gun was there. He reentered the interrogation room a few seconds later.

"We'll just wait here till we hear if the gun is there," Jake said, watching Jenkins's reaction very carefully.

"You can see why we're a bit surprised that you're suddenly so willing to tell us what you've spent hours hiding from us," Scott added, more than a little surprised.

"I guess that's understandable," Robert replied solemnly, not very happy about the fact that he'd had to lie to them.

Thirty minutes later a uniformed officer entered the interrogation room. There was a few minutes of whispered conversation between the three police officers. After which the officer turned and left the room.

"The gun was exactly where you said it was," Jake said, sounding relieved.

"What happens now?" Robert asked, pretty sure that he already knew.

"Unfortunately you're going to be arrested for obstruction of justice," Jake said, not sounding very happy about it.

Jake reached behind him and pulled out his cuffs. He wasn't very happy with this outcome. Because his gut was telling him that Jenkins had a good reason for lying. Glancing at his partner, he could tell he felt the same. Which he told him as he cuffed him and handed him off to an officer.

This case sure hadn't turned out the way they'd been expecting. Sure they'd been glad when they learned about the traffic camera. However, they'd thought they won the lottery when they'd heard on that wiretap that Jenkins had seen where the gun was hidden. Neither of them had ever dreamed that things would turn out the way they did. As glad as they were that the killer was going to jail, it was to bad that a decent man ended up in cuffs too.

A couple of hours later, Robert Jenkins was released because the DA had declined to press charges. A fact that both detectives were quite happy about. The reason that this happened was that the DA and Peter knew each other. Because they'd known each other from when the latter was in the military and Peter was still an agent, the latter was able to tell the former that Jenkins had been forced to lie because of his intelligence work.

A couple weeks later, the two detectives got a very unusual package. Inside was a newspaper that had a headline talking about the downfall of an international crime lord. There was also a cryptic note that said, "You two should listen to your instincts."

* * *

"That is what can happen when spies get tangled up in a murder investigation. Oh boy, did things get tangled," Alicia said, her tone grave, fitting the end of the story.

The crowd clapped earnestly, having enjoyed the story. They all couldn't help wondering what they would have done in Robert's position. A murmur swept over the crowd as they began discussing whether Robert had made the right decision. It was definitely quite the thought-provoking story.

THE END

CHAPTER 6

The Stranger

It was a bright sunny day, the perfect kind of day you'd want during a county fair. A large crowd had formed in front of the band stands. The crowd was practically humming with excitement as a woman walked out on to the stage.

"You all know who's up next. Let's give a warm welcome to Alicia the Storyteller," the announcer said as the band walked off the stage.

A woman walked out onto the stage and up to the announcer. She accepted the mic from the other woman.

"Hello, everybody, on this beautiful day," Alicia said into the mic.

"Hello, Alicia," the crowd replied enthusiastically.

"What kind of story does everyone want to hear?" Alicia asked the excited crowd.

There was a couple of shouted suggestions. However, the one that was the loudest and most widespread was an Old West story.

"Alright, you guys. Let's go on a journey to a time when this country was young. A time of outlaws and lawmen, of cattle barons and homesteaders. Today's tale is about one of those homesteaders who worked tirelessly to build a life for himself and his family. Even more, it's about something that happened which profoundly affected not only this man and his family but many others as well," Alicia said excitedly.

* * *

On a bright, clear day and there was, a gentle breeze blew. Nestled among green trees was a small log home. In front of and to the right side of the house was a corral. The rest of the hundred and sixty acres was dotted with pastures. In those pastures grazed either cattle or horses.

This homestead was owned by a man, his wife, and their son. The man's name was James Everett, his wife's name was Alice, and his son's name was Mark. James was a tall, strongly built man with brown hair and rich deep-brown eyes. Alice was a slight but deceptively strong woman with blond hair and light-brown eyes. Mark was a helpful and energetic ten-year-old with light-brown hair halfway between the colour of his mother's and his father's with brown eyes like his parents.

James and his son were working on the corral fence. They had just replaced a rotten post and were now nailing down a new board. Just as they pounded in the last nail, the front door of the house opened, and Alice stood in the doorway.

"Lunch time," Alice called, drawing the attention of the father and son.

"How's that for timing? Your Ma calls just as we finish this here fence," James commented, smiling at his son.

"You're right, Pa; Ma has the best timing in the whole wide world," Mark replied, excitement clearing his voice.

"You sure about that?" James asked as he packed up his tools.

"Oh right, well, she's got the second-best timing in the whole wide world," Mark corrected, his eyes fixed on his dad.

James smiled fondly at his son as he packed up his toolbox. Father and son walked over to the house. As they neared the water pump, they quickly washed their hands. As they reached the front door, Mark eagerly rushed up to his mom.

"I helped Pa fix the corral. Did you see me?" Mark asked excitedly.

"Yes, I did. You did a real good job helping your Pa," Alice said, smiling lovingly at her son while placing her hand on his shoulder.

"Guess what else? We remembered to wash up all by ourselves," Mark said, beaming up at his mother.

"I saw that too. Why don't we go inside and have some lunch," Alice suggested, holding out her hand to her son.

The cheerful little boy eagerly took his mother's hand and began pulling her toward the door. Naturally, Alice allowed herself to be dragged into the house. James was about a step behind her, enjoying his son's antics. Within a few minutes, the little family were seated around the table. After giving the good LORD thanks for the meal, they started eating. The meal itself was largely silent, everyone busy eating.

"How did mending the corral go this morning?" Alice asked as she stood and began clearing the table.

"It went well," James replied as he stood also.

About twenty minutes later, Alice was weeding in the garden, and Mark was helping. While James worked in front of the barn. He was working on repairing the bed of a buck board.

Just as the homesteader had finished pounding in a nail, he heard a sound coming from the direction of the driveway. This caused him to look in that direction. When he did, he saw a man staggering down the driveway. Instantly he jumped to his feet and got down off the buck board. He took off running in the direction of the possibly wounded man. When he was about halfway, the man collapsed. This caused him to run even faster, and within a second he crouched by the side of the man on the ground.

Sure enough, the man was indeed injured. He had a nasty gash on the side of the head that was bleeding pretty badly. There was also a bleeding wound to the man's side.

"Alice, I need help to get him inside," James shouted after he checked and confirmed that the man was still alive.

Alice quickly told Mark to go inside and get things ready. As soon as she saw him rush into the house, she hurried over to where her husband crouched over the injured man. She reached them just as her husband finished tying his bandana around the injured man's head wound.

"We need to get him inside quickly," Alice said urgently, her voice filled with concern as she looked over the injuries.

"Here, help me get him up," James said, also sounding urgent and concerned as he took a position at the man's shoulders.

Working together the couple lifted the man up off the ground. Moving as quickly as they dared, they got him to the house. Just as they reached the door Mark opened it. Once inside, the couple quickly got him to their bedroom and laid him on the bed.

"I'll send Jake to fetch the doctor," James said as Alice sat on the edge of the bed.

"Once you've done that, I'm going to need boiling water, strips of cloth for bandages, and can you grab the jug of vinegar from the kitchen," Alice said, listing off the things she needed.

James nodded then rushed out of the room. About a minute later, Alice heard the door open and close. The man on the bed shifting and clutching the sheets in pain drew her attention to him. A couple minutes later, as he settled again she heard a horse riding away and the sound of the door opening and closing again. She could faintly hear her husband moving around in the main room looking for the things she'd asked for. It wasn't very long before the bedroom door opening caused her to look up. When she did, she noticed that he was carrying the cloth and the vinegar.

"The water is on the stove," James said as he handed her the jug of vinegar and placed the strips of cloth on the table next to the bed.

Alice nodded and placed the jug on the floor at her feet. Next, the two of them removed the man's jacket. As soon as they got him settled on the bed again, Alice gently removed the unconscious man's gun belt. Next, she carefully unbuttoned his shirt. Trying very hard not to hurt him, she removed the blood-soaked cloth from the wound on the man's side. When she did, she found bits of dirt in the wound.

"I need you to hold him down. Unfortunately, this is going to hurt," Alice said, picking up the jug that was still sitting at her feet.

James nodded and got a firm hold on the wounded man's shoulders. The instant the vinegar touched the wound, he felt the man jerk and try to pull away. Thankfully, his firm hold kept the wounded man still until the wound was clear.

"There I think that should do it," Alice said, putting the cork back in the jug and placing it back on the floor.

"I'll go get the water," James said, hearing the sound of the water boiling on the stove in the kitchen.

"Let me, I need to dry the bandages with the iron. That would be easier to do in the kitchen," Alice replied, standing up from the edge of the bed.

When she was done, she came back into the bedroom with a the clean bandages to find her husband sitting on the edge of the bed. Working together, they managed to bandage the wound well enough that the man wouldn't bleed to death before the doctor came. She briefly returned to the kitchen, returning a few minutes later with a basin of cooled, boiled water and a clean rag.

About an hour later they heard the sound of horses approaching. Figuring it was probably the doctor, James left the bedroom. Just as he entered the main room, there was a knock on the door. The homesteader opened the door and, sure enough, it was the doctor. Dr. Williams was a kindly, grey-haired, country doctor.

"Afternoon, Doc," James greeted, extending his hand.

"Good afternoon, James, I hope Alice and Mark are okay," Dr. Williams greeted, shaking the homesteader's hand.

"Don't worry, they're both fine. They're not the reason we got you out here," James explained as the doctor entered, and he closed the door.

"Glad to hear it," Dr. Williams replied, with his doctor's bag in his hand as he followed James toward the bedroom.

"Right after lunch a wounded stranger showed up," James explained as he reached for the bedroom door handle.

He opened the door, and the two of them walked into the room. As soon as Dr. Williams walked into the room he saw the man lying on the bed.

"Does he have any injuries other than the one on his head?" Dr. Williams asked Alice, while scanning the man on the bed for any wounds other than the obvious one on his head.

"There's also a gunshot wound to his side. It's just a graze, but it was bleeding quite a bit. I cleaned it out as best I could with vinegar," Alice explained, standing up from the edge of the bed and moving to stand by her husband.

The doctor carefully moved the wounded man's shirt aside, thus allowing him to get a better look at the wound.

"How about you two go get a cup of coffee while I finish up here," the doctor said, glancing at the couple before his gaze returned to his patient.

After another worried look at the wounded man, the couple left the room. Once outside the bedroom, they decided to take the doctor's advice.

About an hour later the doctor left the bedroom. As soon as he entered the main room, the couple turned their attention to him. They had been sitting on a couple chairs next to the fireplace but stood up when the doctor walked in.

"How is he, Doc?" James asked, sounding concerned as they walked up to the doctor.

"He's got a fair chance, but he lost a fair amount of blood. It also looks like he's got the start of a fever developing. He's going to need tendin' if he's going to make it," Dr. Williams replied, his tone serious as he looked from one of them to the other.

"Don't worry, Doc; we'll take good care of him," Alice assured with both concern and conviction in her tone.

"I know you will. Send for me if there's any change in his condition," Dr. Williams instructed, then turned and headed toward the front door.

Once the doctor had left, Alice looked in on the wounded stranger. She confirmed that he was sleeping comfortably. Silently closing the door so as not to wake him up, she returned to the main room.

Just then Mark came back inside from doing his chores and walked over to her. When he reached her, he looked up at his mother with a question clear in his expression.

"Ma, will the stranger be okay?" Mark asked, sounding genuinely concerned.

"I really don't know, Mark, but we're going to do everything we can to help him," Alice answered, crouching to his level.

"Is there any way I can help?" Mark asked, sounding hopeful.

"There sure is; you can mention him in your prayers at night," Alice replied with a gentle, loving smile.

"Of course I'll do that. Is there anything else I can do to help?" Mark asked, wanting to do more to help the stranger.

"Alright, how about you run and get a basin of water and bring it to the bedroom," Alice replied, wanting to encourage his desire to help others.

"I'll go do it right away," Mark replied, giving her a brief hug, then dashing toward the door.

"On your way back, be careful not to drop the basin," Alice admonished as he reached the door and opened it.

"I know that, Ma," Mark replied as the door closed behind him.

By the time Mark returned with the basin, Alice was waiting next to the bed. She accepted the basin that he held out to her and placed it on the bedside table.

The wounded man's fever had gotten worse. Alice wet a cloth in the water from the basin. She used the cloth to wet the man's face in an attempt to cool him down.

Over the next few weeks, the wounded stranger's condition worsened. Through it all, the family continued to tend him. Sometimes they stayed up all night to take care of him.

On the third Sunday, the stranger's fever finally broke. Alice checked on him before they went to church. The stranger spent the whole day resting peacefully.

The next morning after breakfast, James and Alice looked in on the wounded man. Just as they opened to door, the man on the bed shifted. The couple moved into the room, closing the door behind them. They both approached the bed, and Alice sat on the edge of it. The man on the bed shifted and moaned, then opened his eyes.

"Where am I?" the stranger asked, his voice so raspy from disuse that it was barely understandable.

"James, help me sit him up so he can have a drink," Alice said, picking up the glass of water on the bedside table.

Working together, the two of them helped the stranger get a drink. Once he was settled back on the bed, he looked between the two people standing by the bed.

"Where am I? Who are you?" the stranger asked again. The question was audible now that his voice was now clearer.

"You're in my home, and my name is James Everett, and this is my wife, Alice," James answered, putting his arm around his wife.

"Can you tell us your name?" Alice asked gently.

"I don't remember," the stranger answered, his voice shaking as he tried unsuccessfully to remember.

James and Alice exchanged concerned looks. After a second, they turned their attention back to the man in the bed.

"What happened?" the stranger asked, sounding confused.

"You were shot in the side, and it seems you hit you head," James answered, sounding concerned.

"I don't remember how that could of happened," the stranger said, his confusion and little bits of fear clear in his voice and in his posture.

"What is the last thing that you do remember?" Alice asked, her concern growing at this revelation.

"Nothing, it's all gone," the stranger answered, running his hand through his hair, despite how tired he felt.

"You might remember something after you've rested for a spell. You've had a real hard time these past few weeks," James suggested, drawing the stranger's attention to him, hoping that his words would reassure the man.

"James is right; you need your rest," Alice agreed, concerned about the stranger's obvious exhaustion.

"I'll try, Ma'am," the stranger replied. While still frustrated, he knew that they were right about him needing rest, and he hoped they were right about getting it possibly helping his memory.

As soon as the couple was sure that the man was as comfortable as he could be under the circumstance, the two of them left the room.

When the door closed behind them, the stranger again ran his hand through his hair, hoping that he would be able to get some sleep. Though he doubted he would be able to, considering the fact that his head hurt and his mind was buzzing like a hive of angry bees.

The next time he woke up, he was much more clear headed. Unfortunately, he still didn't remember anything about himself, which frustrated him a great deal. The fact that his side was still hurting did not improve his disposition any. Neither did the fact that he was still as weak as a kitten from the fever.

Over the next few days, the stranger quickly regained his strength. He still had to be careful about moving around to much, but he at least could get out of bed. A fact that he was infinitely thankful for. There was a knock on the door before it opened.

"How are you doing this morning?" Alice asked with a pleasant smile on her face as she entered the room

"Better than I was a few days ago," the stranger replied, sitting up in bed.

"I'm glad to hear it. Do you think you're up to joining us at the table this morning?" Alice asked hopefully.

"I think so," the stranger said after a second of thinking while, running his hand through his hair.

"I guess we'll see you out there in a few minutes," Alice said with a pleased nod, then turned and left the room

Once he was alone in the room, the stranger looked around. His gaze fell on the clothes that were sitting on the only chair in the room neatly folded. He walked over and picked them up. He returned to the bed and quickly got dressed. After putting on the boots he found under the chair and his gun belt, he exited the bedroom.

"Good morning," James greeted as the stranger walked toward the table next to Jake.

"Morning, Mister," Mark said excitedly.

"Mornin', everyone," the stranger greeted, as he sat down at the table.

"Alice said that you're doing better this morning," James commented, sounding glad.

"Unfortunately I still don't remember who I am," the stranger replied, sounding disappointed by the fact.

"Then what are we going to call you?" Mark asked, drawing everyone's attention to him.

"That is a good point, Son," James replied, not having thought of it, but now that it was brought up, that could be a problem.

Alice glanced up from her breakfast and around the room as she thought about it. When her eyes landed on her Bible sitting on the small table in the sitting area, she had an idea.

"How about Micah," Alice suggested, her gaze returning to the people around the table.

The reason she thought of that name was because that morning she had been reading in Micah in her devotions.

"It's as good a name as any," the stranger replied, vaguely recognizing it as a Bible name.

The four people went back to eating breakfast. After they finished eating, Alice quickly got everything cleaned up.

About ten minutes later, James was standing out on the porch when Micah stepped out of the door. He walked over to lean against the railing next to the homesteader. The two men stood in silence for a few minutes before either said anything.

"What are you going to do now that you're back on your feet?" James asked, breaking the comfortable silence.

"I'm not really sure," Micah replied, staring off past the corral and into the distance, not really looking at anything.

"There's an awful lot of work around here," James said, his gaze still on the horses moving around in the corral.

Micah nodded, his gaze flicking to James for a split second before turning forward again.

"What would you say about stayin' 'round here for a

spell?" James asked, watching the man next to him out of the corner of his eye.

"You offerin' me a job?" Micah asked simply, his gaze never leaving the open space beyond the corral.

"Seems I am. All I can pay you is a dollar a day with room and board," James offered, turning to face the other man.

"Don't got anywhere else to be—that I know of, at least," Micah replied, also turning to face the other man.

With that James and Micah shook hands, sealing the deal. The two of them stepped off the porch, then headed off toward the barn to get some work done.

The first thing that needed doing was some fences that needed mending. Micah hitched up the wagon. While James gathered the supplies into the bed of the wagon. Once everything was together, they got on the wagon and headed out. They were hoping to get the section of fence mended by lunch time. A goal which they were able to achieve with about five minutes to spare.

About a week later James and Micah headed into town. They were going to pick up some much-needed supplies. Fortunately the weather was good, making the trip much more enjoyable.

When the two men arrived in town, James looked around and everything seemed just like it had the last time he'd been in town. He found he wasn't really surprised by that as he pulled the wagon to a stop in front of the general store.

As James and Micah jumped down, a man approached them. He was another homesteader in his late twenties or early thirties. The man had blond hair and green eyes, wearing a white shirt, a light-brown vest, and dark-brown pants.

"Howdy, James, been a while since I seen you," the man greeted, extending his hand toward his friend.

"It sure has, Matt; you weren't in town the last time I was," James replied, shaking his friend's hand, happy to see his friend again.

"Got a might busy moving the herd to the high pasture," Matt explained, clearly also happy to not have missed his friend again.

"It happens," James replied easily.

"Say, where's Jake this afternoon?" Matt asked, expecting to see the hired hand.

"I decided Jake needed some help, so I hired another hand. This here is my new hand, Micah," James introduced, indicating the man standing next to him.

"Well welcome to Ceder Hole," Matt said, extending his hand.

"Thank ya kindly," Micah said, shaking the man's hand.

"How have things been going out at your place?" James asked, hoping that things have been going well for his friend.

"About the same. It sure galls me to have to pay Barrett to use water on my own land," Matt replied, thinking about the man bringing a scowl to his face.

"Yeah, me too," James said, also sounding frustrated and no happier about the situation than his friend.

John Barrett was the grandson of Jack Barrett, the man that first settled the valley and owned about a quarter of the land in the valley. The rest was divided into a bunch of homesteads. Somehow Barrett had managed to buy up all the water rights to the whole valley.

Now those water rights belonged to John since his dad's death. At the time of his dad's death there was a rumour that one of the pages to the will was missing. For days after, the whole town and surrounding area was abuzz with speculation about what was in that missing will page. After about a week, the rumour was dispelled by Barrett's lawyer. He assured both the people and the circuit judge that there was no missing page of the will. However, there were still a few people that wondered if the lawyer was lying and there really was a missing page.

"Well a gotta be goin'," Matt said when he looked at this pocket watch and realized what time it was, knowing he needed to get back to his ranch.

"We gotta get busy too. Can't very well stand around jawin' all day. See ya later, Matt," James said with a friendly pat on the back.

As the other homesteader walked away, James went into the general store. After chatting with the clerk for a few minutes, he ordered the supplies that he needed. While the clerk gathered up his order, he decided to look around and see if they'd gotten in anything new.

Ten minutes later Micah was loading the supplies into the wagon. He was about halfway through with the loading. Suddenly, just as he'd put the bag of nails in the wagon, a shot rang out. The bullet hit so close to him that it ripped his shirt. Reacting quickly, the stranger dove behind a nearby water trough amidst a hail of bullets. As he was doing that he drew his own gun and fired back.

Seconds after the first shot, James rushed out of the general store and ducked behind the water trough next to Micah. He glanced over at the other man as another bullet slammed into the water trough.

The exchange of gunfire lasted for an intense couple of minutes. It ended with Micah managing to hit one of the assailants in the shoulder. The other one helped the wounded one to his feet and quickly got both of them to their horses. After helping his wounded friend get on his horse he got on his, and they galloped off.

"Are you OK?" James asked as they stood up and watched the miscreants gallop away in a cloud of dust.

"Not even a scratch," Micah replied, glancing at James as soon as the two miscreants had disappeared from view.

Working together they quickly got the rest of the supplies all loaded up. While they were working James looked up from what he was doing. When he did, he noticed something that brought a frown to his face. That expression was caused by the fact that he spotted Marcel Cobb. He was a little man, about five feet five inches tall with a weasel-like appearance and disposition. James had long suspected that Cobb was working for John Barrett. Though he'd never had any proof either was up to anything criminal, that's why he'd never said anything. So the fact that Cobb was running around like an overly excited jackrabbit talking to everyone he came across did not bode well for anyone. As soon as they were sure that everything was secured, the two men got on the wagon seat and pulled out.

Unknown to either of them, someone watched the wagon from an alley. While standing in the shadow of the alley, his eyes narrowed as the wagon pulled away from the boardwalk. He stepped out onto the boardwalk as soon as the wagon disappeared.

About an hour and twenty minutes later, James and Micah arrived back at the homestead. James pulled the wagon to a stop in front of the shed. The two men jumped down from the seat and started unloading the building supplies.

Once all of the building supplies were unloaded, the wagon was moved over to the back door of the house. The two of them started unloading food supplies. When they were done, the two men went back to what they'd been doing before.

A couple of hours later, Mark came rushing out of the house. He looked around for a few minutes before spotting his Pa and rushed toward him.

"Ma sent me to tell you it's time for lunch," Mark said, pulling on his Pa's sleeve.

"Alright, Son, we'll be there in a few minutes," James said, ruffling his son's hair before the boy dashed off back to the house.

The two of them followed the eager little boy over to the house. Instead of entering the house, Micah walked over to the porch railing and leaned against it. Less than a minute later James joined him to lean against the rail. After a second of silence, James stood up straight and went into the house.

"How was your trip to town, Dear?" Alice asked her husband as she put the pot of food on the already-set table.

"It was a might bit more excitin' than we figured on, Lice," James replied as he walked up to the table.

"Oh, how so?" Alice asked somewhat distractedly as she sat down at the table.

"While Micah was loading the wagon, someone took some shots at him," James explained as he too sat down at the table

"That's terrible; is he alright?" Alice asked just as she heard the door open.

About a second later, she saw out of the corner of her eye Jake and Micah enter. Jake placed the pitcher of water that he'd filled outside on the table, then sat down.

"Don't worry, Ma'am; I'm fine," Micah replied as he sat down at the table.

"That's good to hear," Alice replied, sounding relieved.

About twenty minutes later, they had just finished eating. Suddenly they heard the unmistakable sound of approaching horses. They quickly rushed out of the house onto the porch. On his way out, James picked up his rifle. Once outside they turned their attention in the direction the sound was coming from.

A few minutes later, half a dozen horses rode up, stopping not far from the house. The man leading the pack was none other than John Barrett. There were six men behind Barrett, all of which were armed and had their rifles in their hands.

"What are ya doin' on my land, Barrett?" James asked, noticing that the men behind Barrett were the ones Cobb had been talking to earlier.

"We know the stranger is staying here," Barrett said, looking disdainfully at the homesteader brandishing his rifle.

"That ain't none a yer concern," James replied, his eyes flicking over the group of men in front of him.

"It is our concern; he's a danger to our community. You're going to hand him over to us," Barrett demanded, sneering at the homesteader.

"What makes him a danger to our community?" James asked with a scowl on his face.

"That scene in town earlier proves my point quite clearly. Someone could have been hurt or even killed," Barrett sneered, glaring at James.

"Gettin' shot at ain't a crime. If yer so all fired concerned 'bout folk's safety, try lookin' for tha man that done the shootin'," James replied, returning the glare.

"We're running that mangy gunslick out of town, and there's nothing you can do about it," Barrett said, hissing like an angry snake.

"Git off my land," James responded, firing his rifle into the air to punctuate his statement, then pointed it at Barrett.

"You can't shoot all of us before someone shoots you," Barrett replied, talking to James as if he thought the man was an idiot.

"That may be, but I shore can hit you," James replied, his aim never wavering.

"You're bluffing," Barrett sneered, his voice filled with arrogant bravado.

"If you're so sure, then why don't you call me," James replied while looking down the sights of his rifle at the man.

There was a tense couple of minutes where everyone wondered what would happen. A few of the riders behind Barrett shifted, uncomfortable with the tension in the air.

"Fine, we'll leave, but know this, if he's still here next month, I won't be renewing the agreement that allows you to use my water," Barrett sneered, glaring at James.

"Just git off my land afor I send Jake for the law," James replied, his voice firm and determined as his intense gaze flicked over each man before returning to Barrett.

With one last glare, Barrett and his bunch rode away. Only once it was certain that they were really gone did the three men relax. The two hands got back to work on what they'd been doing, and James went back inside.

Alice looked up from wiping down the table when James entered and walked up to the table. He told her what had just happened and the threat that Barrett had made. She could tell that the threat was really bothering her husband.

"You know what we need to do, Dear," Alice said, placing her hand on her husband's arm reassuringly.

"Yes I do, Lice," James replied as the two of them sat down at the dining table side by side.

"Dear LORD, may you give us the strength to trust you for those things that we need for life as you told us to in your word in Matthew 6:31-33. Please give us the strength to stand up for what is right no matter what the obstacles or difficulties," Alice prayed, while the five of them had their heads bowed, holding each other's hands.

"Yer right, Lice, the Good LORD, will take care of us as he always has and always will," James said, his voice now confident as he stood up.

James kissed his wife on the check while he put his hat on. After that, he went out to get back to work himself.

That evening Micah found James leaning against the

corral fence. Something had been bothering him all afternoon, but they'd been to busy to bring it up. Now that
things had calmed down, he was going to.

"How long have you known that I'm a gunfighter?"
Micah asked, his tone both certain and curious.

"Didn't know for sure, but I suspected it. As ta why,
while me an Lice was tending you, Jake knocked an empty
kettle off the counter making a fair-sized bang. Even
though you was only half conscious, ya still reached fer
yer gun," James answered, still looking out at the corral.

After about a minute, James turned his gaze to the man
standing next to him.

"When did you figure it out?" James asked, hoping this
meant that Micah's memory was coming back.

"When Barrett called me a mangy gunslick, I had a
flash of him calling me that before. I get the feel that we've
met before, and that it wasn't a friendly acquaintance,"
Micah replied thoughtfully.

"At least that's somethin'," James said, his tone still
hopeful.

"Maybe I should just leave. It seems that my presence
is about to cause you and your family a lot of trouble,"
Micah said, lowering his head and staring at the fence he
was leaning against.

"Just how far do ya think you'd make it before ya fell
off a yer horse," James said, his tone making it clear how
much he disapproved of that idea.

"I can take care of myself," Micah replied, tying to
sound confident.

"'Sides, the doc would have yer head if you bust open

those stitches," James said, then turned and headed back to the house.

After about a minute, Micah headed off to the bunk-house. He was tired and his head was starting to hurt again. Hopefully, things would be clearer in the morning.

Over the next two weeks, there were two more attempts on Micah's life. Fortunately, he was able to escape both of them with nothing more than a scratch on his arm. It was now abundantly clear that someone really wanted their mysterious friend dead.

During the last attempt on his life, Micah got a good look at the man that took a shot at him. Who turned out to be a gun for hire that he'd crossed paths with in an unfriendly manner quite a few times. That night he had a dream about the days leading up to him getting injured. When he woke up the next morning, he remembered everything.

In the morning, the five of them were sitting down at breakfast. As they all sat around the table, things were quiet as people ate. Once everyone was done, Alice started clearing away the dishes while the men poured themselves a cup of coffee.

"How are you feeling this morning, Micah?" Alice asked, breaking the silence as she picked up a plate.

"Last night I had a dream that was actually a memory of the days before I was hurt. When I woke up, I remem-bered everything," Micah answered, drawing everyone's attention.

Mark took a deep breath, prepared to pepper the gun-fighter with innumerable questions. As if reading his mind, his dad looked at him with a stern look.

"One question at a time, Son," James said with a fond smile on his face, successfully stifling a chuckle.

"Alright, Pa. Does that include your name?" Mark asked, eagerly excited to finally find out some of the things that he'd been wondering since the stranger's arrival.

"It sure does; my name is Alex Stone," Alex said, amused by the young man's enthusiastic question.

"What about where you're from. Do you remember that, Mr. Stone?" Mark asked, his next question just as excitedly.

"Now, Son, he might not want to talk about his past," James admonished, gently not wanting his son to pry.

"I know that, Pa; it's fine if he don't wanna answer," Mark replied, then turned his attention back to Stone.

"I was born in a small town in Colorado," Alex answered, not bothered by the question.

"Mark, you know you have chores to do," Alice reminded, her gaze fixed on her son.

"I know, Ma," Mark said, as he stood up and muttered, "They just want to me to leave so they kin talk about important grown up things," as he walked over to and out of the front door

Which was heard by the adults and brought a chuckle from each of them. There was silence a couple of seconds after the door closed behind the boy as everyone at the table gathered their thoughts and considered what they'd just learned.

"I remember who shot me and why. It involves you and everyone else in the valley," Alex said, his tone serious.

"Guess we was wrong it weren't a personal matter," James commented It had been their running theory that

Alex had been shot by someone with a grudge against him from his many years as a gunfighter.

"Yeah, it looks like it. A couple days before I was shot, I rode into Ceder Hole looking for work. I was in the saloon having a drink and playing some poker. Barrett's foreman came in and told me Barrett wanted me to meet him in his office. He hired me to carry a document to the lawyer in the next town. Something felt wrong. I had a bad feeling about both Barrett and the job.

"About halfway there, four men wearing masks jumped me. After they shot me, all but one of them rode away. The one that stayed behind took the document out of envelope and lit it on fire. I managed to get it away from him before it burned. The man was about to lunge at me. Luckily I got my gun and pointed it at him. I told him if he didn't leave, I'd kill him. He left. Unfortunately, he shot my horse before he left. Once he was gone, I hid the paper and started looking for help," Alex explained, running his hand through his hair.

"Do you remember what the document was?" Jake asked, figuring it was probably very important.

"I don't remember; all I've got is a feeling that it's really important," Alex replied, frustrated that he couldn't remember what was on the document.

"How come Barrett would hire a stranger ta take documents ta 'is family lawyer. Why wouldn't 'e jus' send one a his own men?" James asked, confused.

"Why not just give the papers to him when he came to town three days later," Jake asked, just as confused.

"Maybe he didn't want his men to find out what the documents were," Alice suggested thoughtfully.

"Ma'am, if he didn't trust his own men enough to send them, why would he send a complete stranger?" Jake asked, skeptical of her idea.

"The only way we'll know why he did it is to find out what the document is," Alex said, realizing this theorizing was getting them nowhere.

"By that I'm guessin' you remember where you hid it," James said with a knowing look on his face and his sharp eyes fixed on Alex's face.

A supposition that was proven right when Alex nodded. Fortunately, it was also his day off, allowing him time to ride out and find the document.

James tried to convince Alex to let him and Jake ride along. However, the gunfighter pointed out that doing so would leave both Alice and Mark unprotected. He further pointed out that Barrett wouldn't be above kidnapping one or both of them to get what he wanted.

For this reason, about an hour later, Alex rode out, heading in the direction that he'd come from what seemed like a lifetime ago. He road in contemplative silence for a few hours before things started to look familiar. It took about twenty more minutes before he reached the place that he hid the document.

The hiding place was in cluster of three huge rocks. More specifically it was in a crevasse about the width of his hand in the back of the middle rock. Just as he reached it, a bullet struck the rock rim of the crevasse. Which caused him to quickly pull his hand back. Fortunately his hand had already closed around the folded document. Just as he looked down at the paper in his hand, a bullet hit where his head had been a fraction of a second later. He quickly returned fire while tucking the paper in the inside pocket of the jacket he was wearing. After that, the whole situation devolved into a hail of bullets. Alex figured he was up against about five men.

Braving the rain of bullets, Stone ran to his horse. With each step, he fired back in his attackers' general direction. He didn't actually expect to hit anyone, just figured on discouraging them from continuing to shoot at him. A bullet missed him by less than half an inch as he reached his horse. With bullets flying past his ears, he jumped on his horse and galloped away.

As Stone galloped away, he could hear the thundering of hoof beats behind him. Knowing that it was his pursuers, he urged his horse to go faster. Aware of the fact that his horse couldn't keep up this pace for long, he began looking around for somewhere to lay low and come up with plan.

About a minute later, with the hoof beats still thundering behind him, Alex saw a line shack appear ahead of him. The small building was like an answer to a prayer that he only half remembered giving voice to.

Once he reached the shack, he quickly made his way around to the back. Moving quickly, he slid off his horse, tied it to the back rail, and hurried inside. Even though he knew that his pursuers would be here in minutes, he took out the document and unfolded it. As he finished reading the document, a determination hardened within him, and he knew what he had to do. Less than a heartbeat after he refolded the document and put it back in his jacket pocket, his pursuers rode up to the shack.

"Stone, give us the document, and we'll let you live," Barrett shouted from outside the small building.

"Not happening," Alex replied, his voice hard and cold.

"How about I sweeten tha deal some. I'll let you live and pay you five thousand dollars if you hand over the document," Barrett offered, trying to hide his desperation.

"No matter how much you offer me, I'll never give this document to you," Alex replied in the same tone of voice.

"Well, boys, I tried to be civilized about this, but he's unwilling to cooperate. Whoever brings me that document gets the five thousand dollars," Barrett said, shaking his head in mock disappointment.

The instant the words were out of Barrett's mouth his goons opened fire. They peppered the small building with gunfire, getting quite a few in reply.

Alex had just ducked back down from returning fire when he felt a hand on his shoulder. Careful to keep low, he spun around gun up and ready to defend himself. Relief washed over him when he saw it was James and Jake. His look of relief turned into a scowl as the reason they hadn't accompanied him initially returned to the forefront of his mind.

"Afore ya ask, Alice and Mark are stayin' with Matt till this is over," James said, successfully guessing what his friend was thinking.

"You figure out what this is all about," Jake asked, bringing everyone's attention back to the matter at hand.

"Yeah, I did," Alex replied, handing the document to James.

Both James and Jake read the document carefully. As

soon as they were finished, they handed it back with looks of outraged determination on their faces.

"Tha circuit judge's in town t'day. You get tha paper ta him, and we'll cover ya," James said, glancing out the window.

Alex nodded as Barrett and his men began firing again. As the gunfighter darted out the back door, he heard James and Jake start firing. He jumped on his horse and carefully made his way away from the shack, making sure not to be seen by Barrett and his men.

Once Stone was sure that he was safely away, he took off at a gallop. With a renewed sense of determination, he headed toward town as fast as his mount could carry him.

It didn't take very long for the gunfighter to make it into town. When he did, he headed to the livery and took care of his tired horse. Once he was done, he headed off to find the judge.

Turns out it didn't take very long for the gunfighter to find the judge, who was holding court in the saloon. He arrived just as the previous case was ending. The judge was a stern but not unkind older gentleman with grey hair and piercing, green eyes.

"Is there something you need, young man?" the judge asked, his sharp gaze curious as he eyed the gunfighter.

"You need to look at this, Sir; it's real important," Alex said, his tone serious.

"Alright, let me see it," the judge said, gesturing for Alex to come forward and accepting the document that was handed to him.

The judge carefully read the document. Once he was

done, it was clear from his expression that he was not one bit happy about what he had just read.

"Mr. Johnson, please stand up," the judge ordered as his sharp gaze fixed steadily on the lawyer sitting at one of the tables.

"Yes, Your Honour," Johnson said, carefully sensing the judge's anger as he stood up.

"Mr. Johnson, six months ago you stated unequivocally that there was no missing page to Michael Barrett's will," the judge stated, his sharp green gaze glinting like the honed edge of a knife.

"Y-yes, Your Honour," Johnson said as a shudder of pure terror ran though him.

"Yet that very document is right this instant in my hand," the judge said, his knife-like tone cutting into the quivering attorney.

Johnson opened his mouth to try to make an argument in his own defense.

"I'd strongly recommend you choose your next words very carefully," the judge snapped sharply as he glared at the lawyer.

In the end, Johnson made a full confession, hoping that it would buy him lenience. The angry judge pulled his law license and had him arrested for contempt of court while he decided whether to press any other charges.

The missing page of the will left the water rights to the owners of the land. Included in the lawyer's confession was that Barrett was fully aware of the contents of the page. John Barrett was ordered to return all the money and arrested for fraud.

As for Alex Stone, after some heartfelt goodbyes from the Everett family, the gunfighter road away as forever changed as was the town of Ceder Hole and its surrounding area. This change had happened during his time working for the Everetts. He had accepted Jesus as his LORD and Saviour. He knew he could never go back to being a hired gun. While at the same time was equally aware that taking off his gun completely would be tantamount to suicide. He decided to use his gun to protect people. Though what exactly that would look like, he wasn't sure yet. However, he was certain that the LORD had a plan for his life.

* * *

By the end of Alicia's telling of the story, the crowd had at least doubled. All her life Alicia had loved telling stories, not for the applause that she got but because she got to share a glimpse into a world created by someone's imagination with others. Calls for another story rippled through the excited crowd like a wave on the ocean.

THE END

PART 3
Winding Paths

CHAPTER 7
Lost and Found

Alicia's morning had been a busy one. The morning had started when she got a call from her sister. Unfortunately the conversation had been quite tense. After hanging up the phone she scowled at it for a few seconds.

At exactly that instant said phone rang. Alicia looked at the caller ID. When she did, her scowl deepened just slightly. The caller was her manager, though what he wanted she didn't know. She picked up the phone while mentally preparing herself for whatever he was going to say.

"Good morning, Brent," Alicia greeted evenly.

"Morning, Licia," Brent greeted excitedly.

"You sound really excited this morning," Alicia commented, not sure whether it was a good thing or a bad thing.

"You're about to be thanking me," Brent said with a smile on his face as he leaned back in his office chair.

"Really, why is that?" Alicia asked distractedly as she moved papers around on the small hallway table, looking for her keys.

"I've booked you at a charity event this afternoon," Brent said, sounding pleased.

"That's great; you know that I love doing those. Thanks," Alicia said. She was now the one that sounded excited.

Brent happily, if a little smugly, gave her the address

and the time. After giving her the rest of the details, he hung up.

Thirty minutes later, Alicia stepped out onto the stage. As she did so, the frustration of the morning seemed to melt away. This was because she likes supporting a good cause.

"Today, we're going to be telling the story of Emily Caldwell. A woman whose path to the truth is one that has more twists and turns than anyone could have ever imagined." Alicia began looking around at the medium-sized crowd that were clustered around the outdoor stage.

* * *

The quiet of the hospital room and those who were inside it was suddenly shattered. This was done by the sound of a moan from the woman who lay on the bed. At the sound, the doctor rushed forward to the side of the bed.

"Are you alright?" Dr. Blake asked as he pulled a penlight out of his pocket, clicking it on, and shinning it on his hand to make sure it worked.

"I'm not really sure," the woman replied, blinking up at the doctor in utter confusion and then down at her hands.

"Why don't we start with some simple questions," Dr. Blake suggested, then asked several general knowledge questions.

The woman answered all of the questions correctly.

"Now let's take a crack at your name?" Dr. Blake asked while checking her pupal reactions at the same time.

"Of course I can tell you my name. It's," the woman

began, then suddenly stopped mid-sentence with a look of panic on her face.

The instant the woman stopped talking, it was clear that she was panicking. This fact was reinforced by the beeping of the heart monitor accelerating.

"I can't remember my name. Why can't I remember my name?" the woman asked rapidly, her voice getting more panicked with each word.

"What do you remember about yourself?" Dr. Blake asked in a calming voice.

"Nothing," the woman replied. The word was breathed in a voice of total panic, the beeping growing steadily faster.

"First, you need to calm down," Dr. Blake said in his most calming voice.

"Who am I?" the woman asked, turning her gaze to the doctor.

"Your name is Emily Caldwell," Dr. Blake answered in the same voice.

"Who are they?" Emily asked, gesturing to the people that had just entered the room.

"These are members of your family. Do any of them look familiar?" Dr. Blake asked, also gesturing to the group of five people.

"No, I don't remember who any of them are," Emily answered, shaking her head, the look in her eyes was confused and frightened.

The five people shared concerned looks at her statement. However, before any of them had a chance to say anything, the doctor spoke.

"Why don't you rest for a few minutes while we step

out into the hallway for a few minutes," Dr. Blake suggested, putting the penlight back in his pocket.

With that, the group turned and exited the room. As soon as the door closed behind them, all of the family members turned to the doctor.

"What's happening to her?" Mr. Caldwell asked, sounding concerned.

"It's looking like retrograde amnesia. I'll have to do some more tests, and I'd like to keep her for at least another day or two," Dr. Blake said, looking at Emily's chart.

"What can we do to help her?" Mrs. Caldwell asked, sounding upset.

"The best thing to do would be when she does go home to surround her with as many familiar things as possible. That and time is the only thing that we can do," Dr. Blake replied, looking up from the chart.

The family thanked the doctor before they went their separate ways. Dr. Blake had to get back to his rounds. While the family returned to Emily's room.

A couple of days later, a nurse entered Emily's room. She had an encouraging look on her face as she greeted the patient.

"Good morning, Miss Caldwell," the nurse greeted, pushing a wheelchair.

"Morning, Conney," Emily replied, the tone in her voice a little bittersweet.

"Aren't you excited that you're going home today?" the nurse asked, sounding chipper. The only response that she got was a small, unenthusiastic nod.

At exactly that moment, there was a knock on the door.

The doctor entered the hospital room. He gave her one last check, then signed the discharge papers.

The instant the papers were signed, her family entered. When they did, they immediately whisked her out of the room and down to the car. It had been decided that she'd be staying with her parents for a couple of days before returning to her own home.

Emily's mind spun as the car drove. The whole situation was totally insane. It sounded more like something out of movie than something that actually happened to someone. Yet here she was, having to somehow deal with this situation.

Not terribly long later, the fancy car pulled up to an equally fancy house. The house looked a bit like a cabin, only fancier. It was a large colonial-style house with an overhang under which the fancy car parked.

The driver got out and opened the door for them. At exactly that moment, the sky opened up, and it started to rain. The couple headed into the house not really bothered by the change in the weather. Emily sighed at the sound of the raindrops beating all around her as she too walked into the house.

"Welcome home, sweetheart," Mrs. Caldwell said, gesturing expansively around the cavernous room.

"Thank you," Emily said, slightly overwhelmed by her surroundings.

"Let's take this into the day room. There you can ask us any questions that you have," Mrs. Caldwell said, grabbing hold of Emily's arm and practically dragging her in that direction.

"Alice, dear, you might want to let her catch her breath first," Mr. Caldwell cautioned, following the two of them.

"Oh, of course, you're right, Daniel. She can do that in the day room too," Mrs. Caldwell replied, mostly ignoring her husband's advice.

It didn't take very long for the group to reach their destination. Once there the elder Caldwell released her daughter, who immediately sat down on one of the chairs in the sitting room. The other two Caldwells sat down on the loveseat.

"Is there anything that you'd like to know?" Mrs. Caldwell asked, looking expectantly at her daughter.

"Now, honey, remember what the doctor said. We need to let her remember as much as possible on her own," Mr. Caldwell cautioned calmly.

"I know, dear, but that doesn't mean that we can't tell her a few things," Mrs. Caldwell replied, her voice slightly peeved.

"That's okay OK, Dad; I really only have one question anyway," Emily said, sounding a little uncertain, not really sure how she was supposed to be referring to them.

"Go ahead," Mrs. Caldwell encouraged with an equally encouraging smile, though there was something a little sad in the expression.

"How did I get hurt?" Emily asked, watching both of them very closely.

"There was an accident, and you hit your head," Mrs. Caldwell answered, flattening out the wrinkles in her skirt.

"What kind of accident?" Emily asked, noticing that her answer was just a hint vague but not sure what it meant.

"You fell down," Mr. Caldwell answered, being even more vague with a barely noticeable hint of discomfort.

"Is there anything else that you can tell me about it?" Emily asked, hoping to get any information that could help her remember.

"I'm sorry; we don't know all of what happened. All we really know is that we got a call saying that you'd fallen on the sidewalk outside the office and that you were taken to the hospital," Mrs. Caldwell explained, sadness in her voice.

"Could I take a walk in the gardens before lunch?" Emily asked, trying not to sound to disappointed.

"Certainly. Remember, lunch is at noon," Mrs. Caldwell answered, sounding relieved by the change in topic.

With that Emily stood up and left the day room. Not really sure which way was correct, she just picked one at random. Unfortunately that one turned out to be the wrong one. Thankfully, that wrong path led her to a maid who was more than happy to set her on the right path.

As the rather bewildered woman walked down the hallway, she took a look around at her surroundings as she touched her blond hair. She couldn't help notice how cold, empty, and lifeless the huge house felt. The sound of her every step echoed off the walls of the hallway.

It was almost a relief when Emily stepped out of the door into the gardens. The warm sunshine dispelling the cold feeling of the interior of the house. It was actually quite a beautiful day now that it had stopped raining.

Unfortunately, the troubled woman barely noticed either of these facts. This was because her mind was racing as she tried to force herself to remember something, anything. Every time that she did, she came up with the same thing, nothing. It was incredibly frustrating and only resulted in giving her a small headache.

Twenty minutes later, Emily was sitting on a bench disinterestedly, half watching a gardener mowing the grass. A maid walked up to her and got her attention.

"Sorry to interrupt you, Miss Emily, but it's time for lunch, and Mrs. Caldwell asked me to come get you," the young maid said, slightly timidly.

"Sorry, I guess that I lost track of time," Emily replied, standing up.

"It's quite understandable," the young maid replied easily.

"I'm sorry to ask you this, but do I know you?" Emily asked, looking quite uncomfortable asking such a question.

"That's fine, but no, we don't know each other. I started working here after you left. We met for the first time only a few days before your accident," the young maid answered understandingly; the whole staff had been told about her situation.

"Could you tell me anything about my accident that my parents don't know?" Emily asked, watching the maid's reaction closely.

"I'm afraid not. None of us know any more about it than your parents. We really should be going," the maid replied, slightly apologetic.

As the two of them were walking back toward the house someone inside called for the maid. She immediately hurried ahead to enter the house through the kitchen door.

A few minutes later, Emily had just reached the back

door of the house when suddenly there was the sound of a plane flying overhead. She immediately looked up and followed the plane's flight path. Just as it disappeared from sight and before she had a chance to turn her gaze from the sky, she saw a statue falling toward her. Reacting quickly, she dove out of the way. The sound of her alarmed scream intermingled with the resounding crash of the statue hitting the ground. When she jumped out of the way, she landed in a sitting position a foot away. For the next few seconds, she sat there, her eyes fixed on the same spot where the statue fell. Due to this she thought she might have seen a slight wisp of movement on the balcony.

The sound brought the whole household running. When they got there, she was still sitting on the ground and was breathing hard from the fading adrenaline rush.

"Are you alright?" Mrs. Caldwell asked, her voice dripping with concern.

"I think I will be. I'll just need a minute," Emily said, wrapping her arms around herself as she shivered.

"What happened?" Mr. Caldwell asked with the same amount of concern as he handed her a blanket.

"A statue fell off that balcony and almost hit me," Emily answered, pointing up at the balcony, her hand shaking only slightly.

Immediately someone rushed up there to investigate. The man emerged onto the balcony quite quickly and began looking around.

At the same time many of the group on the ground began examining the broken pieces of the statue. They paid special attention to the base of the statue.

"Daniel, isn't that the statue that was loose and almost fell last week?" Mrs. Caldwell asked, looking at her husband.

"You know I think that it might be, but I'm not really sure," Mr. Caldwell said, looking between the remains of the statue and his wife.

"Let's get you inside. A cup of tea is just what you need to settle your frazzled nerves," Mrs. Caldwell said, helping her daughter up and leading her inside.

While that was happening Mr. Caldwell and a few other members of the staff continued their attempts to figure out what had happened, which did include calling the police.

The rest of the day was uneventful. Emily spent that whole time listening to conversation, hoping they'd trigger something. During one of those conversations, they told her about the police deciding that the statue falling was an accident. Their arguments were so convincing she began to wonder about what she had seen.

She also looked at the pictures spread throughout the house. Unfortunately though, none of it worked; she still didn't remember anything.

Bright and early the next morning, the driver took Emily to her house. She thanked him, then walked up to the front door and unlocked it. Stepping into the medium-sized craftsman house, she'd been hoping that her memories would come rushing back. Which sadly didn't happen. Instead the rooms in there were completely foreign to her.

Instead the woman began looking around for any clues. She began looking through everything from the books on the shelves to the papers on the table. It was a strange feeling looking through these things. It felt as if she was invading someone's privacy. The fact she knew mentally that these things belonged to her did nothing to dispel the strange feeling.

By midday, Emily still hadn't found anything and was starting to feel a little hungry. On the way over there, she had noticed a small diner not very far away. She decided that was her best option, so she grabbed her purse and left, locking the door on the way out.

Sitting down at one of the outdoor tables, the blond looked around. It was strange; the world seemed to be flowing around her. They all seemed to have such a definite purpose as they went about their day. Yet, here she sat feeling like a rock at the bottom of a stream. Picking up the menu, she halfheartedly looked through it and picked something at random.

The waitress came, got Emily's order, and returned a few minutes later. Once she was done eating, she paid and left the cafe. As she began to walk back home, she thought about what she'd learned about herself.

Two days had gone by, and Emily again walked to the cafe, which didn't take very long. Feeling a little unsure, the woman watched her surroundings as she sat down. Just as she got settled, a waitress walked up to the table. Her nametag said Mandy.

"Afternoon, Em, the usual," Mandy greeted with a smile as she held the small notebook in her hand.

"Um, I guess so," Emily replied, just a touch of uncertainty in her voice.

"Are you alright, Em," Mandy asked, looking closer at the woman that was one of her regular customers.

"Mostly," Emily replied, trying to sound confident and only mostly succeeding.

The waitress nodded, looking a little unsure as she walked away. She knew something was up but decided not to push it at the moment. As a result, she was distracted as she grabbed the plate with the sandwich and headed back to the table. Because of that she barely noticed a man brush past her and slip something into his pocket as he walked away. She reached Emily's table and placed the plate down without a thought of the nondescript man.

"A ham and cheese with lettuce on brown with a cup of tea," Mandy said, placing the cup in front of the plate, sounding chipper.

"Do I smell a hint of peanuts?" Emily asked as she picked up the first half of the sandwich and was about to take a bite.

"Wait, stop, you're allergic to peanuts," Mandy said, placing her hand gently on her wrist to stop her before she actually took a bite.

"Oh right," Emily said, putting the sandwich down, clearly picking up on the fact that she and this waitress were friends.

"I'll go get you another sandwich, then you can tell me what's going on," Mandy said, picking up the plate and walking away.

The waitress returned a few minutes later with a new sandwich. After putting the plate down, she sat in the chair opposite. She then listened as Emily told her about losing her memory and everything that had happened since getting out of the hospital. When she was done with her story, Mandy was sympathetic. After talking for another minute, she stood up and left to attend to her other tables.

Once Emily was done eating, she stood up and walked up to the register. As she was doing that, she heard the cook and Mandy talking. She told him about the peanut oil on the sandwich. He assured her that he was careful, and he didn't know how it could have happened. Before either noticed that Emily was listening she turned and left, heading home.

Arriving back at home, Emily was practically on autopilot. There was something nagging her at the back of her mind. It felt like every time whatever it was got close to the surface it disappeared again. This went on for about twenty minutes before she decided to drop it.

At that moment the phone rang. She walked over to it and picked up the receiver. It was her boss at work. Apparently she would need to go back to work in a couple of days. That was only if she was cleared by her doctor. She couldn't help but feel something was off as she listened to her boss. There was a strange kind of tension in his voice.

After another couple of hours of exploring her house, Emily found herself in the kitchen. This room felt different somehow. The instant that she entered she walked over to the counter and, without really thinking about it, she turned on the CD player.

"Where did that come from?" Emily asked herself rhetorically.

As the soothing tones of the classical music began floating through the air, the woman began moving around the kitchen. The smells of the spices and ingredients were all so familiar that it ached with a strange combination of knowing and not knowing. The way she prepared everything and cooked the food startled her. It was as if her body knew how to cook, even though at the moment her mind didn't. Before she knew it, she'd prepared an entire meal. It was a strange feeling doing something that she didn't know she knew how to do.

"If I didn't know better, I'd have thought that I was a chef or something," Emily thought out loud.

During her explorations, she had figured out that she worked an oh-so-exciting office job, more specifically a desk job in the records department in the company her family owned. It had definitely not been what she'd been hoping for.

"I almost wish that it had turned out that I was a chef," Emily said as she placed the last dish on the table.

A couple of days later Emily had been cleared to go back to work. Arriving at the bustling office, she was greeted by her secretary.

"Good morning, Miss Caldwell. I've been told about your situation. My name is Melissa. Your office is right this way," Melissa said, leading the way.

The room the two of them entered was smallish. Looking around, Emily couldn't see anything personal. Overall the room was warm but professional. As she sat down at the desk in the centre of the room, sadly there didn't seem to be any pictures. There was, however, one personal item, a rather beautiful cross.

"If you need any help, just call," Melissa said, standing in front of the desk.

"Could you get me a cup of coffee? I think I'm going to need it," Emily requested, lightly rubbing her temples.

"No problem," Melissa replied, her voice chipper, then she turned and walked out the door.

As the door closed, Emily turned her attention to the papers on her desk. For a few minutes she stared at the papers in confusion.

This isn't getting me anywhere, Emily thought, frustrated.

Thankfully Melissa chose that exact moment to return. She placed the cup on her boss's desk with a knowing expression on her face.

"I figured this might happen," Melissa said, pulling a piece of paper out of her pocket and handing it to her.

"What's this?" Emily asked, unfolding the paper.

"Just something that I thought might help," Melissa replied, correctly guessing the cause of her boss's frustration.

The blond took a moment to read what was on the paper. On the paper was an explanation of what she was supposed to do.

"I don't know what I'd do without you," Emily said, getting a flash of a memory the second that she said it.

"Let's hope for both of our sakes that never happens," Melissa replied, with a slightly knowing smirk on her face.

"We've had this conversation before," Emily said, turning her gaze from the paper in her hand to her secretary.

"Yeah, once or twice a week. Including on the day of the accident," Melissa replied, a little surprised at the statement.

"Can you tell me what happened that day?" Emily

asked, hoping she would be able to get some more information.

"No. I'm sorry. I'd already gone home by then. I wish I could have been more help, but at least you're starting to get your memory back," Melissa said encouragingly.

At exactly that moment a man entered the room. When the door opened, both of the women looked up. The man that entered was Paul Collins.

"I heard about what happened and figured I'd come check up on you. It sounds like you've made some kind of breakthrough," Paul said as he walked toward the desk.

"Miss Caldwell might be starting to get her memory back," Melissa reported, sounding pleased.

"That's good to hear. Well I've got to be getting back to work myself," Paul said evenly. His gaze moving from one of them to the other.

Emily had been watching his reactions from the moment he entered the office. Even though his posture was calm and relaxed, she couldn't shake the feeling that something was off. She thought she saw some strange expression on his face when he found out about her getting her memory back.

It's just my imagination, Emily thought, shaking her head. She snapped out of her musing as he asked Melissa for a file, and then she left.

"Thanks for your help. I'll call if I need anything," Emily said with a grateful smile.

Melissa nodded, then turned and left, heading back to her own desk. She hoped that her boss and friend did get her memory back.

Emily read through the list again, just to be sure she had it. Before turning her attention to the stacks of files on her desk. The piles each seemed like they were the size of Mount Everest.

After a few hours of work, it seemed as if every time that the blond took one file off the stack, another would appear to take its place. Even though she knew that this was impossible, it didn't stop it from feeling like it.

Deciding to take a break from the seemingly endless stream of paper, the blond stood up. After stretching, she went off in search of a cup of coffee.

As Emily emerged from the outer office area, she looked around the bullpen for a coffee machine. She spotted one at the other end of the room and headed in that direction. On her way there, many of the people working in the room waved or nodded when she passed. They seemed to really be happy she was back. When she reached the machine, she poured herself a cup, then tried to figure out what to put in it. Thankfully someone came and saved her from the terrifying fate of a bad cup of coffee by telling her how she liked it. Before the young woman left, she reminded Emily about the meeting that was happening in about an hour.

An hour later, Emily entered one of the larger meeting rooms. She sat down and, like everyone else, turned her attention to the person at the head of the table. It wasn't lost on her that when she entered most everyone in the room glanced in her direction for a few seconds before returning it to the front of the room. One thing briefly catching her attention was that two of the executives' gazes lingered on her for a few instants longer than the others.

Throughout the meeting, the blond couldn't help but notice that there was some kind of tension coming from a couple of the people at the table. She wasn't entirely sure that it was a coincidence it was the same two men that had paid her additional attention before. Deciding and hoping it didn't mean anything, she went back to listening to the end of the meeting. When it broke up, everyone filed out of the room.

Emily headed back to her office as quickly as she could without seeming to be hurrying. When she entered the outer office area, Melissa immediately asked her how the meeting went. She replied it was fine on her way past the desk. For the rest of the afternoon, she attempted to escape the very distressing thoughts that were starting to form in the back of her mind. To that end, she proceeded to bury herself in the endless stack of papers and left work as quickly as she could.

It was still light when the mid-level executive left the office building. She walked over to the crosswalk and pressed the button. As she waited for the light to change, she began rooting around in her purse for her house keys that didn't seem to be there. At the same instant she looked up the light came on. Just as she stepped off the curb and onto the crosswalk she remembered hearing something that sounded like keys falling to the ground as stepped onto the sidewalk. She turned around and took a step back toward the curb to go see if it had been her keys that fell. A heartbeat later, an erratically driving car whizzed past her, driving over the exact spot she'd been standing a mere fraction of a second before. She shakily stumbled back onto the sidewalk. When she did, her hand hit something cold and metal. Looking down, she saw that it was her keys that had indeed fallen out of her purse. She stared numbly at them for a few seconds as a small cluster of people formed around her.

"Watch where you're going, Bonehead," one man shouted at the retreating car.

"Are you alright, dear?" A kind older woman asked, placing a comforting hand on her shoulder.

"I think so, but I don't think I'll be walking home after all. I'll see if I can get a ride instead," Emily replied, shakily pulling out her cell phone.

One of the men in the small cluster of people helped her up and over to a nearby bench. Once there, she called her dad and told him what happened. He said he would send a car to pick her up and drop her off at her place. Now satisfied that she was fine and had a ride home, the cluster of people returned to what they had been doing.

Nearly ten minutes later, the car pulled up, and Emily got in. The car ride to her house was deathly silent and as tense as a bowstring. As soon as the car pulled to a stop in front of her house, she jumped out of it as if it was on fire.

The blond immediately rushed up the walkway and up the front steps. As quickly as her shaking hands could, she unlocked the front door and scrambled inside. The instant she was through the door, she turned and locked it behind her. She then retreated to her smallish home office, locking that door behind her too.

All the time Emily's mind raced as the thoughts she'd been avoiding all afternoon came rushing to the forefront of her mind. Just as she'd accepted that the statue had been an accident, the incident at the diner happened. It had been a bit harder, but she'd managed to chalk that up to a coincidence too. How was she supposed to do that again? The quote "Once is happenstance, twice is coincidence, three times is enemy action" popped into her head.

Great, now I'm basing my reaction to a crisis on a quote from *James Bond*. How did I even know that was a James Bond quote? I couldn't tell you my favourite colour but I can remember a quote from a book, Emily thought to herself as her panic level continued to steadily rise.

Looking around at the room that should have been comfortingly familiar, but it only served to heighten the amnesiac woman's fear. In that moment, it truly hit her that there was someone out there that wanted to hurt or more likely kill her. Worst of all, she had no idea who it was or why any of this was happening to her.

The blond began to pace the small room as she tried to force herself to remember. After a couple of minutes of doing that, which only resulted in her getting a headache, she sat down against the wall directly opposite the desk. In that moment, she felt completely, crushingly alone. Not knowing even herself let alone anyone else. She shuddered as she stared blankly straight ahead. When she did, she saw a cross sitting on the desk. As if moving on instinct, she clasped her hands, lowered her head, and began to pray, tears filling her closed eyes.

As Emily finished and looked up, her eyes landed on a picture on the wall behind the desk. It was a painting called "Jesus praying in the garden of Gethsemane." As beautiful as the painting was, she had the feeling that she needed to look behind it. Standing up she did just that. When she did, she found a wall safe requiring both a key and a combination. Hesitantly she reached out and touched it. The instant that her hand came in contact with the cold metal, she had a flash of memory. In the memory she saw herself locking the safe, then taking the key and hanging it on one of the hooks by the front door. She immediately went and got the key. As she walked over to the safe, she looked more closely at the key and realized that there were numbers on it. Inserting it in the keyhole, an idea popped into her head. Taking a chance, she tried the numbers, and there was a satisfying click as the safe unlocked. Inside she found a stack of papers.

Curious, the blond took out the papers and began to go through them. It quickly became clear what this whole mess was about. She also remembered some of the details of the accident where she lost her memory. Making a not-entirely-successful attempt to steady her hand, she picked up the phone and called the police. She asked to speak to a detective in the fraud division. Once she was put through to a Detective Rollins, she told the whole situation to him and about the papers. He sent a squad car to pick her up and bring her to the station.

It turned out that Emily had found evidence of embezzlement. A man had chased her, trying to steal the copy of the papers that she'd been planning to show to her boss, which caused her to slip and fall, hitting her head.

With the information in the papers, they were able to trace the embezzlement to two men: Paul Collins and his boss, Jason Turner. Both of whom were arrested for the embezzlement as well as three counts of attempted murder.

Slowly but surely, Emily got her memories back. It took about a month of getting bits and pieces of her life back before she was pretty sure that she had assembled the whole picture.

* * *

As Alicia stepped off the stage into the backstage area, she took a deep breath. At that moment her phone rang. Looking at the call display, she saw it was her sister and answered it. They both apologized for the argument that morning. Her sister laughingly said she wished they could hug it out. They both said goodbye after making plans for Alicia to come over to their place for supper that weekend.

THE END

CHAPTER 8

A Man and A Mountain

Just like they had planned, Alicia went over to her sister's house on Saturday. After dinner, they were in the living room visiting and relaxing. Carla had just returned from the kitchen with drinks for everyone.

"How about we end the evening with a story from my talented sister-in-law," Mark suggested as Carla settled down on the loveseat next to him.

"That's a wonderful idea," Carla agreed, settling more comfortably and turning excited eyes to her sister.

"One of these days, someone should pull that on you, Mark," Alicia said, with a teasing tone in her voice.

"I'm a dentist. I don't think that would really work," Mark replied, with a teasing smirk on his face.

Mark got an immediate response to that statement coming in the form of Alicia throwing a pillow at him. This caused both women to giggle, which brought a smile to his face.

"So Licia are you going to," Carla asked hopefully.

"Alright, let's see; I got it. How about a tale of adventure and adversity. About one man who's forced to test his will against a mountain," Alicia said, looking between the two of them.

* * *

On a bright, crisp morning, the air was clean and clear. A gentle breeze blew across a small country airport. A small charter plane sat waiting on the runway, waiting till it could once again touch the skies. Two men walked out of the hangar's small office. One was the pilot, whose name was Jack Spencer, and the other one was the manager of the airfield.

"Looks like a beautiful day for a flight," Jack said, looking up at the sky and across at the distant mountains.

"I'm not sure. There are reports of a possible storm front coming in in a few hours," the manager said, looking at the clipboard in his hand.

The two men walked over to the waiting plane. They got there just as the last of the cargo was being loaded up.

"Is everything good to go?" Jack asked, his gaze going from the man next to him to the plane in front of them.

"Yeah, you're good to go," the manager said, looking up from the clipboard.

With that the pilot climbed into the plane. He double checked the cargo to make sure that everything was secure. Once he was done, he entered the cockpit and started the preflight checks. As soon as he finished, he began taxiing the plane down the runway. Before the plane went very far, he waved to the manager of the airfield. The plane took off smoothly into the sky.

The first few hours of the flight were smooth, with only a few minor pockets of turbulence. Suddenly clouds began to roll in, and the plane shuddered violently as it hit a pretty nasty patch of turbulence. The wind began to pick up and whip in all directions.

This made it hard for Jack to keep the plane on course. As he fought with the controls, the wind picked up even more. By the time he managed to get the plane back under control, he realized that he'd been blown way off course. Looking around, he tried to figure out what his direction and heading were. Before he could he hit another patch of turbulence. The plane rocked as the sky turned a dark, ominous grey as storm clouds closed in and covered the sky like a shroud. He tried to climb out of the weather, but every time he tried, the wind would knock him back down.

A couple of minutes later, Jack's already lousy afternoon got even worse. This happened when a combination of snow and ice began to fall. With the swirling snow, his visibility was pretty much obliterated in seconds. The ice hitting the plane feeling like it was the size of a baseball, even though they were in reality much smaller.

All around the cockpit lights were flashing and alarms were blaring. The pilot tried to keep the plane level as one of his engines began to fail. He reached for the mic as the failing engine gave up.

"Mayday, mayday, I've lost one engine and am dealing with extreme weather," Jack shouted over the blaring alarms.

All the pilot got in response was static. The disheartening sound cut through the blaring alarms. He hung up the mic as the plane shuddered again.

Suddenly out of the swirling snow a mountain seemed to appear out of nowhere. Jack tried to turn the plane, but it was like trying to fly though molasses. Looking down at the control panel, one specific alarm caught his attention. That alarm warned of a steering system malfunction.

That's just what I need, Jack thought as the mountain got closer and closer. He flipped the switch for the emergency locator beacon.

By the time Jack got his hands back on the controls, the mountain was to close to avoid. Instead, he tried his level best to soften the inevitable crash as much as he could. An effort that was mostly effective as the plane hit the snow.

After skidding a significant distance, the plane came to a screeching, grinding halt. But not before it plowed a significant trench behind it. There was also a trail of twisted and mangled metal.

Jack groaned as he came to, still strapped in his pilot seat. His head pounded like a bass drum pounding out a steady rhythm of sharp, piercing pain. When he opened his eyes, he found that he was slumped against the control panel. He moved his sore arms to brace under him and tried to push himself into an upright, seated position. Which turned out to be a mistake as the instant that he did a searing pain shot though him. It felt like every inch of his body was hurting.

The pilot reached for the mic even though he knew that there was next to no chance it was still working. Despite this, he still had to try. No matter how slim the chance, it was still a chance. He took a deep breath as he pressed the button on the mic.

"Mayday, mayday," Jack said, his voice slightly breathless from the pain of moving.

The instant that Jack released the button he'd been expecting to hear static. Instead, the radio started to shoot sparks all around the cockpit. In a frantic attempt to keep the plane from catching on fire, he grabbed handfuls of snow and threw it on the still sparking radio with one hand. While he released the latch on his belt with the other. Once free of the belt, he grabbed the radio, pulled it off the panel, and tossed it out of the cockpit into the snowbank. The copilot seat was still smoking in a couple of places, and he threw snow on them till they stopped smoking.

Finally fairly confident that the plane wasn't going to burst into flames in the next few minutes, the pilot looked around. He was a little surprised when he found that his backpack was still there. Picking it up, he stumbled out of the cockpit. He began looking around in the cargo hold. Looking at the writing on each box to see what was inside. Barely able to believe his luck, he had to do a double take as he read what was in a couple of the boxes. In one of the boxes was apparently survival rations. Another one, according to the writing, had warm winter clothing.

Grabbing a crowbar off a nearby crate, Jack walked back over to the crates that he was interested in. The lid of the first crate was quickly pried off and tossed away. He placed his backpack down next to the crate and opened it. Standing up, he began looking through what was inside the crate. He quickly put as many of the ration packs in his backpack as he could carry, as well as a few reusable water bottles.

Moving quickly, or as quickly as he could, Spencer opened the other crate. Sure enough, there were indeed winter clothes inside, more specifically, snow-pants, jackets, and boots. He quickly found some that were in his size. Moving carefully, he put them on.

Digging deeper in the crate, Jack found a couple of

boxes of matches, which he quickly stuffed in his backpack. He checked over what was in his pack to make sure that everything was as ready as it could be. Once he was done, he zipped it back up and put it on. When he did, he let out a grunt of pain at the added weight on his back.

Pulling the hood of his jacket up, the pilot walked over to the door. He took a deep breath and reached over to the handle and pulled as hard as he could. Unfortunately, it only moved a little bit, so he just pushed it harder. It still didn't move as much as it should have.

Looking closer, Jack noticed that the door and the frame was bent. Changing strategy, he began using his shoulder to force the door open. It took three hits before the door finally gave way to the force of the last hit, causing it to fly open.

The instant that the door opened, a bitter cold wind blew in. Immediately causing Spencer to pull his jacket closer around himself. Shivering slightly, he jumped out of the door. His boots crunched on the snow as his feet hit the ground.

"Now where do I go?" Jack asked rhetorically as he looked around at the frigid, tree-covered landscape.

After a few minutes of thought, the pilot decided to head down the mountain. The bottom won't get any closer from standing here, Jack thought as he began walking. The wind whistled and the snow swirled in his wake.

Soon the plane faded from sight, and the sun began to sink toward the horizon. Jack knew that he needed to make camp as soon as possible. He looked around for a good spot. Finding one a couple of yards away, he made his way over.

That spot was an open space in the centre of a ring of trees, which would quite nicely break the wind. He made his way over to the clearing. Quickly he set up camp, including a small fire in the centre of the clearing, then made a small shelter out of tree branches.

Once Spencer was done, he quickly checked himself over for injuries. He found only a few superficial injuries but nothing serious. All of which he quickly took care of. There was also a soreness that seemed to permeate his entire body. As soon as he was done, he curled up and tried to get as much sleep as he could, considering the situation.

A couple of days later, Jack was travelling at a steady pace. He had once again stopped for the night and had just finished his evening meal. Sitting by the campfire, watching the flames dance, he tried to think about something else other than the night noises that surrounded him. When that stopped working, he decided to look through the things in his pack. Looking through the pockets on the sides, he found something he hadn't been expecting. This unexpected find was a Bible from 1902. Suddenly he remembered why he had it. The Bible had belonged to his girlfriend's family and had been somehow lost. He'd spent months looking for it so he could give it to her for her birthday in an attempt to patch things up with her. Things hadn't been going so well with her because they'd ironically been fighting about how important this religious stuff was to her. As he looked at the Bible he couldn't help wonder if he'd ever get the chance to give it to her.

Jack ran his hand over the two words on the cover of the leather-bound book. All this God stuff had never really made any sense to him. He couldn't figure out what a book that was written two-thousand years ago had to do with his life now. After all, life was so incredibly different from how it was back then. As for whether there was someone up there, he didn't really know nor did he really care. His opinion was that if there was, he didn't think that person could possibly be affecting their lives down here.

Due to this, the pilot had never even read a word of the Bible. For lack of anything better to do, he decided to read it for a bit. He opened the book to a random page in about the middle, which turned out to be Ezra 10, and he began reading.

About fifteen minutes later, Jack evidently found something that he really didn't like because he not so gently closed the book. He angrily stuffed the Bible back in his pocket. Once he zipped the pocket closed, he glared at it for a few seconds before he laid down with his back to his backpack and went to sleep.

The next morning, the stranded pilot got up with the sun and was a bit stiff. This was because the temperature dropped a bit over night. Again he started a fire with the manuals and other books that he salvaged from the plane. This morning, it was the FAA regulations' turn. Once the fire was started, he got another of the ration packs out.

A few minutes later, the ration pack was warmed and ready to eat. Just as he took the ration pack off the fire, Jack heard a sound coming from the bushes.

The sound came again, and Jack surged to his feet, reaching for a tree branch as he did. Unfortunately, his hand met nothing but air. Looking around, he spotted the branch on the other side of the campsite. His empty hands clenched in frustration at not having anything to defend himself with when he needed it.

Before the man could make a move toward it, the sound, which was a growl, sounded again and it was getting closer. Those growls sounded like they were canine. Maybe a coyote or it could even be a lone wolf. Either way, it was almost sure to be something dangerous. A still closer growl sounded, and he got ready to defend himself. He'd no sooner gotten ready when a single wolf jumped out of the bushes. Its teeth bared, and it snarled at him. The wolf began to stalk forward toward him. It looked to be a young male, probably only a year old. Its eyes locked on him as it again snarled. A heartbeat later, the wolf launched itself at him.

Having seen this coming, Jack managed to avoid the attack by jumping to the side. Due to this the wolf landed face first in a snowbank. As he began slowly moving toward the tree branch, the animal pulled itself out of the snowbank. Once out of the snow, it turned to him and snarled. He noticed that the animal looked even angrier then it did before. It was even snapping its teeth at him as its eyes glared at the man. As he kept moving to the side, the wolf extended its front paw and swiped at him, just barely missing while at the same time snapping its jaws at him. Just as the wolf lunged for him again, he dove for the branch, grabbing it just before he hit the ground.

Pushing himself back to his feet, Spencer turned and faced the charging predator. Despite this, it kept getting closer, clearly not the slightest bit worried. The instant it was close enough, he swung the branch like a baseball bat as hard as he could. He hit the wolf in the side, hard, just as it jumped up, its bared teeth aiming at his neck. The wolf hit the ground with a yelp.

After about a minute, the wolf got up favouring it's side significantly. It snarled one more time before disappearing off into the bushes, clearly deciding to go find an easier meal somewhere else.

Once sure that it was gone, Jack breathed a deep sigh of relief as he collapsed against the log that he'd been sitting on, which was next to his almost-dead fire. As soon as his heartbeat returned to normal, he picked up his forgotten breakfast. While he ate, he reached over and pulled a different leather-bound book out of the pocket on the other side. This book was his journal. He'd started writing in it the day after the crash. He figured if he did die on this stupid mountain, on the off chance that anyone ever found him, he might as well leave something behind.

This morning was a little more exciting than it has been for the last couple of days. First, I played a little tag with a wolf. We both decided that we didn't like that game, so we figured that we'd try some batting practice instead. That was a bit more of a smash, but he decided to go find breakfast some-where else after the first swing. I do hope that is the extent of the excitement for today

On another topic, I still don't understand why Ruth lets her life be dictated by some old book. I guess the only way I'll understand is if I read some more.

As he closed the journal and put his pen back in the loop, his thoughts strayed to what he'd read the night before. He still didn't like it. Thinking about this caused him to remember something that Ruth had said. "Since God made the game, he gets to set the rules."

While the pilot packed up his campsite, he decided that when he stopped for the night, he'd try reading the first chapter of the book. He wanted to know whether it really claimed that God created the world. For now he started off on another exciting day of walking.

The snow-covered trees around Jack glistened in the sunlight, like they were covered in diamonds. The air was still, and the only sound in the air was the clomping of his own footsteps. Idly, he wondered how something as soft-looking as the snow could make it feel like his feet were made of lead. He was sure glad that the legs of his snow pants were over his boots, or he'd have about six pounds of snow in them by now. He couldn't help noticing that you sometimes think about the strangest things when you do something as monotonous as walking, especially when you were doing it for an extended period of time. He was so focused on those thoughts that he failed to notice something important.

The stranded pilot had emerged from the tree line and walked into what he thought was another clearing. That, however, was not the case. A fact that was made abundantly clear shortly after he stepped foot in the open space. This open space was in fact a rather large lake. A fact which was revealed by the rather ominous cracking sound at his feet. A sound that only decided to start after he'd gone nearly three feet onto the ice. The sound sent a searing spike of terror through him. If there was one thing that he knew about wilderness survival in the snow, that was "wetness was your enemy." If you and or your clothes got wet, that was when the danger of hypothermia was at its greatest.

Since back the way Jack came was closer than the other side, he took a step back. The instant that he did even worse and numerous cracking noises erupted. Quickly deciding that wasn't a good idea, he carefully picked up his foot. Instead, he tried to take a step forward. When he did, there was only a slight cracking even after he put his full weight on it. With his other foot, he began looking for another slightly stronger piece of ice. He heard that same cracking sound in the first few places that he put his foot, before he found what he was looking for. He continued this careful pace across the six or so feet. Once he reached the other side and got his pounding heart to slow down a bit, he realized two things simultaneously. One, that was probably not the correct or safest way to cross a cracking frozen lake. The other was he was incredibly lucky he'd made it across without falling in.

After catching his breath for a few minutes Spence stood up and headed into the trees once again. He wanted to get out of the wind. Once safely under the relative shelter of the trees, he pulled out his compass and the aviation chart from the plane. While not nearly as helpful as either a topographical map or even a regular map, it was better than nothing. He needed to know whether he was still going in the right direction.

It took about twenty minutes for the pilot to figure it out. When he did, he found that he was in fact going in the right direction. A fact that was a great relief as he put both compass and chart back in his pack. He decided he needed a drink of water. Pulling out his water bottle and taking a drink, emptying it. Realizing that he should fill it before he left and grabbed a rock and walked back over to the side of the lake. Just as he was about to hit the ice, he recognized the irony of now seeking to cause the very thing that he'd only a few minutes ago been doing everything he could to avoid. It only took a couple of hits from the rock to create an opening. Being careful to get as little water on his gloves as he could, he filled up his water bottles. Once they were full and safely back in his pack, he set out again.

That evening, a couple of hours before sunset, the crash survivor again made camp. This time he used a particularly bushy fir tree as his shelter instead of making one. That night dinner was a rabbit he'd managed to catch, which was a nice change from the ration packs. Just like he'd planned after dinner, he again picked up the Bible. He read for about twenty minutes before closing it again. It was quite clear the book actually did say what Ruth had told him it did. *Just because he made the rules doesn't mean that I have to follow them, Jack thought with a defiant scowl on his face. He was still thinking about it when he went to bed.*

The next morning, Jack took off again. Each breath he took formed a misty cloud. Those puffs of mist were quickly swept away by the wind. A wind which was quickly picking up to the point that the trees were waving.

Several hours and quite a few miles later, snow began to fall. It swirled around in the gusting chaotic winds. That blowing snowfall quickly escalated to blizzard-like conditions. This made it really hard to keep moving forward.

As conditions continued to get worse, Jack decided to

find somewhere to hunker down till this storm passed. An effort that was made much more difficult by the fact that visibility was continuing to worsen to the point he nearly couldn't see his hand in front of his face. Which also caused him to completely lose track of what direction he was supposed to be going. In order to keep his hood up, he had to hold it with both hands.

"I've got to get out of this really quickly," Jack said, his words were quickly stolen away by the whipping wind.

The pilot began wandering, totally disoriented, in a seemingly endless blanket of white. It felt as if there was nothing but white no matter which direction he looked. The gusting wind blocked out any and all other sound. From every direction the snow seemed to bombard him, covering his face despite the hood. The ever-deepening snow on the ground was also making moving forward quite difficult. In fact, it got so bad that he even ran into a couple of trees because he couldn't see them till it was to late.

Suddenly out of that endless whiteness, a solid wall of rock seemed to rise up out of nowhere. Jack shivered as he examined the imposing wall of rock. He looked both directions for any sign of a nook or cranny that he could possibly hide himself in. His heart sank as he couldn't see anything in his admittedly limited field of vision. Stumbling forward, he tried to walk along the wall to see if there was one that he just wasn't seeing.

After about ten to fifteen minutes of walking, it felt like he'd never find anything. He stumbled over a rock and fell against a tree. As he pulled himself back up to his feet, he looked up. When he did he spotted something that did a better job at freezing him in his spot than the weather. There before his eyes was the mouth of a cave. If he hadn't fallen, he'd have walked right past it. This was because it was tucked behind some trees and bushes.

Wiping the snow off his face, Jack pushed his way through the mounds of snow toward the mouth. The instant that his feet hit the rock inside the cave, he nearly stumbled and fell. It felt as if about fifty pounds of weight was suddenly lifted off his feet. Once he regained his balance, he began looking around. When he did, much to his great relief, he saw quite a bit of wood, definitely enough for a fire.

At least I don't have to go back out into that, Jack thought.

The storm raged for the next two days without stopping. By the time the snow finally petered out, the pilot was starting to run low on water. That is why he decided to venture out of the safety of the cave. The snow had partially blocked the mouth of the cave. So it took a bit of digging before there was a hole big enough for him to get out. Once he got out, he immediately began looking around. When he did, he spotted a small stream not that far away. He also noticed that everything all around him was covered in a foot deep layer of snow. The branches of every tree were sagging quite significantly from the weight of the snow. This trip over to the stream was an arduous one. With the wind still pretty bad, he filled his water bottles as quickly as he possibly could. Before he returned to his shelter, he looked around trying to figure out where he was. More specifically he was trying to figure out which way was down the mountain yet again. A task that didn't take very long for him to do. He reentered the cave and sat back down by the dying fire to finish the last swallow of his now cold coffee. Once he packed up his camp, he headed out again.

As the morning wore on, it was really starting to feel as if the pilot was never going to reach the bottom. It seemed as if the expansive winter landscape would go on forever. Stopping for a few seconds to catch his breath, it seemed as if nature itself did that as well. Right then there was, a moment of stillness that seemed to encompass everything. Not even the wind blew; there was none of the sounds of wildlife that he'd become accustomed to. There, in that moment, his surroundings were breathtakingly beautiful.

How can something be so beautiful and so deadly at the same time? Jack silently wondered as he began walking again.

About an hour later, Spencer sat down on a boulder and pulled out a granola bar for his lunch. When he did, he pulled something else out as well, his journal. It felt as if every muscle in his body was on fire, and he would like nothing more than to never move again.

Well, the storm is finally over and I'm moving again. It is better than sitting on my hands waiting. Or at least that's what I keep telling myself. I've got to say that something's been on my mind for quite a while. Even though I've been reading the Bible quite a bit during the storm. There is one thing that I still don't understand. Why is it that if there is a good God up there somewhere, how can he possibly let bad things like this happen? Is this some kind of punishment for some wrong that I did? Or is my number simply up? Jack wrote as his frustration surged, then put the journal away.

In that moment he knew that it had never been a matter of not believing God existed. It was always that he was angry at him. This train of thought brought him back to that fight he'd had with Ruth. He'd asked her to marry him, and she had said that she couldn't because they would be unequally yoked. Which lead to a screaming match about what that meant. At the end of which he'd stormed out slamming the door behind him. Now he was sure that he'd said some things he regretted and was wondering if he'd get a chance to apologize.

To shake off those depressing thoughts, Jack turned his train of thought back to wondering what unequally yoked meant. The only thing he knew was that it was something from the Bible. It took a couple of minutes to remember what verse she'd mentioned during their fight, but he did end up remembering it, which was in 2 Corinthians, more specifically chapter 6 verse 14. Which was about saved and not saved people not being romantically tied together. Shaking his head, he dismissed the whole idea as ridiculous.

Pushing all of this out of his mind, the pilot stood up, even though that was the last thing he wanted to do. He stuffed the wrapper in a pocket of his pack as he started out again.

The trees towered around Jack on every side as he walked. There were also numerous large rocks that he had to scramble over despite the fact they were covered in snow and slippery. It wasn't very hard for him to make it over, but it was a bit nerve racking. Every time his hand slipped, he thought he was going to fall. Once on the other side, he saw something incredible. It was a beautiful grove of trees with a small mountain spring in the centre. The angle that the sun shone into the clearing made the snow and the water glitter. It looked like something that you'd see in a photograph used as a wallpaper or something like that. Though he doubted a picture could really capture something so amazing. It took a couple of minutes before he could pull himself away, back on his path down the mountain.

Spencer was starting to get really tired, which was making it hard for him to get his feet to move correctly, resulting in him not watching where he was going. Due to this, he stumbled and rolled toward the edge of a cliff. He just barely managed to grab hold of the edge of the cliff and was holding on for dear life. The first thing that he did was try to find any footholds. Unfortunately there didn't seem to be any in his first attempts. About a foot away, he saw a spot with better holds that he might be able to climb up. He took a steadying breath and started very carefully moving sideways by holding tightly with one hand and carefully moving the other. Each time he moved his hands rocks fell, and he wondered if he was going to join them. When he reached the spot that he was aiming for, to his great relief, the holds were indeed solid and he was able to climb back up. Just as the ledge that he had been holding onto gave way. After pulling himself to safety, he pulled out his journal while he sat down to catch his breath.

I almost found a considerably faster way down this stupid mountain. It was close, but I managed to avoid taking it. On the upside, I think that I'm getting close to the bottom of the mountain.

Standing up, Jack put his journal away. After which he did the last thing his aching body wanted to do and that was, to start walking again.

As the pilot walked, the dense forest suddenly parted. When he emerged from the tree line, he stumbled across what was clearly an abandoned mine. He decided to stop and take a better look around. Stepping into the cleared area, he saw numerous rusted pieces of old mining machinery. Examining these machines closer, he quickly realized they'd been there for a really long time. These once top-of-the-line revolutionary feats of engineering were now little more than rusted heaps of metal.

Turning his attention to other parts of the site, he spotted an old cabin. Curious, he decided to take a look inside. When he stepped into the small wooden structure, the air was musty. Thus reinforcing the idea that this place had been abandoned a long time ago. It was a simple one-room structure with a stove on one side of the room and a bed on the other. On the same side of the room as the kitchen was a small table. He noticed that there were some papers on the small table. Walking over, he took a look at the papers. One of these papers was an old newspaper that was dated March 17, 1876. After looking around for a few more minutes, he went back outside.

Once outside Jack looked around again. When he did something caught his eye. That something was the opening of the mine shaft. He walked over to it so that he could get a closer look. The shaft was boarded up, and there were a bunch of signs nailed to the boards. These signs read things like "Keep out," "Danger," and "Warning, Risk of Tunnel

Collapse." Instead of listening to those wise warnings, he found a metal bar and pried the boards off. When he went and got the metal bar, he also found a torch which he lit. He shined the light into the expanse of blackness. *I wonder what's in there, Jack wondered his eyes fixed on that very blackness. He made what would likely turn out to be the rather big mistake, of entering the shaft.*

As Spencer walked deeper down the tunnel, the inky blackness enveloping him, a blackness that was only kept at bay by the flickering light of the torch he carried. That light created a ring of light around him. He looked around at everything the light revealed. Things that no one had laid eyes on for over a hundred years. A fact that excited him every time something new was revealed. He was so focused on all the interesting things he was seeing he didn't notice how deep into the tunnel he was getting.

Suddenly, there was a crash so loud that it felt as if the mountain itself shuddered. One minute Jack was standing on the seemingly firm floor of the tunnel. The next there was nothing under him, and he was falling. Only to land with a really painful thud on the floor of the shaft below the one that he'd just been in. With a pain-filled groan, he tried moving his limbs. His already tired and now certainly bruised limbs didn't like that very much. However, thankfully, he could move all of them without any shooting, searing pain. For this reason, he was reasonably sure that none of them were broken. Though how that was possible he wasn't sure.

Hey, I'm not going to look a gift horse in the mouth, Jack thought, trying to move his right arm. When he did he found that it was slightly pinned by a support beam. With his other free hand, he found a smaller piece of wood and used it as a lever to get his arm free. Right away, he scrabbled backward out from under the hole. The instant he started moving, his ribs screamed at him with a sharp, shooting pain. It looked like something was broken after all. He was nearly out of breath from the pain by the time he reached the wall.

The pilot leaned his head against the wall as more dust fell from above. He carefully wrapped his arm around his middle as his breathing returned to something resembling normal. Something which took a few minutes, all things considered. Nearly out of instinct, he reached into the pocket where he'd kept his journal. Panic surged through him when it wasn't there. Looking around, he spotted it on the other side of the hole. As carefully as he could, he went over to get it and made his way back.

Since the crash this mountain has thrown everything it could at me. Now I've finally hit rock bottom both literally and figuratively. After all, there doesn't seem to be any way that I could get any lower than this.

He stared at the words for a few minutes as the truth of them really hit home. After that he slowly closed the book and put it away as he leaned his head against the wall again.

The pilot couldn't help thinking about the painful, tragic irony of him, a born flyer, dying like this, deep underground, surrounded by rock. He'd always thought and hoped that when his end came he'd at the very least be able to see the sky, the very sky that had been his home for the vast amount of his life.

As Jack sat there staring at the ceiling, one of the verses he read while waiting out the storm popped into his head. That verse was about God humbling the proud and giving grace to the humble. In that moment it occurred to him that his current predicament was different from all the other troubles that he'd had after the crash. All those other situations, there was either nothing or precious little that he could have done to prevent them. This time, however, he was only in this situation because he didn't listen to the warning signs and decided he knew better. It just hit him that, that was what he'd been doing with God all his life.

Right then and there, Jack Spencer lowered his head and clasped his hands. Most importantly, he opened his heart.

"Jesus, I've reached rock bottom and realize that I can't go it alone. Please come into my heart and forgive my sins. Amen," Jack prayed, with all his heart.

Once the pilot was finished he looked up and opened his eyes. When he did, he stood up and began looking for a way to get out of this place. Looking around he realized that he needed his torch, which he picked up. After making sure it wasn't damaged, he relit it and started off down the tunnel. Each step he took echoed off the walls of the dark, dank tunnel.

After ten minutes of walking, Jack came to a fork in the tunnel. He lowered his head and prayed, asking for wisdom on which tunnel to take. Suddenly a beam of light appeared in one of the tunnels. Curious, he walked down that tunnel. When he reached the beam of light, he looked up and saw an air shaft. Which he figured was the source of the light. He decided to keep going and see where this tunnel led.

Each step he took sent a searing pain through him originating from his ribs. Despite this, he kept going by focusing on putting one step in front of another. This ultimately led to him reaching the end of the tunnel.

When the pilot did, he looked up from his feet and focused on what was in front of him. It took his sluggish, exhausted brain a couple of minutes to process what he was seeing. There before him was an exit. Just as he stepped out into the cold evening air, he heard a slightly distant rumbling. As he began moving further down the barely there path, it eventually led past the opening of the ventilation shaft he'd seen earlier inside the tunnel. What drew his attention was it was completely closed by debris. He couldn't tell when this happened; it could have been two minutes ago or twenty years ago.

Jack kept following the path leading away from the mineshaft, which turned out to be a confusing, winding path. As he walked the sun continued to sink lower in the sky. While there was still enough light to see, he noticed some foot prints a couple feet off the barely there path. Deciding to check it out, he left the path and walked over to the trail. In the rapidly diminishing light he could tell the footprints were fresh.

This proved to the stranded pilot someone was or had recently been in the area. Encouraged by this development, he decided to begin following the trail. As he did so, the sun set and the light level began to drop a lot more rapidly. He hoped that the light didn't give out completely till he found the end of the trail.

A short time later, it got pitch black. Just as that was

happening Jack saw the faint glow of a campfire ahead of him. With renewed determination, he started walking quite a bit faster toward that light, making it his new goal.

Meanwhile, in the campsite, a medium-sized group of six people were staying there, though only four of them were sitting around the campfire. They were chatting amongst themselves. The leader of the group was a man named David. He stood up to put wood on the fire. Sitting on the log next to where he'd just been was a man named Adam, and the person sitting next to him was a woman named Rachel. The last person was another woman named Sarah.

"What direction do you think we'll be going tomorrow?" Rachel asked, sounding like she was looking forward to it no matter what the answer.

"Don't know yet; our fearless leader hasn't told me yet," Adam said, pointing to the man that was over by the fire.

"You'll find out in the morning, along with everyone else," David said as he walked back over to the log and sat down.

Before any of them could respond in any way, there was a sound in the bushes. At the sound, a silence fell on the group around the campfire

"Did any of you hear that?" Sarah asked, her eyes fixed on those very bushes.

"Obviously we all heard that," Adam replied, his gaze briefly flicking to his friend before they returned to the bushes.

"You don't think that it's the monster from John's story, do you?" Rachel asked, a touch of trepidation in her voice.

"Of course not. That was just a story," David answered,

his voice carrying a complete certainty as he too watched the same spot.

Suddenly a man stumbled out of the bushes. He was unsteady on his feet with his eyes fixed on their campfire. As he entered into the ring of light created by the campfire, he turned his exhausted gaze on them. When he saw them, he stood there for a few seconds before he started to fall to the ground.

Moving quickly, David and Adam rushed forward. They just managed to catch him before he hit the ground. The two men helped him over to the fire. Working together, they helped him sit down on the log.

"Sarah, grab the canteen," David instructed urgently.

Immediately the woman stood up and ran over to the truck parked not far away. As she was doing this David started to try to assess the man's condition. It was quite clear the man was exhausted and was probably dehydrated as well. Just then, Sarah returned with the canteen and handed it to him.

"Mister, are you alright?" David asked, placing the canteen in the man's hand while watching his reaction.

Jack took a drink from the canteen. He just barely managed to stop him from drinking the whole thing. The last thing his aching ribs needed was for him to get sick to his stomach.

"I'm pretty sure that I'll, somehow, live," Jack replied as he lowered the canteen and looked around at the group of people.

"You look like you've had a rough go of it, friend," David commented, eyeing his ripped and dirt-covered clothes. He also noticed the way the man was holding his ribs.

"You have no idea," Jack agreed as he tried to concentrate on the conversation as his head started to hurt.

"Could you tell us your name?" Adam asked, not liking the way he was wincing every few minutes.

"Yeah. My name is Jack Spencer," Jack said, rubbing the bridge of his nose.

"Well, Jack, do you think you could sit here for a few minutes? I'll be right back," David said, calmly as he stood up from his crouched position.

"Sure, I'll just take a quick nap," Jack said, his eyes dropping, and he was starting to sway sideways.

"Adam, can you keep an eye on him and make sure he doesn't go to sleep," David said before walking over to the truck.

Once the off-duty coast guard commander reached the truck, he picked up the CB mic. He called in for an ambulance and reported their position as well as that they were dealing with a possible head injury. The response they got was that they were sending an air ambulance and paramedics. After signing off, he put the mic away and walked back over to the campfire. When he got there, it was clear that the man was just barely keeping his eyes open.

"So would you mind telling us how you got in this situation?" David asked, sitting down next to the man as the others also sat down.

"My plane went down near the top of the mountain, among other things," Jack replied, not really wanting to go over everything.

"Was it in that big storm at the beginning of the week?" Adam asked, surprised by the implications of his question.

"Yeah, it was," Jack replied, his gaze flicking to him.

"You are one lucky man," Adam commented, surprising the pilot.

"How's that?" Jack asked, blinking at the other man in confusion.

"We were supposed to be hiking another mountain this trip. If it hadn't been for the road to that mountain being closed by an avalanche, we wouldn't be here," Adam explained with a thoughtful look on his face.

"And if you hadn't been here, I probably would have died," Jack said, thinking about the implications.

"When you were hiking down the mountain, did you find anything interesting?" Rachel asked a bit eagerly.

"Yeah, I found an abandoned mine," Jack replied, turning his attention to the brown-haired woman.

"Really, could you tell us where," Rachel asked; for some reason she now sounded even more excited as she pulled out a map.

Rachel stood up and walked over to a nearby rock. She spread the map in her hand over the rock. There was definitely a sense of anticipation about her.

"Sure, I'd be happy to," Jack said, standing up and walking over to where the map was and began looking at it. It only took a few seconds for him to find the location and point it out on the map.

"Thank you," Rachel said, as she pulled out a pen and marked the spot that he indicated on the map.

A couple of minutes later, the group heard the sound

of an approaching helicopter, the lights of which seemed to suddenly appear out of the darkness. Mere seconds later, the whirlybird touched down in the parking area. The instant that the skids hit the ground the door opened and two men quickly jumped out. Both men quickly ducked their heads and began rushing toward the campfire where the group was waiting. Just before they entered the ring of light, David intercepted them and told them what he had observed. They thanked him and walked over to the injured pilot. The two paramedics crouched next to Jack, their attention focused on him.

"Mr. Spencer, I'm going to ask you some questions. They might seem a little silly, but I'm going to need you to answer them anyway," the first paramedic said, then asked his assessment questions, most of which he was able to answer fairly well.

Once the first paramedic finished the questions, he took out a small penlight. He used it to check Jack's pupil reaction, which was slightly sluggish, a fact that brought a frown to his face as he shared a concerned glance with his partner.

"Can you tell me if you're hurting anywhere else?" the other paramedic asked, turning his attention back to the patient.

"My ribs hurt the most, and I've probably got some bruises too," Jack answered while trying to force his eyes to stay open.

The two of them began doing some other assessments before deciding that he was dehydrated and probably had a concussion. They started a couple of IVs and loaded him

onto the stretcher, then onto the chopper. The two paramedics quickly jumped in after him. Once the door was
closed, the chopper took off.

As soon as the chopper disappeared from view the
group decided that now was as good a time as any to go to
bed. After saying goodnight to each other, they headed off
to their tents.

After a short flight, the helicopter landed on the roof
of the hospital. There were doctors waiting for them. The
second the stretcher was unloaded it was quickly wheeled
inside as the doctors began moving around it like excited
bees.

The doctors determined that he was indeed dehydrated
and he also did have a concussion. They decided to keep
him for a couple of days for observation during which time
he'd be given IVs to deal with the dehydration.

The next day, Jack had been settled in a room. He was
watching TV when there was a knock on the door causing
him to look up. When he did, he saw that it was Rachel, one
of the women from the campsite.

"Mind if I come in for a moment?" Rachel asked,
sounding just a little bit hesitant as she quickly scanned
the room.

"Yeah, sure," Jack replied, muting the TV.

Rachel walked in and sat down in one of the chairs.
She took a moment to gather her thoughts before she said
anything.

"I heard that you were getting out of here today. I figured that I'd come and thank you," Rachel said earnestly.

"I'm quite sure that it should be me that's thanking

you," Jack said, sounding totally confused as to what she was talking about.

"Let me explain. My great grandfather owned that mine you found. When he was thirty years old, he disappeared. Everyone said that he just abandoned his wife and baby. Despite the fact that she said that he would never do that. The family never knew what happened to him. The morning after you left we hiked up to the place that you showed us. When we got there, we found the mine just like you said. While we were looking around, we found great grandfather's journal. His wife was right; he didn't run out on them. Thank you for helping us. Now we finally know what happened to him. The funny thing is that I wasn't even supposed to be there. Sarah invited me at the last minute," Rachel explained as she fiddled with the hem of her shirt.

"I'm glad that happened," Jack said, his mind reeling a little in astonishment.

Right then the doctor entered the room, and she quietly excused herself. The doctor quickly did the checks that he needed to do and signed the discharge papers. Within about twenty minutes, he left the hospital and headed home.

About a week after Jack got out of the hospital, he was walking down the sidewalk. He was still thinking about everything that had happened. Especially what Rachel had said at the hospital. The odds of that happening by accident were so astronomical that it boggled the mind.

Those contemplative wanderings surprisingly led Jack to the steps of a church. After a couple of minutes of debating whether he should go in. He ended up deciding to enter the place of worship. Each step he took down the aisle running down the centre between the pews echoed around the cavernous space. He ended up sitting down on one of the front pews. His eyes fixed thoughtfully on the cross at the front of the room. Something else that had been on his mind was weighing quite heavily on him at the moment.

"I hope I'm not disturbing you, but you look like you have something that you want to talk about," the pastor said, walking up to the pilot.

"Yeah, you could say that, Reverend," Jack said, running his hand through his hair.

"I've been told that I'm a good listener. If you want to talk about it, I'd be more than happy to listen," the pastor replied, making sure it was an offering and that he was not pushing.

"It's a bit of a long story," Jack said, not really sure.

"I've got the time," the pastor replied simply.

The pilot told him the whole story of the plane crash and all troubles that came after it. A momentary silence fell when he stopped talking.

"Sounds like you've had a good deal of trials of late," the pastor commented after a few seconds of thinking.

"That's sure the truth, but that's not what's bothering me. After all of that, I asked Jesus to forgive my sins. Now I'm wondering if it was just the stress of the situation or if I really meant it," Jack explained, leaning forward with his elbows on his legs and putting his chin on his clasped hands.

"That is a question that only you can answer. Was that

something that you'd ever considered before?" the pastor asked thoughtfully.

"No, I was so strongly against anything to do with God that it broke up me and my girlfriend," Jack replied with total certainty.

"It seems that the LORD has used these troubles to get your attention. Now you need to decide where you're going to go from here. If you're interested, there are people here that are willing to help you," the pastor said, his voice kind and understanding.

"I'll think about it. Thank you, Reverend," Jack said with a thoughtful tone of voice before standing up and heading back down the aisle. A few minutes later the sound of the door opening and closing echoed through the room.

A couple of days later, Jack Spencer realized that him giving his life to the LORD was very real. When he told Ruth this, she was so happy. Not long later, they ended up getting engaged. A year after that the two of them were married.

* * *

"Well, what do you think?" Alicia asked, glancing between the two of them kind of hopefully, with just a trace of nervousness.

"That was amazing, Licia," Carla replied, sounding pleased.

"Yeah that was a really good story. Just the right blend of excitement and heart," Mark agreed, sounding impressed.

"Thanks, guys, I sure hope the audience next week likes it too," Alicia replied with a slight smirk on her face.

"So we're guinea pigs now," Carla said, with mock hurt in her voice as she threw a pillow at her sister.

"Why of course, Dear Sister," Alicia said, with a smile and a barely concealed laugh in her voice.

At that, the three of them shared a good laugh. They spent the rest of the evening having fun playing board games.

THE END

CHAPTER 9
On the Run

During one of the breaks, Alicia took a few seconds to catch her breath and took a drink out of the water bottle the stage hand gave her. When the break was over, she walked out onto the stage and up to the mic. As soon as she picked up the mic, a hushed anticipation settled over the crowd.

"Is everyone having a good time?" Alicia asked, trying to get the crowd excited as she stepped up to the front of the stage.

"Yeah," the crowd shouted, excitement crackling like static electricity.

"This is the story of a wife and mother who got herself into a situation that was filled with danger and adventure. It all started in a dark back street in the dark of night," Alicia said, trying to build anticipation in the crowd.

* * *

A woman was walking down a street well after dark. The woman's name was Carley Trent, who had light-brown hair and dark-green eyes. She pulled her topcoat closer as she looked nervously around her. She was headed to the nearest gas station with a jerry can clutched in a white-knuckle grip.

Why did my stupid car have to pick this neighbourhood to run out of gas? Carley asked herself as she walked.

Twenty minutes later, Carley arrived at the nearest gas station. Looking around, she quickly recognized that it was definitely one of the rundown ones. She tried unsuccessfully to find someone to help her. Seeing the lights were on in the building, she headed in that direction. As she got closer, she saw through the window that there was no one behind the counter.

Just as she reached the building, she heard voices coming from the side of the building. After another unsuccessful glance around looking for someone, she decided to investigate. When she stepped around the corner, she saw two men arguing. One was dressed like a regular workman wearing a high-vis vest, a button-up shirt, and jeans. The other was dressed like a high-end businessman wearing a suit that probably cost as much as her car. The workman who's back was toward her shoved the businessman who was facing her, causing him to take a couple steps back. An instant later, the businessman pulled out a gun and shot the first guy.

The sound of the gunshot caused Carley to gasp and drop the gas can in her hand. The clatter of the gas can hitting the ground caused the man with the gun to look up. When their eyes met, they both got a good look at each other. In that instant, Carley felt like a deer caught in the headlights.

Suddenly the sound of the gas station door opening and closing woke her from the misty haze of shock. In the next heartbeat, she bolted toward the gas station door.

A decision that turned out to be a good idea because an instant later another bullet hit the brick wall of the building right next to where she had been standing.

In her fright, the woman ran right into the owner of the gas station, who had come out to see what was going on. When she collided with the man, he reached out to steady her and could feel her trembling.

"What's wrong, Ma'am? Were those sounds gunshots?" the man asked the clearly frightened woman.

"Yes, they were gunshots," Carley replied, to frightened to say much else.

The man guided Carley to a chair in front of the gas station. The two of them looked up just as a car sped off into the night. The gas station owner, who had gotten out his phone to call the police, managed to get a picture of the license plate.

Within a few minutes, two patrol cars pulled up in front of the gas station. Two sets of uniformed officers got out of the cars. One set started looking around while the other walked toward the gas station owner and Carley.

The officers separated the two people so they could get their statements. One of the officers took the station owner's statement. Once he was done, he was told he could leave.

Carley gave the other officer her statement. By the time she was done, it was clear that she was really shaken. To keep her from going into shock, the officer gave her a blanket. Just as she finished her story, the other two officers found the body.

The officers called into dispatch and reported the

murder and that there was a witness. They were told to inform the witness that she'd need to accompany them to the station.

"Ma'am, we'll need to you to accompany us back to the station," the first officer informed her in a calm, reassuring tone.

"It's really important, isn't it," Carley said as she looked from one officer to the other, still sounding frightened but starting to calm down.

"Yes, Ma'am, the detectives just need to talk to you about what you saw," the second officer replied in a calming, professional tone.

"What about my car? I can't just leave it there. I think I dropped my gas can over there," Carley replied, her hand shaking just slightly as she pointed back toward the side of the building.

"It's going to be alright; you don't need to worry about your car. One of these officers will take care of it. You just need to tell us where it is," the first officer said calmingly.

Carley agreed to go with them and gave them her car keys. When she stood up, she shivered and pulled the blanket that she had wrapped around herself a little tighter. The officers gave her a ride to the station.

Once there, Carley was shown to the desk of one of the detectives. When she walked up to the desk there was as, a man sitting behind it and another man leaning against it.

"Mrs. Trent, I'm Detective Morris, and this is my partner, Detective Mathews. Why don't you have a seat," Morris suggested, gesturing at the chair in front of his desk.

"Thank you, Detective," Carley said, unwrapping the blanket from around her, neatly folding it, and placing it on the other chair in front of the desk. Once she was done, she sat down in the chair the detective had pointed to.

"We're going to need you to walk us through what you saw this evening," Detective Mathews said, drawing her attention back to the matter at hand.

"Certainly, Detective. I was headed home from the office. I'd just passed the city limits, and my stupid car decided that would be a wonderful place to run out of gas. So I grabbed the gas tank from my trunk and started back the way I came. I was looking for a gas station. Because it was already dark, I was praying all the time I walked. The Lord must have been listening, because I found one that was still open.

"As I got close to the station, I heard the voices of two men arguing. Since there didn't seem to be anyone inside the building, I decided to find out if either of the men could help me. Just as I stepped around the corner of the building, one of the men shot the other. I was so shocked that I dropped the gas can in my hand. The sound of it clattering on the ground caused the man with the gun to look up. When our eyes met, I felt like a deer caught in the headlights of a car. I couldn't stop thinking that I'd just seen this man kill someone and that he'd seen me seeing him," Carley explained, her voice and hands trembling. At the end of the story, it was very clear that she was terrified.

"It's okay, Mrs. Trent; you're in a building full of police officers. You're safe here," Detective Mathews said, hoping to calm her down.

"Do you think you could identify the man with the gun?" Detective Morris asked, his voice calming.

"Oh most definitely," Carley replied with certainty, despite the lingering fear in her voice as her eyes settled on the surface of the detective's desk.

"Good. What we're going to do is get you to look at some books of mugshots," Detective Morris explained as he motioned for another detective to grab the books.

"But, Detective, that won't be necessary; that's him," Carley said, pointing to a picture that was pinned to a file on the desk.

The partners both looked at the picture she was pointing at. They shared an astonished look for a few seconds before Mathews picked up the picture.

"Are you certain this is the man you saw?" Detective Mathews asked, holding up the picture.

"Completely certain, Detective," Carley replied, her voice as certain as her words.

By this time it was getting really late, and she was starting to get really tired. It was now half past midnight, so that was not very surprising.

"Would it be alright if I go home?" Carley asked, barely able to stifle a yawn as she blinked sleepily at the detective.

"That would be alright, but you'll have to come back first thing in the morning," Detective Morris replied, easily seeing how tired she was.

"I'll just call a cab. I'm not sure where my car is," Carley commented, trying to work out a plan on how to get home.

"Your car is probably in the lot," Detective Mathews assured, entering the conversation.

"Oh I'll take the cab anyway. I'm far to tired to drive safely," Carley replied sleepily.

"You're right. If it's alright, these officers will give you a ride home. They'll also stay to keep an eye on things," Detective Morris agreed, gesturing to one of the officers standing off to the side.

"Alright," Carley said, standing up and following the officers out of the room.

The next morning, Morris and Mathews entered the captain's office. When they did, there were two other detectives in the room. The tension in the room was so thick that it crackled like static electricity.

"Do you think that Mrs. Trent will be willing to testify?" Captain Miller asked, looking between the two detectives.

"We'll ask her when she comes in. She called and said she'd be here about an hour from now," Morris answered, looking at his watch.

"When she gets here, offer her protective custody. We both know that Lowell won't care whether she's willing to testify or not; he'll still kill her," Captain Miller said, his voice grave and his eyes looking like he was recalling a bad memory.

"Don't worry, Captain; we will," Mathews said with certainty.

"We'll make sure that she understands how serious the situation is and how much danger she's in," Morris added, also remembering what happened the last time they had a witness against this guy.

"Davis, Lewis, I want you to bring Adrian Lowell in," Captain Miller said, turning his attention to the other two detectives.

"Since he knows we have a witness that saw him murder someone, he's going to go so deep underground that he's going to get in a traffic jam with groundhogs," Davis said, sounding a little skeptical.

"I don't care if you have to dig so deep that your shovels melt. I want Lowell in cuffs," Captain Miller instructed firmly.

"Let's go. We've got a lot of digging to do, D," Lewis said, nudging his partner.

Lewis and Davis both stood and left the office. As the door closed behind them, Captain Miller turned his attention to the remaining two detectives.

"Don't you two have some arrangements to make before your witness arrives in about thirty minutes," Captain Miller said, dismissing them.

"Sure do, Captain," Mathews replied, taking the hint.

The two detectives stood up and also left their captain's office. Once they reentered the bullpen, they headed straight to their desks. As soon as they sat down, they started making arrangements for a safe house.

Thirty minutes later, just as the two detectives finished, an officer brought Carley Trent into the bullpen. They looked up as she walked over to their desks.

"How are you doing this morning, Mrs. Trent?" Morris asked, remembering how distraught she had been the night before.

"Much better, thank you, Detective," Carley replied,

feeling much more herself after a mostly restful night's sleep.

"There's something important that we need to ask you," Morris said, his tone serious.

"Would you be willing to testify against the man that you saw last night?" Mathews asked, his tone just as serious.

"The man that I saw is really dangerous, isn't he," Carley said as she sat down on the chair that was sitting next to the desk.

"I'm going to be straight with you. Yes, he's a very dangerous man," Morris said, leaning against the desk.

"If I don't, will he get away with killing that other man?" Carley asked, looking between the two detectives.

"That would be the most likely outcome. Because there isn't really anything to connect him to the murder except your testimony," Mathews answered, sitting behind his desk.

"Alright, I'll testify," Carley said after taking a deep breath.

The two detectives shared a slightly surprised look. Both had expected it to be harder to convince her to testify, though they were glad she was willing.

"We'd like to offer you protective custody till after the trial," Mathews said, knowing what the implications were and hoping she wouldn't change her mind.

"You mean he'll try to kill me to keep me from testifying," Carley replied, her tone just as serious as the detective's.

"He'll certainly try. That's why it's so important that

you let us protect you," Morris answered, trying to impart just how important it was.

"Alright, I'll go into protective custody," Carley agreed, after glancing at each of the detectives.

With that the two detectives stood up, and Carley followed suit. The three of them headed out of the bullpen and down to the garage. They got into the detective's car and started the engine.

"Where are we going?" Carley asked as the car pulled out of the parking lot.

"We're going to your house to pick up some things that you'll need. After that, we're going to a safe house," Morris answered as they pulled out of the garage.

It didn't take very long for them to reach Carley's house. The detectives and Carley got out of the car. As they approached the house, the detectives carefully watched their surroundings, looking for potential danger. Once inside, the detectives began clearing the house, looking for any possible threats. They split up, one taking the upstairs and the other the down. As Mathews checked some of the rooms upstairs, he noticed something that was a cause for concern.

"Tim, we might have a problem," Mathews said, sounding concerned as he walking down the stairs and into the living room.

"What kind of problem, Alex?" Morris asked, reentering the living room after having just finished checking all the downstairs rooms.

"The potentially bad kind. Half the master bed hasn't been slept in and neither has the kid's," Mathews replied, sounding concerned.

About a second later, Carley walked into the room from the kitchen. The worried looks on the two detective's faces made her worried too.

"Mrs. Trent, your husband and son aren't here, and it seems they are missing," Morris said, trying to come up with a plan

"Don't worry, Detectives; they're not missing. They're in a remote cabin in Iceland. The cabin is so isolated that no one but the old man that owns it even knows where it is. They're safe there. They have been there for the past week," Carley replied, surprising the two detectives.

"Okay if that's the case, how come you're not with them?" Morris asked, slightly skeptical.

"Oh, that's right; I forgot to tell you that part. I had some things I needed to finish up at work before my boss would let me take a vacation. That stuff was supposed to take two weeks, so we talked about it, and it was decided the boys would go, and I'd join them when I was done. Last night I managed to get it finished early and was going to get a flight out this morning," Carley explained, alleviating the detective's concern.

The two detectives talked about what they had just been told as Carley got the last of the things she wanted to take with her. Both detectives were just glad that her family was somewhere safe.

She carried her backpack as the three of them exited the house. They were about half way to the car when the first shot sent all three people scrambling for cover. That turned out to be the waist-high stone wall surrounding Carley's front lawn. As they crouched behind it, bullets pinged off the stones every few seconds. Each one causing Carley to flinch.

"We've got to get to the car, preferably before they figure out that there are more of them than there are of us," Morris said as he stood slightly to return fire.

"At the count of three, you two make a break for it, and I'll cover you," Mathews suggested, trying to figure out which direction the shots were coming from.

"Alright," Morris replied, not really liking the idea but not having any choice.

"One, two, three, go, go," Mathews said. He half stood and began firing in the direction that the bullets were coming from.

The instant that Mathews began firing, Morris and Carley started moving. They moved toward the car as quickly as they could while half crouching. With every step that they took, bullets hit the ground at their feet and flew by them, missing them by mere inches. As soon as the two of them made it to the car, Mathews quickly began moving to join them. While he did that, Morris laid down cover fire.

"I vote that we get out of here," Mathews said, dropping down next to the others behind their car, taking cover.

"I second that," Carley agreed, flinching as another bullet hit the car.

"The motion carries. Let's get a move on," Morris said, reaching up and opening the passenger door of the car.

Morris carefully crawled into the car and began trying to get into the driver's seat, while at the same time he reached for the radio.

"Officers under fire, expedite," Morris said, into the

radio, then gave their current position as another bullet hit the car.

A couple of units acknowledged the call over the radio. Within a few minutes, they could hear the distant sound of sirens. As the sirens got closer, the amount of gunfire began to lessen. In minutes two other units pulled up. The officers managed to apprehend two suspects.

After giving their statements to the officers they left for the safe house. It didn't take long for them to reach the safe house, an open-concept, two-bedroom apartment with the two bedrooms in the back. When they got there, the two detectives again cleared the apartment.

"Who gets the bedrooms and who gets the couch?" Carley asked, trying to think about anything other than what had just happened.

"How about Mrs. Trent takes one of the rooms and we rotate who sleeps on the couch. I'll take the couch tonight," Mathews suggested evenly.

"Sounds good to me. Mrs. Trent, how about you pick your room, and we'll take whatever is left," Morris suggested, gesturing to the hallway that lead to the bedrooms.

"Alright," Carley said, picking up her backpack.

Carley walked down the hall. There were two doors across from each other. After glancing at each room, she picked the one on the right. As she unpacked her clothes, she tried to wrap her mind around what just happened. She'd never been shot at before, and it was an experience that she didn't want to repeat. Though considering the predicament that she currently found herself in, that was probably quite unrealistic. While she thought about these things, she put her backpack on the bed.

Just as Carley was about to unzip the zipper of her backpack, she heard glass breaking coming from the main room of the apartment. She also heard the sound of gunshots. An instant later, the door opened, and she spun around to see who it was. There standing in the door was Detective Morris.

"We have to get out of here now," Morris said urgently.

"What's going on?" Carley asked, picking up her backpack again and following.

"We've got some unpleasant company," Morris said as they made their way to the back door while keeping an eye out for danger.

When they ran down the hallway, a couple of people stuck their heads out their doors to see what was happening. Morris motioned them back inside to keep them out of harm's way. As they reached the back door, they could still hear gunfire.

Just as he was about to open the back door, the door behind them opened and closed. Reacting quickly, the detective spun around to face the door, bringing his weapon up. While at the same time, he pushed Carley behind him for protection.

"Relax, it's me, but there's some unpleasant company right behind me, so we should hurry," Mathews assured, his weapon pointed at the ground.

"Try knocking next time," Morris said, lowering his weapon.

Just as he again reached for the doorknob, they had

to duck as more bullets were shot at them. The detective reached out and opened the door. As soon as it was open, all three of them rushed through the door. All three of them jumped behind a concrete barricade as another hail of bullets chased them out.

"Where did you park the car?" Morris asked as a bullet hit the barricade.

"It's over there," Mathews said, indicating toward where he had parked the car.

"Do you think we'll make it?" Carley asked, not particularly liking the amount of space between them and the car.

"We will because we don't have any choice," Mathews said confidently and calmly.

With that, together the three of them stood. As they made a break for the car, the two detectives returned fire. While they ran, bullets pinged off the asphalt at their feet. Just as they reached the car, it quickly got a few extra holes in it.

"Well that got the blood pumping," Morris said with a slightly sardonic half grin as he opened the passenger door.

"I prefer a good jog for that, thank you," Mathews replied, nearly rolling his eyes as he returned fire again.

Morris slid into the driver's seat just in time for a bullet to hit the side window, raining tiny shards of glass on him. At that exact moment, Mathews and Carley also got in the car.

The instant that both doors closed, the car took off. Within seconds, the tires squealed as they sped out of the parking lot like a shot. As they did so, the bad guys were hot on their heels.

"The safe house has obviously been compromised.

What are we going to do now?" Mathews asked, alternating between staring out the back window, keeping an eye on the bad guys, and glancing at his partner.

"Do you really think that it would be a good idea to try our luck with another department safe house?" Morris asked, sounding worried.

"It doesn't really seem like a chance we can afford to take considering the circumstances," Mathews said, shaking his head, not liking that idea at all.

"I agree," Morris said, frowning as he wove around the car in front of him. Unfortunately his actions were immediately mimicked by the bad guy's car.

"If we can't go to another police safe house, what are we going to do?" Carley asked, looking between the two detectives from the back seat.

Before either detective had a chance to answer, there was a thud as they were rammed by the bad guy's car. Morris tried to swerve to avoid the other car. Much to his frustration, however, his efforts were unsuccessful as the other car stayed with them.

"Not sure I'm going to be able to lose them," Morris said, gritting his teeth as they were, yet again, rammed by the other car.

"Why don't you try telling them one of your jokes? It sure worked with your last date," Mathews replied as the car yet again swerved.

As the car again swerved just in time to avoid being rammed again, Carley lowered her head to pray. "LORD, please protect us and provide us a way to escape those who wish to harm us." She continued praying this prayer as they continued their evasive maneuvering. Out of seemingly nowhere, a big eighteen wheeler truck pulled out between their car and the bad guy car. Seeing an opportunity to get away into a parking lot, he then slid into a parking space in the middle of the lot where he couldn't be seen from the road.

Just a second later, the bad guy car passed the entrance to the parking lot. A couple seconds after that, a black and white stopped the bad guy's car. Within a matter of a few minutes, the occupants of the car were cuffed and put in the back of the police car.

As soon as the coast was clear, Morris pulled out of the parking spot. Both detectives kept a close look out as they pulled out of the parking lot.

"Where to now?" Mathews asked as they drove.

"Plan B," Morris answered simply.

A little while later, the car pulled up to a medium-scale hotel. Once they checked in, they quickly made their way to their room.

In minutes, the three of them stepped through the door. The instant the door closed behind them, Carley flopped on the couch. She wrapped her arms around herself and began quietly praying for the strength to get through this. After a couple minutes, she stood up just as the two detectives turned in her direction.

"After that, I don't think I'm even going to bother unpacking my backpack," Carley said, crossing her arms.

"That's probably wise, Mrs. Trent," Mathews agreed, also figuring that they probably wouldn't be here long enough for unpacking to be worth the effort.

"Do you think that it's safe enough for us to go get some groceries?" Carley asked, looking at the clock and realizing how late it was getting.

"Ordering pizza would probably be safer. The last thing that we need is for you to be spotted out on the street," Morris said, shaking his head.

"Great, restaurant food for the next week," Carley replied, a slightly annoyed tone in her voice as she kept her arms lightly crossed.

"Most of the time not having to cook is the only part of being in protective custody that people actually like," Morris said, a slight half smile on his face.

"What can I say, I like to cook, and I prefer food I've cooked myself," Carley replied, finding a little confidence in this familiar topic.

"I'm sorry, Mrs. Trent, but that won't be an option for the next few days," Mathews said in a tone that brokered no argument.

"I think I'll manage to survive somehow," Carley replied lightly, trying to lighten the mood and cheer up the frustrated detective.

Morris picked up the phone and began dialing the closest pizza place. While he was doing that, he picked up the TV remote with his other hand and tossed it to Carley. Once he was done making the phone call, she turned on the TV.

She began flipping through the channels looking for something interesting to watch. She ended up settling on a rerun of *Matlock*. She was really happy when she realized that it was just starting.

Both detectives settled around the room to wait. Morris

sat in the chair that was near the large window in the front of the room. Mathews sat in the chair on the other side of the TV that was in the middle of the room against the wall. As he did so, he pulled out a deck of cards and began playing solitaire.

When the pizza arrived Morris paid the delivery boy while also taking the opportunity to glance down the hall in both directions. The three of them quickly ate supper then the two detectives switched who was on guard at the window.

Afterwards Carley retreated to the bedroom. When she did, she got her Bible and devotion book out of her backpack. She sat down on the bed and had her devotions. Once she was finished, she quickly changed clothes and went to bed.

The next morning when she emerged from the bedroom the two detectives were already deep in discussion. They were sitting at the small table that was on the side of the TV farthest from the door.

"What is the plan for today, Detectives?" Carley asked as she walked up to the table, drawing their attention.

"As of right now, the plan is to stay here and be as invisible as possible," Morris answered evenly.

"Although that is subject to change depending on the situation," Mathews added, running his hand through his hair.

"What do you mean?" Carley asked, slightly confused.

"We still don't know how our safe house was compromised, so we have to be ready to move at a moment's notice," Morris explained, sounding concerned.

"That man I saw wants to kill me really badly," Carley said, a slight tremor in her voice as she thought about her situation.

"Yes, he does. Your testimony will put him away for the rest of his life. It may even put him on death row. However, don't worry; we'll protect you," Mathews replied, not wanting to scare her but knowing from experience that it's best to be honest.

"I'm sure glad my boys aren't having to deal with this because of me," Carley replied, shaking her head.

With that she decided that she needed to get her mind off her situation. To that end, she turned on the TV and began flipping through the channels.

After a brief discussion, the detectives decided to call their captain. They'd tell him that they were all still alive and that Carley was with them. However, they wouldn't tell him where they were.

The atmosphere in the room was tense. It felt a little like the calm before a storm. It was almost as if everyone in the room was waiting for something to happen. While at the same time it was as if all three of them were simultaneously hoping or in Carley's case praying that nothing would.

A few hours later, they'd just had lunch when there was a knock on the door. Morris went to the window to see who it was. Mathews went to the door and got ready to open it if necessary. Both of them had their guns in their hands, ready for trouble.

"Who is it?" Mathews asked, trying with only limited success to keep the tension out of his voice.

"A package arrived for you," a male voice on the other side of the door replied immediately.

Morris looked out and saw it was the bellhop, as well

as confirming that the young man was carrying a cardboard box. He quietly relayed his information to his partner.

"There is a Do Not Disturb sign on the door. Could you leave it at the front desk? We'll pick it up later," Mathews replied, his instincts telling him that something wasn't quite right.

"The gentleman that delivered it said it was very important that the package be delivered to you right away," the bellhop replied, clearly torn between hotel policy and what he had been told.

"Alright, bring it in," Mathews said, opening the door stepping to the side to allow the young man in, while keeping his weapon pointed at the ground.

"Where would you like it, Sir," the bellhop asked, regarding the gun slightly nervously.

"On the table would be just fine, young man," Mathews said, slightly suspicious of both the young man and the box in his hand.

The young bellhop walked over and placed the box on the table that the detectives had just vacated. When he turned back toward the door, he eyed Morris and his gun warily.

"Will that be all, Sirs," the bellhop asked, relaxing significantly when he noticed the detective badges on their belts.

"Yes, thank you," Mathews said, slipping him a five-dollar bill as the bellhop left.

Once the door closed, both detectives turned their attention to the box on the table. There wasn't anything particularly menacing about the box. It was just a plain, ordinary, cardboard box. Still neither detective could shake the bad feeling they got when they looked at the mundane object.

"There seems to be a note taped to the top of the box," Morris commented as he walked up to the table.

"What does it say?" Mathews asked as he watched the bellhop walk down the hall through the window.

"A little parting gift from your friend from the gas station. RIP, rest in pieces, Mrs. Trent," Morris read after removing the note.

"How much do you want to bet that there's a bomb or something equally nasty in that box," Mathews said, rhetorically.

"Why that evil psychopath. He really thinks he can get away with anything, doesn't he," Morris said, seething as he glared at the note, then at the box.

"We need to be careful not to touch that thing and call in the bomb squad," Mathews said, picking up the phone.

"You really think there's a bomb in that box," Carley said, eyeing the box with a mixture of disbelief and nervousness.

"Unfortunately, there's a good chance of that," Morris said, running his hand through his hair with a frustrated look.

"But if a bomb went off in this room, wouldn't that hurt, maybe even kill, the people in the rooms on either side of us?" Carley asked, totally horrified.

"It probably would, but Lowell doesn't care who else gets hurt as long as he kills you," Morris said grimly.

"That's terrible," Carley said, a combination of sadness and anger replacing the fear in her bright eyes.

"The bomb squad will be here in a few minutes," Mathews said as he hung up the phone.

A couple minutes later, the three of them heard the sound of approaching sirens. After a few minutes there was a knock on the door. Before any of them had a chance to move the door opened. In walked their captain with a bomb squad guy right behind him.

"What have we got?" Captain Miller asked, his gaze flicking over his two detectives and then Carley.

"As I told you on the phone, seems we got a little gift from Lowell," Mathews said, gesturing at the box on the table.

"So this is the suspicious box," the bomb squad guy said, walking up to the table dressed head-to-toe in his green suit.

The bomb squad guy took a quick look at the exterior of the box, which unfortunately didn't help him very much.

"First off, I'm going to need everyone out. Second, I'm going to need some rooms evacuated on this floor and the one above us," the bomb squad guy said as he turned his attention to the other people in the room.

"How many on each floor are going to need to be evacuated?" Captain Miller asked, figuring how many units it would take.

"Since I don't know how powerful the device is. I'd say, on this one two rooms on either side. The same goes for the second floor. Might need more once I get a look at the device. We'll just have to wait and see," the bomb squad guy replied after a moment's thought.

"I'll get some more units down here and get it done,"

Captain Miller said in a serious tone, then turned and left the room.

The two detectives and Carley immediately followed him. As they made their way to the lobby Morris considered something that had been bothering him for quite a while. That thing was how the bad guys were always finding them. By the time they reached the lobby, he was pretty sure he had the answer. The first thing he did when they got there was make a phone call.

It turned out that the device was a simple one with a small blast radius. This meant they didn't need to evacuate more rooms. It didn't take very long for the device to be safely disarmed and removed.

As the bomb squad was leaving they passed a police technician. The tech walked over to Mathews, Morris, and Carley who were waiting off to the side to avoid getting in the way. Morris had called in a favour to get help confirming a hunch.

"Thanks for coming, James," Morris said, extending his hand.

"Glad to. I hope I can help you figure it out," James said, shaking the detective's hand.

Morris had come to suspect that Lowell had somehow planted a tracking device on one of them. That was why he'd asked James to help. The four of them went back to the room the two detectives and their witness had been staying in. Once there, James got his equipment and quickly scanned both them and their stuff. Within a few minutes, the tech was able to find something. There was a tracking device attached to Carley's backpack. The three of them thanked the tech, then started trying to figure out what to do about it.

"What are we going to do with it?" Carley asked, staring at the square, black piece of plastic and metal with a blinking red light on the top sitting on the table.

"I got an idea that might just work," Morris said, reaching for a piece of paper that was sitting on the table.

"I feel deeply frightened by the look on your face," Mathews said, the tone in his voice making it abundantly clear that it was the exact opposite.

On that note, they decided that they needed to move again. As Carley picked up her backpack, she hoped that they'd be able to stay in one place for a while. Just as they were leaving the room, Morris made a quick phone call.

As they were leaving Morris asked an officer to take the envelope that had the bug and a note to the hotel a few blocks away. The officer entered the room Morris had rented for the rest of the day and placed the envelope on the small, round table.

About twenty minutes after the officer left, two armed men broke the door down with their guns drawn. They searched the entire room and found nothing except the envelope. One of them picked up the envelope and opened it. He pulled it out and began reading the short note. "Close but no cigar" is what the note read.

Meanwhile, on the other side of the city, the detectives and their witness arrived at a hotel just as the sun was setting. After they checked in, they headed to their room. All three of them were exhausted as Mathews unlocked the door.

Once inside, Carley put her backpack in the room. After spending a couple hours watching TV, she went to bed.

The next morning after breakfast, the phone rang. Mathews talked for a few minutes, all the time with a serious look on his face. After a few minutes, he hung up and turned his attention to the other people in room.

"What's going on?" Morris asked, concerned by the look on his partner's face.

"The trial will be taking place a bit sooner than we thought it would. It'll be happening in about five days," Mathews answered, not sure what to think about the situation.

"You're right; that is awfully fast," Morris agreed, sounding a little confused.

"The DA wants to get the trial over before Lowell has another chance to kill me," Carley said grimly.

Neither detective really liked it, but that was essentially the case. Finding themselves without any reply, they both chose to say nothing at all. On that grim note, the three of them went about the rest of their day.

Over the next six days, the three of them managed to lay low and not get shot at even once. A fact that surprised both of the detectives, but neither were complaining. During that time they'd been staying at a cabin just outside the city.

The next morning, Morris, Mathews, and Carley were headed back into the city. The reason for this was that they had been notified that Carley was going to be testifying that afternoon. They were only a couple blocks from the courthouse when someone shot out their front two tires, causing them to swerve wildly. Luckily, Mathews managed to steer the swerving car into a nearby parking lot they happened to be passing at exactly that second.

A second later, another car pulled into the parking lot. Four armed bad guys jumped out of the car and began moving toward the detective's car. As they got closer, they opened fire at the three fleeing people.

Within a second of the car entering the parking lot, Morris and Mathews got a bad feeling and decided it would be wise to ditch the car. The three of them quickly made a break for it on foot. By the time the bad guys got out of their vehicle, the three of them were already on the other side of the parking lot.

Just as the bad guys opened fire, the three of them managed to duck around a corner into an alley. Together the detectives rushed Carley down the alley while keeping an eye out behind them. As they neared the end the bad guys entered the alley and began firing. This forced the three of them to take cover to avoid getting shot.

A few minutes into the gunfight a car squealed to a stop at the entry of the alley. As the firing continued, two people from the car entered the alley.

"Thought you could use a couple hands," Lewis said, as he took cover next to the other detectives and fired at the bad guys.

"Can't say I'd turn them down," Morris said, sounding slightly relieved as he too returned fire at the bad guys.

"What would you ever do without us to save you damsels in distress," Davis added, also firing at the bad guys.

A couple minutes later, Mathews ducked behind cover to reload. As he slid the clip into his gun, he glanced at his watch and didn't really like what he saw.

"She needs to be in that courtroom in fifteen minutes," Mathews said, looking up at his partner worriedly.

"Get her out of here," Lewis shouted, over the gunfire before Morris could say anything.

Neither detective liked the idea of leaving their friends in the middle of a gunfight. However, as the minutes ticked by, the chances of Lowell getting away with murder loomed larger. A few minutes later, they reluctantly left. As they ran, Carley prayed for the safety of the two brave detectives.

After a frantic race, the detectives got Carley to the courtroom door with just seconds to spare. She entered just as the judge called the courtroom to order.

The two detectives were standing outside of the door when a man in an expensive business suit walked up to the door. As the man approached, both detectives glared at him.

"I see that you two are still in good health, so I can assume that the young lady is as well," Lowell said, hints of disappointment entering his mild tone.

"That's right; three strikes, you're out," Morris said, still glaring daggers at the murderous businessman.

"How very mature," Lowell replied, dryly sarcastic.

With one last nasty look at both of them, Lowell entered the court room. Neither they nor Lowell himself were very optimistic about his chances of winning. Sure enough by the end of the day Lowell was found guilty of murder. A finding that absolutely no one was surprised about. The only thing that surprised anyone was that the jury was only out for about an hour.

* * *

As Alicia finished the story, the crowd clamoured to find out what happened to the other detectives. All of them wanted to know if they survived or were killed by Lowell's thugs.

"If you wonderful people would stick around after the intermission, you'll find out," Alicia said excitedly into the mic.

This announcement was met with equally excited applause. Sure enough, once the intermission was over, everyone was back in their seats.

THE END

CHAPTER 10

The Chase

Once the intermission was over, Alicia walked back out onto the small stage. The second that she did, the crowd started chanting, "What happened?"

"Since you guys have been so awesome, I'll tell how Lewis and Davis found and arrested Lowell, as well as how they come to be in that alley," Alicia suggested, stepping forward on the stage as the crowd fell into an anticipatory silence.

* * *

For Detectives Lewis and Davis, the shift had started like hundreds of others. After rollcall, they grabbed a cup of coffee from the breakroom. The two detectives then headed toward the bullpen. Lewis had short blond hair and green eyes. On this particular day, he was wearing blue jeans, a light-blue button-down shirt, with a dark-grey blazer. Davis, on the other hand, had black hair and grey eyes, wearing a forest-green t-shirt under a tan leather jacket and grey jeans.

"You get the rest of the papers on the Philips case to the DA that he wanted," Lewis asked as they walked down the hall.

"Yep, took them over yesterday," Davis replied just as they reached the door to the bullpen.

"Do you think he'll be satisfied with them this time?" Lewis asked as he opened the door while trying not to spill his coffee.

"You've got to learn to be a little more positive," Davis said, shaking his head as they sat down at the desk that they shared.

With that the two of them got busy doing the paperwork that was left over from yesterday. Just as they were starting to make progress, the captain's secretary walked up and put another stack on their desk. She just smiled as they scowled lightly at her.

"Whatever did we do to deserve such a thing, Emma?" Lewis asked with a look of mock hurt on his face.

"I'm sure you'll think of something if you try hard enough," Emma replied, placing her hands on her hips.

"You wound me deeply," Lewis replied, placing his hand over his heart to accentuate the look of mock hurt still on his face.

"I try," Emma said without missing a beat, not at all phased by the look.

Davis couldn't take it anymore and started laughing quietly at his partner. Said partner realized he was being laughed at and picked up a piece of paper, crumpled it into a ball, and threw it at his friend.

"Lewis, Davis, get in here and make it snappy," Captain Miller barked, sticking his head out of the door to his office.

Hearing the tone in their captain's voice, the two

detectives immediately stood up. As soon as they entered the office they closed the door.

A few minutes after they entered, two other detectives joined them, Morris and Mathews, if they remembered correctly. They only half listened as the captain talked to them. The only thing they really picked up on was that there was finally a witness against Adrian Lowell, a fact which both of them were quite happy about.

"Davis, Lewis, I want you to bring Adrian Lowell in," Captain Miller said, turning his attention from the other two detectives.

"Since he knows we have a witness that saw him murder someone, he's going to go so deep underground that he's going to get in a traffic jam with groundhogs," Davis said, sounding a little skeptical.

"I don't care if you have to dig so deep that your shovels melt. I want Lowell in cuffs," Captain Miller instructed firmly.

"Let's go. We've got a lot of digging to do, D," Lewis said, nudging his partner.

Lewis and Davis both stood and left the office. As soon as they entered the bullpen, they went straight to their desks. The first thing that they did was picked up their phones and start making phone calls.

When the phone calls yielded nothing, the detectives turned their attention to their computers. They were trying to see if they could find anything helpful on the system. Including past associates and places he had hidden in the past.

After about an hour, Lewis and Davis had again not

found anything. The detectives decided to try a different angle. So they figured they'd hit the streets to see if they could find anything that way.

It took a little over ten minutes of driving around before anything shook loose. This development came in the form of car driving recklessly, who the detectives immediately pulled over. Once the car pulled over to the shoulder, both detectives got out and walked up to it.

"What do we have here?" Davis said, looking into the driver's window.

"Looks like its Philip Rogers, who happens to be Adrian Lowell's driver," Lewis added as he looked into the passenger window.

"How about you jump out of there; we need to have a little chat," Davis instructed as he took a couple of steps back.

"If you're okay keeping an eye on things, I'll run him," Lewis said, gesturing back to their unmarked police car.

Rogers got out and walked to the end of the car under the cautious watch of Davis, passing the other detective as he did. Lewis slid into the driver seat of the car and ran Rogers. What came up on the screen was quite interesting. The detective slid out of the car and walked up to his partner.

"Find anything?" Davis asked, having just finished checking Rogers for weapons, a search that came up empty.

"I'd say so, our friend here has six warrants," Lewis said, shaking his head in mock disappointment.

"Looks like someone's taking a ride downtown," Davis said, making a circle motion with his hand, indicating for Rogers to turn around. While the detective did that, he also reached behind him and got his cuffs out.

"Put your hands behind your back," Lewis added as the criminal turned around.

"You can't do this," Rogers protested, starting to get upset and pull away.

"Yes, I can. You're under arrest," Davis said as his cuffs clicked closed around both of the criminal's wrists.

While Davis put Rogers in the back, Lewis slid into the driver's seat. Once he was inside Davis got in the passenger seat.

Not long later, they arrived back at the precinct with their prisoner. After booking, he was taken to one of the interrogation rooms.

Rogers sat on one side of the table and glared at the two detectives. They sat on the other side of the table staring unconcernedly back at him.

"What is it you guys want from me?" Rogers demanded, angrily glaring at them with his arms crossed.

"What makes you think we want something from the likes of you?" Davis asked, seemingly unconcerned.

"Cause I doubt you guys would haul me into an interrogation room over some traffic warrants," Rogers said, scowling at the two detectives.

"The man has a point, don't you think, D," Lewis commented, glancing from the criminal to his partner.

"Yeah, I do, and guess what, you're right," Davis agreed, calmly staring at Rogers with a thoroughly unimpressed look on his face.

"It's very simple, Rogers; what we want is for you to tell us where we can find your boss," Lewis said simply as he crossed his arms.

"I can't do that," Rogers said, shaking his head emphatically.

"Sure you can. We have faith in your ability to roll over like a good lap dog," Davis said while standing up and walking around to the other side of the table. He leaned against the table and crossed his arms as he stared down the crook.

"Except I don't have any reason to roll over for you boys," Rogers said, crossing his arms as he stared at the two detectives.

"That's where you're wrong. You're forgetting the warrants that we arrested you for," Lewis reminded, as if talking to a small child.

"Those were just traffic stuff, nothing to worry about," Rogers replied, waving his hand dismissively.

"You're right. Five of them are, but guess what lucky number six is," Davis added, still leaning against the table next to the criminal.

"I don't remember," Rogers said evasively as he shifted uncomfortably.

"Well in that case, why don't we help jog his memory. The sixth warrant was for possession of stolen property," Davis said, walking around behind Rogers and leaning against the table on the other side of the table.

"If you tell us where your boss is and anything else you know about him, we'll talk to the DA about knocking some years off your sentence," Lewis added, still sitting on the opposite side of the table.

"I don't know where he is, but I do know of someone who probably does. Steven Sinclair always knows where

Mr. Lowell is. That's all I know," Rogers said, sounding a bit desperate, knowing that he was looking at a ten-year prison sentence.

"There, was that so hard," Davis said, shaking his head as he stood up.

With that the two detectives left the room. A few minutes later, an officer came and took Rogers to the holding cell.

The detectives quickly ran the name Rogers had given them. Turns out Mr. Steven Sinclair has a rap sheet a mile long. That wasn't even the best part, which was that Sinclair had been last seen with Lowell less than a week ago. Sinclair was Lowell's accountant, so if anyone knew where the crime boss was, it would be him.

They were certain they had something to work with when they looked up his last known address. They decided that a stakeout was the best bet, hoping Sinclair would lead them to Lowell.

So the next morning Davis and Lewis parked outside the apartment building. The towering building was like any number around the city. The structure was all made of glass and steel from top to bottom.

Of all the things they did as police officers, stakeouts were by far the most boring. They watched as a seemingly endless stream of people came and went from the building. None of whom were the person that they were looking for.

It was four mind-numbing hours before the two bored detectives caught sight of the man they were looking for.

Finally, Davis thought as they saw the accountant exit the apartment building. As the man got into his car, Lewis started theirs. As their suspect's car pulled out, they waited a few minutes before following.

"Do you think he'll lead us to his boss?" Davis asked, keeping an eye on the suspect's car that was two cars ahead of them.

"We'll have to wait and see, but it's more than likely that he will," Lewis said as he worked to maintain the tail while avoiding being seen.

"We just have to not get caught before he does. Which won't happen if you keep driving that close," Davis added as they came pretty close to getting seen.

"If you think you can do better, why don't we switch places," Lewis snapped good-naturedly, keeping his eye on the target.

It took about twenty minutes of following Sinclair before he eventually stopped somewhere interesting. They watched as Sinclair stopped at an abandoned storefront. As the accountant went in, the detectives noticed that there was another car in the parking lot.

"Who do you think that our mystery guest is?" Davis asked curiously.

"Not sure, but it might be someone connected to Lowell," Lewis replied, feeling a bit optimistic.

"It might even be Lowell himself," Davis suggested, also hoping for the best-case scenario, though he was almost sure that they wouldn't get that lucky.

The detectives sat and watched the building for another twenty minutes. When still nothing happened, they started to get a little uncomfortable with how long it was taking.

"Do you think we should get out and see what's

going on?" Lewis asked, still watching the entrance to the storefront.

"I'm a bit curious about what their little chat in there is about," Davis agreed, glancing from the building to his partner.

With that the detectives got out of the car both getting out on the passenger's side to avoid being seen. Once they closed the door behind them, quietly they made their way to the back of the store, all the time being extremely cautious, very much aware of the bad guys inside.

As they crept closer to the building, they began to hear voices coming from inside. It wasn't until they got closer that they could begin to hear what was being said. There were two men talking inside the store. One of them they instantly recognized as Sinclair and the other was a man that they didn't know.

"Word on the street is that the cops are after Mr. Lowell again," the unknown man said, as if he were talking about something as inevitable as the weather.

"We both know how this one will end," Sinclair replied, sounding quite exasperated with the situation.

"Will these dumb cops ever learn that they'll never take down Mr. Lowell?" the unknown man asked, sounding flatly unimpressed.

"In order to figure that out, they'd have to have a brain," Sinclair replied, sounding as if he was talking about a particularly slow sheep.

The listening detectives shared unhappy looks. Neither thought much of what they had just heard the bad guys say. As the bad guys started laughing, both detectives knew that they were going to get the last laugh when the witness testified.

"Did you finish the arrangements that the boss wanted to be made, Mr. Moore," Sinclair said, bringing the conversation to the business they'd come here to discuss.

"Yes, I got the last of them done this morning," Moore replied, sounding quite pleased with himself in a really despicable way.

"Good, Lowell needs you to deliver these papers to the address on the envelope, and then he wants you to report to him," Sinclair instructed, not sounding very happy.

"Fine," Moore replied, sounding slightly annoyed.

After that the detectives heard the sound of footsteps heading toward the door. Realizing that the bad guys' meeting was over, they quickly got back to their car. Just as they got into their car, the two bad guys exited the building.

"We should definitely follow Moore. It seems it'll be more productive?" Lewis said as he watched the bad guys get into their car.

"Yeah, sounds like he might even lead us right to Lowell," Davis agreed as the bad guys pulled out, and they waited a few minutes before doing so as well.

The two of them followed Moore for about fifteen minutes before he stopped at a store. They waited as Moore went into the store for a few minutes. When Moore left the store, he took a quick look around before getting into his car and driving away. There was something about the look on Moore's face before he got into his car that made the detectives uneasy as they followed.

That uneasy feeling worsened as they followed Moore

into the warehouse district. It got even worse when they followed the bad guy into the largely abandoned area. The shadows had begun to lengthen, causing it to seem more ominous.

"I don't like this one bit, D," Lewis said, not liking how deserted this area was.

"Yeah, me neither. Say, partner, are you thinking what I'm thinking?" Davis asked, as the suspect pulled up in front of an abandoned warehouse.

"Yep, he definitely knows that we're following him," Lewis agreed, watching the suspect enter the warehouse.

"What are the chances that he's not very happy about it?" Davis asked, watching the windows of the warehouse.

"A hundred percent, I'd say," Lewis replied, glancing at his partner for a second before returning his gaze to the door that their suspect had just walked through.

"Let's go say hi," Davis said, reaching for the door handle with a mischievous smirk on his face that never ended well for anyone.

"You know I hate it when you get that look on your face," Lewis said, also reaching for his door handle while glancing at his partner.

Davis shot his partner his most innocent expression as they both got out of the car. The look on Lewis's face as their gazes met over the top of the car clearly conveyed his total disbelief.

"How about we call for backup instead of whatever crazy idea is bouncing around that crazy head of yours," Lewis suggested, the lightness in his voice taking any sting out of his words.

"That is a better idea," Davis agreed easily.

Lewis reached back into the car and picked up the radio mic. He called in for backup, requesting the backup units to park two blocks away and approach on foot. While they were waiting for their backup, the detectives worked out a plan for how they'd be going into the warehouse.

A few minutes later, four uniformed officers walked up. While being careful to not be easily seen by anyone inside the warehouse.

"Here's the plan. Mike, Jack, you guys will stick with my partner. Billy, John, you two are with me. You and your guys will take the back, while we'll take the front," Davis outlined. Once he got a nod from each of the four uniformed officers they split up.

Before they got very far, the man in the warehouse started firing at them. All the police officers scrambled for cover behind the unmarked car. Based on the number of bullets being fired at them, it quickly became clear that they were outnumbered.

"If you'll cover us, we'll try to make it around back to flank them," Lewis suggested as another round of bullets hitting the car punctuated the sentence.

"Alright, on the count of three," Davis suggested, making eye contact with his partner, wordlessly admonishing him to come back with no extra holes.

Lewis replied with a nod, signifying that he'd do his best. On the count of three, after a very sincere heartfelt prayer, the detective rushed from behind the car and toward the nearby concrete barricade followed a fraction of a second by the two officers. As they ran, bullets zipped past them and impacted the ground at their feet.

As he stood up to return fire, Lewis and the two officers slid behind the barricade. As soon as he did, he was met with increased fire. The last thing the detective saw as he ducked back down was a bullet that came uncomfortably close to his partner.

A couple seconds later, he chanced a glance around the car. When he did, he saw his partner and the two officers with him disappear around the corner of the building.

You better be careful, Davis thought, as he ducked back behind the car.

"Let's keep these guys busy," Davis said, glancing at the two officers while he changed the clip in his gun.

"Sounds good to us," John said after sharing a look with his partner and checking the ammunition in his own gun.

With that the three police officers simultaneously stood and again fired at the warehouse. Which unsurprisingly caused an increase in the fire coming from the bad guys.

A couple minutes later, they heard gunshots inside the warehouse. As soon as they did, they rushed toward the building. To their surprise, as they rushed up to the building, only a few shots were fired at them.

"Looks like whoever's inside is a little to busy to pay attention to us," Billy commented, sounding a little surprised.

"How about we get in there before those boys have all the fun," John commented as they ran toward the building.

It only took them about a minute to reach the

warehouse door. Davis immediately checked to see if the door was locked. Unfortunately it was, though none of them were very surprised about that.

"Billy, you go left; John, you're on the right; and I'll take the centre," Davis instructed as the three of them stood ready on either side of the door.

After receiving a nod from the two officers, Davis kicked in the door. As soon as the door gave way, they stepped into pure chaos. The first thing they did was find cover while locating the position of their fellow officers. The bad guys clearly heard them enter, causing them to turn and start to fire at the officers.

The fire fight didn't take very long after the three other officers entered. After about ten minutes, all the bad guys wisely decided to surrender and were taken into custody. The four uniformed officers transported them to be booked.

As soon as they secured the scene, the detectives began looking around for clues. There were papers covering the table and quite a few on the floor as well. They both began looking through each and every one of those papers, looking for any mention of Lowell's location.

"Do you think that Sinclair knows where Lowell is hiding?" Lewis asked while looking through a handful of papers.

"Probably, we'll just have to ask him when we get back to the station," Davis replied without looking up from the papers he was reading.

"The tough part will be getting him to tell us," Lewis replied thoughtfully.

"I don't think that we're going to need to have that

chat with Sinclair after all," Davis said, his eyes fixed on the paper in his hand.

"Why, what did you find?" Lewis asked as he put down the papers he had been looking through.

Lewis stood up from where he had been sitting on the opposite side of the long table. He walked over to where his partner was sitting. Whatever his partner had found it must be pretty important.

"According to this, Lowell will be visiting several of his front businesses this afternoon," Davis said, holding up the piece of paper in his hand.

"You know what I think? A big shot like Lowell deserves a welcoming committee," Lewis suggested, quite certain Lowell wouldn't like the welcome that he had in mind.

"Good idea, and I know just the guys to do it," Davis agreed, hoping he would get to be the one to slap the cuffs on the crime boss after what had happened with the last witness they had that was willing to testify.

With that Lewis and Davis left the job of going through the papers to the other detectives. They headed to the first business on the list. Unfortunately they missed Lowell by a matter of just a few minutes. As they headed to the next location, they hoped that they'd have better luck. The next location was a dry cleaner that was suspected of cleaning a lot more than just dirty clothes. Just as they pulled up across the street, a black sedan parked in front of the dry cleaner's shop. The first people out of the car were two bodyguards, followed less than a second later by Lowell himself. After the crime boss looked around at his surroundings, he and the rest of his group quickly piled back into the car. The second they were all back inside, the car screeched off, leaving nothing but burnt rubber in its wake.

"Yuh know what, I think he recognized us," Lewis commented as the car sped away.

"And he left without even saying hi. Now that's just rude," Davis said, shaking his head in mock disappointment as he started the engine.

The next instant the unmarked police car took off after the fleeing criminal with lights and siren. They determinedly followed as the sedan weaved in and out of traffic, trying desperately to lose them. When that inevitably didn't work, the pursued car sped up significantly. Unfortunately that meant the police car had to speed up as well or risk losing them. To make matters worse, the fleeing vehicle again started weaving through traffic, only this time going much faster. This caused multiple near misses with surrounding cars. The fleeing car sometimes missing the other cars by a fraction of a second and mere inches.

"That driver was already going to be taking a ride for failure to stop. Now we can add reckless driving," Lewis commented as the car they were chasing just barely missed sideswiping another vehicle.

Not long into the pursuit, some black and whites joined in. Together they tried to box in Lowell's car. However, just as the car in front was manoeuvring into position, but before it had quite gotten there, the suspect's vehicle managed to slip past. Unfortunately in the process of doing this, he tapped the back bumper of the police car.

"Now he's going to get charged with damaging police

property," Davis commented as the car that was hit dropped out of the chase and pulled over to assess the damage.

Within about ten minutes, the chase had moved from the city centre and onto the highway. Since all the police officers involved with the chase knew without a shadow of doubt that this car wasn't going to stop of its own accord, they knew they had to do something to stop it. Davis called into dispatch requesting a spike strip be deployed, a request that was quickly granted. Their luck held as it turned out there was a highway patrol unit a couple of miles ahead of them that agreed to deploy the spike strip.

A few minutes later, the detectives heard over the radio that the spike strip had been successfully deployed. It wasn't very long before the highway patrol unit reported Lowell's car had finally pulled over to the side of the road. They advised the highway patrol unit to keep an eye on the suspect's car but not to approach without backup.

It took the unmarked and the three black and whites only a few minutes to reach the scene. When they got there, the three PD cars and the patrol unit quickly surrounded the suspect's car. The occupants of the car were instructed to stick their hands out the windows. Instead of following said instructions, they began firing at the officers. Fortunately, suspecting that this might happen, Lewis had called into dispatch and had traffic redirected so no innocent passing motorists would be injured or killed.

A few minutes into the exchange of fire, Davis noticed a figure moving away from the car out of the corner of his eye. Turning his attention fully to the retreating figure, he realized it was Lowell. Who clearly planned to slip away while his bodyguards and driver kept the cops busy. A plan that the detectives intended to totally ruin.

While being careful not to be seen by Lowell's bodyguards or driver, the partners moved out from behind the car. They quickly made their way into the field next to the highway. Once they were sure they were far enough away so as not to be seen by the bodyguards, they picked up their pace in an effort to catch up with Lowell.

It didn't take the detectives very long before they caught up with Lowell. As the crime boss came into view, Lewis put on a burst of speed. Just as the detective got within arm's reach of the criminal, he tackled him to the ground. As the two men struggled on the ground, Lowell elbowed Lewis in the ribs in an attempt to get free. Unfortunately for him, that attempt was quite unsuccessful as the detective's hold remained firm. In another bid for freedom, the criminal tried to reach for the detective's gun that was in a holster at his side. Just as the crime boss's hand touched the rough-textured grip of the gun, he heard something that made him freeze, the click of the safety of a gun being disengaged.

"Don't even think about it," Davis threatened; he was about two steps away from where the detective and the crime boss were struggling with his gun aimed at said crime boss's head.

"Are you saying that if I try to kill your partner, you'll kill me?" Lowell asked with a hint of mockery in his voice.

"Do you really want to find out?" Davis asked simply, his tone of voice cold.

"No, I don't think that I do, Detective," Lowell replied, that same note of mockery still present in his voice.

"Good. Now get off of my partner. Get down on the ground with your arms straight out to your side," Davis instructed, glaring at Lowell.

"You surely can't expect me to lay sprawled on the ground in this suit. Why it's worth more than both of you make in at least a month," Lowell protested, his tone dripping with put-upon superiority as he gazed condescendingly at the detective standing over him while he got off the other detective and began to stand up.

"Why not? You were more than happy rolling around on the ground in it when you were trying to kill me," Lewis replied, standing up.

"Now get on the ground with your hands out to the side," Davis instructed, his gun still pointed unwaveringly at the smug criminal.

While glaring venomous fire at the two detectives, the crime boss reluctantly followed the instructions. All the while silently planning his vengeance.

"Mind if I do the honours?" Lewis asked, reaching behind him and pulling out his cuffs.

Davis made a go-ahead gesture, and Lewis walked over to the silently seething crime boss. The blond detective proceeded to cuff the criminal while his knee rested lightly on the small of the suspect's back. Once the cuffs were securely around Lowell's wrists and locked, Lewis helped the man to his feet. As soon as they were both standing up right the detective searched the suspect for weapons or anything else illegal. When he'd finished, he didn't find anything.

"What do you say we go see how the others did with

this guy's friends," Lewis said, holding on to his prisoner's arm.

"Good idea, then we can take him to the station, get him booked, and in his cell before our shift ends," Davis agreed, gesturing to Lowell while his eyes never left his partner.

The three of them headed back across the field toward the flashing lights of the police cars. As they got closer, they noticed that the gun fire had completely stopped. Though whether that was a good thing or not was still to be determined, as they were not yet close enough to see who had won the gunfight.

A few minutes later, the group reached Lowell's car. The two detectives were relieved to find a uniformed officer searching it. The officer must have heard them approach as he stood up and turned in their direction.

"I see you got him," Billy commented, seeing Lowell standing with them in cuffs and sounding quite pleased with that fact.

Both detectives nodded, then turned their attention to the car.

"Find anything interesting in there?" Davis asked, gesturing to the car with a curious expression on his face.

"Not much; just an unregistered firearm near the driver's seat. No drugs or anything like that," Billy replied, gesturing to the 9 mm handgun sitting on the roof of the car.

"Looks like the driver is going to be charged with that as well," Lewis added, his eyes following the officer's gesture.

"How did things go here?" Davis asked, glancing around, looking for Lowell's lackeys.

"The driver and the bodyguards are in custody," Billy reported, pointing at the other black and white.

"The only casualty was Billy and J's black and white," Mike commented, gesturing to the police car that had quite a few bullet holes.

"I already called a tow truck since it won't start," John added, pointing to the bullet holes in the engine area of the police car.

It didn't take very long for the officers to get things settled at the scene. Once that was done, the detectives took in Lowell while the officer took the driver and bodyguards in.

All the way back to the station something did not sit well with Davis. The something was the look on the crime boss's face when they put Lowell in the back of their car. What was bothering him was the smugness of the criminal's expression. The detectives couldn't figure out what a crook who was sitting in the back of a police car in cuffs could look so smug about. However, one thing was completely certain, whatever it was, it wasn't anything good.

Not very long later, the unmarked police car arrived back at the station. As Lewis helped Lowell out of the back of the car, the criminal smirked smugly.

"You really should just release me now and save us both time and me a lot of money," Lowell said, his voice dripping with superior smugness.

"If we did that, you'd miss out on the joys of being booked and tried for murder," Lewis replied, completely dead pan.

"Such a pity, you could have saved the taxpayers a lot of money," Lowell said, shaking his head in disappointment.

"Contrary to what you clearly believe, you are not better than anyone else," Davis stated bluntly, while glaring at the criminal.

"On that you are very sadly mistaken, Detective Davis," Lowell replied, sounding as if he was talking to a particularly annoying flee.

The two detectives made eye contact as they silently fumed about what the criminal had just said. When they broke eye contact, they, not exactly gently, led the smug criminal into the station. They handed him over to the officers as quickly as they could. Neither of them wanting to be around the smug murdering crime boss any longer than they had to.

When they had done that, they headed to the bullpen to do their reports. As soon as they were finished with their reports they headed to the captain's office to hand them in. On top of that, they needed to talk to the captain about something important. Lewis knocked on the door of their superior's office.

"Come in," Captain Miller said, looking up from the papers he was going through on his desk as his detectives entered.

Both detectives had grave and serious looks on their faces as they entered. Together they put their completed reports on the captain's desk.

"Good job bringing in Lowell," Captain Miller commended, not liking the looks on the faces of his two detectives.

"About that, something is very wrong," Davis said thoughtfully as he leaned against the file cabinet next to the door.

"What is it," Captain Miller said, not liking the sound of this at all.

"When we brought Lowell in, he was really confident that he'd be out of here in no time," Lewis said, scowling as he leaned against the wall on the other side of the door.

"Yeah, and he was totally certain that he'd get away with that murder," Davis added, not sounding any happier about it.

"He's already tried to kill the witness twice. You think that he's going to try again," Captain Miller stated with a scowl.

"Yes, Captain, we do," Davis said, crossing his arms with a scowl of his own.

"Alright, I want you to find out who, how, and when. Get on it. The trial starts tomorrow morning," Captain Miller instructed, while also dismissing them.

"We intend to do just that," Davis said, straightening from where he was leaning.

"That's exactly what we plan to do," Lewis agreed, also standing up straight.

With that the two detectives left their captain's office. As they did so, they shared a determined look. Neither wanted to see that smug crook get away with murder again.

As soon as they entered the bullpen, they headed straight for their desks. When they reached them, they noticed that there was a stack of papers on each of their desks. They immediately began looking through them. It didn't take very long for them to realize that they were the papers from the warehouse they hadn't looked through yet.

"Do you think that we'll find anything in here?" Davis

asked, indicating to the stack of papers on his desk with the ones in his hand.

"I sure hope so, 'cause we're running out of other leads," Lewis said, looking up from the papers in his hand.

On that encouraging note, they got back at it. They began going over every single line of each and every document. Unfortunately most of said documents were purchase orders or maintenance reports, which weren't particularly helpful.

Nothing seemed to happen for about twenty minutes, and the only sound coming from the two detectives was the sound of shuffling paper. That was why it was so startling when that silence was broken rather abruptly.

"I think I found what we're looking for, partner," Lewis said, sounding both excited and hopeful, his eyes still fixed on the paper in his hands.

"What did you find?" Davis asked, standing up from his chair and walking around the desks till he was standing next to his partner.

"According to this, Sinclair hired four guys for a hit that is supposed to take place in a parking lot," Lewis explained, finally looking up at his partner.

"Now we just need to find out which parking lot and when," Davis commented, tapping his chin thoughtfully as he leaned against the desk.

"Why don't we just ask Sinclair? I'm sure if we ask nicely, he'd be happy to tell us," Lewis suggested, holding up the oh-so-incriminating piece of paper.

"Good idea. Let's go see what our criminal acquaintance

has to say," Davis said with a smirk, clearly looking forward to the little chat.

Not very long after that, the two detectives were on one side of the table in one of the interrogation rooms. With the criminal lieutenant was on the other, looking quite confident. A look that they were about wipe away completely.

"You cops don't have anything on me," Sinclair declared confidently as he glared at both of the two detectives.

"Are you so sure?" Davis asked, while opening the file in front of him.

"Yes," Sinclair replied sharply, still totally confident.

"Then what do you call this?" Lewis asked, picking up the top document in the file and sliding it in front of the criminal.

"But you can't possibly have this," Sinclair said, after reading the document.

"And yet we do," Davis replied, crossing his arms as he glared at the not-so-confident criminal.

"If that witness dies, you'll go to prison while your boss walks free," Lewis threatened, standing up, placing his hands on the table, and leaning forward.

"The only way to keep that from happening is to tell us where and when the hit is going down," Davis added, staring down the criminal.

"Alright, the hit is going down in a parking lot three blocks from the courthouse tomorrow morning when the trial starts," Sinclair said, sounding defeated.

The next morning, Davis and Lewis arrived at the parking lot. Unfortunately, the only thing they found was the car that Morris and Mathews had been using. Luckily it was empty; however, there were a good many bullet holes in it.

Just as they were starting to get worried, they heard gunfire. So they followed the sound to an alley not very far way. The tires screeched as they pulled up. Seeing their fellow detectives and the witness in trouble, they immediately jumped out to help them.

"Thought you could use a couple hands," Lewis said as he took cover next to the other detectives and fired at the bad guys.

"Can't say I'd turn them down," Morris said, sounding slightly relieved as he too returned fire at the bad guys.

"What would you ever do without us to save you damsels in distress," Davis added, also firing at the bad guys.

A couple minutes later ,Mathews ducked behind cover to reload. As he slid the clip into his gun, he glanced at his watch and didn't really like what he saw.

"She needs to be in that courtroom in fifteen minutes," Mathews said, looking up at his partner worriedly.

"Get her out of here," Lewis shouted over the gunfire before Morris could say anything.

The instant the other detectives left, the fire from the bad guys intensified. Clearly, said bad guys wanted to get rid of them as soon as possible so they could go after the witness. A plan both Davis and Lewis had every intention of totally ruining.

When Davis stood up to return fire, he got a graze on his arm. That caused him a jolt of pain in his arm while returning fire. Just as he ducked back behind cover, he saw one of the bad guys go down. Though how badly said bad guy was hurt he didn't know.

"Surrender and we'll get medical help for your buddy," Davis called from behind cover, not really expecting for them to actually do it.

However, much to the surprise of both detectives, a few minutes later the bad guys did surrender. True to their word, they called for EMS. It turned out that two of the other bad guys were also injured. All the wounded bad guys were treated and taken to the nearest hospital under the guard of a uniformed officer.

"Guys, my partner is hurt," Lewis said, calling the paramedics over.

The two paramedics walked over to the partner. Their attention was instantly on the detective that was sitting on a crate.

"It's just a scratch," Davis protested, his gaze flicking between the paramedics and his partner.

"How about we take a look at it anyway," one of the paramedics suggested, spotting the rip in the detective's jacket with blood on the edges.

Davis opened his mouth to object, but the sharp look his partner shot him caused him to close it. Sure enough, it was just a scratch, which the paramedics quickly bandaged.

Once that was done, the two detectives headed over to the courthouse. They sat in the gallery in of the courthouse. When the jury returned a guilty verdict, Lowell didn't look at all smug or superior anymore.

* * *

The conclusion of the story was met with relieved clapping. The crowd was quite happy that the two detectives made it out of that hairy situation. They also quite enjoyed the whole story.

Alicia asked the crowd what they thought of Lowell. The response was immediate and resounding as boos filled the air. After that she asked what they thought about what happened to him, which got a resounding cheer.

"You guys have been an amazing crowd. Goodnight, everybody," Alicia said as she put the mic back on the stand.

The crowd applauded again as Alicia waved and left the stage. Everyone was still buzzing with excitement as the lights on the stage faded.

THE END

PART 4

Fantasy & Legacy

CHAPTER 11

A Light in the Shadows

Alicia arrived at the museum banquet hall a little early. Today she was going to be telling a story at a medieval-themed fundraiser. When she got there, her manager went off to talk to someone on the other side of the room.

A whole bunch of people were busily buzzing around the large room. Those people were getting the large room ready for the event. It quickly became clear that something was wrong. Apparently one of the people that was supposed to be helping had called in sick. Because of that they were now shorthanded. They weren't sure whether they were going to be able to get it all done in time.

When Alicia found out about this, she immediately offered to help. With her help they were able to get the last of the preparations done. The last centerpiece was put in place just as people started to file in.

After the dinner was done, a chair was placed on the small, slightly raised platform in the front of the room. Alicia walked up and sat on the chair as she was handed a mic.

"Join me as we travel back to a time of knights and castles, only with a fun sci-fi twist. However, our adventure today will have little to do with either of these things. This story is focused on the ordinary everyday life of an ordinary little village. What is ordinary in the world in which this village exists is vastly different than what we'd consider ordinary. Unfortunately, things don't stay ordinary in this village for very long," Alicia said, introducing the story.

* * *

The bright sun was shining that afternoon in the small medieval village of Rosevale. Despite the early hour, the town was already bustling with activity. People went to and fro, most of them were in a bit of a hurry seeing as it was lunch time. This village was like any of the numerous ones dotting the landscape.

There was something that we would find quite unusual about the population of not only this village but the whole world. There is a percentage of the population that has special abilities. These abilities weren't magic or anything like that. Instead, they are genetic and passed though certain families. Abilities that can take any number of forms, depending on the person. These abilities had their limits and varied in strength from person to person.

One of the busy townspeople was a young woman named Cyrila. Her brown hair was long and straight with a small braid going down the middle in the back. She had matching brown eyes that took in the world around her. The young woman was the daughter of the innkeeper, whose name was Edith. At the moment, she was headed to get some bread for her mother. As she walked down Cook's Street, she looked around, seeing many of her friends. Many of whom waved to her as she walked past. She also stopped at a couple of shops and talked to a few of them for a few minutes. Once she finished, she continued to her actual destination which was, the baker. As she was headed in that direction, she saw another of her friends, the man who owned the pie shop.

"Good morning, Peter," Cyrila greeted as she walked past.

"Morning, Cyrila," Peter said, seeming a little distracted as he focused on what he was doing but still happy to see her.

"You seem quite busy this morning," Cyrila said cheerfully as she watched a lot of people stop at the shop.

"Yeah, it's really busy this morning," Peter replied as he put a new pie in the place of a pie that had just been bought.

The two of them chatted for a few minutes. Before Cyrila walked away, and Peter returned to his kitchen to go back to work.

Before the young woman had taken more than a couple of steps, another young woman about the same age stepped out of the shop across the street. The second that she saw Cyrila, she walked quickly across the street.

"What brings you out and about on this fine morning, Cyrila?" the other young woman asked as she walked up.

"Mother has sent me to the baker's. You wouldn't by chance want to come with me, Floretia?" Cyrila asked hopefully.

"As a matter of fact, I would. I'm sure Mother won't mind if I pick up a few loaves for us too," Floretia replied, happy to spend a little time with her friend.

The next shop was the baker, and the two of them entered, chatting about something that happened the day before. When they entered, they were immediately greeted by the delicious smells of freshly baked bread. Looking around, they saw the baker, Humbert, standing in front of his oven. He had just opened it, so they could see a tray of loaves inside. The tray suddenly floated about an inch off the bottom of the oven. Then an instant later, it floated out of the oven and over to the counter. Once there, the individual loaves floated up and onto a nearby cooling rack.

"I bet you're glad you don't have to reach into that hot oven or touch that hot tray," Cyrila commented once the last loaf was safely on the rack.

"Most definitely," Humbert agreed, turning to the two young women.

"How is the best baker in Rosevale on this fine afternoon?" Cyrila asked with a warm, friendly smile on her face.

"Quite good, and need I remind you that I'm the only baker. How are two of my favourite customers?" Humbert asked, returning the smile.

"About the same as always," Cyrila replied easily.

"Yeah, me too," Floretia added simply.

"I don't suppose there is any interesting news at the inn that you'd like to share?" Humbert asked hopefully.

"Now if you want to find that out, you'll just have to come down to the inn," Cyrila replied, her smile turning into a smirk.

"You, my dear, are much to strict," Humbert responded, shaking his head.

"Don't blame me. It's Mother's rule, and you know it," Cyrila replied, shaking her finger, her smile taking the sting out of her words.

"Speaking of your mother, I have her order right here," Humbert said, gesturing toward the pile of loaves with a wave of his hand.

"They look wonderful as always," Cyrila said, holding out the basket she had in her hand as she turned her gaze to the bread.

With an expression of concentration on his face, the baker's gaze focused on the loaves, causing them to float up and follow his gaze into her basket. She then handed him a small pouch of coins.

"And what can I get for you today, Floretia," Humbert asked, turning his attention to her.

"Just a couple of loaves," Floretia replied, handing him the coins and holding out her basket. A second later two loaves floated into it.

The two young women and the kind baker said their farewells, then the ladies left the shop. Once outside, the two of them parted ways as well.

Cyrila quickly left Cook's Street and headed back toward the inn. When she got there, she nodded to Godard who was manning the gate. Once inside the walls, she circled around the main building and entered through the backdoor, which opened into the kitchen. She was greeted by a delicious smell. That smell was coming from the large pot hanging over the fire in the hearth.

"How was Humbert?" Edith asked as she entered the kitchen while drying her hands with a small towel.

"He's just fine, Mother; here's the bread," Cyrila answered, while placing her basket on the table in the middle of the room.

"That's good. Remember we'll be getting in that large group of travelers this evening. I do hope that everything is ready," Edith said, fretting just a little.

"Everything's ready. I checked it all before I left. The bread was the only thing missing," Cyrila reminded as she took the loaves out of her basket and put them in a bowl.

"That's good," Edith replied, sounding relieved as she checked on the pot of stew, which was just about done.

"Do we know who they are?" Cyrila asked curiously.

"No, the messenger just said to expect a large group of travelers," Edith replied, shaking her head as she stood up.

"Would it make you feel better if I went out to the stables one more time?" Cyrila asked, indulging her mother.

"Thank you, dearest daughter. This is the first year that I've been running this place without your father," Edith said, a deep sadness in her voice.

"Yeah. I miss him too," Cyrila replied with the same sadness in her voice.

In the heavy silence that followed, Cyrila turned and disappeared through the door that she had entered through just minutes before. Her mind swirled with those painful thoughts as the door closed behind her.

It was only a couple of minutes' walk to the small stable building. When she entered the timber building, she saw a young man who looked to be a couple years older than her. The man had red hair and green eyes. He looked up from what he was doing when the door closed behind her.

"Any special reason you're checking up on me twice in one day?" the man asked as he placed his hand on the head of the horse he was standing next to, hoping that he wasn't in trouble because he really liked this job.

"Don't worry; it's nothing you did, Jerome. Mother's just worried because there's a big group coming in tonight," Cyrila explained, putting to rest his concerns.

"I'll be ready," Jerome replied, stepping back away from the horse. When he did, the horse made an annoyed sound. The horse handler told the horse to settle down.

"I've always wondered what it's like to talk to animals the way you do," Cyrila asked, her gaze flicking from the horse to the man.

"It's not much different than talking to a person. At least to me it isn't anyway," Jerome explained as best as he could.

"Well I'll let you get back to work. I've got to be getting back to the main house," Cyrila said, more cheerful than she had been when she'd entered.

The young woman nodded as the horse handler waved goodbye. Then he turned his attention to what he had been doing. Cyrila also turned and left the building.

Once outside, she walked over to and entered the back door of the main house. She made her way through the kitchen and into the main room. When she did, a couple of the cleaning staff was finishing tidying up the room. She spent the next couple of hours helping them make sure that everything was ready.

Just as the three of them finished, two locals entered through the front door. Unsurprisingly, both of them were people that she knew. They chatted as they sat down at one of the tables.

"Evening, Cyrila," Hugh greeted when she walked up to them.

The other one who's name was, John, raised his hand in greeting as his eyes locked on the front door.

"You two found out that we're getting in a large group of travelers, didn't you," Cyrila commented knowingly.

"Guilty as charged," Hugh said, not the slightest bit repentant.

About ten minutes later there was the sound of approaching horses. Sounds that were quickly followed by that of the gate opening, then there was a pause before it closed again. Accompanying that sound was horses coming closer.

A few minutes later, there were footsteps walking up the three steps to the front door. The door opening let in a gust of cool autumn wind. On the heels of that wind, the group of travelers entered and quickly closed the door behind them.

Cyrila watched as the fifteen men walked further into the room. She watched as they walked up to the small table she was standing behind. An older middle-aged man seemed to be the leader of the large group.

"My brother and I will be needing separate rooms. The rest of our men will stay in the common room," the leader said, barely looking at her.

"Will you be needing separate rooms or would you like a single room with two beds?" Cyrila asked, her eyes flicking between the two men.

"One with two beds will be fine," the leader replied shortly.

"Very well, if you'll follow me," Cyrila said, leading the two men up the stairs leading to the second level where their room was.

After returning downstairs, the young woman noticed that some locals had arrived and were talking to the travelers. She heard some talk about the fact that it was market day tomorrow. However, most of the talk was unsurprisingly about what was happening outside of their little town. Her attention was suddenly drawn away from the conversations when the group's leaders returned to the main room.

Throughout the evening, Cyrila had learned a couple of things about the group of travelers. The most clear of them was that she didn't care for the leader's brother. She wasn't really sure why, but there was something about him that felt off. Just the sight of him made her skin crawl, and she wanted to get as far away from him as possible. The man's name was Lothar. He and his brother were traveling merchants, at least that's what they said they were. She wasn't really sure whether or not she believed them.

It appeared that others didn't share the young inn keeper's opinion. The man had a silver tongue and had managed to ingratiate himself with quite a few of the locals. She was almost glad when the gate closed behind the last local at the end of the day. She was exhausted by the time it was time for everyone to go to bed.

The next morning when the young woman emerged from her room for breakfast she got some news that wasn't very good. The group was going to be staying for an unknown amount of time.

After breakfast, Cyrila headed out to the market square.

She decided that she was going to enjoy market day and not think about creepy merchants as she walked around the paved circular area that was lined with many booths.

After walking around for quite a while, the young woman decided she was getting a bit hungry. Looking around for something to eat, she noticed a huckster she recognized.

"Hello, Sten," Cyrila greeted as she walked up to the young man.

"Afternoon, Cyrila. Do you want something?" Sten greeted, holding out the tray with straps around his shoulders, carrying pies and other food.

"Are they still warm?" Cyrila asked, her question only partially serious.

"You wound me. Of course they are," Sten said, putting his hand over his heart with a look of mock hurt on his face. As he did this, he ran his other hand over the food on his tray, using his abilities to heat up the food.

"I'll have a beef pie," Cyrila requested, pointing to the one she wanted.

Sten handed her the pie, and she handed him the money. He walked away as she looked around and found somewhere to sit to eat her food. She quickly found one and walked over to it.

After the young innkeeper was done with lunch, she continued walking around. When she walked up to the carpenter stall. She looked at the items on display. As she did, something caught her eye.

"You have a good eye, Miss Cyrila. That is quite a beautiful piece," the owner of the stall said, noticing that she seemed quite focused on a small wooden box with a pretty flower pattern carved on the lid.

"I'm trying to decide if I should buy it," Cyrila replied with a slight smile on her face.

"Would you like a closer look?" the owner asked, picking up the small box and holding it out to her.

"I think I will buy it," Cyrila said. After that they began discussing how much it cost. When they reached an agreement, she handed him the money.

As Cyrila put the box in her satchel, she pulled out the list her mother had given her. Unrolling it, she mentally ticked off the things she had already bought. There were only a little under half the things left on the list.

About twenty minutes later, she was nearly done with her list. She only had one item left. As she looked for it, she again saw something that she had noticed a couple of times throughout the day. In that time, she saw that creepy guy Lothar skulking around and talking to quite a few people. Sometimes it was in groups of three or four; other times it was one on one. She still wasn't sure what it was about the guy that she didn't like. That's why she tried to shake off the feeling and finish off her shopping.

Once Cyrila finished her shopping, she headed home. When she arrived home and took her cloak off, she looked around for her mother. Just as she was about to call out to her, Edith walked down the stairs.

"How was market day?" Edith asked as she walked up to her daughter.

"The crowds were impossible, but I managed to find everything on the list," Cyrila replied, sounding tired.

"Clearly they weren't impossible seeing as you got everything," Edith replied, with a playful smile on her face.

"You are the impossible one, I see," Cyrila countered, shaking her head as she walked into the back kitchen area.

"I try," Edith replied, following her daughter.

"Did anything interesting happen here while I was gone?" Cyrila asked as she put her basket on the table.

"That's not quite the word I'd use to describe it," Edith said, a slight scowl on her face as she thought about it.

"What happened?" Cyrila asked, not liking the sound in her mother's voice.

"That man Lothar pushed Elia for not getting out of the way fast enough. All the girl was doing was using her abilities to clean up any dust in the main room," Edith explained, still not looking even the slightest bit happy about that.

"She has to concentrate really hard to gather the dust together and throw it away. He should of been considerate of that," Cyrila said, scowling unhappily.

"I told him if he continued to behave like that, he and his group can find alternative accommodation," Edith said, crossing his arms. She immediately got a nod of complete agreement from her daughter.

After that their conversation turned to more trivial things. As they were chatting they put away all the things that were in the basket.

About two and a half weeks went by with nothing out of the ordinary really happening. However, during that time when she'd walked around town, something had felt off. It felt almost as if there was a dark cloud hanging over the town. Every day it seemed like that cloud seemed to be getting worse. It seemed as if the whole town was getting angrier and angrier. So throughout that time, she did the only thing that she really could and that was pray.

To make matters even worse, the two supposed traveling merchants who didn't seem to have anything to sell were still in town. A fact that no one at the inn was really happy about. They'd all been hoping the group would be gone by now.

Cyrila was walking down the street. She could feel a tension in the air that had never been there before. There wasn't the chatting, laughing, and just general hum she had grown accustomed to. She thought about all these things as she stepped into the baker's shop.

"Good morning," Cyrila said as cheerfully as she could while looking around as a frown appeared on her face.

If anything, the tense atmosphere was ten, maybe fifteen, times worse in here. When the young woman entered, the baker turned his attention to her. When he turned around, she was expecting the friendly expression that she had seen on his face so many times. Instead he regarded her with suspicion until he realized who she was. His expression changed to one that was quite heavily tinted with sadness.

"Morning, Cyrila," Humbert greeted with that same sadness in his voice as he placed a tray of loaves on the counter.

"So how is business for my favourite baker?" Cyrila asked, with considerably less enthusiasm than she had before.

"Not so good anymore," Humbert replied, wishing that this woman's attitude was still shared by everyone else.

"That's really awful. Why would that be?" Cyrila asked, her concern for her friend thick in her voice.

Before the baker could answer, a man came in. It was someone she recognized as a local farmer who lived next to her friend Floretia. The instant he entered the shop, it was abundantly clear that something was very wrong. There was a nearly tangible tension between the two men as their eyes met. Which was quite odd considering the fact that they had always been quite good friends.

"What can I get you?" Humbert asked, sounding more reserved than he had ever been in his entire life.

"Just three loaves," the man said, looking like he wanted to be anywhere but where he was as he walked over to the counter.

The baker reached over, picked up the loaves, and handed them to the man, who immediately turned and walked out of the shop.

"I don't understand. The two of you have always been such good friends," Cyrila said, looking completely confused.

"That's what I thought too, but it appears that's not the case," Humbert replied, sounding deeply sad as his eyes slid down to the counter.

"I'll just have our usual order," Cyrila said, the look on her face clearly showing that she still thought of him as her friend.

The baker motioned the young innkeeper forward toward the counter. When she did he quickly looked around to make sure no one was watching. Once he was sure that no one was watching, he carefully used his abilities to put the loaves in her basket.

"Thank you. I'll see you later," Cyrila said, with a reassuring smile.

"Yeah," Humbert said, with the slightest hint of a smile on his face.

With that the young woman turned and left the shop. When she stepped out onto the street, the sun had started to set.

As Cyrila began heading back to the inn, she thought about everything that had happened in the baker's shop. That's when she realized something that sent a cold chill down her spine. She suddenly realized that he had been trying to hide the use of his abilities.

This led the young woman to another startling realization. As she had been walking down the street, she realized she hadn't seen anyone openly using their abilities. In fact, now that she thought about it, it had been quite a while since she had seen anyone doing so. Though why this was happening she didn't know.

There was one thing that was very clear to the young innkeeper, whatever was happening was slowly tearing her home apart. It was extremely painful to watch her friends turn on each other this way. The worst part of the whole situation was that no one seemed to want to do anything to stop it from happening.

One moment Cyrila was about to walk past the opening of an alley, the next thing she knew, someone lunged out from the darkness and put their hand over her mouth. He then pulled her into the alley. When they were deep enough into the alley that they were hidden from the light of the torches lining the street, the man shoved her against one of the walls. He then held a knife to her throat with a hate-filled look in his eyes.

"If I take my hand off your mouth, will you scream?" the man asked, voice just barely above a whisper.

Cyrila shook her head as much as she could while being careful of the knife as she looked into his eyes.

"That's good to hear, 'cause you and me've got to have a little chat," the man said, taking his hand off her mouth.

"I don't know about your conversation skills, but you're sure good at getting someone's attention," Cyrila replied, trying desperately to hide how scared she was.

"You are a spunky one, arn't you. I've been watching for a while now, and you seem awfully friendly with those people," the man said, pure hatred dripping off the last two words like slime off of a slug.

"What people?" Cyrila asked, totally confused, having no idea who he could possibly be talking about.

"I'm talking about the people with those wretched powers. That think they're so much better than us regular folks," the man sneered, that same hatred burning in his eyes.

"None of them have ever thought that they were better than anyone," Cyrila countered, her voice shaking ever so slightly.

"You better listen and listen good, Girly. You need to decide whose side you're on. Either you're siding with them or your own kind," the man said, holding the knife blade just a little closer to her neck.

Without saying another word, the man let her go. As she sank to the ground, he turned and walked away without a single backward glance.

After a few seconds, the young woman stood up from the ground. She managed to push herself up onto her legs, which felt like they could barely support her. As soon as she did so, she made her way home as quickly as she could. All the time she tried not to think about what just happened.

When the welcome sight of the inn gates came into sight, she didn't think she had been so happy to see anything in her entire life. As soon as she reached the gate, she immediately knocked on it. Right away she could hear Godard on the other side moving around for a few seconds before the gate was opened.

"It's awfully late to be out, Miss Cyrila," Godard commented, as soon as he opened the gate and saw who it was.

"I guess it is," Cyrila replied, still trying not to think about it and being only marginally successful at it.

"Mrs. Edith is really worried about you being so late in coming home," Godard informed, noticing that something was not right as he stepped aside to let her in.

"Thanks for telling me. I'll go find her right away," Cyrila replied as she stepped through the gate.

As the young woman began walking toward the main building, she heard the gate close behind her. In order not to disturb any of the guests, she headed around to the kitchen, noting idly that she went in that way almost more than the front door. The instant that she walked through the door, she saw her mother standing there with her arms crossed and worry burning in her eyes.

"And where have you been, young lady," Edith asked, her voice stern with very strong undertones of worry.

"I'm sorry, Mother," Cyrila said, her voice trembling just slightly.

The tone in her daughter's voice caused Edith to rush forward and draw her into a hug. The instant that her arms encircled her daughter, she shuddered. The innkeeper gently guided her daughter over to a chair and got her to sit down. Once seated, the young woman pulled out of the hug and wrapped her arms around herself.

"Now start at the beginning, and tell me what happened," Edith said, pulling another chair alongside the other one.

Cyrila took a deep breath as she collected her thoughts. She then explained everything that happened in the alley. Including what the man had said to her and that he had threatened her. By the time that she was finished her hands were shaking.

"Could you tell who this man was?" Edith asked, putting her arm around her daughter as concern and anger warred inside her.

"No, he was dressed all in black and the alley was dark," Cyrila answered, shaking her head with a disappointed look on her face.

"What about his voice? Did it sound at all familiar?" Edith asked, hoping for any way to identify the man.

"I'm afraid not, he had a cloth around the lower half

of his face, which changed the sound of his voice," Cyrila answered, shaking her head again.

"Is there anything that you do remember about him?" Edith asked gently.

"The only thing that I remember about him is that he has brown eyes. Which is unfortunately very common," Cyrila replied with a frown.

"That's alright; why don't you go off to bed," Edith said, gesturing off toward her daughter's bedroom.

"Alright," Cyrila replied, having to blink to keep her eyes open as she stood up from the chair and gave her mother a hug.

After that, the young woman drowsily made her way to her room and prayed before getting into bed. Once in bed, she was so exhausted that she went right to sleep.

The next morning Cyrila woke to the unpleasant sound of breaking glass. That was, followed by the sound of something wooden breaking. She sat up and slipped her shoes on. As soon as they were on, she rushed out of her room, through the kitchen, and into the main room. The sight that greeted her was that of an all-out brawl.

"Just what is going on here?" Edith demanded, her stern voice raised to be clearly heard over the din of the fight.

At the sound of the innkeeper's voice all movement in the room stopped. Everyone immediately turned their undivided attention to her.

"Someone had better tell me who and what started all this," Edith demanded, her voice making it clear that if the guilty party didn't speak up, there would be consequences for all of them.

"That girl dared to use those wretched abilities right in front of me," the leader of the group of travelers said, with disgust clear in his voice.

In the strained and tense silence that followed, you could have heard a pin drop. The thunderously angry look on the innkeeper's face made it so no one wanted to be the one to break the silence.

"Such behaviour is not allowed here. I'm afraid that you'll have to seek accommodation elsewhere," Edith said, her voice tight with barely contained anger.

"Fine," the leader said through gritted teeth as he prepared to turn and head out the door with his cronies.

"Before you leave, you still owe me for your two and half week's stay. You'll also be paying for all of the damages," Edith said, a touch of vindictiveness entering her voice as she held out her hand while staring the man down.

"Why should I give you anything?" the leader asked, with a sneer.

"Because if you don't, I'll send someone for the under-sheriff," Edith replied, sounding very much like there was nothing she'd like more than to see him hauled away in chains.

The leader of the miscreants gritted his teeth as he threw a bag of coins at her. With that he and his trouble-makers turned and left the inn. It was quite safe to say no one there would miss them, even a little bit.

Once they were gone, Edith, Cyrila, and the three maids got busy cleaning the place up. It took them a couple of hours, but they managed to get the place into some semblance of order. However, they were going to need to buy a couple of new chairs and a table.

Cyrila decided to head over to the carpenter's shop to see if he had the furniture. She brought Godard with her to carry them. As the two of them walked down the streets, much to her great sadness things didn't seem any better than they did the day before. The only good thing that happened during the whole trip was that she was able to get the furniture.

Over the next week, things in the little village continued to get worse, with animosity toward those with special abilities getting worse with every passing day. It had gotten so bad that none of those with special abilities dared use them unless their doors were locked and their shutters were closed. Even then they didn't use them very often. Throughout this time, she continued to pray.

Cyrila and the maids had just finished cleaning up after some other travelers that had just left. Even Elia seemed frightened to use her abilities, even though she knew she was safe there. It was as if she was beginning to believe that there was something wrong with her because she had these abilities. Something neither of the innkeepers were very happy about.

Suddenly a frantic pounding on the door broke the subdued silence that had engulfed the building. Nearly as one, the five of them looked over at the door. After a second, the banging came again. This broke them from their surprise, and Cyrila rushed over to the door. When she opened it, on the other side was her best friend, Floretia, shaking like a leaf, breathing hard, and looking like she had been crying. Edith instantly sprang into action and led the trembling young woman over to the nearest chair.

"Go get her some water," Edith ordered, glancing at her maids before turning her attention to the clearly upset young woman.

"Yes, Ma'am," the oldest of the maids replied before the three of them hurried off to do as instructed.

"How about you tell us what happened to get you in such a state?" Edith asked, with motherly concern in her voice.

"This morning an angry mob showed up at our farm," Floretia began, her voice hitching a little as she remembered.

"What happened? What did they do?" Cyrila asked, knowing full well that she was not going to like the answer.

"They burned down our barn. Papa tried to stop them, but they wouldn't listen," Floretia answered, a single tear streaking down her cheek.

"Were you able to get the animals out?" Cyrila asked, placing her hand on her friend's shoulder, her voice both concerned and sad.

"Yes, we got the animals out, then I came here for help. I knew we wouldn't get it anywhere else," Floretia answered, her voice dripping with sadness.

"Don't you worry; as soon as you finish this, Cyrila, Godard, and Jerome will go with you to make sure that everything is alright," Edith said reassuringly as one of the maids handed her the cup.

Floretia took a deep breath and nodded as she accepted the cup. As soon as she was done with the water, she stood up.

The four of them immediately headed out together. When they reached the farm, all that was left of the barn was a smouldering pile of ash. Thankfully the house was still intact and the harvest hadn't started yet. Best of all, Floretia's father, Luke, was unharmed as he stared morosely at the ruins.

First, the group from the inn made sure that the fire was completely out. After that, they helped the farmer build a temporary enclosure for the animals. There really wasn't much else that could be done till the farmer got enough money to buy the materials for a new barn. However, he couldn't do that till he harvested his crops, which he couldn't do without a barn to put them in. This left him with a bit of a chicken and an egg problem. On that sombre note, the farmer thanked them for their help, and they returned to the inn.

That night before climbing into bed, Cyrila knelt by her bed and began to pray. As she had done every night since this whole mess had started, she prayed that God would help their village out of this terrible situation. She also asked if he wanted her to play a role in saving her home, that He'd tell her what that was and give her the courage and the wisdom to be able to do it. Once she was done praying, she stood up and slid into bed, hoping that tomorrow would be better, but somehow knowing that it wouldn't be.

The next morning, everyone was awoken to the frightening sound of an angry mob pounding loudly on the thankfully still closed gates. All of those living and working at the inn scrambled out of their beds to try and figure out what was going on. When they approached the gate, they could hear the mob talking about how they were going to run all the people with special abilities out of town. Something that was only possible because none of them were serfs.

"Open up! We know that you got some of them hiding in there," someone shouted from the other side of the gate as the pounding continued.

"Why don't we come back for them after we take care of these ones," another of the angry mob suggested between the banging sounds.

It seemed that the rest of the mob agreed with him. The pounding stopped and they could hear the large group of people moving away.

"I'm going out there to talk to them," Cyrila declared as she reached to remove the bar from the gate.

"You should let the undersheriff handle it," Edith suggested, her real worry that she could be hurt left unsaid but nonetheless understood.

"He's not here. Someone has to go out there and talk some sense back to them before something terrible happens. More importantly, I know this is what the LORD wants me to do," Cyrila said with complete certainty.

"Since I can't stop you, alright," Edith replied, sounding totally terrified.

"Make sure that you bar the gate after me, and please pray for me," Cyrila said, then pushed the gate open and stepped out.

Once the young woman was through, they closed and barred the gate. After that they all went into the middle of the main room of the inn and began to pray. As much as they wanted to help her, they also knew that if the mob wouldn't see her as a threat, it increased the chances that they'd actually listen. The same couldn't be said if they all went out.

Meanwhile, outside Cyrila quickly spotted the larger group that had a small group in front of them. The mob was prodding the smaller group forward with sticks. As she got closer, she could see who was leading the group it was, those two creepy merchants. Now she knew that they were merchants of hate. She could also hear what the mob said. Things like how it was unfair that they could do things no one else could, and that they thought they were better than regular folk. Not wasting another moment, she picked up the pace.

"Wait," Cyrila shouted, stepping between the two groups.

"What do you want?" Lothar asked with a sneer.

"Yeah, this has nothing to do with you," someone in the mob shouted from near the front.

"Go back to your inn, or better yet, bring us those two that you're hiding," someone else shouted from further back.

"I'm here to talk some sense into all of you. These are our friends and neighbours. Name one time any of them have ever, in word or deed, given the impression that they thought they were any different than anyone else, let alone better," Cyrila challenged, looking into the eyes of as many of the locals as she could.

There was a murmur in the crowd as they each tried to think of something. None of them could think of a single time.

"You talk about fairness, how many times has Luke used his ability to make plants grow on your fields and only asked for one or two bushels in payment. When you were able to grow twice as many bushels than you'd otherwise be able to grow because of it. Another thing, you talk about these people being able to do something that you can't, so what. Lydia, you can sing like an angel, while Henry over there sounds like a strangled toad. We all have things we're good at; the things that they can do are no different," Cyrila said, gesturing to the people behind her.

Many of the local people started nodding as they thought about what she'd said. While others laughed at the toad comment.

"Everything is so easy for them," one of the merchants' men shouted, not really liking where this was going.

"Easy? I can't count how many times Humbert got a headache after a particularly busy day. I can think of many times any number of these people have been so exhausted by the end of day from over taxing their abilities. I'm sure you can too," Cyrila challenged, again focusing her attention on the locals in the group.

There was a murmur of agreement that swept though the crowd. Many of them began to question if what they were doing was right.

"These outsiders come to our village and spread their poisonous hate. Now all of you have to decide whose side you're on. Theirs or that of people you've known all your lives," Cyrila said, her challenging gaze sweeping over the crowd.

One by one people began walking over to stand behind Cyrila. Before long all that was left of the angry mob was the hate merchants and their men, who were the only people to be run out of town that day.

It took some time for the bonds of trust and friendship to be rebuilt. To that end, all those who had been involved in burning down Luke's barn rebuilt it out of their own pockets. Slowly but surely, the little village returned to the happy place it had been. Leaving that whole incident as both a memory and a lesson.

* * *

The end of Alicia's story was met with soft clapping. It was clear that those in the crowd were still a bit lost in thought, but nonetheless still enjoyed the story.

THE END

Labyrinth of Shadowstone Manor

The chatter of the milling crowd filled the brisk, early October air. Today she was at an event called Dragon Days. The crowd was buzzing with excitement as Alicia stood in the backstage area of the outdoor stage. She closed her eyes as she savoured the music the medieval musicians were playing. One of the stage managers walked up to her, breaking her out of her revelry.

"You'll be up as soon as they're finished," the young woman said absently while going over something on the clipboard.

"I'll be ready," Alicia replied confidently, her voice chipper and her eyes sparkling with anticipation.

The woman nodded, then immediately turned and walked away. As she did she said something into the head-set that she wore.

Still enjoying the music, the storyteller picked up the stack of papers on the small table. She began going over the pages, making sure she was ready.

As the last notes of the last song floated in, she fin-ished with the last page. Simultaneously the announcer stepped onto the stage as the musicians finished. She called for a round of applause for the musicians. Once the clapping died down, they gathered up their instruments and left.

"Next up, we have something that I'm sure many of you are really looking forward to. Join me in welcoming Alicia, one of the most well-known storytellers in the country," the announcer said, gesturing to the opposite side of the stage.

At the gesture, Alicia stepped onto the stage. Looking out at the crowd, she walked to the middle of the stage as the announcer walked off.

"Considering the theme of this event, I'm sure that this will come as a surprise to none of you. I'm going to tell you a story about dragons," Alicia said, waving to the crowd.

The crowd chuckled and clapped in response.

"Together we are going to delve into a world of dragons and sword fights, where there lives both men and monsters. We will be entering the country of Vaner. More specifically, our story takes place in the town of Langer. In that small town a family not unlike any other lived in a modest but sturdy house among the beautiful rolling hills a short ride from the town," Alicia began, the introduction drawing more people's interest.

* * *

On a bright sunny day, a small family was heading home. They'd spent the day gathering berries and other food in the forest, none of them aware that they were not alone in their journey.

Upon reaching their home, the father helped his wife,

who was holding their two year-old-daughter, down from her horse. He then led both horses over to the barn.

While her husband took care of the horses, the mother took their daughter inside. The young girl was asleep in her mother's arms.

"Are we home, Mommy?" the little girl asked, gently rubbing the sleep out of her bright-blue eyes as the door closed behind them.

"That's right, sweetie," the mother replied, with a fond look in her matching eyes as she first slipped her own shoes off, then those of her daughter.

"Is Daddy outside taking care of the horses?" the little girl asked, her blond hear mixing with the woman's own golden strands.

"That's right. He should be in soon," the mother replied as she walked further into the house and toward the small kitchen, after putting her daughter down.

About ten minutes later, the door opened and closed. The sound was quickly followed by the little girl excitedly exclaiming "Daddy."

"I see you're awake, Aldith," the father said, catching her as she gleefully rushed into his arms.

The little girl giggled as she was picked up.

"Now where did my lovely Anwen get off to?" the father asked, his voice warm while making a show of looking around.

"In the kitchen, Carron," Anwen replied, her voice just as warm, with a smile on her face.

"That smells good," Carron said as he walked into the kitchen and up to his wife, hugging her from behind.

"Well that's good because it's ready," Anwen said as she felt the comforting feeling of her husband's strong arms encircling her.

Both parents laughed as they felt small arms wrap around their right legs. Looking down, they found blue eyes looking back up at them. Patting her daughter's head, Anwen grabbed two pot holders and picked up the large pot. Stepping out of the comforting embraces, she carried the pot over to the table and put it down. As she did that, the other two sat down at the small table. After a prayer of thanks for their food, the happy little family ate their evening meal. Once finished, the three of them headed off to bed.

A couple of hours later, Carron suddenly and unexpectedly sat up straight, coming awake in an instant. Less than a heartbeat later, he knew why he was awakened.

"What's wrong, My Love?" Anwen asked, rubbing her eyes after having been woken up by her husband's abrupt movement.

"I heard a noise coming from Aldith's room," Carron answered, sounding concerned as his feet hit the floor.

Hearing that, Anwen was instantly wide awake as well. She quickly slipped out from between the blankets and stood up.

Together the two of them silently slipped out of their room and made their way to the room next to theirs. Carefully opening the door, they entered the room. As quickly as it had arisen their concern faded.

The sight that greeted them melted both of their hearts. There on the bed was the most adorable white and blue dragon that ever lived, which looked to be about the same age as Aldith. The adorable little lizard was wrapped around their daughter and both were sound asleep.

"What do you think, Carron?" Anwen asked, keeping her voice low as she watched the sleeping pair.

"It's uncommon for a connection to be formed at such a young age, but it has happened," Carron answered, his voice a gentle whisper.

"They say that the longer a pair are together, the closer they will become," Anwen commented, a fond smile forming on her face.

"I suspect that these two will be together for the rest of their lives," Carron replied with his own fond smile.

Their talking apparently woke the little dragon up because it let out a couple of protective little squawks, which were almost as adorable as the little creature itself. In response they each held out their hands for the little one to sniff. When it did, it apparently realized who they were as it resumed its previous position and went back to sleep. Following its lead, the couple retreated to their own bed and were quickly back to sleep themselves.

The next morning the three of them found out the Magistrate had caught some dragon poachers not far from them. The poachers had just killed a mother dragon that had been seen with a blue and white female pup. They informed the Magistrate the pup was with them and had formed a connection with their daughter.

Sixteen Years Later . . .

Aldith and her dragon Acha had just landed in a field a couple of miles from their home. After sliding off her back, the young woman reached into the saddlebags and pulled out the lunch that her mother had packed. She sat down in the soft grass. An instant later, Acha laid down behind her, the dragon's smooth scales a pleasant warmness against her back. Opening the small basket, she couldn't hold back a smile finding a note from her mother sitting on top of the food.

"Double A, don't forget that you need to get home early today because your uncle is coming over," Aldith read aloud, smiling fondly at the nickname.

Acha let out an amused rumbling reverberating through her slender, graceful body. At the same time the dragon licked Aldith's hand that was holding the paper. Afterward, the amused dragon placed her head back on her front paws and continued to enjoy basking in the sun as her human friend put the note in her pocket and ate her lunch.

About thirty minutes later, Acha's head shot up and she let out a warning growl. The dragon's sharp blue gaze locked onto the surrounding bushes, her powerful muscles tense and ready to strike at the first provocation.

This roused Aldith from her pleasant half doze. Her hand immediately grasped the handle of her sword that was at her waist even before her eyes were fully open. Once they were, she quickly followed her dragon's intense gaze to a cluster of bushes about four feet away.

Four men slithered out of the bushes, all of them armed with various weapons. Two carried maces, another an axe, and the last a short sword. Their clothes were shabby, only slightly above rags, and smelling of the rotting vegetation of the forest floor.

"Hand over your dragon, Girly, or we'll kill you and take her," the leader sneered, his eyes greedily taking in the beautiful dragon as she surged to her feet.

"I got a better idea. You take your bunch and crawl back under the rock you came from," Aldith suggested as Acha's front legs planted on either side of her.

Acha growled menacingly as fire ignited in her mouth.

"Will ya look at that, looks like she likes my idea too," Aldith added mockingly, tense and ready to draw her sword.

With an enraged snarl from the leader, the four men charged at the pair. If that wasn't bad enough, two more groups of four slithered out of the bushes on the other two sides of the roughly triangular clearing.

The snarl was intertwined with the sound of Aldith drawing her blade. Unsurprisingly the leader charged at her with his mace raised high above his head. As she swung her sword, skillfully deflecting the blow, it caught the sun and glistened.

As the leader's blow continued its downward path into the ground, one of his lackeys charged her with a short sword. Their blades crossed, forming an x. Thinking quickly, she kicked her opponent's legs out from under him to break the standoff. After that, the two began slashing at each other. Neither side landed a blow till Aldith managed to get in a lucky blow, hitting her opponent in the side of the head with the pommel of her sword, knocking him out.

At exactly that moment, the leader managed to pull his mace out of the dirt where it had gotten stuck. He quickly spun to face the young woman. Aldith instantly spun around to face him with a fiery glare aimed at him. The two of them again faced off.

While her human fought, Acha attempted to defend herself from the nasty, smelly, evil human attackers. Her whip-like tail was nearly continuously striking out. With each swing, she knocked at least a couple of the attackers off their feet. Suddenly three or four of the attackers jumped onto her tail, trying to pin it down. Frustrated at the uncomfortable weight on her appendage, she roared and threw them off, sending them flying back into the bushes from whence they had come.

At the same time, the dragon swiped at the attackers with her razor-sharp claws. With every swipe, the men were barely able to avoid getting cut to ribbons. If that wasn't tough enough, they had to scramble out of the way of streams of fire that were shot at them.

In the chaos of the fighting, the dragon failed to notice

one lone attacker crouched in the bushes. A dart from that attacker flew past all the human combatants. Unnoticed by anyone, it hit the dragon in the neck. She immediately began feeling disoriented. Shaking her head in an effort to clear it had absolutely no effect on the feeling.

Before Acha could regain control and focus on her surroundings, a huge net was thrown over her. Her efforts to dislodge the net knocked the dart in her neck loose, and it fell to the ground at her feet. She sniffed the dart and found that it was dipped in a herb mixture that had a sedative effect on dragons. The drowsy feeling began to get worse, and she began swaying on her feet.

As the dragon fell to the ground, barely awake, she saw her human place herself between her and the men. When the young woman reached her, she held her sword defiantly. As she slipped into unconsciousness, she felt her friend place her hand on her head reassuringly.

"Put them both in the cage," the leader instructed, almost sounding disappointed that he wouldn't get to kill the young woman.

"What for?" one of his lackeys asked, sounding confused.

"The boss might be able to use her to control the beast, you brainless halfwit," the leader said, as if he was talking to a clod of dirt.

"You better put your sword down if you want to stay with your dragon, Missy," Another lackey suggested, as if talking to a small child with his arms crossed.

The leader scowled as the young woman glanced at each of them. It was clear by his expression that he wasn't happy about the delay. Finally, after just under a minute, she dropped her sword, clearly realizing that she had no chance against so many by herself. As her sword clattered to the ground, she was knocked unconscious from behind.

After what was, in his opinion, way to long, both the dragon and the girl were loaded into the cage that was mounted on the back of a wagon. The instant the door clanged loudly shut, the wagon rumbled forward.

Nearly fifty minutes later, the two unfortunate occupants of the cage woke up. The swaying motion of the wagon was the first thing Aldith became aware of as she returned to consciousness, quickly followed up with the pounding pain in her head. Each bump of the road sending a spike of pain into her brain that felt like a white-hot poker.

The intermittent hisses of pain coming from Aldith caused Acha to force herself back to wakefulness a little faster than she would otherwise have. As she forced her eyes open, she let out a concerned whine at another hiss of pain from her friend.

"I'm alright," Aldith said reassuringly, patting the dragon's head.

The dragon let out the most disbelieving shriek she could muster.

"You worry to much," Aldith said with fond exasperation.

For that, the young woman got a puff of smoke blown in her face.

"Was that really necessary?" Aldith asked, blinking from the smoke.

Based on the expression on the lizard's face, she thought it was.

After that the two of them lapsed into a tense, worried silence. Neither of them knew what faced them at the end of this journey. Each mile that the wagon traveled brought them that much closer to that uncertain fate.

Somewhere around two and a half days later, the wagon stopped and a group of soldiers approached it. Once the poachers received a bag of coins, the wagon was turned over to the soldiers. As the poachers disappeared back into the bushes, the wagon was driven away.

Darkness had completely fallen when they finally reached their destination. It was a dark and foreboding manor. The dark structure seemed to absorb every bit of moonlight that hit it. The only light escaping the building was the little bit of lamp or candlelight coming from the windows.

The cage was quickly brought inside and placed in one of the largest rooms. Suddenly the dark ebony door opened, and a man walked into the room. As the door closed behind him, he walked over to the cage. He then slowly walked around the cage like a hungry predator. As his eyes took in the dragon, they filled with a greedy desire to possess. The man was in his early forties with brown hair and cold green eyes. He wore the fine clothes of a nobleman.

"And what is this?" the man asked in a mocking, condescending tone.

"My name is Aldith, and Acha is my dragon," Aldith answered, glaring at the man while clenching her fists so hard they were shaking.

"In that case, allow me to introduce myself. I'm Lord Dunstan," Lord Dunstan introduced with a mocking flourish of his hand.

"Can't exactly say it's a pleasure," Aldith replied, her tone biting.

"Since this beautiful and rare dragon has already formed a connection with you, you'll just have to renounce that connection. Once you've done that, I'll form one with the beast myself, and she'll become the finest jewel in my collection," Lord Dunstan said as if what he was saying was a forgone conclusion and was simply the way things were.

"Never," Aldith replied, her voice showing that she'd rather die than comply with his demand.

The greedy nobleman stared at her in astonishment, clearly not having expected her refusal. He could hardly believe that an ordinary peasant girl would dare refuse him anything. This astonishment quickly turned into a burning, consuming fury.

"Chain them and take them to the dungeon," Lord Dunstan bellowed at the guards that were standing off to the side.

Immediately the guards began moving toward the cage. The men bound both of them in chains. In the process of doing so, they got hissed and growled at. As soon as they both were secure, they were forced out of the cage.

"You will never step foot outside that dungeon till you follow my order," Lord Dunstan shouted after them as the two of them were led away.

The actual trip down to the dungeon happened in a foggy haze. A haze that only lifted when the heavy metal door clanged shut. As both of them turned to face the door one of the guards stood there with the ring of keys in his hand.

"You really should have done what His Lordship ordered, girl," the guard said, looking at her like she was stupid.

With that the guard turned and walked away. As he was walking away he whistled a smug-sounding tune.

Once the guard left, darkness engulfed their small, dank cell. The darkness encompassing them was so oppressive that it felt like it would smother them. It was almost as if it was a physical, tangible thing that they could reach out and touch.

"Well it looks like we really got ourselves in a real predicament this time," Aldith commented, looking around.

With the combination of a look, a squawk, and a snort, the dragon replied, which clearly said, That, Dear One, is quite obvious.

In an effort to dispel the darkness even a little, Acha ignited a low flame in her mouth. The soft golden glow quickly spread around the room. Though the light that was emitted was dim, it was definitely enough to see by. After a quick glance around the room the dragon settled down at the back. Her human friend nestled against her, and she gently covered the young woman with her wing as the two of them drifted off to sleep.

One Week Later . . .

During that time both of them got a little lost in their seemingly hopeless predicament. Breaking out of that dour cycle, Aldith stood up and began looking around again. This time she was taking a much closer look. She was looking for anything that could help them get out of there. Unfortunately there was nothing in the small space but straw and a little water that dampened the cold, stone floor.

Not finding anything, the young woman began looking to see if she had anything on her person that could be helpful. For a few tense seconds, as she kept coming up empty, it looked like this search was going to have the same results as the last. Thankfully, after a couple of minutes, she found a small, narrow length of metal about the width of a fencing wire.

"Look what I found," Aldith said, holding up the piece of metal.

Acha had a skeptical and unimpressed look on her face. She seemed to be asking, What are we supposed to do with that?

"Hopefully we'll be able to use this to get out of these chains," Aldith said, rattling the chains binding her wrists.

The dragon made a happy chirping sound, clearly liking that idea a lot.

It only took a couple of minutes of trying for the young woman to realize the metal wouldn't be enough. It only took her a second to come up with the idea of Acha using her smallest claw in combination with the piece of metal. Working together, the two began working on the chains around her wrists. It only took a couple of minutes for the first one to click open. Now that they knew what they were doing, the other opened even quicker. As soon as she was free, the two of them quickly opened the chains binding the dragon.

Now able to move around freely, the pair turned their attention to the locked door. Looking down at the piece of metal in her hand they couldn't help wondering something.

"What do you think; should we give it a try?" Aldith asked, looking between the door and improvised lock pick.

With a chirp of approval, Acha nudged her human friend toward the door.

Taking that quite correctly as a "yes," the two once again got to work. They made quick work of the door lock. As the door swung open, they shared a victorious look. Though they both knew that this was only the first step in their efforts to escape.

As the two of them stepped out of their cell, the sight that greeted them was not very encouraging. The only thing that either of them were really aware of during their trip down to the dungeon was that it was a confusing labyrinth of tunnels. Now they had to tackle the difficulty of having to figure out which way to go. In front of them were no more than four different directions they could go. To make matters worse, there was no indication which way was the right one.

"Well, standing here staring at them isn't going to help anything. So I guess we'll just have to pick one and see where it goes," Aldith suggested, glancing at her friend.

Acha took a step forward, then looked searchingly down each tunnel. After a couple of minutes, she indicated the middle one on the right.

"That one's as good as any other," Aldith said as the two of them began walking down that tunnel.

The pair had been walking down the tunnel for about twenty minutes. Suddenly the two of them stopped in their tracks. The reason for this abrupt stop was that they heard noises from up ahead. The noise was the sound of men talking. Being extremely careful not to make even the slightest sound, they crept forward.

When they were close enough, they carefully peeked around the corner. What they found was four guards sitting around a table. They laughed and drank while playing cards. It was clear that the men didn't seem to be expecting any trouble.

Silently the pair slipped back into the hall. As they slipped back into the darkness, they were intent on coming up with some trouble that they could provide to the guards.

In the deserted hallway, Aldith found a small, empty, ceramic jar covered by a small cloth. An excited smile lit up her face as an idea popped into her head. She quickly explained her idea to her dragon friend.

First the young woman ripped a fairly narrow strip of the cloth. Next she poured some of the black powder that she carried to start campfires into the jar, while holding the strip of cloth in the centre to serve as a wick. Once there was enough powder in the jar to serve her purposes, she stuffed the rest of the cloth into the jar around the wick to hold it in place. Finally she picked up the lid of the jar, which Acha had already carefully cut a hole in. That hole was just the right size for the wick to pass through. The wick stuck out of the jar about four inches. Holding her little firecracker in one hand, Aldith picked up a sturdy-looking stick.

With that the pair were ready to put the plan into action. Just as they got into position and peeked around the corner, they found that all the guards were so engrossed in their game they weren't paying any attention to their surroundings. That was Acha's cue to light the fuse. As soon as it was lit, Aldith carefully tossed it in an arch so that it landed in the entrance to the other hall that was directly across from them, past the open area where the guards were. Thankfully, and a little surprisingly, it didn't break and rolled a couple inches down that hall. Even better, the fuse was still burning.

A couple of seconds later, the small explosion went off. Curious about the source of the small pop, two of the guards stood and headed off down that hall. At exactly that moment, the pair struck. Acha's tail lashed out and knocked one of the guards unconscious. Simultaneously Aldith hit the other guard on the head with the stick also knocking him unconscious. The two of them shared a slight victorious smile as the two guards hit the ground.

A couple of minutes later, the other two guards reentered the open area. Unknown to either of them, the two escapees waited on either side to the entrance to the tunnel. Before either of them knew what had happened they, too, were rendered unconscious.

After sharing a look, the pair began heading down the tunnel. When they reached the next junction, there were three branching tunnels this time. This time they decided to try the left tunnel.

The two of them had been walking for about an hour before they were again stopped dead in their tracks. Only this time it was a dead end that stopped them.

After a couple of seconds of glaring at the stone wall, the pair turned around. They headed back the way that they came. The plan was to try one of the other tunnels, certain that one of them was the right one.

Meanwhile in the manor house above their heads, a monk stormed down one of the many dark hallways. He had his fists clenched and he glared at the floor in front of him. It was quite clear that something was really bothering the man.

"I heard you were looking for me, Brother Gerallt," Lord Dunston said, stepping out of one of the doors that lined the hallway.

"Indeed I was," Brother Gerallt replied, with barely controlled frustration.

"What seems to be distressing you so, Brother?" Lord Dunston asked, his voice dripping with false sincerity and concern.

"You have the nerve to ask me what is distressing me. When just yesterday you lied to the Abbot and to all of us," Brother Gerallt accused, sounding frustrated.

"That is an awfully serious accusation to be throwing around, Brother. Just what was it that I'm supposed to have lied to you about?" Lord Dunston asked, his voice sickeningly smooth.

"You told us that the young woman that you have locked up in your dungeon tried to steal one of your dragons. That was a lie. The dragon with her is hers.

They have been connected since they were two years old. Before you try to deny it, I got a record of the connection from the Magistrate of Langer," Brother Gerallt accused, holding up a scroll.

"May I see that?" Lord Dunston said through clenched teeth.

"Certainly, this is only one of the many copies that are in my possession," Brother Gerallt replied calmly as he handed the scroll over.

"I see," Lord Dunston replied, his teeth still clenched as he halfheartedly examined the document.

Once the vile nobleman had finished his perusal of the document he handed it back. All the time he was desperately trying to come up with a way to salvage the situation. Suddenly a rather despicable idea popped into his equally despicable brain.

"Surely these uncomfortable facts don't have to go any further than the two of us," Lord Dunston said, his voice dripping with silky smooth persuasiveness as he pulled a medium-sized velvet bag out of his pocket.

Before the slightly bewildered monk could say anything the nobleman held out the bag, clearly offering it to the monk. There was a very distinctive clattering coming from inside the bag. As the monk stared at the bag as if transfixed, his lips were moving. When he took the bag out of the nobleman's hand, he got a sickly victorious smile on his face.

"You can keep your sparkly stones," Brother Gerallt said, dumping the jewels inside the bag on to the tile floor.

"We can't all be as virtuous as you, Brother Gerallt," Lord Dunston sneered, a look of such pure contempt on his face.

"That's where you're wrong. I do not possess any virtue, not even the smallest measure. Every bit of goodness in me comes from my Lord, Saviour, and Friend Jesus Christ," Brother Gerallt replied, his voice firm and confident.

The nobleman just stared at him, not really sure what to say. The last thing that he'd been expecting the monk to say was that.

"Do you have any idea how hard it was to refuse those jewels? Do you realize how many ways my mind came up with to justify it? It was only through His strength that I was able to refuse," Brother Gerallt replied, staring down the stunned man standing in front of him.

"What are you going to do now?" Lord Dunston asked, finally finding his voice once again.

"I'm going to do anything that I can to help free that young woman," Brother Gerallt answered, his voice filled with certainty.

"I could order you killed," Lord Dunston threatened, grasping at straws.

"But you won't," Brother Gerallt replied with absolute certainty.

The nobleman lowered his head and clenched his fists. As he watched the monk turn around, he now knew without a doubt that he'd lost this round.

"It is my sincere prayer that one day you realize that no amount of wealth or dragons will ever satisfy you.

When that day comes, I'll be more than happy to show you what will," Brother Gerallt said before walking away.

Meanwhile back down in the dungeon, Aldith and Acha reached yet another dead end. The two of them had been hitting a whole bunch of them for a couple of hours.

Aldith pounded the stone wall in utter frustration. After which she slid down the wall to a sitting position. She then drew her knees up and wrapped her arms around them. It had been a frustrating and discouraging couple of hours.

Acha cooed worriedly as she rubbed her head against her friend's shoulder. It had been a rough couple of hours. The worst part was that they had been doing so well when they took down that first group of guards. In a further attempt to cheer up her human, she nudged her friend's hands and cooed reassuringly. When she did the young woman looked up.

"Do you think that we'll ever get out of this place?" Aldith asked, sounding a bit discouraged.

The dragon nodded her head, certain that together they'd make it out. Seeing the unconvinced expression on her friend's face, she blew a puff of air at her human.

"You're right. Sitting here feeling sorry for myself isn't helping anything," Aldith said, running her hand over the smooth, warm scales on the dragon's head.

Putting action to that sentiment, the young woman stood up. After taking a deep breath, she picked up her stuff that had fallen to the ground.

Together the pair headed back the way they had come yet again. Both hoping that this would be the last time they'd have to do that.

Within about twenty minutes the two of them reached the intersection again. This one only had three branch tunnels. They decided to try the middle one.

This tunnel led to yet another intersection, this time with only two choices. The two of them took a few seconds to look between their choices. After which they decided to take the tunnel on the left.

To the pair's surprise, this tunnel was considerably shorter. As they neared the dead end of the tunnel, the dragon suddenly stopped in her tacks. Even more surprising was when Aldith tried to take another step forward, Acha gently pulled her back with her front paw.

"What's wrong?" Aldith asked once she regained her footing.

The dragon flicked her gaze to the ceiling and then it flicked meaningfully to the stone that the young woman had been about to step on.

Looking closer the young woman realized something quite startling. There was a pressure plate on the floor that would have dropped a grate a couple of feet behind them, which would have left both dragon and young woman trapped.

Being careful of any further traps, the two of them headed back to the fork. For what felt like the millionth time, they took the other tunnel.

About thirty minutes later, Acha suddenly perked up. She was suddenly at full alert and constantly scanning the area for danger. The dragon kept sniffing the air, and every time she did, she got even more alert and concerned.

"What is it that you smell?" Aldith asked, not liking her dragon's reaction and gripping the stick in her hand even tighter.

The dragon's only response was to growl and glare at the tunnel ahead of them.

Both of them were considerably more cautious as they continued down the tunnel. There was an almost menacing stillness in the air.

About ten minutes later Aldith finally knew what had upset her dragon. Distantly she could hear the sound of dogs barking. These weren't the kind of dogs that people kept as pets. These were either hunting dogs or attack dogs. No matter which they were, the escapees had to be very careful because both were very dangerous.

The instant Aldith and Acha rounded the corner they were greeted by vicious barking. Six rather large vicious-looking attack dogs charged at them. Reacting quickly, they turned and ran.

As the pack began to gain on them, Aldith desperately climbed onto her dragon's back. Just as one of the dogs leaped up to try to bite down on her foot, she pulled it up out of reach. The dog crashed to the ground and immediately jumped to its feet, angrily growling at the pair..

The pair ran down the tunnel as fast as they could. Both of their hearts were pumping whether it was from fear of exertion neither could really tell.

While the two of them were running a slightly crazy idea began forming in Aldith's head. By the time that they reached the fork, the idea was completely formed. The instant they entered the slightly open area, they darted down the tunnel leading into the fork. Seconds later the pack of attack dogs joined them.

As soon as all the dogs were in the open area, the dragon shot a stream of fire at the tunnel that the dogs had just left to keep them from going back that way. Once they'd done that, they began to use fire to push the pack down the other fork. They pushed the angry, snarling animals all the way down to the end of the fork.

With a satisfying clang, the grate fell, trapping all six dogs, unharmed. Clearly enraged by being denied access to their prey, several of the dogs snarled and threw themselves against the solid metal barricade. Which unsurprisingly had absolutely no effect on the barrier. With the angry pack's snarls echoing behind, they turned around. They were intending to check out what else was down that other fork.

Quickly reaching where the pair had been confronted by the dogs, they were met by yet another unpleasant surprise. This time it was six guards that were armed to the gills. All of them watched both of them with a condescending look.

"You think you're so smart, don't you, girly," the leader sneered, talking to her as if she was a small child.

"Only compared to some," Aldith replied, her grip on her stick tightening.

"Really, and who are they?" one of the others challenged, crossing his arms.

"Sorry, Fellas, I don't have a mirror on me at the moment," Aldith remarked, a slight mocking smile on her face.

"You're really going to get it now, girly," the leader said, his hands clenched so hard that they were shaking while he glared at her.

"Then come and collect instead of standing there talking," Aldith challenged calmly.

Before another word could be spoken, the six soldiers charged forward. They were all determined to recapture both of the escaped prisoners.

The only thing that gave our heroes a fighting chance was that the tunnel was quite narrow. In fact it was narrow enough the soldiers had to attack them two at a time.

The first pair of soldiers fell fairly easily, with both dragon and human working together in harmony. The giant lizard attacked with her tail, using it like a whip to knock the weapon out of the men's hands, as well as snapping at any soldiers that got to close. While the young woman's stick served to be a surprisingly effective weapon. She ducked and parried the soldier's strikes. While, attacking as many of his vulnerable points as she could manage. This continued till both of them were unconscious.

Immediately after they'd knocked the first two out, the next lucky soldiers stepped up. When they did the dragon roared, the sound filled with menace and warning. The two men tried to take a step back out of fear of the angry reptile. Unfortunately for them, their friends pushed them back forward. Realizing that there was no escape, they attacked. This fight was a bit harder for the two escapees, but in the end they won.

The third fight was the hardest of all. Due to the fact neither of them had gotten very much sleep or decent food for the last week. Unfortunately this was a disadvantage that their opponents were more than happy to take advantage of. Despite these difficulties, the two friends never gave up and fought furiously to protect each other. Their determination was rewarded as they surprisingly managed to win. None more surprised than the two of them.

As the last soldier collapsed unconscious the dragon and rider collapsed against each other in total exhaustion. Both counted their survival just short of a miracle.

"That was fun, but let's never ever do it again," Aldith said, her voice slightly breathless.

Acha replied with a slightly tired-sounding, amused snort.

"I have an idea; why don't we sit here for a little while and catch our breath," Aldith suggested, while reaching up and pulling her canteen off the saddle.

The dragon clearly liked that idea as she lay down behind her friend.

About fifteen minutes later, they were woken from their half doze by the sound of someone coming. This caused both of them to push themselves to their feet.

Out of the shadows stepped a man. This man was not who either of them had been expecting. The unexpected arrival was a monk.

"Who are you?" Aldith asked suspiciously.

"My name is Brother Gerallt," Brother Gerallt answered calmly

"I guess now that you found us, you're going to hand us over to Lord Dunston," Aldith said, gripping her stick a little harder.

"I would never dream of doing such a thing," Brother Gerallt replied, instantly sounding appalled by the notion.

"Then what are you here for?" Aldith asked, not having expected that response.

A growl from Acha served to reinforce the young woman's question.

"I'm here to help you escape," Brother Gerallt answered, as if it was the most obvious thing in the world.

"Won't you get into trouble?" Aldith asked, sounding concerned.

"Do not worry, Sister; nothing will happen to me. Come, we must go before those soldiers' reinforcements arrive, " Brother Gerallt replied, touched by her concern for his well being while beckoning her toward the direction that he'd just come from.

The monk led our heroes down the tunnel as quickly and quietly as they could, wanting to put as much space between the soldiers and them as possible.

Within about ten minutes they reached one of the few exits from the labyrinth. It was the only one that was outside of the manor.

Unfortunately news of the pair's successful escape quickly reached Lord Dunston. To no one's surprise, he was really mad about it. He glared accusingly at the soldier that had just done the unenviable task of informing him.

"Kindly, explain to me how one eighteen-year-old peasant girl evaded and or defeated many of my highly trained and supposedly highly skilled soldiers," Lord

Dunston said, his voice calm and cold with restrained fury.

"We tried our very best, Your Lordship," the soldier replied, his voice somehow steady despite the fear that was pouring off him.

"That has been made abundantly clear. Now get out of my sight," Lord Dunston ordered, his voice cold and threatening. He watched coldly as the soldier scurried out of the room.

Ten minutes later the nobleman stormed into his dragon stable. His long black coat billowed out like angry storm cloud as his angry strides carried him down the aisle between the eight dragon enclosures.

"Bring back that dragon, and kill that girl," Lord Dunston bellowed to his many dragons lining the room.

As the bellowed order echoed around the cavernous room, all eight of them stepped out of their enclosures. All of the giant lizards quickly left the stable building. Once outside, the powerful animals took flight.

A few hours earlier, Aldith and Acha excitedly emerged from the dark, cavernous tunnel system for the first time in over a week. Despite knowing that they weren't in the clear yet, they couldn't help the surge of excitement filling them. Each savouring the feeling of the sun shining down on them.

The instant that they were out in the open, Acha spread her massive and majestic wings. She let out a crone of pure enjoyment as the gentle wind caught them. It felt so wonderful to stretch her muscles after having to keep them folded for so long.

Aldith was just as happy to be outside again. She spread her arms and turned her face to the sun with her eyes closed. The sun on her skin felt like a warm hug from nature itself. A gentle, warm breeze ruffled her hair. She could hear the chirping of song birds off in the distance.

"I apologize for interrupting you. However, the two of you really should leave before more soldiers come," Brother Gerallt said, breaking them out of their revelry.

"You are correct. I don't know how we can ever thank you, Brother," Aldith said, gratitude in her voice.

"The only thanks that I require is that you promise to return safely to your family," Brother Geralt said, kindly handing her the saddlebags the guards had taken from her.

"That we promise," Aldith answered for both of them, accepting the bags and putting them behind her dragon's saddle.

With that Aldith got on her dragon's back. As soon as she was settled in the saddle, the dragon again extended her wings. With a few beats of her powerful wings, she launched them into the air.

In less than a minute, they were out of sight of the dark imposing manor house. Once they were, the monk also left.

The pair flew for about thirty minutes before they stopped. They needed both food and some clean water. The dragon landed in a small clearing in the midst of a forest. Once the young woman jumped down and grabbed her canteen, the dragon darted off into the forest. While she was gone, the young woman filled her canteen and took a long drink of water. Once she returned to the clearing, she started a small fire in the centre.

About thirty minutes later, the dragon returned with a deer. As she placed it near the fire, she felt the saddlebags removed from her back. She watched as her friend pulled out the tools needed for her to prepare her portion of the meat. While this was happening the dragon headed down to the river for a drink of water.

A couple of hours later, the two of them had their supper. Once they were finished, they curled up and went to sleep.

Early the next morning, Aldith and Acha were woken quite suddenly. Their abrupt awakening was caused by the sound of growling from the bushes. In an instant, both sprung to their feet, their eyes scanning their surroundings. When the growling came again, Aldith jumped on Acha's back. The instant that she was in the saddle the dragon took to the sky.

Once the pair got aloft, they were immediately surrounded by seven dragons, who were joined quickly by the eighth one. They were all growling at them menacingly. Two of them were green, another was a deep brown with wisps of green, two others were stone grey with a few sparkles of jewel tones, and finally the last one's pitch-black scales glistened in the sun. They were all circling the two of them like they were prey.

Before either of them could react, the entire group of enemy dragons began attacking them. The most distressing part was that they were majorly going after Aldith. Acha let out a distressed squawk as she narrowly dodged a ball of fire aimed at her friend. All of the other attacking dragons began shooting fire at them as well.

The dragon couldn't even enjoy the rush of the wind over her wings as she dodged out of the way of yet another attack. She gracefully manoeuvred around her opponents' attacks. Her beautiful blue and white scales sparkled in the sunlight as she flew through the sky like water. Just as a fire ball was about to hit her she dropped into a steep dive. This caused the attack to hit another enemy dragon instead.

Just as Acha dodged the next attack, the black dragon dove toward Aldith with its claws bared, intending to snatch the young woman off of her dragon's back. In order to keep this from happening she barrel rolled out of the way. When the black dragon's claws were met with nothing but air, it roared in anger at having its prey snatched away.

The aerial battle continued like this for another hour and a half. Thankfully the younger dragon's superior speed and stamina allowed her to escape the older, slower dragons. Unfortunately she didn't make it out of the fight unharmed. They couldn't afford to land to assess the severity of the wounds as they flew frantically toward their home.

In their mad dash for home, the pair flew through the night. Dawn was just touching the sky and lighting it up in its brilliant display of colours when they at long last reached their greatly missed home.

The exhausted dragon landed heavily in front of the porch. When she did, she let out a hiss of pain from the bite mark on her right front paw, which caused her to lift it off the ground.

Hearing the commotion outside, Carron and Anwen

stepped out onto the porch. The instant they saw who it was, they rushed toward the pair. Upon seeing that the condition of the pair, their concern skyrocketed.

"Mamma, Papa," Aldith said, tears in her eyes as her parents reached her.

"What's wrong, dearest? How did you get hurt? What happened to Acha? How did she get injured?" Anwen asked, worried tears in her own eyes.

"Just where have you been all this time, young lady?" Carron asked, his concern not very well hidden by the gruff sound of his voice.

Aldith tearfully explained the whole situation to her parents. The whole time she was trembling from the letdown of the adrenaline high that she'd been running on since she stepped out of that dungeon cell.

After the story ended, the parents shared a heartbroken and concerned look. Anwen was the one to break the look as she led her daughter into the house. While at the same time Carron led the injured dragon to the barn. Once they were safely inside, he assessed the dragon's wounds. Thankfully all of them were minor and would heal with no problem.

Inside Anwen made her daughter a cup of tea. While her daughter drank it, she prepared a bath for her and set out some clean clothes. After both of them, Aldith felt massively better.

A couple of months after the ordeal, things for the small family largely returned to normal. That is until one day the Magistrate paid them a visit. As they invited him in, they could tell that whatever he had to say was serious.

All four of them sat down at the small dining table. As Anwen got them all a cup of tea, the Magistrate took a moment to gather his thoughts. He explained that His Majesty the King had ordered an investigation into Lord Dunston, not only his actions to Aldith and Acha but how he acquired all his dragons. It was determined that he gained seven of his dragons through coercion or murder. The King, wanting to make an example of the wicked lord, stripped him of his title. He was then tried for the two murders he personally committed and was sentenced to death.

During the disgraced nobleman's last days, Brother Gerallt regularly visited him. He tried to lead the man to the LORD till the end. The Magistrate didn't know whether he was successful or not.

After talking to the family for a few minutes, the Magistrate left. All three of them were a bit surprised about how things had turned out.

* * *

There was a round of applause. After that died down, Alicia stepped off the stage. As the first notes of another medieval song started, she took a deep breath. When she stepped further into the backstage area, she couldn't help but wonder if she'd be able to do what Brother Gerallt had.

THE END

CHAPTER 13

The Quest for the Treasure of Wisdom

Alicia was travelling in a bus on a really, really long trip. She and everyone around her were bored to tears. It was nighttime, so no one could read, and there was very little else to do. One of the people sitting in the row of seats in front of her thought he recognized her. He turned to confirm his suspicion about who she was. When he did, sure enough, he found out that he was right.

"You're Alicia, the storyteller," the man said, sounding hopefully.

"That's right," Alicia said with a friendly smile.

As soon as she said that, the attention of everyone instantly turned to her. They all hoped for something to relieve the boredom.

"Could you tell us a story?" another man requested from behind her.

"Sure, let me see. I know just the thing. The story of a young archaeologist that went on an adventure to recover the necklace, arm rings, and circlet of Karina the Wise, who was the leader of a Viking tribe that lived on a small island off of Norway," Alicia began, already captivating the attention of those around her.

* * *

About midway through the morning a young man sat in a library. He was alternating between examining a piece of parchment and the book that was next to it. Also, he was making notes about what he was studying. His study was interrupted when two men entered the library and walked up to him.

"We are looking for a man named Allen Chase?" the first man asked, trying to get the young man's attention.

"Well congratulations, you found him," Allen said, looking up from his studying at the two men who'd interrupted it.

"You're Allen Chase," the second man commented with no small amount of surprise as he regarded the young man sitting at the table.

"Let me guess. You were expecting a scholarly, white-haired, older man of fifty or more, instead of a young man of barely thirty-two," Allen replied, barely hiding his annoyance.

The two men at least had the decency to look ashamed. He was of course used to reactions like theirs, so he mostly ignored it.

"Let's get down to business, gentlemen," Allen suggested, only the slightest hint of impatience in his tone.

"Certainly. This rune stone was found last week near a Viking settlement on Arnholm," the first man said, pulling a stone tablet with writing on it out of his bag.

Allen stood from his seat as the first man placed the stone on the table. The man took a step back as the young archaeologist began examining the tablet. He took a few minutes to examine the tablet before looking up at the two men.

"This seems to be a reference to Karina the Wise," Allen said, sounding both excited and intrigued.

"We believe that it could lead to where her treasures were hidden after her death," the second man added, his gaze darting from the tablet to Allen.

"I think you're correct. This line here says, 'Those who seek the treasure of wisdom must start under the beginning,'" Allen read, excitement creeping into his voice.

"We were hoping you could find the legendary treasures of Karina the Wise in time for them to be included in the exhibition of the greatest Viking leaders," the first man stated, sounding hopeful.

"When is the exhibition?" Allen asked thoughtfully.

"Two months' time," the second man replied, hoping that would be enough time.

"That should give me plenty of time," Allen replied confidently.

"Does that mean you'll help us?" the first man replied, needing the confirmation.

"How could I say 'no' to finding the treasures of one of the few female Viking leaders that is known to have existed?" Allen replied rhetorically.

"Thank you, Mr. Chase," the first man said, shaking his hand.

"Yes, thank you so much," the second man agreed, also shaking his hand.

With that the two gentlemen turned and left the room.

Their departure was barely noticed as Allen was already again leaning over the table.

Allen examined the tablet, more specifically, the sentence that he'd read earlier. He was trying to decipher the meaning of the beginning. This could be in reference to multiple things. It could be anything from where she was born to the place she first gained leadership of the tribe. Even the house she lived in when they first settled the island or the location of the battle in which she died.

The archaeologist stood up and walked over to a nearby bookshelf. He was in search of a particular reference book. The book he was looking for was about the early life of Karina the Wise. As his intelligent brown eyes scanned the titles, he ran his hand over the back of each book.

After a couple minutes of looking, he found what he was looking for. When he did, he picked it up off the shelf.

Immediately he opened the book and began reading it. As he read he began to make his way back to the table. He walked with his nose in a book. Due to that, he just barely managed to avoid tripping over a chair that was left pulled out from the table. He had a brief thought about needing to watch where he was going before he was once again completely engrossed in what he was reading. By the time he reached the spot at the table, he found what he was looking for.

Allen closed the book and reached for the phone. He booked himself on the next flight to Norway. The archaeologist spent the entire flight doing more researching. When the plane landed and he stepped outside of the airport, he hailed a cab. What he failed to notice was the man in the black overcoat following him out of the airport.

"Where to?" the cab driver asked as soon as he got in.

"The next ferry to Arnholm," Allen replied distractedly as he took a book out of his bag and began reading it.

"You got it," the driver replied, pulling out into traffic.

The only response the driver got from the archaeologist was a distracted "hum." As the taxi navigated the busy afternoon traffic, the same black rental car stayed one car behind the taxi.

Once the taxi arrived at its destination, Allen paid the driver and paid for his passage to the island. When he got there he checked into a hotel.

In all his researching, the archaeologist couldn't find anything that narrowed down where his beginning point was. Because of this he decided he'd check them all. He was going to start with the one that was most likely to be the right one. It was the ruins of the house where Katrina was born. He was considering all this as he walked down the stairs and up to the front desk.

"How do you like your room, Sir?" the woman at the desk asked with a warm smile.

"It's just fine, Ma'am. I heard that the house where Katrina the Wise was born was recently found," Allen commented, excitement entering his voice.

"Yes, it was," the woman replied easily.

"Could you tell me where to find it?" Allen asked eagerly.

"Certainly, Sir," the woman replied. Then she gave him directions.

After thanking the lady behind the desk, the archaeologist turned and walked out. He hailed a cab and told the driver where he wanted to go. Unknown to either the archaeologist or the driver, two cars back there was a black car following them. It took about ten minutes for them to get there. He paid the driver, then got out.

He began to examine the ruins as the taxi drove away. There really wasn't much left of the house. With his height at five eleven, the external walls defining the perimeter of the house were about six inches above his waist level. Inside, the stone floor was still in remarkably good condition. One thing that he quickly noticed was the house was bigger than the ones around it. Another odd thing about this house was that there were stone walls inside separating distinct rooms. What remained of the internal walls were only about half the height of the external ones. There were three distinct rooms, a large main room and two small rooms in the back. One of the rooms in the back was slightly bigger than the others. Making it unlike most of the rest of the houses in the village that were made up of just one room.

According to the notes he found written by the last researchers to study the site, the back two rooms were bedrooms. If he had to guess, he'd say that the smaller one had belonged to Karina. He entered that room and began examining it. Allen was looking for something to back up his theory. Sure enough, at the base of one of the walls was a rock with *Karina* inscribed on it.

The archaeologist's thoughts went back to the inscription on the rune stone. *Those who seek the treasure of wisdom must start under the beginning.* He was at the spot that was most likely to be the beginning referred to in the riddle.

Now he just had to figure out what the reference to "under" meant.

Unless, Allen thought as he spotted what looked like a carved stone embedded in the floor. What drew his eye was that it was slightly blue in colour. He began moving aside the dirt, debris, and dried leaves.

Clearing the area revealed the design of a wave made out of a bluish stone. He began a close and thorough examination of it. The majority of the design was made out of large stones. However, in the very centre there was a collection of twelve smaller ones. Intrigued, he carefully ran his hand over the stones. When he did, he noticed that there was a rune on each one. He pressed lightly on one of the stones, and it moved just slightly.

"Could it be some kind of combination lock?" Allen wondered to himself as knelt on the ground, never taking his eyes off the stones.

Around the combination lock was the phrase "That which defined her." He figured that it was likely a clue as to what the combination was. There was really only one word it could be. The archaeologist pressed the runes, spelling out the word *wisdom*.

As soon as he did, there was the grinding sound of rocks scraping against each other. The stones below the wave design moved aside. When they did, it revealed the entrance to some kind of underground structure. Standing up, he walked over to it. He took out his flashlight and turned it on. Shining the light down the hole revealed a set of stairs. He took a step forward and the top step was sound, so he carefully walked down the stairs.

What the archaeologist found at the bottom of the stairs was a small underground area. The area was round and lined with stones. In the centre was a stone pedestal with more runic writing on it. On the wall near the bottom of the stairs was a torch. He picked it up, took a cigarette lighter out of his pocket, and lit the torch.

Walking up to the pedestal, he brought the torch closer to the writing. There were two rings on the pedestal with writing on it. On the outer ring there was an inscription. The inscription said, *Only by virtue can one obtain the key to the treasures of wisdom.* The inner ring seemed to be a list of character traits, each on its own stone.

"In Viking culture there are nine noble virtues. They are courage, truth, honour, fidelity, discipline, hospitality, industriousness, self-reliance, and perseverance," Allen said to himself as he pressed on each of the stones with those traits on it.

When he did, the stone in the centre of the pedestal retracted and another stone rose up with the key on it. The key itself had a handle with the same wave shape that was on the floor upstairs. The end of the key's shaft was about an inch and a half long. While the head looked kind of like a triangular flag with three small holes in it. He picked up the key and headed up the stairs.

Allen quickly reached the top of the stairs. The instant he reached the open air, he felt the unmistakable feeling of the cold metal of a gun barrel being pressed against his left temple.

"Hand over the key," a voice that was just as cold demanded, coming from just behind and to the left of him.

"Alright," Allen replied, reaching into his pocket, taking out the key, and handing it to the man threatening him. The man took the key from his hand, then shoved him to the ground. As Allen hit the ground, he picked up a fist-sized rock, being very careful that his attacker didn't see. He half turned so he was looking up at his attacker while keeping the rock in his hand hidden by his body.

"Now, Mr. Archaeologist, you're going to tell me where to find the treasure, or I'll blow your head off," the man threatened, pointing his gun at Allen's head.

"No, I don't think I am," Allen replied, throwing the rock at the attacker's head.

The miscreant dropped to the ground like a sack of potatoes. The archaeologist scrambled to his feet and rushed over to check on his downed attacker. Luckily it turned out that the man was simply unconscious. Allen quickly retrieved the key, then put it safely back in his pocket. After that he pulled out his cell phone and called for a cab. A few minutes later, the cab arrived and took him back to the hotel.

Something told him it wasn't the last he'd see of his attacker. He was sure the pounding headache the man was going to have would make the man very disagreeable when they next met each other. However, there wasn't really anything he could do about that at the moment.

That being the case, he decided to do some more research. After all, he needed to translate more of the rune stone inscriptions to figure out the location of the treasure. He pulled the rune stone and a book on runes out of his bag and set to work.

A couple hours later, Allen had translated another section of the rune stone. That section read *"The first step on the journey of wisdom is to prove one has true courage. To do this you must follow the path of the warriors of the past."*

The question was what could the inscription mean? Could it be referring to the site of a famous battle? He continued to ponder the question as he walked down the stairs. To try to get the answer, he decided to head to the local library.

"Mr. Chase, there's a message for you," the woman at the front desk said to him as soon as he reached the bottom of the stairs.

Allen turned and walked over to the desk. By the time he reached the desk, the woman had retrieved the envelope and was holding it out to him.

"Do you know who left the message?" Allen asked as he accepted the envelope.

"A man in a black overcoat," the woman replied after a second of thought.

"Did he leave his name?" Allen asked, his attention turning from the envelope to the woman behind the desk.

"Unfortunately he did not," the woman responded, sounding like she wished she had a different answer for him.

"Did you recognize him?" Allen asked, tapping his chin in thought.

"No, Sir, I did not," the woman answered immediately.

"Was he from around here?" Allen asked, sounding both concerned and curious.

"No, he was an American like you. I did not see which

way he went either," the woman replied, anticipating his next question.

"Thank you for your assistance, Ma'am," Allen replied, with a grateful smile on his face.

"You're most welcome, Sir," the woman replied, returning a smile.

With that Allen turned and left the hotel. As he walked, he opened the envelope and looked at the letter inside. When he reached the curb, he looked up and hailed a cab. After he closed the door of the cab behind him, he pulled out the letter and began to read. It read, *"Take me to the treasure, or I'll kill you. I'll be watching you, and I'll find you."* It seemed he was right about being in contact with his adversary again. That contact was about as friendly as he suspected it would be.

As the cab pulled away from the curb he told the driver he wanted to go to the university. At the university he was planning to do some research that would help him decipher the clue. He had a friend at the university he hoped would be able to point him in the right direction. It didn't take very long before the cab pulled to a stop in front of the university. He distractedly paid the driver and got out, his mind still going over the clue.

Once out of the cab, he pulled the piece of paper out of his pocket he'd written the clue on. He read it over again as he walked toward the entrance of the building. As soon as the archaeologist stepped foot in the building, a man with greying hair spotted him and walked over to him.

The man was of course his friend at the university who happened to be the head librarian. As they headed to the library they began discussing important battles that took place before or during the time of Karina the Wise. By the time they reached the library, the two of them had assembled a list of the most significant battles from around that time. Allen thanked his friend for the help just before he was called away.

Once his friend left, Allen got started on his research. He found quite a bit of information about all of the notable battles on his list. The question now was which one is the rune stone referring to? After placing the paper with the passage from the stone next to the book he was reading, he tapped it with the end of his pencil thoughtfully a few times.

I wonder, Allen thought as he circled the word *journey* in the clue. Looking through the list of battles he found the one furthest from the village ruins. He quickly found what he was looking for. There was a great battle about ten years before Karina was born. Excited by this new lead, he nearly jumped from his chair to get the book on that battle. As he walked back to where he had been working he opened the book. In that book he found a map showing the route taken by the warriors from the village to the battlefield.

After making a copy of the map, he rushed out of the library and the university building itself. Once outside, he hailed a cab and asked to be taken to the village ruins. As soon as the door closed behind him, the cab left, heading back to the city.

The archaeologist looked around the site as he pulled out the copy of the map. After he looked at it for a few seconds and compared it to what he saw, he headed over to the gate that the warriors left the village through. He walked over to the gate. The only thing left of it was an archway. At about waist height there was a stone on each side made of the same blueish stone. They were each about the same size and shape. On the sides facing away from the village the crest of Karina was carved into each of the stones. The crest looked like a cross in front of a long boat. The bases of the arch were each about two feet wide and came to about his shoulder. The curved part was about the same two-foot width. The arch was made of a grey stone; while the surface was weathered, the structure was still sound.

Just as he was about to step through the arch, he noticed an inscription on the side of the right base at the same level as the blueish stones. The inscription read, *"Beware the perils of the beginning of a journey."* Looking closer at the inside of the arch while being careful not to step under it, he found signs of a trap. He spotted three lines of holes that ran the entire inside of the arch. In an effort to find the trigger, he brushed away the dead grass and leaves. This revealed three lines of paving stones. These stones were made of either the same blueish stone or a reddish orange stone. The lines went from one base to the other. With the two types of stones alternating across the space. These lines of stones matched up with the lines of holes exactly.

Allen figured the blueish stone with Karina's crest on it was an indicator that he should step on the blue stones. Testing his theory, he stepped on the first blue stone. When he took the next step, his foot slipped and brushed over one of the red stones. A fraction of a second later, he heard a click. In less than a heartbeat, he knew he had to make a decision. Should he jump back or forward? This was a test of courage, which to the Vikings was going forward even in difficult times, so that meant he should jump forward.

Suddenly arrows started flying from the line of holes in the middle of the arch. Just in the nick of time, he jumped forward, landing precariously balanced in a crouched position. He carefully stood up straight. As he did so, he noticed a cut in his sleeve from one of the arrows.

A couple inches to the right and that would have been most unpleasant, Allen thought, examining the cut and finding no wound. He even more carefully stepped off the last blue stone and onto the dirt path beyond.

Immediately he began to walk down the dirt path. The path that now seemed to be used as a hiking trail for both locals and tourists interested in the history. As he walked along the path he watched his surroundings very closely. Not only for possible clues but also to look out for any signs he was being followed. He knew his antagonist was likely not far behind him. The last thing he wanted to do was get caught by surprise again. As he walked, he found neither a clue nor a sign he was being followed. It wasn't until he was about halfway down the path that he found something interesting.

At exactly the midway point, there was a large rock right next to the path. The large rock was round and weathered till it was almost smooth. On the side facing the trail, there seemed to be writing on it. He crouched to get a better look to see if he could tell what was written. However, it was covered up by moss growing on the rock as well as dirt that was caked on the rock. Being careful not to damage the writing below he removed the obstruction. Underneath was written, Only by continuing forward no matter what can one prove his courage. As he stood up straight, he began to ponder what the inscription meant.

As he continued walking down the path, he quickly became lost in thought trying to work out this new puzzle. That turned out to be a mistake. He heard a slight sound behind him. It was a good thing to because less than a second later he barely managed to dodge out of the way of a blow to the back of his head that would have knocked him unconscious. Instantly he spun around to face his attacker, who he instantly recognized.

"It's you again," Allen said, scowling at the man.

"You really should pay more attention, Professor," the man admonished with a mocking shake of his head.

"I don't take advice from nameless, common, and thieving ruffians," Allen shot back as he glared at the man that had now attacked him twice.

"You wound me deeply, Professor. I may be many things, but I'm certainly not common or nameless. Jason Black, purveyor of ancient treasures to the fabulously wealthy," Black replied, shooting the archaeologist a thoroughly affronted look.

"You didn't deny being a thief," Allen responded, raising an eyebrow.

"I'll do whatever it takes to get what I want. If that makes me a thief, then so be it, just as long as I'm a rich thief," Black replied, not the slightest bit bothered by Allen's accusation.

"What is it you want?" Allen asked, his sharp eyes watching Black's every move.

"That really is simple, Professor. First, you're going

to hand over the key you found in the ruins. After that, you're going to lead me to where the treasure is hidden," Black replied as he circled around till he was blocking the archaeologist's path.

Allen mirrored his adversary's every move till they again faced each other. His adversary had black hair and cold brown eyes. He was about average in height and build. Black was very unimaginatively wearing a black leather jacket with a brown shirt peeking out from underneath. He wore dark-brown pants and black hiking boots.

"And what if I don't?" Allen asked, glaring at the thief.

"Now that I would not recommend, Professor," Black replied as he glared back at the archaeologist while pulling out a knife and pointing it at Allen.

"As good as that advice is, I'm not going to take it," Allen said calmly as he dropped into a fighting stance.

"And here I thought you were intelligent," Black said, shaking his head in mock disappointment.

With that Black lunged at Allen, who dodged smoothly. Next he tried slashing the archaeologist across his chest. Allen grabbed his attacker's wrist, pulling it off to the side and twisting it till the man dropped the knife. Black nailed Chase in the ribs hard enough to distract the archaeologist. Thus allowing the thief to wrench his wrist free. Both combatants backed up a step and glared at each other. As they glared at each other, Allen kicked the knife out of reach, taking it out of play. The archaeologist then returned the favour, nailing Black in the ribs just as hard. They fought for a few more minutes before Allen scored a lucky hit, knocking Black to the ground.

"I think that's about enough of that," Allen said as he pulled a revolver out of the holster attached to his belt and aiming it at Black.

"This isn't over. I told you I'll do whatever it takes to get what I want," Black said, glaring up at the archaeologist.

"That may be, but it's over for now," Allen replied, unfazed as he too glared down at his temporarily defeated foe, knowing full well the man was telling the truth.

The archaeologist's aim never wavered as he watched the other man's every move as he got to his feet. The thief shot Allen a scathing, sneering glare while retrieving his knife and put it back in the sheath clipped to his belt. He turned away from his destination to watch the man walk away. In the distance, he spotted a car and saw Black get in and drive away.

He didn't turn back to his destination till the car was out of sight. When he did, he continued down the dirt path. As he walked, he went back to considering the inscription on the stone, more specifically the meaning of it.

When he reached the end of the dirt path, he found it led to a statue. Which was surrounded by a ring of knee-high stones. Based on the inscription at the base of the statue, it was of Karina's father, Olaf the Bold. According to legend, that battle was the one he was most remembered for.

He walked up to the statue and looked closer at the base, looking for any other inscriptions. On the base under the inscription about Olaf's bravery in battle was another inscription. This one seemed to be slightly younger than the other one. Above the younger inscription was the crest of Karina the Wise. This inscription read "What lies beneath will lead to the answer, but only for those that have the courage to seek it." Looking closer at the crest and inscription, he noticed something unusual. The crest was upside down and there was a circular wear pattern around it. As if it was something that was turned repeatedly.

"Hm, I wonder," Allen said to himself thoughtfully.

On a hunch, he carefully turned the crest right-side up. As soon as the crest was in the correct position, there was a clicking sound. Immediately after the click, there was a grinding sound, which told him something was happening. The grinding sound was coming from two locations. The first location the sound came from was one of the stones that made up the stone ring. The second was the base of the statue, and it seemed like the statue itself was moving. Though whether it was good or bad he wasn't sure yet. He supposed he was about to find out.

The archaeologist turned his head in that direction to see what caused the sound. In doing that, he accidentally released the crest. The instant he did, the crest began turning again back to its previous upside-down position. His attention instantly snapped back to the crest as he took hold of it again. He again turned it back right-side up and held it there. As soon as he did, the grinding sound started again. Out of the corner of his eye, he saw the stone in the ring, that he noticed before move aside slightly. When the stone stopped moving, a loaded spear thrower rose out of the hole under the stone straight up and down. As soon as it completely emerged from the hole, the top began moving backward toward the ground, preparing to fire.

At the same time this was happening the statue began to move, revealing a hidden compartment. As the statue moved, Allen could begin to see something inside. Just before the compartment was open enough for him to be able to reach in, the spear thrower was ready to fire. Now he was in a bit of a predicament. If he released the crest, thus stopping the spear thrower, the compartment would close. He only had a split second to make a decision. Suddenly he remembered that according to the Vikings courage was to continue even when it's dangerous. In light of that, he knew what he had to do.

He stood firm and held the crest in place. He stayed perfectly still as the spear thrower released launching the spear. The spear flew past his back, missing him by only about a little less than an inch. He only allowed himself to breathe again when he heard the thud of the spear hitting the stone. After taking a deep breath, he reached in the compartment and took out what was inside. He looked down at an item in his hand. It was an oval-shaped stone with notches around the edges and writing in the centre. Looking closer at the notches, he noticed they were evenly spaced. He turned his attention to the writing in the centre. The writing in the centre was in an obscure dialect he was not very familiar with. Because of this, it would take him some time to translate the writing in the middle.

When he left the ruins, Chase took a cab back to the university. Once he got there, he headed straight to the library. As soon as he got there, he immediately started working on the translation.

About an hour later, the archaeologist sat at a small

table in a back corner of the room. He had a book on one side, the stone on the other, and a notebook in the middle. Despite the difficulty of the translation, he was starting to make progress. He was so engrossed in his work that he didn't notice when someone sat down across from him.

"Hello again, Professor; it's good to see you hard at work." Black said, bringing the attention of the archaeologist to him.

"I can't say it's good to see you at all," Allen replied, glaring daggers at Black.

"That's hardly a very friendly attitude toward someone seeking expert counsel," Black replied, with mock disappointment in his tone.

"I won't help you find the crown jewels of Karina the Wise so you can sell them," Allen responded, the last few words were laced with venom.

"In that case, I'll just take that stone you found and what you've completed of the translation so far," Black said, pointing at the stone and the notebook.

"Not happening," Allen replied, pulling the stone and notebook closer to him.

"I'm afraid I really must insist," Black said, pulling out a gun and pointing it at the archaeologist.

Black smiled menacingly at Allen while he picked up the notebook and the stone. While he was doing this, his aim never once wavered.

"What a pity you couldn't be more reasonable. It's been a pleasure," Black said with a smirk as he stood up.

"Not even a little bit," Allen replied, his glare still firmly in place.

"Till the next time, Professor," Black said, then disappeared between the bookshelves.

Allen glared venomously at the spot where Black had disappeared. What galled him the most was that he'd only translated the part that said it would lead him to where treasure was. However, he hadn't yet translated the part that told him where the hiding place actually was. Black was going to be really mad when he realized this. That thought cheered Allen up a little bit; though, he was still not very happy about the situation.

It didn't take very long for him to figure out how he was going to get the stone back. The answer lay in the fact that Black would need to get the translation of the writing on the stone finished. With his plan worked out, he stood up and went to find his friend. It only took a few minutes for him to find his friend who was in his office. He knocked on the door, and a second later he entered the office. The man behind the desk stood, walked up to Allen, and extended his hand.

"Hello, Mark," Allen greeted, shaking his hand.

"I hope you found everything you needed to complete the translation," Mark said as he took a seat behind the desk.

"I did, but a man named Jason Black stole the stone from me before I finished the translation," Allen replied, not sounding very happy about it as he sat down.

"That's terrible. I'll do anything I can to help you get it back," Mark offered, sounding no happier about it than the archaeologist.

"Thank you, Mark. Do you know anyone that can translate this dialect of Old Norse?" Allen asked, placing the book he'd been using for the translation on Mark's desk.

"There is someone, Dr. Fredrick Larson. He's done a few translations for the university a few times. This is his address. I hope he can help you," Mark answered, writing down the man's address on a small piece of paper.

"Is he known for doing that kind of work," Allen asked, accepting the piece of paper.

"Yes, he is," Mark answered, not sure of the reasoning behind his friend's question.

"That's good," Allen replied, clearly encouraged by his friend's reply as a plan began forming in his mind.

"I hope your idea works and you get the stone back, Allen," Mark said, seeing the plan forming in his friend's expression.

"Yeah, me too," Allen said, standing up.

The two men said a brief goodbye and shook hands. After that Allen turned and left his friend's office. Right away he called for a cab and gave the driver the address that Mark had given him.

Once Allen arrived at the address, he took a quick look around the parking lot looking for Black's car, which thankfully wasn't there. He cautiously entered the office building and made his way to the elevator. He pressed the button for the floor and waited as the doors closed. As the elevator moved, he ran though his plan in his mind again. His plan would only work if he got to Dr. Larson before Black did. A second later, the door opened and he stepped out. He walked down the hall stopping at the door with Dr. Larson's name on it, and knocked, hearing, "Come in," from inside.

As Allen entered, he saw a man in his thirties sitting behind a desk. Larson had light-brown hair, blue eyes, and wore a light-brown suit. The archaeologist knew that the linguist was watching him curiously as he walked up to the desk and extended his hand. Larson shook his visitor's hand.

"Please, have a seat," Larson said, indicating one of the chairs in front of his desk as he sat back down behind the desk.

Allen nodded and sat down in the offered chair. As he did this, he contemplated what he was going to say.

"I'm Dr. Allen Chase. Mark Beck at the university said that you were the best person to translate a certain Old Norse dialect," Allen said, watching the other man's reaction.

"He is correct. Obscure Old Norse dialects are my specialty," Larson replied evenly, raising an eyebrow.

The linguist wondered where Chase was going with this. He knew for a fact the other man had a rather extensive knowledge of obscure Old Norse dialects.

What does he want with me when he can just do the translation himself? Larson wondered as he observed the adventurer across from him. As if the archaeologist had read the linguist's mind, Allen explained his plan.

Two hours later, Jason Black walked into Dr. Larson's office. He sat down in the chair in front of the desk. The dishonest antiquities dealer regarded the linguist with a critical eye. He knew that he had to carefully phrase what had to say next. If the man on the other side of the desk suspected the stone was stolen, he'd refuse to help.

"Dr. Larson, I understand that you are an expert in

obscure Old Norse dialects," Black said, watching the other man's reaction.

"That is correct," Larson replied evenly.

"Excellent, I'm in the antiquities trade. A piece has recently come into my possession. There is text on the item that I need translated," Black explained smoothly.

"I'd need to see the piece," Larson replied, being careful not to show any reaction.

"Certainly," Black responded, a little surprised that was Larson's only reaction.

Black reached into the inside pocket of his suit jacket. He pulled out a velvet pouch and leaned forward to place it on the desk in front of the linguist.

Larson reached forward, picked up the pouch, took out the stone, and examined it for a few minutes. After a few minutes, he carefully placed the stone on the desk. Less than a second later he looked up and glared at Black.

"I'm afraid I can't help you," Larson replied with barely restrained anger in his voice as he continued to glare at the thief.

"Really, why is that," Black asked, looking like he wanted to roll his eyes.

"I have good reason to think that this item has been stolen. I cannot in good conscience assist you," Larson replied, crossing his arms.

"Oh, I think you will, Dr. Larson," Black said, glaring as he pulled out his gun, pointing it at the linguist.

"I wouldn't recommend that, Mr. Black," Allen said, entering through a side door while the police came flooding behind him and through the other door.

All the police had their guns out and pointed at the thief. They were all watching the man in the black suit's every move.

"Ah, Professor, I wasn't expecting to see you here. I see you brought some friends with you," Black commented, glancing at Allen while keeping his gun pointed at Larson.

"I'll be taking the stone back," Allen said, walking up to the desk while Larson slipped the stone back in the velvet bag.

"Sir, lower you weapon and place it on the ground," the lead policeman instructed, the tone of his voice was firm.

Allen watched as Black quickly placed his gun on the ground. The archaeologist reached over and picked up the velvet pouch with the stone inside, then turned to leave. He stopped in the doorway and turned around to face the antiquities thief.

"This time it was a pleasure, Mr. Black," Allen said, flashing the thief a smirk before turning around again.

"Till next time, Professor," Black said as the door to the office closed.

"That likely won't be for quite a while, Mr. Black," one of the other policemen commented as he walked up behind Black and cuffed him.

"Yeah, probably about twenty years," another policeman added, while he reached down and secured Black's gun.

"I wouldn't count on it," Black sneered as he was led out of the room.

The archaeologist walked down the hall. He quickly made his way outside while the police took Dr. Larson's statement.

Allen headed back to the hotel to finish the translation. Within about ten minutes, he was in his room. As soon as he closed the door behind him he pulled the book out that he had been using before. He sat down at the table and got busy on the translation.

The archaeologist started on the next section of the text. It took him a couple of hours to translate the rest of the text. It turned out he was right. This portion of the text detailed the location of the treasure.

The text read "Your journey to seek wisdom is nearing the end. To find the treasure you seek you must look under the seat of power." What would have been considered the seat of power in a Viking village? That was the Great Hall. It was where feasts, festivals, and meetings would take place. It was also the centre of the village's social life. As well as being the place where the chief would meet with the other high-ranking members of the village to discuss important decisions. Which meant the treasure was likely hidden in an underground chamber like the one he had found the key in.

Excited by this new revelation, Allen took a cab back to the village ruins. After he got there, it didn't take very long for him to find the Great Hall. That was because it was the largest building and in roughly the centre of the village. It was also the most intact building in the village. The reason it was so much more intact was because it was made of stone instead of wood.

Inside the archaeologist found little remaining from what he knew had once been there. The only things left were the long fire pit that extended the length of the hall and what appeared to be a stone throne. The throne was on a raised dais at the far end of the hall. He walked over to get a better look. When he did, he found that the dais extended across the width of the hall and was about six inches high. However, the part that was under the throne was two inches higher.

He began examining the dais and the throne. He was looking for another inscription that would tell him how to open the entrance to the underground chamber. Sure enough, he quickly found an inscription on the dais. It read, "The beginning of wisdom will show you the way." Under the inscription were three pictures. The first was Thor's hammer, second was a cross, and third was an axe. Recognizing the first part of the inscription, he got his Bible out of his bag. After reading the verse, he knew the answer. Turns out that the answer to the inscription was in Proverbs 9:10. With a triumphant smirk he pressed the cross. As soon as he did, the part of the dais under the throne moved backward, revealing a set of stairs.

The adventurer cautiously made his way down the stairs. At the bottom there was a hallway ending in a round medium-sized chamber. There was a stone pedestal in the centre of the chamber that was about waist high. He walked across the chamber up to it. On the surface of the pedestal was a space the size and shape of the stone. There was also a seam going down the middle of the surface of the pedestal on either side of the space and along the right edge of the space itself. He placed the stone in the space so it was in there horizontally, then he turned it till it was vertical. When he did, the seam opened and another circle of stone rose up.

At the top of it there was an inscription. The inscription read "What did she seek like silver and searched for like hidden treasure?" Under the inscription there was a line of tiles with various things that people valued. Beneath that were two spaces the same size as the tiles. Again he recognized the reference in the inscription. Once again he took out his Bible and opened in to Proverbs 2:4-5. He looked at the tiles again and picked up two of the tiles. One of the tiles he picked said "The fear of the LORD" and the other said "The knowledge of GOD." He placed the tiles in the spaces.

A second later there was a rumbling sound and an alcove lined with stone opened. He walked over to the alcove. Inside was a flat wooden box with a key hole in the front. He took out the key he'd found in the beginning and unlocked the box. With a sense of anticipation, Allen opened the box revealing the circlet, necklace, and two arm rings. The three pieces were beautiful, made of gold with sapphires. The circlet was a ring of gold dotted with small sapphires and a larger round sapphire in the centre. The necklace was a pendant with Karina's crest which was, a cross in front of a longboat. There was a sapphire in the centre of the cross. The pendant was on a gold chain. Lastly, the arm rings looked like smaller versions of the circlet. He closed and relocked the box, then left the underground chamber.

When he got back, he called the men from the museum who had asked him to find the artifacts. He told the men on the other side he'd found the artifacts.

A week later, Allen arrived at the exhibition with a

sense of anticipation. It gave him a feeling of satisfaction and excitement to see the treasures of Karina the Wise displayed alongside the artifacts associated with the other great Viking leaders. He managed to slip in and out of the event without drawing the attention of reporters or any of the other annoying people that frequent such events.

* * *

As Alicia concluded the story, it was met with excitement. The rest of the trip was filled with excited chatter about the story that they'd just heard. Some people looked up the Bible verses mentioned in the story. While others wondered if Black had managed to escape. It was safe to say that the rest of the trip was anything but boring.

THE END

PART 5
Final Reckonings

CHAPTER 14

Dust on the Wind

The convention centre was alive with the hum of excitement and anticipation. There was a small stage set up in one of the bigger rooms of the centre. Alicia was in the curtained-off backstage area. She was about to go on, and for some reason she found herself feeling a bit nervous. The reason for this feeling was that she was telling a brand new story that she'd never told before. As she stepped out onto the stage, she clutched the mic in her hand as she took a deep, calming breath.

"How many of you are having a good time so far?" Alicia said, as she walked to the centre of the stage.

"Yeah," the crowd cheered uproariously in response.

"As I'm sure you all know, I'm going to tell you a tale of murder and mystery. Only today it's going to be a little different than you might be expecting. Instead of a sprawling city, it'll be the vast, seemingly endless grassland. Towering skyscrapers will be replaced by equally towering pine trees. The bustling noise of cars and trucks exchanged for horses and wagons. That's right, folks; we're taking a ride back to the days of the Old West. Join me in a murder mystery, cowboy style," Alicia said, her statement followed by a hushed silence filled with anticipation.

* * *

Dust swirled down the main street of the small, one-horse town of Silver Springs, Texas. As the sun set, it glittered off the floating dust. Those last rays of sunlight also illuminated a cowboy stumbling out of the saloon. In the quickly fading light, he staggered down the board-walk. Abruptly he turned and walked down a narrow alley between the barbershop and the general store.

Just as the man reached the middle of the alley, there was a wisp of movement from the growing shadows at the mouth of the alley. Slowly that movement materialized into a shadowed figure approaching the man that was fac-ing the end of the alley. That figure revealed itself to be a man dressed in clothes so average that it seemed almost intentional. The mystery man noiselessly advanced on the drunken man like a stalking predator. He stopped only a couple of feet away from the drunk man. With a kind of menacing smoothness, he pulled out his knife.

"I told you that you'd pay. Well that payment has come due," the man said, his voice cold, threatening, and down-right deadly.

The instant the threat was uttered, the man to whom it was directed stiffened, causing a small malicious smile to appear on the other man's face.

Good; he remembers me, the man with the knife thought. Without a trace of hesitation or mercy, he threw the knife. With a sickening thud, the blade embedded into the other man's back. As the other man dropped to the ground, the murderer walked away, never once looking back.

The next morning the town was bustling with early morning activity, the people completely ignorant of the evil deed that had been committed the night before. Among that bustle of activity was a man riding into town. As he rode down Main Street, the early morning sun glinted off the silver, star-shaped badge on his vest. This badge identified him as a Texas Ranger. The ranger came to a stop in front of the saloon. After getting off his horse and tying it to the hitching rail, he took off his hat and ran his hand through his damp blond hair as his bright, intelligent, blue eyes scanned his surroundings meticulously. Once he was done, he walked into the saloon.

"Howdy, Caleb," the bartender said as the ranger walked up to and leaned against the bar, his eyes flicking around the room.

"Howdy, Sam, whisky," Caleb said, dropping some coins on the worn, scuffed, oak bar.

"It's been a few years. How have you been?" Sam asked as he placed a glass in front of the ranger and poured.

"You know, the usual, ride for endless days, then get shot at," Caleb said, picking up his drink and downing it.

"Ya get any new holes in that stubborn hide a yours?" Sam asked with a laugh and a fond shake of his head.

"A few," Caleb replied, with a smirk pulling at the corner of his mouth.

Before either could say anything else, a loud, female scream shattered the peace of the morning. Both men rushed out of the building and onto the boardwalk.

The second that they did, they spotted a crowd of people across the street and a couple stores down. They headed in that direction, along with everyone else. Both of them were pretty sure what they'd find when they got there. Sure enough, when they got over there, they saw that someone had been killed.

When Caleb made his way to the front of the crowd, he was quite happy about what he saw. There was a deputy standing in the mouth of the alley stopping anyone from getting any closer. There, at about the middle of the alley, the dead man lay on his front. As the ranger tried to take a step forward, the deputy held out his hand, halting him.

"Ya ain't allowed in there. None a tha rest a ya are allowed neither," the deputy said, his gaze locked on Caleb for a few seconds. When a couple of the men in the crowd tried to take a step forward, his gaze flicked to the rest of the crowd.

Instead of replying, Caleb moved his jacket aside, showing his badge. As the deputy stepped aside, the ranger turned his gaze to the dead man. The instant he entered the alley, there were indications that this man had been murdered. Before he took another step, he looked around at the ground for boot prints. He instantly noticed the two sets of prints going into the alley but only one that went out. While being careful to disrupt things as little as possible, he moved toward the body.

When he reached the body, the cause of death was pretty obvious. The knife, still embedded in the victim's heart, was a dead giveaway. The next thing he noticed about the body was that it was covered in dust as if the man had just come off the trail. Standing from his position crouched next to the body, he turned his attention to the deputy.

"Deputy, do ya recognize this fella?" Caleb asked, his sharp eyes watching the deputy very closely.

"Ain't never seen 'im in m' life, Ranger; probably just some drifter," the deputy replied, instantly and without hesitation.

"Mind going ta fetch the doctor and the undertaker. Might want ta rustle up the sheriff too," Caleb instructed with a thoughtful look, something about the deputy's conclusion not sitting right with him. Though what it was he wasn't sure yet, which also bothered him.

"Alright, Ranger," the deputy replied, casting a stern look at the crowd before hurrying off to do as he was told.

"Do any a you people recognize this fella?" Caleb asked the curious crowd. His gaze flicked among them, looking for any sign of recognition.

Unfortunately, he didn't find even a trace of it. Replies to the negative and the shaking heads rippled throughout the small crowd.

"Alright you people need ta move on now. There's nothing ta see here," Caleb said with a disappointed sigh that he couldn't quite stifle.

The people moved along with minimal grumbling. This was a fact he felt quite thankful for. He had no doubt that within a few hours everyone in the town would know what had happened. By the end of the day, news would spread to the surrounding area as well. Whether this would make his investigation easier or harder was yet to be determined.

Deciding that was a question for later, he turned his attention back to the body and the scene as a whole. As he was looking around the body, he noticed where the man's hat where it had fallen off when the man fell to the ground. Just as he was about to turn his attention elsewhere, something caught his attention. He could just make out what could be a piece of paper in the main part of the hat. Reaching over and picking it up, he pulled out some papers. The papers turned out to be several letters, a telegraph receipt, and a land deed. All of which identified the dead man as one James Marshal. The deed showed that Marshal was from the other side of the state.

That certainly explained why no one recognized him, Caleb thought to himself as he examined the documents. He put all the documents into the inside pocket of his jacket as he stood back up from his crouched position. While he was doing that, he pulled a small notebook out of his inside pocket where he put the victim's papers. He quickly wrote down everything that he'd observed from the body and scene so far.

Just as he finished this, two men walked up. Not only was the sheriff not with them, they'd even lost the deputy. This was a fact that he was not very happy about.

"Hello, I'm Dr. Jenkins, and this is the undertaker, Mr. Richards," Dr. Jenkins introduced with slight annoyance in his voice.

"Where's tha sheriff an tha deputy?" Caleb asked, crossing his arms, not looking any happier than the doctor seemed.

"The deputy gave me this note, then rode away with the sheriff," Richards replied, holding up a folded piece of paper.

Richards handed the note to Caleb, who unfolded it. The note said, "Had ta leave town ta chase down some rustlers. Probably be gone a couple a weeks, at least. Figured with you bein' a big time Ranger, ya could handle a couple a drifters killin' each other." He glared at the note in annoyance as he refolded it.

He bristled internally at the sheriff's assertion. He never liked it when lawmen jumped to conclusions.

How could he possibly know what happened? Caleb wondered, while silently fuming.

"I don't see why you wanted me here," Dr. Jenkins said, breaking the ranger out of his contemplation.

"Well, Doc, I was hopin' you'd tell me if there's anythin' about the body that could help figure out who did this," Caleb explained as they both crouched next to the body.

The doctor nodded, then began looking over the body. It only took a few minutes for him to finish his examination.

"Find anythin', Doc?" Caleb asked the instant that the doctor finished.

"From the look a things, this poor fella didn't even see it coming. There aren't any signs of a fight," Dr. Jenkins replied, shaking his head in pity.

"You can take the body away now. Just be careful of those boot prints," Caleb said, pointing at the boot prints.

As Richards carefully walked into the alley, Caleb turned his attention to the new bunch of people who had gathered. There were about fifteen, all wanting to get a better look at the murder.

"Move along, people. There ain't nothing ta see here," Caleb said, his stern gaze sweeping over the entire crowd. He was not really happy that he had to do this again.

"Was it murder, Ranger?" a woman in the crowd asked from the front of the crowd.

"Did he really get stabbed in the back?" a young man asked from the back of the crowd.

"Yes, it was, and yes, he was. Now y'all need ta move along," Caleb said, gesturing for them to move along.

With only minimal grumbling, the crowd again quickly dispersed. As the people began to move away, he headed over to the hotel. As he walked, he once again pulled out his notebook and wrote down everything the doctor had told him. Just as he was about to step up on the boardwalk in front of the hotel, something drew his attention out of the corner of his eye.

That thing was the livery stable as it occurred to him that he should head over there. As he walked over, a question popped into his head.

Just as he reached the stable door and his hand touched the door handle, it suddenly slid open with a scraping sound. The unexpected sound and movement caused his hand to fly to his gun. When he noticed the other man wasn't wearing a gun, he moved his hand away.

The man who opened the door was older than him with brown hair that had streaks of grey. Both of them were about the same height. However, the other man was quite a bit more strongly built than the ranger.

"Didn't mean ta startle ya, Ranger," the man said in a deep voice as he noticed the ranger's hand move away from his gun.

Caleb nodded as the two of them walked a few steps into the barn. He took a few seconds to size up the other man who, he guessed, was the livery man.

"I'm sure ya heard about tha murder last night," Caleb commented, hooking his thumbs in his gun belt.

"Sure did," the livery man replied, crossing his arms.

"Do ya know when tha murdered fella came ta town?" Caleb asked, watching his reaction.

"He rode in day afore yesterday just afore sunset," the livery owner replied, after he thought about it for a second.

"Did ya notice anything about 'im?" Caleb asked as he pulled out his notebook, wrote down what he'd been told, and got ready to write down the answer.

"Now that ya ask, I did notice somethin'; I ain't real sure why. It looked like that fella had ridden hard an' long. Cause he were covered in dust from 'is hat ta 'is boots. His horse looked mighty worn. That fella musta been pushin' that poor critter awful hard," the livery owner said, shaking his head in disappointment at the treatment of the animal.

"Thank ya kindly fer yer help," Caleb said, extending his hand.

The livery owner shook his hand, then touched the brim of his hat.

Caleb closed his book and slipped it back into his jacket pocket as he turned toward the door. As he left the stable, he went over what he had just learned. It was quite obvious that the victim was running. The only question is whether he was running toward something or away from something.

As soon as he left the stable, he resumed his course to the hotel. When he entered the lobby of the hotel it was abuzz with people talking about the murder. As he walked up to the register, it occurred to him to check the register for the victim. When he signed his name, he glanced at the names above it, and sure enough there was the name of the murdered man. Just to be thorough, he took note of all of the names from the day of the murder. When he was sure he had them memorized, he turned his attention to the clerk.

"Do ya know about when this man checked in?" Caleb asked, pointing to the name right above his.

The clerk turned the register around toward him and looked at the name.

"Ah, yes, Ranger, that gentlemen checked in day before yesterday. It was around sunset when he came in," the clerk replied, turning his attention to the lawman.

"What did he do after checking in?" Caleb asked, not really surprised by the answer since it lined up with what he'd already been told.

"I'm afraid I cannot disclose the activities of my guests," the clerk answered, crossing his arms defiantly.

"This time ya can," Caleb said, staring the clerk down.

"You mean that is the gentleman that was killed last night," the clerk guessed, sounding quite surprised.

"He was," Caleb confirmed simply.

"And to think that he was staying in this very hotel. Though he wasn't here for very long," the clerk commented, sounding astounded, as if it was big news.

"What do you mean he wasn't here very long?" Caleb asked, needing more information about that comment.

"When he checked in, he went up and put some saddlebags in his room, then left again," the clerk answered, his gaze flicking to the stairs.

"I'm going to need to take a look at his room," Caleb said, his voice amiable with just a hint of steel behind it.

"Oh certainly, Ranger; it's room two, and yours is eleven. Right this way," the clerk said, picking up the both of the keys from the hooks and walking around the desk. The clerk led the ranger toward the stairs. As he followed the bespectacled man to the stairs, he could feel someone watching him. When he stepped onto the stairs, he took another glance around the lobby. Unfortunately he couldn't see anyone paying him any special attention. The feeling went away when they reached the top of the stairs and turned the corner down the hallway with rooms on either side. It took less than a minute for them to reach room two. The clerk handed Caleb the key to this room, as well as the one for his, excused himself, and hurried back down the hall.

In the interest of being thorough, but without really expecting to find anything, Caleb crouched to examine the lock. He was looking for any sign the lock had been picked or forced open. However, much to his surprise, there were scratches around the lock like someone had tried to pick it. Whether they had been successful or not he didn't know.

When he stood from his crouched position, out of the corner of his eye he saw someone open the door directly across from the one he was standing in front of. Turning around to see who it was, he noticed that it was a woman right before the door closed.

"Ma'am, my name is Texas Ranger Caleb Turner. I need to ask you a few question," Caleb said, knocking firmly on the door.

"Oh, my apologies, Ranger Turner. I thought you were that ruffian returned to make another dreadful scene," the older woman said, opening the door again.

"Could ya tell me what happened, Ma'am?" Caleb asked, his gut telling him that this could be very important.

"Let me see. It was day before yesterday at a thoroughly uncivilized hour. The gentleman that was staying in that room was just leaving his room. Suddenly, out of nowhere, this brute showed up and started yelling and carrying on. At one point, that ruffian even pushed the other man," the lady said, shaking her head, sounding totally appalled.

"Did you hear what tha man was sayin'?" Caleb asked, now even more certain that this was important.

"If I remember correctly, he kept shouting something about demanding the payment of some kind of debt," the lady answered after a moment's thought.

"Do you recollect what he looked like?" Caleb asked firmly, putting this unknown man in the suspect column.

"Let me see. He was about your height with a little stockier build. I never got a good look at his face. He did have brown hair though. He was dressed in clothes very similar to what you are, Ranger. I'm afraid that is all I remember," the lady replied, disappointed in herself for not taking a better look at the miscreant.

"You've been mighty helpful; thank ya, Ma'am," Caleb said, touching the brim of his hat.

"You are most welcome, Ranger Turner. I'm glad to have helped," the lady replied, nodding her head, then turned and went back into her room.

Once the door closed behind her, the ranger turned and entered the murdered man's room. The second he stepped foot in the room, a frustrated scowl appeared on his face. It was instantly apparent someone had been in here. He walked over to the bed where the saddlebags sat. It was immediately clear that someone had gone through both of them. With an annoyed sigh, he picked up the saddlebags. He would go through them in his room later, but he wasn't particularly optimistic about finding anything. After a last quick look around the room he left.

He quickly went to his room and put both sets of saddlebags inside. As soon as he closed the door behind him, he made sure to double-check that the door was locked before heading back downstairs.

When he reached the bottom of the stairs, he glanced around and headed across the lobby toward the door. Just as he stepped out onto the boardwalk, a man walked up to him looking like he wanted to say something.

"Ranger, last night I saw tha murdered fella in tha saloon. He were real liquored up by tha time 'e stumbled out a there," the man explained, taking a quick glance around before returning his attention to the ranger.

"Did he talk to anyone or seem to be meeting someone?" Caleb asked, intrigued by this new information.

"I ain't rightly sure. The barkeep more 'in likely would be able ta tell ya," the man answered, tipping his head in the direction of the saloon.

"Thank ya, Mister," Caleb said, touching the brim of his hat.

"Glad ta help, Ranger," the man replied, returning the gesture.

With that the two men went their separate ways, the man headed in the direction of the general store. Caleb, on the other hand, changed his direction and headed toward the saloon. As soon as he walked through the batwing doors, he walked up to the bar.

"Can I get ya anything?" Sam asked, walking over to stand in front of Caleb.

"Not this time, Sam," Caleb replied, leaning against the bar.

"So this visit is official like," Sam replied, not sounding the least bit bothered.

"'Fraid so, Sam. You wouldn't happen ta remember a fella by tha name a James Marshal in here last night," Caleb asked, his tone making it clear that the question was really important.

"Now that ya mention it, I surely do. He had quite the load on by tha end of tha night," Sam said, while wiping out a glass.

"Ever seen him in here afore?" Caleb asked, wanting to confirm what he was pretty sure he already knew.

"Can't say I have. He sure ain't from these parts, that's for true and certain," Sam said with complete certainty.

"What makes ya say that?" Caleb asked, curious as to what made him so certain.

"Cause there ain't no one in these parts that woulda talked back ta Mr. Roberts the way he done. Ya shoulda seen tha look on Mr. Roberts's face. I'm right surprised that he left here alive. I thought for sure that his gun was goin' ta shoot 'im dead right then an' there," Sam said, shaking his head as he picked up the bar rag.

"What did he say?" Caleb asked, his intense gaze fixed on his friend, waiting for an answer that could be very important.

"By tha time it happened, that Marshal fella was real drunk. Tha whole time he was in here, Mr. Roberts seemed ta flinch a little. Finally he told Marshal that he'd had enough. Boy, Marshal didn't take that to kindly. He told 'im ta mind his own busyness and to stay outta his. That's what set off Mr. Roberts's hired gun. At tha time, I thought he was real lucky that the slick didn't shoot 'im dead. Guess I was wrong considerin' what happened after he left," Sam answered, sounding sympathetic.

"Did ya notice whether he met with anyone?" Caleb asked a little distractedly as he contemplated what he had just learned.

"He weren't meeting anyone, that's for certain sure. No one approached him tha whole time," Sam replied thoughtfully as he considered the question.

"Did he do anything else in particular?" Caleb asked, still slightly pensive.

"Come ta think on it, he did make an effort ta join tha poker game Mark Jackson was in. He had ta go clear across tha room," Sam answered after about a second's thought.

"Did ya notice who was tha big winner that night?" Caleb asked, fiddling with an empty glass on the bartop.

"'Fraid not, sorry, Caleb," Sam replied, shaking his head.

At the other end of the bar, someone signaled for Sam's attention. With a parting nod to Caleb, the bartender walked away. With that the ranger turned and left the saloon, making a mental note to ask around for this Mike Jackson.

As soon as he stepped through the batwing doors and out onto the boardwalk he ducked as a bullet hit the doorframe. In the same fluid motion, he drew his own gun. While he dove for cover, all the bystanders also scrambled for cover. He'd only just taken cover behind a water trough when more shots flew through the air where his head had been just seconds before. When more shots slammed into the water trough, he finally managed to figure out where the shots were coming from.

During the next pause in the barrage of bullets, he popped up and returned fire. He had to quickly duck back down again as more bullets flew by his ears. This time they were coming from a slightly different direction.

Great, two against one, just what I need, Caleb thought with a scowl.

As the bullets flew over his head, he tried to narrow down the places the two barrages were coming from. After a couple more shots, he was finally able to figure it out. Less than a heartbeat later, there was another pause in the fire, causing him to pop up and return fire.

When his gun was empty, he ducked back down expecting another round of fire. The seconds ticked by with no gunfire being aimed at him. Just to be cautious, he waited a few more seconds before deciding it was over.

Figuring that whoever the shooters were had taken off, he left his cover. Still being cautious, he began to make his way in the direction of where the shooters had been. He figured that both of them were pretty close to each other. When he reached the spot one of the shooters had stood, he took a quick look to see if there was anything. Unfortunately there wasn't anything that could tell him who it was that was shooting at him.

Shaking his head, he next made his way to the spot where the other shooter had stood. This time when he looked around he found something quite interesting. On a post right behind the boot prints of the shooter was a note pinned to it by a knife. The note said, *Asking questions can turn out to be downright lethal if you're not careful, Ranger Turner.*

Not even the slightest bit worried by the threat, he pulled the knife out. With both items in hand, he headed back over to the hotel. When he got there, he had the hotel manager lock both pieces of evidence in the hotel safe.

Once he stepped out onto the boardwalk again, he began heading over to the general store. As he walked over, everyone was whispering about either the murder or the firefight. He passed two couples who were just leaving as he entered the store.

"Afternoon, mind if I ask ya a few questions?" Caleb asked, walking up to the counter.

"I'll certainly help in any way I can, Ranger," the clerk answered, returning back behind the counter, having just put something away.

"That's good ta hear. Has a fella by tha name James Marshal bought anything here," Caleb asked, his sharp eyes watching the clerk.

"The name sounds vaguely familiar. When about would he have been in here? I'll just check my ledger and find out," the clerk replied as he pulled out a large book from under the counter.

"Figure it woulda been some time yesterday," Caleb

answered, leaning on the counter in such a way that he could see the door in the reflective surface of something on one of the shelves.

The clerk opened the book and began looking through the entries. It only took him a few seconds to find what he was looking for.

"Marshal was here. He bought a bag of flour and one of sugar," the clerk said as he closed the ledger book.

"Do you remember if'n anythin' interstin' happen?" Caleb asked, his sharp eyes flicking between the clerk and the reflection of the door.

"Just that he had a bit of a shovin' match with another fella," the clerk replied, as if he didn't think it was very important.

"Was tha other fella about my height, bit bigger, with brown hair?" Caleb asked firmly, of the opinion that it was in fact important.

"No, he was couple inches shorter, with a slight build, and black hair. In fact, I'm pretty sure it was Mark Jackson," the clerk replied without hesitation.

Just as Caleb was about ask where he could find this Mark Jackson, he stopped and his hand twitched just slightly. Without saying another word, he touched the brim of his hat, then turned and left the shop.

Once outside he began walking down the boardwalk. After only taking about a dozen steps, he all of a sudden stopped in his tracks.

"Mind tellin' me why yer followin' me," Caleb said. Though he phrased it like a question, in reality it was nothing of the kind.

"You are a sharp one," a man said, from behind the ranger, sounding amused with just a hint of impressed.

"I guess he ain't bad fer a lawdog," another man said, stepping out from the between two buildings in front of the ranger.

"What is it y'all want?" Caleb asked, his hand resting on his gun.

"Ain't no need ta get all proddy, Ranger. We're just a couple a public-minded citizens out ta hep the great state a Texas," the guy behind him said, calmly.

"And how do ya plan on doin' that?" Caleb asked, his voice dripping with suspicion.

"Givin' a certain Texas Ranger a piece a advice tha might keep 'im from gettin' lead poisonin'," the one in front said, a cool threat in his voice.

"I'm listenin'," Caleb said, his voice steady and calm.

"You see, we like tha sheriff's view a things right well," the man behind said, his voice filled with false cheer.

"It really would be fer the best if'n ya leave it at that an' ride out," the one in front added, his voice still cool.

"An' what'll happen if'n I don't take yer advice," Caleb replied, his voice as cool and steady as a mountain pool in the spring.

"Ya never know when lead poisonin'll crop up," the one behind threatened, his voice about the same temperature as an iceberg.

"Did ya know that stubbornness is a leading cause of lead poisonin'?" the one in front asked, though it was more of a threat.

"Seein' as you boys have bin kind enough ta give me all

this advice, I reckon I should return tha favour. Tha thing about lead poisonin', it can be catchin' if ya ain't real careful," Caleb said, a threat in his voice that was as cold and hard as his gun.

With that the ranger started walking forward again. He calmly walked past the hired gun as if he had not a care in the world. That impression was belied by the fact that his hand was still on his gun. Less than a minute later, he heard footsteps heading in the opposite direction.

Once he was sure they were gone, he decided to get some supper and go over the evidence he'd gathered so far. To that end, he crossed the street and entered the small cafe. He sat down in one of the tables in the back.

"Evening, Ranger," the waitress greeted, walking up to the table.

"Howdy, Ma'am," Caleb greeted, starting to stand up till she gestured for him to sit back down.

"There's a real good soup today. So what kin I get ya?" the waitress asked, pulling a small notebook out of the pocket of her apron.

"I'll have the soup and a cup a coffee," Caleb replied, taking off his hat and putting it on one of the other chairs at the table.

"Comin' right up, Ranger," the waitress said, writing down his order, then scampering off back toward the kitchen.

As soon as she was gone, he pulled out his own notebook. Opening it, he began going through what he'd found out so far.

One thing is for true and certain is that someone

doesn't like tha questions I've been askin', Caleb thought as he looked through the last page of his notes.

"Somethin's got ya focusin' real hard," the waitress said as she placed the bowl of soup and the cup of coffee in front of him.

"Reckon so, Ma'am," Caleb said, looking from the cup and bowl in front of him to the young woman.

"Is it that murdered fella? Cause everyone's talking about it. You see, nothing ever happens in this town, so a murder is real big news," the waitress said with eager anticipation.

"Yer right it is. There's somethin' you could do to help me ifn' yer willing," Caleb said, then took a sip of his coffee.

"Sure, I'd be right happy ta," the waitress replied eagerly.

"Would I be right in guessin' that ya know 'bout everyone in these parts?" Caleb asked, figuring that her eagerness to help had more to do with wanting to be part of something interesting happening than anything else, but he'd take what he could get.

"I reckon so, seein' as this is tha only cafe in town," the waitress answered, just as eagerly as before.

"Does that include a Mark Jackson?" Caleb asked, watching really closely her reaction to the name.

"It surely does. His folks live a couple miles out a town to tha north," the waitress said, recognition sparking to life in her brown eyes.

"Do ya know if'n he's livin' on his folk's place?" Caleb asked, as he drank the last swallow of his coffee.

"Far as I know," the waitress said simply.

"When was the last time ya saw 'im?" Caleb asked, not really sure what to expect.

"Last time I saw 'im he was gettin' in a shovin' match with a stranger by the name a Marshal," the waitress answered, sounding like she wasn't sure if it was important or not.

Caleb had already been planning to talk to this Mark Jackson. However, this man just made it to the top of his "to talk to" list. While he'd been doing his thinking, the waitress had gone and got the coffee pot and returned.

"Ya wouldn't happened ta have seen a man a bit stockier than me, about as tall, with brown hair around?" Caleb asked, not really expecting an affirmative answer.

"Sure have. Was in here yesterday 'bout ten minutes after that Marshal fella left," the waitress answered, holding out the pot, offering him another cup.

"I don't suppose ya caught his name?" Caleb asked a little hopefully as he held out his cup.

"Sure did. His name was John Davis," the waitress answered, refilling his coffee cup.

"He a local boy?" Caleb asked, then took a sip of his coffee.

"Yep, he shore is. Though his folks was from somewhere on t' other side a the state. He was born just after they moved here. Been gone for a couple months though," the waitress answered immediately.

"Any idea where he's stayin'?" Caleb asked, glad to finally have a name for all three of his suspects.

"Last I heard, he was stayin' in one a tha rooms above tha saloon," the waitress replied hurriedly as she was called away.

The ranger spent the rest of the time it took to finish

his meal thinking. He was trying to figure out which of his suspects that he would talk to first. Finally, just as he finished the last spoonful of soup, he decided to head out to the Jackson place in the morning. With that he stood, tossed a few coins on the table, put on his hat, and walked out. He crossed the street and headed over to the hotel to get some sleep.

The next morning he got on his horse and headed out of town. As he rode down the main street, there was a restlessness in the air that made him uneasy. The feeling didn't really go away till he passed the last of the buildings.

A passing cowhand gave him more precise directions. There was something in the expression of the cowhand when he mentioned the Jacksons that gave him a bad feeling. The look was one of a strange combination of sadness and fear. Though what the cause of the look was he had not the faintest idea.

About three quarters of the way to the Jackson's place, there was a group of five riders about fifty feet ahead of him who were heading toward him. As they got closer, he began to be able to hear some of what was being said. From that, he was able to quickly figure out that they were the infamous Mr. Roberts and some of his cronies. It was a bit more than slightly tense as he rode past the group. Once past them, he didn't let himself relax till they were a good distance away.

Nearly twenty minutes later, he rode up to the Jackson's place. What he saw didn't sit well with him one bit.

There in front of the farmhouse was a young man whom he figured was Mark. The problem was that he was saddling his horse as fast as he could with some very full-looking saddlebags strapped on.

Caleb rode up to the hitching rail at the other end from the young man. He got off his horse, looped the rains around the rail, and walked over to where the young man was.

"From tha looks a things, yer goin' on a long trip," Caleb said, leaning on the hitching rail next to the young man's horse.

"I don't see how that's any of your business," Mark replied, scowling at the man to hide his startled surprise.

"Reckon this makes it my business, kid," Caleb responded, pulling back his jacket to reveal his badge.

"What do you want, Ranger?" Mark asked, glaring at the ranger behind the look there were hints of nervousness.

"Were you in town day before yesterday?" Caleb asked, just to find out if the young man would lie to him.

"It ain't none of your business where I was and when," Mark replied, crossing his arms and glaring at the lawman.

Another man walked up to the two of them. When he reached them, he stood between the ranger and the young man.

"I'm makin' it my business. Now answer m' question," Caleb responded, staring down both men, daring them to lie.

"Mark was with me all day repairing fences," Mr. Jackson lied, while looking the ranger right in the eye without blinking.

"Pa's right," Mark added his own lie.

"What is all this about, Ranger?" Mr. Jackson asked, crossing his arms, glaring defiantly.

"Just ta ask ya a few questions about tha murder a James Marshal," Caleb answered, crossing his arms loosely.

"Is that all of your questions?" Mark asked, sounding impatient.

"I was told that tha two a ya didn't get along real well," Caleb commented, ignoring the young man's question completely.

"Didn't know him well enough ta have much of any feelin' about him," Mark said in an attempt to be evasive.

"That ain't what I heard. From what I've been told, you had a shovin' match with 'im," Caleb said, raising an eyebrow.

"He owed me money from a poker game the night before. I needed that money to pay my folks' mortgage," Mark replied, sounding a shade defensive.

"If you really want ta talk ta someone that had cause ta kill that Marshal fella, tha one ya should be talkin' to is Jeremiah Roberts," Mr. Jackson said, stepping out of the house.

"Really, and why is that?" Caleb questioned, eyeing the older man slightly skeptically.

"There was something 'tween that Marshal fella and Roberts that he didn't want nobody knowin' about," Mr. Jackson answered, crossing his arms.

"Any idea what that mighta been?" Caleb asked, considering the older man's words.

"Ain't got no idea. Just know that when he heard that Marshal was comin' to town, he got real nervous," Mark answered, thinking back.

"When did he find this out?" Caleb asked, narrowing his eyes slightly.

"Middle a last week someone came up to him in the saloon and told him," Mark answered, not sure that it was important.

"Did you see what this stranger looked like?" Caleb asked, getting a strange feeling.

"No, sorry, Ranger," Mark replied, running his hand through his hair.

"Then how do you know it was a stranger?" Caleb asked with just the right amount of skepticism.

"I saw him for a few second as I was leavin' the saloon. Didn't get a good enough look to describe 'im, just enough to know that I never saw him before," Mark said, scowling at the ranger.

Caleb wasn't sure how much he believed their story. On the one hand, their story was a little convenient. On the other hand, it would explain why the first thing that Marshal did was seek out Roberts.

"Son, don't leave town till this whole thing is settled. I'd really hate ta have ta put a poster out on ya. 'Specially if'n you're incorrect," Caleb warned, staring down both of them.

"Fine," Mark said, crossing his arms.

With that Caleb turned and got back on his horse. As he got on his horse, he saw Mark unsaddling his horse. He touched the brim of his hat. The only response he got from the gesture was a pair of scowls, then he turned his horse and rode away.

As he rode back toward town, he scowled and glared at the dusty trail ahead of him. His staring contest with the desert sand continued till he reached town. Unfortunately the buildings rising from the barren landscape did nothing to lighten his mood.

The restlessness in the air was still present as he rode into town. As he rode up to the livery stable, he finally figured out what the restlessness was. It was as if the entire town was waiting for something. He sighed as he handed his horse over to the livery man.

Stepping out of the stable, he decided to ask around some more. He wanted to see if he could confirm the Jacksons' story. Unfortunately he didn't find anything helpful, even though he talked to the rest of the shop owners in town, as well as quite a few other people in town.

After the last fruitless interview, he decided to get some lunch at the saloon. He walked through the batwing door into the mostly empty room. By the time he walked up to the bar, Sam was already waiting for him.

"Find any trouble yet today?" Sam asked with a slight smirk.

"Not yet," Caleb replied with mock surprise in his tone.

"You must be slipping," Sam replied, shaking his head in mock disappointment.

"Reckon you can rustle up something that at least approximates grub?" Caleb asked, a smirk tugging at the corner of his mouth.

Sam chuckled as he disappeared into the back room. Returning a few minutes later with a plate of food in hand.

"Even made sure ta burn it real good for ya," Sam said, placing the plate in front of his friend with a slight laugh in his voice.

Caleb chuckled as he started eating while going through

the facts of the case. He was about halfway through his meal when a question occurred to him. When he asked the bartender, the answer he got was just what he needed to tie up a loose end that had been bothering him. As Sam began wiping down the bar, Caleb turned and headed to the door.

Hours later, he was in the sheriff's office. At the moment, he was trying to wear a hole in the floor with his pacing. The reason for this action was that he just couldn't shake the feeling he was missing something important in the investigation. Something in his gut told him he'd seen something important. He just couldn't figure out what it was, no matter how hard he tried, and it was very frustrating.

After about twenty minutes, it became apparent that the pacing was accomplishing nothing. So he left the sheriff's office. As he looked around, his gaze was drawn to the church that was two buildings down on the other side of the street. Stepping off the boardwalk, he crossed the street.

Walking up to the building, he got a good look. It was a beautiful country church with a cross on the steeple.

When he entered, the sound of the door closing behind him echoed around the main room that was bigger than he expected. At the sound, the preacher turned his attention to him.

The minister was around forty and of a slight build. The coloured light filtering through the stained-glass window contrasted his grey eyes.

"Welcome, Ranger," the pastor said, walking up to him.

"Howdy, Preacher," Caleb greeted with a friendly smile, taking off his hat.

"I understand that you're investigating the murder of

the unfortunate stranger," the pastor said solemnly, with clear sympathy for the victim in his voice.

"That's true," Caleb replied just as solemnly.

"So what brings you here today?" the pastor asked as they sat down on a pew.

"I'm afraid I'm runnin' a little low on answers in the investigation. When that happens, I like ta come an see if tha One with all tha answers can spare me a few," Caleb answered, his gaze traveling to the front of the church.

"I sincerely hope He gives you your answer," the pastor replied, pleased by the answer.

"He always does. It just ain't always the answer I want, but it's always the one I need," Caleb said thoughtfully with, his eyes fixed on the cross at the front of the church.

"That is so very true," the pastor said, then stood and left the ranger to his prayers.

Once Caleb was alone, he bowed his head, clasped his hands, and prayed. When he was done, he felt a sense of peace that hadn't been there when he came in. With a nod to the preacher, he picked up his hat and walked out.

As soon as he stepped out of the building, he headed back over to the sheriff's office. Just as he sat down behind the sheriff's desk, the doc walked through the door.

"Afternoon, Doc," Caleb greeted, only half interested as he pulled out his notebook and other papers pertaining to the case.

"Afternoon, Ranger," Dr. Jenkins replied, walking up to the desk with a box in his hand.

"What can I do fer ya, Doc?" Caleb asked, looking up from his papers.

"Just dropping by the items that were on the body of the murdered man," Dr. Jenkins answered, placing the box on the desk.

"Thank ya, Doc, I'm sure it'll be real helpful," Caleb said, his curious gaze flicking from the doctor to the box.

"Hope so. I've got patients to attend to, so I better be going," Dr. Jenkins said, then turned and walked out of the building.

Caleb reached across the desk and picked up the box with one hand. With the other he moved the papers that he'd been looking at aside. Placing the box in front of him. He opened it and began looking through the contents. Most of what he found was to be expected. He didn't find anything interesting till he reached the bottom of the box. There, wrapped in a strip of white cloth, was the knife that was the murder weapon. Unwrapping it, he took a closer look at it. After examining it for only a few seconds, he hastily closed the lid of the box and rushed out of the building.

"I can't believe I didn't see this sooner," Caleb said, chastising himself as he left.

The instant the door closed behind him, he hurried across the street. As soon as he reached the other side, he made his way to the general store as quickly as he could.

When he approached the store he noticed that the door was slightly open. He could hear what was being said by the two men inside.

"I heard tell that the ranger was askin' questions about John Davis," the customer commented curiously.

"That's right. He was," the clerk agreed easily, not sure what the other man was getting at.

"Do ya reckon that he knows that Davis was the one that told Roberts that Marshal was coming to town?" the customer asked, tapping the surface of the counter.

"He does now," Caleb said, leaning against the table just inside the door.

Both of the other men in the store jumped just slightly in surprise. Neither of them had heard the lawman enter. Before the ranger had a chance to say anything else, the customer quickly left.

"Is there something I can get you, Ranger?" the clerk asked as the ranger walked up to the counter.

"Did ya sell this here knife?" Caleb asked, having noticed the display of specialty knives.

"Yes, I did, Ranger; that particular item was sold half-way through last week," the clerk replied immediately.

"Who did you sell it to?" Caleb asked, the gears in his head turning.

"I'll have to consult my ledger," the clerk said, pulling out a large book.

Once Caleb had the name, he swiftly left and headed back to the sheriff's office. Sitting back down behind the desk, he again began going through the papers. While doing that, a man entered the office wanting to see the sheriff.

"I've got some information for him. When will he be back?" the man asked apprehensively.

"Maybe I kin help," Caleb offered, looking up from his papers.

The man nodded, figuring that one lawman was as good as another. He didn't think that what he told the ranger was particularly important. However, the other man seemed to think it was, if the look on the lawman's face was anything to go by.

The ranger's mind raced as the last piece of the puzzle clicked into place. He was slightly preoccupied when he thanked the man for reporting the incident. The man said goodbye and left.

Halfway through the next morning, Caleb entered the saloon. When he did, he looked around at the sparsely populated room. His sharp gaze was looking for someone. He nearly smirked as he placed his hand on his weapon, having not only found the one he was looking for but a few others as well.

"Roberts, Davis, and Jackson, I'm goin' ta need the three of ya ta move ta this here table," Caleb said, pointing to the empty table a foot in front of him.

"Might we assume that the reason for the change of seating arrangements is that you intend to reveal which of the three of us is the murderer," Roberts said as he sat at the indicated table.

Caleb nodded as he watched the other two sit at the table. The three suspects sat alongside of the circular table and the ranger on the other side facing them.

"It was John Davis that murdered James Marshal," Caleb said, his gaze locking onto Davis with a burning intensity.

"Really, why would I want to kill some drifter that ain't never been here before," Davis asked, crossing his arms.

"Cause ya think that he stole some land from yer pa," Caleb explained, his hand resting on his gun.

"That's because he did steal our land right out from

under us," Davis said; there was a seething anger in his voice as he said each word.

"'Cept he didn't. It was returned ta him by tha court. Tha man that sold it ta yer pa stole it from the Marshals. After he killed James's folks fer tha deed. That land had been in their family fer three generations," Caleb replied, staring down Davis.

"That's tha pack a lies that thieving no good fed tha judge," Davis replied, glaring right back.

"He had documentation ta prove it," Caleb said, his voice level.

"I don't believe you, but tha only thing you've managed to do is prove that I have a motive just like everyone else at this here table," Davis replied, his tone turning smug.

"Ya sure as shootin' did a right fine job a arrangin' that," Caleb said, the tinniest hint of a smirk appearing on his face.

"What do you mean, Ranger?" Roberts asked, his eyes narrowing.

"What in tarnation are you talkin' about?" Mark asked, glaring between Davis and the ranger.

"A week and a half ago, Davis is the one that told you, Roberts, that Marshal was coming to town. I'm guessin' 'e told ya a few other things too," Caleb said, raising an eyebrow.

Roberts nodded mutely as he glared at the other man. Remembering when Davis told him that Marshal was planning to get drunk and tell everyone about his father being a deserter.

"An' Mark, do ya remember that Davis was tha dealer

during the poker game the day before the murder," Caleb said, his gaze shifting to the young man.

"Yeah. What of it?" Mark asked, crossing his arms.

"He was making sure that you'd win by cheatin'. Knowing that Marshal would bet more money than he had," Caleb said, mirroring the gesture and crossing his arms.

"So that he'd owe me money, giving me a motive," Mark said as realization dawned on him.

"You don't got a single shred a proof again' me," Davis snapped, outraged that his brilliant plan had been discovered.

"On the same day that you talked to Roberts, you bought a one-of-a-kind knife that was the murder weapon," Caleb replied, uncrossing his arms and his hand moving back his jacket and resting on his weapon.

"My pa always wanted a knife like that one. Thanks to Marshal, he didn't ever get to own one. So I figured that it would be appropriate to kill that thief with one," Davis sneered, glaring at the ranger.

With that near confession, the other two former suspects stood up and backed away from the table. As they did, Davis stood up, still glaring at Caleb. For a few tense seconds, it looked like the murderer would try going for his gun. Sure enough, after about a minute, he did, and the ranger shot the gun out of the killer's hand, then the ranger led him away.

* * *

"That is how a cowboy solves a murder," Alicia said with a joy-filled smile as she held up her arms.

A flood of relief surged through Alicia at the response. She hadn't been sure about this story since it was so different than most westerns. However, the crowd seemed to have enjoyed it, which was the most important thing.

THE END

Flags Among the Stars

It was midmorning and Alicia rushed into the convention centre. The reason why she was in such a rush was that she was fifteen minutes late for a meeting with the convention organizer. What caused her tardiness was that all morning everything that could possibly go wrong did. As she hurried down the hallway, she looked around for the administrator's office.

After about fifteen minutes of fruitless search, she finally found the right office. With an interesting mix of relief and nervousness, she knocked on the door before entering. After she apologized for being late, the two of them went through a few last-minute details.

As she stepped out of the office, she looked at the sign directing her where to go. Emerging from the relative quiet of the administrative wing and onto the floor was quite daunting. The sounds of the sci-fi convention buzzed around her as she wove through the crowds.

Despite the busyness of the main room, it didn't take her very long to reach the largest of the event rooms that were off the main room. Glancing at her watch as she entered, she realized she was fifteen minutes early this time. Looking up, she saw some technicians setting things up. So she found an out-of-the-way place to wait and get herself ready.

Exactly fifteen minutes later, people started to file in and take their seats, quickly filling up the room to capacity. All of them were excitedly talking about what story they were about to hear. Some even wondered if it was going to be a new one. The excited chatter stopped abruptly as Alicia stepped out onto the stage.

"Is everyone having fun at the convention so far?" Alicia asked after picking up the mic while looking out at the crowd.

"Yeah," the crowd cheered, clapping.

"Good. Who wants to join me on an adventure to a future of spaceships that traverse the stars?" Alicia asked, stepping to the edge of the stage.

"Let's go," the crowd replied, in an excited roar.

"This science-fiction adventure will be unlike anything you have heard before. It all centres around a single ship and her crew that learn just because something looks mundane and ordinary doesn't mean that it is," Alicia began, causing everyone in the crowd to lean forward just slightly in anticipation.

* * *

Our story is set in a future where humanity has colonized the stars. You might be expecting that Earth would be under some one-world government like so many of the science-fiction books and movies you've read and seen. That most certainly is not the future you will be hearing about today. In this future humanity managed to reach the level of technology that allowed them to travel to the stars without losing the richness, beauty, history, and culture of the individual nations. Because of this, humanity painted a beautiful tapestry across the stars instead of it being one homogeneous blob. With each country of the world having claimed their own section of space.

Today's adventure begins with a mid-sized exploration cruiser belonging to the Canadian Space Service. The cruiser is named CSS *Acadia*, Which was currently docked at a space station. The cruiser was there for routine maintenance and refitting.

While this happened, most of the crew were on leave. That included Captain Adeline Price, who was relaxing in one of the station's visitor lounges. She was quite enjoying one of the green areas, sitting on a bench under a tree reading a book. Unfortunately before she could finish her book, Lt. Thomas Farran walked up to her and saluted. With a barely suppressed sigh, she closed her book and lowered it to rest on her lap.

"Yes, Lieutenant Farran," Captain Price asked, standing up and saluting back.

"Is that an actual paper book," Lt. Farran asked, his eyes landing on the book with no small amount of astonishment.

"Digi pads are fine for work, but there's nothing quite like the feel of a paper book to draw you into a story," Price replied, glancing fondly at the book in her hand before returning her attention to the young officer still standing in front of her.

"That's very interesting, Ma'am," Lt. Farran replied, not really sure that he agreed with her.

"I don't think that you came all this way to talk to

me about literary formats," Captain Price said, not in the slightest phased by the young officer's reaction.

"The maintenance and refitting on the *Acadia* is complete, Ma'am," Lt. Farran informed with his hands clasped behind his back.

"Good. We'll be able to get underway right after I get our orders in the meeting with Admiral Simmons," Captain Price said, nodding with approval in her voice.

"I'll make sure that everything will be ready," Lt. Farran said. Then he saluted. When it was returned, he walked away, headed back the way he had come.

About ten minutes later, Captain Adeline Price stood in front of Admiral Simmons' office. Reaching over, she pressed the chime button on the panel next to the door. When the light on the top of the panel turned green, she stepped forward and the door opened. Stepping inside, she saw the admiral sitting behind the desk. After a brief greeting, at the admiral's request, Adeline sat in a chair in front of the desk.

"You'll be taking the *Acadia* to this area of the border regions," Admiral Simmons said, as a screen rose from the desk at the push of a button.

When the screen stopped rising, a grid map of the pertinent region appeared. One of the grid points flashed red.

"One of the border patrol interceptors detected some anomalous readings coming from here," Admiral Simmons said as the image zoomed in on the red square, showing what appeared to be a nebula.

"What kind of anomalous readings? Was it energy or matter?" Captain Price asked, looking at the image in front of her.

"Unknown. It was to far away from the Border Protection Grid to pick up anything, and the interceptor couldn't leave its post to run more detailed scans," Admiral Simmons replied, also contemplating the image.

"That's where we come in. You'd like us to go take a look and see if there's anything interesting there," Captain Price guessed, her eyes still fixed on the image of the multi-coloured cloud of dust and gas.

"That is correct, Captain Price. All additional information will be sent to the *Acadia*. You are to leave immediately," Admiral Simmons ordered, dismissing her as he pushed a button causing the picture to disappear off the screen and for it to retract.

"Yes, Sir," Captain Price said, standing up and saluting.

When the salute was returned, she headed out of the office. As she walked out the door, she felt a sense of anticipation grow inside her. Missions like these involving the possibility of finding something that no one had ever seen before were her absolute favourites.

From the looks of things, this one could be especially interesting. Because it involved something as seemingly ordinary as a nebula hiding something interesting and unique. She just couldn't wait to see what that nebula was hiding.

As these thoughts raced through her head, she walked over to the telepoint. Stepping onto the circular platform that was raised a couple inches and reaching forward, she pressed a few controls on the pedestal-like control panel. She programmed in her desired destination. Less than a second later, a round curtain of energy rose from the edges of the platform all around her till it was a couple of inches over her head. Once it reached that point, the energy curtain began going back down.

In under a second, the same thing happened on an identical platform miles away. When the energy curtain disappeared, she stood in its wake.

Stepping off the platform, she took a few minutes to survey the expanse of the docking bay. All around her, workers rushed about like worker bees in a giant beehive. Among the dozens of ships that were being worked on, she quickly found the one she was looking for.

There in front of her gleamed her beautiful ship, the *Acadia*. Its sleek, graceful design was a stark contrast to the boxy freighter next to it. Walking closer, she gently ran her hand over the feather-like engravings in the hull that could only be seen up close. The feather motif was because the design of the ship so resembled a raptor diving for its prey.

I can hardly wait for you to fly again, old friend, Price thought as she looked up at her ship. She had been the captain of the *Acadia* for the past four years.

Before that train of thought could go any further, a beeping noise came from a device on her sash-like belt. Reaching down, she unattached her communicator that looked like a silver disc about two inches across and half an inch wide. She placed it in the palm of her hand. When she did, a hologram appeared above it. The image that appeared showed Lt. Farran. The image, though tiny, was crystal clear.

"Ma'am, are you ready for us to bring you onboard?" Lt. Farran asked, his own eagerness to get underway clear in his voice.

"Just port me directly to the bridge," Price ordered with her own barely concealed eagerness in her voice.

"Right away, Ma'am," Lt. Farran said before his image disappeared.

An instant later, the same round curtain of energy appeared around her again. The next she knew, she was standing on the familiar bridge of her ship. Looking around, she saw that all the bridge crew were at their stations.

"How did the refitting go, Commander Varley?" Price asked as she sat down in her command chair, looking at the main viewer.

"Very well, Ma'am," Cdr. Ryan Varley replied as he walked up to the captain's chair.

"What's the status of engineering?" Price asked, starting a roll call.

"The engines and all engineering systems are up and running," LCdr. Lucas Jeffers reported, monitoring the readouts on the console in front of him.

"Tactical status?" Price asked calmly.

"All tactical systems online and ready," LCdr. Brandon Kemp replied, looking up from his console and at the captain.

"What about the sensors?" Price asked, glancing to the right at the mentioned station.

"Fully functional, Skipper," Lt. Chester Haden replied, standing up a little straighter.

"Communications?" Price asked, her eyes flicking over to that station.

"Online and waiting," Lt. Duncan Farran replied, after finishing the last check.

"And finally, what about the helm?" Price said, concluding the roll call.

"Ready and raring to go," Lt. Evan Pratt replied eagerly from his station.

"Ma'am, all decks report ready for launch," Varley replied, holding a digipad in his hand showing the reports.

"In that case, we really should get underway," Price commented, with a slight smile tugging at the corner of her mouth.

"Yes, Ma'am," Varley replied, his green eyes lighting up.

The mere thought of finally getting back out there filled him with excitement. After all, three months was an awful long time to be stuck on a space station. The entire crew was all eager to get back out into open space.

"Communications, contact station administration. Have them open the docking bay doors," Varley ordered, his eyes fixed on the main viewer.

"Aye, Sir," Lt. Farran said, his hands flying across the controls.

"As soon as the doors are open, take us out nice and easy," Price ordered, her own blue eyes sparkling with anticipation.

"Nice and easy, aye, Ma'am," Pratt replied, his gaze fixed on the small screen that was on his console.

Within a few minutes the ship emerged from the docking bay. The doors closed behind them. The instant they were clear and far enough away, they engaged their FTL drive.

It took just over a month for them to reach their destination. When they arrived, the day shift had just arrived and the captain had just stepped onto the bridge. Just as she sat down in the command chair, they rendezvoused with the *Fremont*, the border patrol interceptor that had found the unusual readings.

"Ma'am, the *Fremont* is signaling us," Farran announced. His attention focused on the console in front of him.

"By all means, open up a channel, Lieutenant," Price said, glancing from the officer to the main viewer.

Within less than a second, the BP's insignia of a maple leaf in a ring of stars with a shield in front of it flashed on the screen for a couple seconds. To be replaced by a grey-headed man who looked to be in his late thirties.

"Good morning, Captain Travers, I'm Captain Price of the Space Service Ship *Acadia*," Price greeted calmly and professionally.

"Morning, Captain Price, and welcome to the border regions," Travers replied in the same tone of voice.

"We were sent to investigate the unusual readings that you picked up. Is there anything that you can tell us that wasn't in the report or you've learned since?" Price asked, going over what they did know in her head.

"While our report was very thorough, we have been able to pick up something on the outermost edge of our sensor range," Travers answered, thoughtfully.

"Anything that you can tell us would be helpful," Price replied, just the smallest hint of eagerness in her voice.

"We were able to detect some spacial and gravitational anomalies coming from the edges of the nebula that our sensors could pick up," Travers explained, looking at a digi pad in his hand.

"It would be a great help if you could send over your sensor data," Price said, thinking over what she had just been told.

"Certainly," Travers said, gesturing to someone off to the side.

Within seconds the *Acadia* was receiving the information from the interceptor. Just as they received the last bit of data, a red light began flashing on the other ship.

"Well, duty calls. Safe travels, Captain Price," Travers said, after one of his officers said something in the background that wasn't picked up.

"Thank you for all your help, and I wish you the same, Captain Travers," Price said with a nod. The BP's insignia appeared on the screen for a second as the channel closed.

An instant later, the interceptor moved off at maximum pre-light speed. When they were far enough away, they jumped to FTL and disappeared.

"Helm, how long will it take to reach the nebula?" Price asked, turning her attention to the officer in question

"About three hours at normal cruising speed," Pratt answered, after inputting the coordinates they'd just gotten.

"Then by all means," Price said with a go-ahead gesture.

The young officer's hand skillfully glided across the console. Causing the ship to gracefully turn, then an instant later, it seemed to disappear in a streak of light.

"Haden, I want you to analyze every bit of data that we just got from the *Fremont*. I want to know as much as possible about what we're getting into by the time that we arrive," Price ordered, sitting back in her chair.

"Yes, Ma'am," Haden replied, his attention turning to his console as he accessed the data they'd just gotten and began analyzing it

In the time it took them to reach the nebula, they had gone through every byte of sensor data. They hadn't been able to learn much except that the anomalies were confined to the borders of the nebula. Learning anything else would have to wait until they got closer and ran more in-depth scans.

"Ma'am, we've reached the nebula," Pratt said as they dropped out of FTL and came to a full stop a couple hundred thousand km from the nebula.

"Bring it up on the main viewer; let's see what we're dealing with," Price ordered, her gaze fixed on the viewer.

An image appeared on the screen, drawing the attention of the entire bridge crew. Most nebulae were static and unchanging, like a beautiful painting painted by the hand of the LORD. This one, however, was very different. The colours swirled, pulsed, and changed location every few seconds. "It's breathtaking," Varley commented, almost mesmerized by the shifting kaleidoscope of colours.

"Alright people, what we're going to do is fly around the perimeter and do thorough in-depth scans of every inch of that cloud," Price ordered, breaking the bridge crew out of their momentary trance.

"Yes, Ma'am," Pratt said, bringing the pre-light engines online.

Some of the bridge crew were a little disappointed that they weren't going straight into the cloud. However, they all understood that when dealing with the unknown, it was always wise to gather as much information as possible.

When they finished their survey of the cloud, the information that they were able to gather, while interesting, was limited. The instants of a portion of the cloud disappearing and reappearing in another place in the cloud weren't a case of matter being moved from place to place. Something far more interesting was happening. It seemed that the space which the matter inhabited was what was moving. There were also these strange, wave-like, gravitational anomalies hinting at what might be a fairly predictable pattern. They didn't have enough observational data to be certain that the pattern would repeat.

"What are we going to do now, Ma'am," Varley asked as they returned to their previous position.

"Since we weren't able to determine either the cause or the source, we'll be taking the *Acadia* in," Price said with an odd mix of anticipation and unease.

"Increase structural support fields to maximum." Varley instructed, turning his attention to the engineer.

"Structural fields are at maximum. I also increased the motion compensation system by 10 percent," Jeffers reported, his hands skillfully gliding over the controls.

"Good thinking, Jeffers," Varley commended, impressed by the foresight.

"Helm, take us in one quarter pre-light speed," Price ordered, her eyes fixed on the image displayed on the main viewer.

"Yes, Ma'am," Pratt replied as the engines hummed to life.

"Sensors, I want you to run continuous in-depth scans in all directions as we make our way inside," Price ordered as they began moving.

"Right away, Skipper," Haden replied, initiating the scans and setting up so the results would be automatically sent to the captain's viewer.

Within seconds, the sleek ship began moving into the nebula. The instant it did, the ship shuddered as it was hit with one of the gravitational anomalies. When that happened, they were all glad for the increased motion compensation system.

"Damage report," Price barked as soon as the shaking stopped, and they were completely inside the nebula.

"Structural fields are down by 1 percent. No other damage detected," Jeffers replied, after getting himself back to being straight in his chair.

"Good, I want the computer working on predicting the gravitational anomalies so we can avoid them," Price ordered as she and the rest of the bridge crew righted themselves also.

"I'll do my best, Skipper," Haden replied as he began working on predicting the gravitational anomalies.

"Move us ahead at one-quarter pre-light. Let's take

a good look around," Price ordered, looking over the data that she was receiving from the deep scan.

The next couple of hours were very frustrating for the bridge crew. Every last external sensor decided that right at this moment was a wonderful time to have a nervous breakdown.

"Jeffers, what is wrong with those sensors?" Price asked, turning her sharp gaze on the chief engineer.

"I don't know, Ma'am; according to these readouts, all the sensors are functioning normally," Jeffers replied, sounding nervous.

He took a deep breath, knowing full well he shouldn't be nervous. The reason he was so nervous was that he didn't want to let down his new captain.

Just a fraction of a second later, the ship shuddered as another anomaly hit. This time it was a lot stronger and knocked everyone off their chairs. It also caused the lights to go out and then flickered a few times.

"Let's find out if those readouts are right. Pratt, take us out," Price said as she got back into her chair.

"Uh oh," Pratt said, as a dinging emanated from his console.

"I don't like that combination, Mr. Pratt," Price said, pinching the bridge of her nose while closing her eyes for a second.

"What's happening, Lieutenant? Why aren't we moving?" Varley asked, pinning the young helm officer with his steely grey gaze.

"The engines are functioning, but I'm having trouble getting them to engage," Pratt said, not able to figure out what was wrong.

"What's the cause?" Varley asked, his eyebrows drawing together as his eyes flicked from the helm officer to his console.

"It seems that we've found our way into one of those pockets of spacial instability. The navigational sensors are having a hard time trying to identify our current location. Because of that, we can't seem to plot a course," Pratt said, his hands still flying over the console as he tried unsuccessfully to compensate.

"Since we can't just plot a course out of here, let's try finding a stable patch of space. From there, we'll hopefully be able to figure out where we are in the nebula. So let's see where a ninety degree turn and moving forward at a quarter pre-light for ten minutes takes us," Price ordered, glancing up from the data to the main viewer.

"Come about ninety degrees and ahead one quarter PL, yes, Ma'am," Pratt said as he began turning the ship.

"Haden, has the deep scan shown any sign of stable space in that direction?" Price asked, turning her attention to the station in front of her and to the left.

"Not yet, but I'll keep a close eye out," Haden replied, his eyes fixed on the readout in front of him as the data scrolled.

With that the sleek ship began moving through the kaleidoscopic colours of the cloud. As they started moving, it was at half the speed they had been trying to go. The reason they were going so slow was that it was like they were trying to fly though half-frozen maple syrup.

To make matters worse, a few minutes after they started moving, there was another jolt. This one was some stronger than the last one. The ship shuddered and came to a full stop.

"That one hit a bit harder this time, Ma'am," Jeffers reported as he pulled himself off the floor and back into his chair.

"Yeah, I noticed," Price said flatly as she and the rest of the bridge crew all got up and back onto their chairs.

Over the next hour, the Acadia jumped a total of four more times. The structural support fields were now down 20 percent. With them dropping around 5 percent on the rough jumps, which was what the last four had been, while the smoother jumps only dropped the field by between 1 and 2 percent.

"Ma'am, we've been analyzing the data on the jumps, and I think we've figured out a pattern," Haden said, his eyes fixed on his screen.

"Finally some good news," Price said, sounding tired, while turning her chair so that she was facing the sensor operator.

"What have you found?" Varley asked, also turning his attention to Haden with an intrigued look on his face.

"So far, the closer we got to the edges of the nebula, the more intense the jumps. All the smoother jumps happened when we were near the middle," Haden explained, lifting his gaze from the scene.

"Basically this nebula is like a mouse trap; easy to get in but nearly impossible to get out," Price commented with a frown.

"Now we just have to find a way out of this mouse trap," Varley added, as he went over the data himself.

"Which will likely be much harder than it sounds,"

Price agreed, standing up and walking in a circle around her chair deep in thought.

The captain completed the circle before sitting down in her chair. Just as she sat down, the ship shuddered again.

"Have you gotten any closer to figuring out the cause of the disturbances?" Price asked, holding on to the armrest.

"Unfortunately not, Ma'am; the interference from the anomalies is scrambling the sensor readings," Varley answered with a frustrated sigh.

"Keep me updated," Price ordered, just barely able to keep the worry and frustration out of her voice.

About ten minutes later, the day shift ended. Smoothly the day shift officers handed their stations over to the night shift. Within a few minutes, the handover was complete and the night shift officers were the only ones on the now largely silent bridge.

Instead of heading off to bed right away, Adeline headed to one of the less-frequented green areas on deck four. She leaned against the railing running along one of the walkways. Closing her eyes she listened to the sound of the tree leaves being rustled by the climate control system, a sound which never failed to relax her. On paper, these areas were trees, grass, flowers, and other plants, were grown to lighten the load of the CO_2 scrubbers and oxygen generators. However, she was absolutely sure it was also for maintaining the whole crew's sanity, including her own. She'd always thought of them as an oasis of life in an ocean of stars.

"I knew I'd find you down here, Ad," a voice behind her said. There wasn't even a trace of formality in his voice.

"I figured that you would," Adeline answered, turning to face the person, already knowing it was Varley.

"So are you going to tell me what's bothering you?" Ryan asked. He moved to stand next to her and also leaned against the railing.

"If we don't get out of here soon, the structural support fields are going to fail. When that happens, those distortions are going to crush us like a tin can," Adeline answered, sounding really frightened.

"That won't happen. After all, the LORD never gives more than you can handle," Ryan replied, trying to reassure her.

"Ya know, I really think that is an often misquoted and misunderstood verse. Because there have been many things in my life that I couldn't handle," Adeline said, turning to face the man standing next to her.

"Then what do you think the verse means?" Ryan asked thoughtfully as he pondered her words.

"That the LORD never gives us anything that He can't handle if we let Him," Adeline answered with a tiny, shy smile.

"In that case, we really have nothing to worry about. Because there's nothing that this perplexing cloud can throw at us that can top that," Ryan replied, with a small, reassuring smile.

"You're right, Var," Adeline replied, feeling much lighter.

The two of them stood there silently for a few minutes just enjoying their surroundings. After about a second ,Adeline's face got serious again.

"We still haven't heard back from the review board," Adeline commented, her tone just as serious as she stared down at the flowers.

"No, we haven't. I hope they don't split us up. We make such a good team," Ryan said in the same tone, his eyes also fixed ahead.

"Me too, but they might now that they know that we're half siblings," Adeline said, running her finger over the smooth surface of the rail.

"Even before we knew we were related, we were a good team," Ryan commented, thinking back on the time before they found out.

"How long has it been since we found out?" Adeline asked, again turning her gaze to her brother.

"It's been almost six months," Ryan answered, after thinking for a few seconds.

"Hard to believe that it's been that long. It seems like just yesterday that we got that surprise," Adeline commented with a fond smile as she thought back on it.

"That wasn't exactly what I was expecting either," Ryan commented, as he too thought over the day that they found out.

"It's truly amazing how one day can change so much," Adeline commented, with a thoughtful look on her face.

After that, a comfortable silence fell on the room, broken only by the sound of the trees. A few seconds later, they said goodnight and left to finally get some sleep.

Somewhere in the neighborhood of six hours later, Captain Price's peaceful slumber was abruptly disrupted. This abrupt disruption came in the form of the hardest jolt yet. Said jolt was so strong that it knocked her out of her bed. The thud of her hitting the ground was accompanied by the beeping of the internal con system. After untangling herself from her blankets, she reached up to her bedside table, feeling around for the button to answer. She blinked her eyes open just as she found and pressed it.

"Captain, there's a situation up here," LCdr Davis reported, his voice tense as it seemed to fill the room.

"I noticed that, Davis," Price said, half sleepy and half annoyed about being woken up at four in the morning.

"You're needed on the bridge," Davis responded, with urgency in his voice.

"I'll be up there ASAP," Price replied, her voice now tight with worry and an edge of urgency entering it.

Price got up and dressed in record time. Once she was done, she hurried out the door. On her way to the bridge there was another jolt. This one was so strong that the hallway tilted, causing her to stumble into the wall. With far more difficulty than there should have been, the captain finally made it to the bridge. When she did, the day shift was there.

"Report," Price ordered, as she nearly stumbled onto the bridge. Her gaze took in the controlled chaos.

"We're stuck in two pockets of unstable space with half the ship in each pocket," Haden reported, not looking up from his controls.

"If we don't get out of this soon, it'll tear the ship in half," Jeffers said, his statement punctuated by another jarring jolt.

"Solutions, now," Price ordered, as she made her way as steadily as possibly across the pitching deck to her chair.

"We could ramp up the structural support fields to 5 percent above max and use the PL engines to pull us out of both pockets. There seems to be a pocket of stable space half a spacial unit ahead of us," Kemp suggested from his station at tactical.

"We could engage the engines on one side and push us into one of the pockets," Farran suggested, as the ship pitched back and forth like it was a sailing ship caught in a storm.

"I don't like the idea of overtaxing the support fields, which are the only things keeping us from being crushed like a tin can. However, I don't really want to go through another jump if I can avoid it," Price said thoughtfully.

"How about instead of ramping up the structural fields we use the tactical shields to reinforce them," Kemp suggested, working out in his head how the shields would need to be recalibrated, knowing he'd need to do it quickly.

"Do it and quickly. I like being in one piece," Price ordered as the ship groaned under the strain, causing the entire bridge crew to wince.

"Jeffers, help Kemp with the recalibration, and get it done quickly," Varley ordered, gripping one of the rails as the ship shuddered again.

It only took the two men a couple of minutes to get the shields recalibrated and brought online. However, the tension that permeated the bridge made those few minutes seem like an eternity.

"We're ready," Jeffers said, breaking the tense atmosphere.

"Punch it," Price ordered, gripping the armrests of her chair tighter in anticipation.

An instant after the order was given, the engines flared to life and grew brighter with every passing second. When they didn't immediately begin to move, nervousness began to permeate the now silent bridge. Just when everyone was becoming certain that it wasn't going to work, the normally graceful ship lurched forward. Suddenly, like the snapping of a strained rubber band, they broke free and glided into the pocket of stable space. The bridge erupted into cheers, and the tension lessened considerably.

"With that settled, the night shift can take over again, and you have the bridge, Davis. I'm going back to bed. I'll see you in the morning," Price said, standing up from the command chair.

"Good night again and sleep well, Skipper," Davis said, standing at attention and saluting.

Price nodded and returned the salute. After which she turned and left the bridge and headed back to her quarters. In that moment, she wanted nothing more than to curl up in her bed and sleep for the next week. Alas, she'd have to settle for just a few hours.

After those few hours, Price got up and headed to the bridge. Just seconds after she arrived the nightshift left.

"Good morning, everyone," Price greeted, as she sat down in the command chair and her eyes scanned the bridge.

Good mornings came from the entire bridge crew as they settled at their stations. They all got busy with their morning tasks.

"Now that this nebula isn't trying to shake us apart or tear us in half, let's figure out what's been causing all this trouble," Price instructed with a sense of anticipation in her voice.

With that everyone began pouring over the sensor data.

Haden began running further scans focusing on the centre of the nebula. When he did, he found the readings were considerably clearer now that they were in stable space.

It took a couple of hours for Haden to sort through the readings to find something. He could barely believe what he saw displayed on the screen.

"Skipper, I found something that you should take a look at," Haden said, his astonishment clear in his voice.

"What did you find?" Price asked, anticipation, curiosity, and just a hint of worry in her voice as she turned her attention to the sensor officer.

"The scans of the centre of the nebula revealed something quite unusual. What they showed was a wormhole being sucked into a black-hole," Haden explained, sounding surprised, concerned, and a little excited about the discovery.

"That is likely the cause of the spacial instability," Varley said, sounding thoughtful as he tapped his chin.

"Bring it up on the main viewer. I think we'd all like to see what's been causing us all this trouble," Price ordered, a little steel entering her voice as she remembered her ship almost being ripped apart last night.

"Right away, Skipper," Haden replied as his fingers flew over the controls, also wanting to get a look at what had almost killed them all.

Less than a second later, the CSS logo flashed on the screen for a few seconds before being replaced. What appeared on the main viewer was the wormhole and the black hole. The former looked like a luminescent blue tunnel being warped and twisted as it was getting sucked in. The black hole looked like a swirling vortex with a ring of matter and energy that was in the process of being sucked in. As you looked closer at that ring, you could see splotches of blue which were pockets of energy from the wormhole. All of this matter and energy swirled into the pitch-black centre that gives the phenomena its name. It looked like only the edge of the wormhole had been consumed by the black, swirling mass.

The eyes of everyone on the bridge were fixed on the main viewer. To see two of space's most powerful forces converge like that was truly amazing.

"Check the CSS database. I want to know if someone else has come across something like this," Price said, her tone serious.

"I checked. There is no record of something like this in any database in the country," Jeffers said, having run it through every Canadian database, even the civilian ones.

"If possible, run it though the databases of the US and as many of our other allies as you can. See if any of them have seen anything like this," Price ordered, hoping to get some helpful information that way.

Several of the bridge crew began running the checks, each officer taking a different country to contact. They ended up contacting five countries. As soon as the last inquiry was sent, a tense silence engulfed the bridge as they waited for the answers. Suddenly five beeps pierced the silence, and all the officers quickly checked the results.

"Ma'am, unfortunately we got a negative result from all the databases," Jeffers reported, after receiving reports from the others.

"How far are we from the edge of the nebula?" Price asked thoughtfully, deciding to take a different route.

"Pretty far. The pocket we're in is three quarters of the way to the centre," Varley said, his eyes fixed on the digipad in his hand.

"How are our structural integrity systems holding up?" Price asked, remembering the beating they took the night before.

"The structural support fields are down 30 percent while the tactical shields are only down about one and a half percent," Jeffers reported, sounding slightly distracted as he got his crew busy repairing the support fields.

"We can't just sit here in this bubble. I want options, people" Price asked, her stern gaze flicking over everyone on the bridge.

"What if we try to recalibrate the forward sensors to detect these stable space pockets and leap frog from one to the next till we get out," Pratt suggested, sounding confident as he turned his chair around to face the captain

"That might work if we could count on these stable pockets being navigable," Varley replied, sounding a little skeptical.

"What could make them un-navigable?" Price asked, turning her attention to her first officer.

"As you know most of the stable space pockets are littered with gravitational anomalies," Varley explained, his statement was punctuated by the ship shaking at just that moment as a gravitational anomaly hit.

"Are the stable pockets that you're wanting to use navigable?" Price asked, not really sounding to impressed with the plan.

"How long will the sensor modification take?" Varley asked, looking up from his digipad and toward Pratt.

"Somewhere between twelve hours and two days," Jeffers said, after conferring with Pratt for a few seconds.

"We're not spending that long just to go back the way that we came," Price ordered, rejecting that idea.

"Captain, I have an idea. It's either brilliant or completely insane," Farran said, slightly nervous.

"Let's hear it, Lieutenant," Varley said, sounding intrigued.

"I think that we should head toward the centre and go through the wormhole," Farran suggested, after taking a deep breath.

"You're right. That is crazy, Kid," Haden said, shaking his head.

"If we did that, we'd have no idea where we'd end up," Jeffers countered, voicing a potential problem with the idea.

"At least we'd be out of here," Farran said, defending his idea.

"Whatever we'd face on the other side I'm sure that we can handle," Kemp said confidently.

"Good job. Sometimes a brilliant and crazy plan is just what is needed," Price said, sounding impressed.

"What needs to be done so we can attempt this?" Varley asked, directing the question to Jeffers as another jolt hit the ship.

"All the structural support systems will have to be repaired. The tactical shields should be brought back up to a hundred percent also," Jeffers answered, after bringing up current statuses of both systems.

"How long will it take to make the repairs?" Varley asked, just as eager as everyone else to get out of this stupid cloud.

"A couple of hours, three at the most. That is, as long as we don't get to many more of those jolts. If we do, it'll slow us down a bit," Jeffers answered, already going through what needed to be done in his head.

"Do it," Price ordered with a decisive nod.

Jeffers handed his bridge station to another member of his team. Afterward he headed down to engineering to get the repairs started. Entering engineering, he was greeted by the familiar and welcome sound of the hum of the engines. That sound was one thing that he dearly missed when he needed to be on the bridge.

"Listen up, people; we've got two to three hours to get every system responsible for keeping this ship in one piece back up to one hundred percent," Jeffers instructed over the bustling activity that mixed with the sound of the engines.

"Why the hurry?" Crewmen Jacobs asked, looking at his commanding officer with confusion and a twinge of concern.

"Because that's how long we have before we're going to attempt something crazy," Jeffers explained with the tiniest hint of a smirk.

"There's a surprise," a passing crewman muttered, shaking his head.

The entire engineering team got busy with the repairs. Half of them were assigned to each of the shield systems that needed repaired. When the crew working on the tactical shielding finished they went over and helped the crew working on the structural shielding. Working together, they got all the repairs done on time.

Ten minutes later the bridge officers were at their stations. Price stepped out of her office onto the bridge. As she did, there was a distinct hum of nervous energy in the air.

"Status report," Price said as she sat down in the command chair.

"The repairs are complete and all stations report ready," Varley answered immediately.

"Jeffers, will your repairs handle what we're about to put them through?" Price asked, her tone serious as she met her chief engineer's gaze.

"It'll be a bit of a rough ride, but we'll make it through, Ma'am," Jeffers replied with as much confidence as he had in any part of the plan.

"Alright, Mr. Pratt, come about and head for the wormhole at one quarter PL," Price ordered, her voice grave.

"Yes, Ma'am," Pratt said, his tone as serious as the situation.

"Bring the wormhole up on the main viewer. I want to see it," Price ordered, the same serious tone still in her voice.

As the ship began to come around an anomaly shook the ship. Causing everyone to brace themselves by holding onto their consoles. When the shaking passed, Pratt had to make some minor course modifications. As if the nebula wanted to remind them of how dangerous this situation was, though none of them really needed that reminder.

A few minutes later, they reached the border of the pocket. When they tried to go through, they were met with resistance they weren't expecting.

It's like flying through syrup again, Pratt thought as

he tried to keep them on course. After a couple of minutes, they managed to get through.

"Increase our speed to one-half PL," Price ordered urgently as soon as they emerged in the pocket of unstable space.

The increase of speed allowed them to make it out of the pocket before it jumped. They made it out by only a few seconds to spare.

Within a couple of hours they were finally closing in on the wormhole. As they moved closer, everyone began to wonder where they would end up. One thing all of them knew was that they were looking forward to getting out of here.

"Ten km and closing, nine km, eight km, seven km, six km," Pratt reported, trying to keep them on course despite the jostling.

As predicted the ride toward the wormhole was a rough one. As each number in the countdown progressed, the rougher it got. It seemed that each number was followed with significant jolts of turbulence.

"Five km, and counting, four km, three km, two km," Pratt continued, his skilled hands moving even faster over the control in order to keep them on course.

The image of the wormhole on the screen got bigger as they got closer. As the image on the screen grew, so did the tension.

"And one," Pratt said, concluding the countdown.

"All hands brace for entry into the wormhole. We're going in," Price ordered over the internal com system, sounding urgent.

Entering the wormhole felt like hitting a brick wall. The jarring impact knocked everyone off their chairs and to the floor. Even though the trip through lasted only a few minutes, it felt considerably longer. When they emerged on the other side, the lights were dim and blinking. The smoke was so thick in the air that coughs could be heard in the background.

"That was fun," Price said sarcastically, pushing herself to her feet.

"Let's not do that again," Varley agreed wholeheartedly.

"Damage report," Price ordered, sitting down in the command chair as she held her aching head in both hands.

A few minutes later the damage reports began to appear on her screen. She moved her hand to pinch the bridge of her nose as she read the list. It would take far, far less time to list the things that were working than the things that were not. Unfortunately the FTL engines, shields, weapons, and most of the sensors were not among the former. To make matters worse, the PL engines were down to 25 percent.

"Where are we?" Price asked, looking up from the depressingly long list scrolling on her screen as the lights blinked ominously.

"Fairly deep inside British space," Varley answered, his voice as neutral as he could make it, not really liking being defenseless, even in an ally's space. Especially considering their less than conventional arrival.

"Ma'am, there's a ship approaching," Kemp said, his voice tense. "They're signaling us, Ma'am," Farran said urgently.

"Open a channel," Price said, sitting up straighter.

"Attention unknown vessel. My name is Captain Henry

Marshall of the HMS *Trent*. Please identify yourself," Captain Marshall said as soon as the image of a man in his late thirties with brown hair and blue eyes appeared.

"My name is Captain Price of the CSS ship *Acadia*," Price explained, her voice calm.

"Looks like you ran into a spot of bother," Captain Marshall commented with understanding in his tone.

"You're quite right; we apologize for our abrupt arrival. We were dumped here by a wormhole and got banged up in the experience," Price explained, the lights and consoles blinking behind her punctuating her point.

"So I see," Captain Marshall said, a strong note of concern in his accented voice while standing tall with his hands clasped behind his back.

"We are requesting assistance with repairs," Price said, the flickering lights behind her going out and some sparks flying from a couple of consoles.

"Certainly, we'll escort you to the nearest space station capable of assisting with your repairs. After which you're free to return to your nation's space," Captain Marshall agreed, after reviewing sensor data that confirmed what they were saying.

With that the two ships began moving toward the space station. Despite their restricted speed, it didn't take very long for them to get there. Once both ships reached their destination, they went their separate ways. It didn't take very long for the *Acadia*'s repairs to be completed. After which they returned to Canadian space.

* * *

"What do you amazing people think of the blending of a thrilling space adventure with vibrant national cultures?" Alicia asked, a glowing smile on her face.

Her question was answered by cheering from the excited crowd. The story got people in the crowd thinking about what was great about their countries. She told them that this was only the first of these adventures, a fact that the crowd seemed quite happy about.

THE END